Pearl

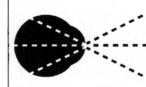

This Large Print Book carries the
Seal of Approval of N.A.V.H.

Pearl

Mary Gordon

Thorndike Press • Waterville, Maine

Published in 2005 by arrangement with Pantheon Books, a division of Random House, Inc.

Thorndike Press® Large Print Basic.

The tree indicium is a trademark of Thorndike Press.

The text of this Large Print edition is unabridged.
Other aspects of the book may vary from the original edition.

Set in 16 pt. Plantin.

Printed in the United States on permanent paper.

Library of Congress Cataloging-in-Publication Data

Gordon, Mary, 1949–
    Pearl / by Mary Gordon.
        p. cm.
    "Thorndike Press large print basic" — T.p. verso.
    ISBN 0-7862-7644-4 (lg. print : hc : alk. paper)
    1. Students, Foreign — Northern Ireland — Fiction.
2. Upper West Side (New York, N.Y.) — Fiction.
3. Americans — Northern Ireland — Fiction.   4. Mothers
and daughters — Fiction.   5. Protest movements —
Fiction.   6. Northern Ireland — Fiction.   7. Hunger strikes
— Fiction.   8. Large type books.   I. Title.
PS3557.O669P43 2005b
    813'.54—dc22   2005005049

FOR

Enda McDonagh

Eileen Tobin

National Association for Visually Handicapped
------------------------ *serving the partially seeing*

As the Founder/CEO of NAVH, the only national health agency solely devoted to those who, although not totally blind, have an eye disease which could lead to serious visual impairment, I am pleased to recognize Thorndike Press* as one of the leading publishers in the large print field.

Founded in 1954 in San Francisco to prepare large print textbooks for partially seeing children, NAVH became the pioneer and standard setting agency in the preparation of large type.

Today, those publishers who meet our standards carry the prestigious "Seal of Approval" indicating high quality large print. We are delighted that Thorndike Press is one of the publishers whose titles meet these standards. We are also pleased to recognize the significant contribution Thorndike Press is making in this important and growing field.

Lorraine H. Marchi, L.H.D.
Founder/CEO
NAVH

* Thorndike Press encompasses the following imprints: Thorndike, Wheeler, Walker and Large Print Press.

ACKNOWLEDGMENTS

In researching the history of the I.R.A., I began, as everyone must, with the work of Tim Pat Coogan. I am also indebted to Ed Moloney's *A Secret History of the I.R.A.*, and Padraig O'Malley's *Biting at the Grave*. I have, as well, consulted more personal accounts, most especially Bobby Sands's *Writings from Prison* and Gerry Adams's autobiographical work, most particularly *Falls Memories*. I was greatly helped by Silvia Calamati's *Women's Stories from the North of Ireland*. I consulted video footage of the Omagh bombing from both English and Irish sources.

Most important were the many conversations with Irish friends, particularly Martin Byrd, Barbara Fitzgerald, Enda McDonagh, Cliona Ni Cheallaigh, and Ronan O'Ceallaigh.

My medical advisers, Dr. Patricica Kauffman and, as always, Dr. Maureen Strafford, were generously available with their expert knowledge.

To my patient readers, my endless thanks: Penny Ferrer, Kathleen Hill, David

Plante, Claudia Rankine, Jan Zlotnik Schmidt — and with special thanks for her special attentions, Fran Kiernan.

For her careful and enthusiastic support, my thanks go to my editor Deborah Garrison and, as always, to my agent, Peter Matson.

CONTENTS

The Call

Travelers

Dubliners

The Call

• 1 •

We may as well begin with the ride home.

It is Christmas night, 1998. The ending of a day that was not unseasonable, except in its failure to fulfill the sentimental wish for spur-of-the-moment snow. The sky: gray; the air: cold, with a high of 33 degrees Fahrenheit. Palpable winter but not winter at its worst. Fewer of the poor than usual died on that day of causes traceable to the weather. Perhaps the relatively unimpressive showing of weather-related deaths was due to the relative clemency of the air, the relative windlessness, the relative benevolence that could be counted on by the poor to last, perhaps, nine days, December twenty-fourth through the first of January.

Ten o'clock Christmas night. Four friends drive south on the way home after a day of celebration. They have had Christmas dinner at the house of other friends, a weekend and vacation house in the mountains north of New York. One couple sits in the front of a brown Honda Accord, the other in the back. They are all in their fifties. All of their children are on other continents: one in Brazil, working on an irrigation project; one in Japan, teaching English; one in Ireland studying the Irish language at Trinity College. They were determined not to have a melancholy Christmas, and for the most part they have not.

They leave Maria Meyers off first since she lives in the most northerly part of the city or, as they would say, the farthest uptown.

She opens the door of her apartment on the sixth or top floor of a building on the corner of La Salle Street and Claremont Avenue, a block west of Broadway, a block south of 125th Street, on the margins of Harlem, at the tip end of the force field of Columbia University. Before she takes off her brown boots lined with tan fur, her green down coat, her rose-colored scarf, her wool beret, also rose, she sees the red light of her answering machine.

Her heart lifts. She reads the red light as a message from her daughter, who has not, after all, forgotten to call on Christmas. She probably thought her mother would be home all day; Christmas has never been spent anywhere but at home.

In the darkness, seeing with clarity one

thing only, the blinking red light that means her daughter's voice, Maria knows that when she flips the light switch she will be illumining a place nothing like the house she grew up in. Purposely, deliberately unlike. Walls painted orange-yellow. Woven fabrics from Guatemala, carved wooden angels — green and pink — from Poland, and from Cambodia a tin demon, her protector.

She drapes her coat, her hat, her scarf over the chair covered with a slipcover the color of a green apple. She sits on the footrest in front of it, on woven triangles of magenta, cobalt, rust. She takes off her boots, which made her feet so uncomfortably overheated in the car. She is greedy for the sound of her daughter's voice, her greed a tooth that bites down hard. Her stocking feet are slippery on the pine floor. She'd been more hurt than she wanted to admit that Pearl hadn't returned her call, hadn't made contact before she left for the countryside. But that was what she wanted, wasn't it? A daughter who did not feel obligated, who felt free to pursue her life, her interests, her pleasures, her adventures. She'd imagined Pearl sitting in a basement kitchen around a table of students toasting one another with cheap red wine, filling plate after plate with spaghetti they had made together. Or maybe it wasn't spaghetti; she didn't know what cheap meal Irish students chose to celebrate their liberation from the domestic cliché of family Christmas. Pearl had said she would be with friends. No one's family? Maria had said. "I don't know anyone's family here," Pearl had said, and Maria had thought, Well, that is being young.

But it is not her daughter's voice she hears on the answering machine. It is a strange voice, a woman's voice, a voice with a southern accent.

"This is the State Department in Washington. We're looking for Maria Meyers, the mother of Pearl Meyers. This is an emergency. You can call toll-free."

★ ★ ★

E-M-E-R-G-E-N-C-Y

The word makes Maria believe she has lived her life all wrong. The familiar walls, the furniture of the apartment are threatening to her, offer her no comfort.

State Department. The official world. Run by men like her father. And where is her father now? She wants her father, dead twenty-four years, dying thousands of miles away from her, estranged. She says

16

the word: Father. Then tries to unsay it. She tells herself to be calm. She breathes in and out, the breathing technique she learned for giving birth. She focuses her dislike on the voice on the machine — what kind of voice is that for the State Department? — and the name of the person she is supposed to call: Lynne Craig. *Lynne Craig?*

She tells herself she has never liked anyone named Lynne. What kind of name is that for a diplomat? If you were expecting a serious future for your daughter, would you name her Lynne?

Her daughter's name has always been something she was proud of. She always relished people's surprise when they heard it.

What's the baby's name?

Pearl.

A disappointed look. Wanting to say, That's no name for a baby, people would say, "Unusual."

"It's my mother's name," Maria would say.

Then people would say, "Oh, yes, of course." Forgiving her for something.

A toll-free number. As if paying the toll would prevent someone's making a call to the State Department when they'd been told it was an emergency. She tries to imagine a person for whom a toll-free number would, in such circumstances, make a difference. She cannot. She loses confidence in the ability of someone who would invent such a procedure to save her child. This frightens her: she cannot trust the people who are said to be in charge. And, unusually for her, Maria does not know what to do.

She dials the number. The tone beeps. She tries to imagine the State Department. She sees official buildings but they could be anywhere, in any city, at any time since the mid-nineteenth century. She sees her young self and her friends demonstrating in front of such buildings in the 1960s. In those dark years, the people in the buildings had been the enemy. Now they are her only hope. Therefore they are dear to her. Therefore she hates them. They know something, possibly unbearable, that she does not know. Something about her daughter. Something she needs to know.

She gets, on the fifth ring, Lynne Craig.

"Mrs. Meyers —"

"It's Ms. I'm not married."

This is the kind of woman Maria is. She has heard the word *emergency*, and yet she insists on not being misnamed. She is not married; she wants to make that clear. No husband for a second opinion. She is a person who believes it is one of her strengths: making things clear.

"Yes, well, Ms. Meyers, ma'am, we have a bit of a situation over there in Dublin. A little bit of an unusual situation that your daughter's gotten herself involved in."

"Is she all right?"

"Well, we hope she will be."

"What exactly do you mean by that?"

"Well, as I said, your daughter's gotten herself into a little bit of an unusual situation. She's chained herself to the flagpole in front of the American embassy in Dublin. She says she hasn't eaten in six weeks, and she's refusing food and drink."

"Why is she doing it?" Maria knows she must try to understand. If there is a logical progression, it will be comprehensible. Therefore, some action can be begun.

"Well, at first, Ms. Meyers, because it's Dublin and because of the particular situation over there with the Irish politics and all, we supposed she was involved with the IRA. You know, there's a group that's very opposed to the peace treaty that's being worked out, very vocal about their opposition, more than vocal in some cases. But this doesn't seem to be the case with your daughter — IRA involvement, I mean. She wrote a statement that she left on the ground by where she's lying. It's a bit confusing, Ms. Meyers. We think she's doing what she's doing because some young boy died and she considers herself responsible. And then she's in favor of the peace treaty; she says her act is in witness to it. We can't make much sense of this, and she won't talk. Now she's written a letter to you and another to a Mr. Kasperman. It says *personal and confidential,* but if you were willing we could read it to you now."

"She's getting medical help?"

"Yes."

"In that case, we must respect her wishes. If the letters are confidential, it means they're for our eyes only. Mr. Kasperman is an old friend of the family. Just take the proper medical steps and wait for me to get there."

"Yes, ma'am, whatever you say. Does she have any history of mental instability?"

"Of course not."

"Well, Ms. Meyers, as this is a kind of unusual situation, we'd have to ask that kind of question. Any political involvement?"

"As long as I've known her she's been only marginally aware of politics. She's interested in language. She's studying linguistics. She's in Ireland to study the Irish language."

"Yes, ma'am. Well, you see, she has some connections there that are of some concern. There's a young man, a kind of involvement, who has interests, connections, with certain radical groups. But they all seem to disavow any connection with what your daughter's doing. They say it's just the isolated act of a disturbed individual."

"My daughter is not disturbed. She's in danger, and I'd like to know what you're doing about it."

"Well, right at the moment, ma'am, we're trying to be in dialogue with her. But she doesn't seem very receptive. I'll tell you the truth, ma'am: she's very weak, and we're afraid of injuring her if she resists when we try to remove the chains by force. She's chained her wrists, you see. So we're sort of hoping she'll remove the chains herself."

"Isn't it cold there?"

"Yes, ma'am, we have some concerns about that. They seem to be taking measures; I think some heaters have been set up. But our greatest concern is that she won't drink. You know, they can survive this kind of thing without eating, but the drinking's crucial. We're worried about de-hydration. We've set up heaters around her so she's warm. She can't stop us doing that."

"Then get the chains off without hurting her."

"That seems to be the problem right now. She's resisting us pretty strongly there. We're trying to avoid force. Of course, if she gets much weaker, she won't be able to resist."

Maria doesn't know what to hope for: that her daughter will weaken enough so she can't resist or that she will retain her strength. How is it possible to wish that your child will weaken? Yet she knows that is what she must do, if only she knew how to form the wish. She has never had this experience before; she has always known exactly what to wish for. She has often believed that her wishes would be granted or that, if not, she would be able to live with their having been refused. But now she does not know how she must live. Or how she would live if anything should happen to her daughter. Her daughter who is in danger now.

"We were hoping you might have some kind of leverage if you were on-site."

"I'll be on the next plane."

"I've taken the liberty of booking you a seat; I'm afraid there's only first class left on the six p.m. flight tomorrow. And I've taken the liberty of booking you a hotel, the Tara Arms. Any cab at the airport will know it. Of course, you'll want to stop by the embassy first. Speak to Miss Caroline Wolf."

Maria wants to vomit, as if, opening her mouth, the horror of what she's heard might spill out as in a medieval allegory: a sinner spewing out devils, sin.

But she can't waste time thinking of herself as a figure of allegory. Her daughter is in danger. Her daughter is doing something she doesn't understand. She can't even form a picture. Why can't they remove the chains? Maria is an impatient woman, and not being able to understand has always made her feel trapped, suffocated. She wants to claw against this incomprehension. She wants to make Lynne Craig say something that will allow her to understand. So, although she doesn't want to hear her voice anymore, she asks another question. In case it will unlock something.

"First class?" she says.

"I'm afraid that's all that's available. The flight leaves JFK at six p.m. tomorrow night."

Tomorrow night. Six p.m. First class. Thousands of dollars. Nineteen hours.

She packs her bag.

★ ★ ★

Maria waits until midnight, when it is 6 a.m. in Rome, to call Joseph Kasperman, her oldest friend. Joseph Kasperman, to whom Pearl addressed the other letter.

And now I will tell you the story of Joseph and Maria. Your first thought might be that they are lovers. Having learned they are not, you might imagine they are blood relations: perhaps brother and sister. They are neither lovers nor blood relatives, they are friends. More than friends. Neither has a memory of life without the other. And what is a life without the memory of a life?

Joseph's mother was housekeeper to Maria and her father, Maria's mother having died before Maria was two years old and Joseph's father having abandoned him and his mother before Joseph reached his first birthday. Two half-orphans, brought up together: a tie not of blood or sex, a tie of friendship. Friendship from the start of memory. Joseph cannot forget that he is the son of a servant. Maria almost never thinks of it.

Maria has a little Italian, enough to ask

24

for Mr. Kasperman in the hotel Santa Chiara, where she has stayed many times, first with her father, then with her father and Joseph, then with Joseph and his wife, Devorah, most recently with Joseph and Pearl. Now Joseph is there alone. Devorah and her father are dead. She will not allow herself to think that Pearl might be dying.

Joseph answers the phone, and she tells him what Lynne Craig said. How she dislikes Lynne Craig, how she dislikes the State Department and its toll-free number, how she dislikes having to depend on the State Department for anything. Particularly anything important.

"Why is she doing it?" Joseph asks.

"It's something about a boy who died, whose death she feels responsible for. And something about being a witness to the importance of the peace treaty. I don't understand."

Now she will ask a question for the magic value of the spoken words. Joseph has always wanted to make her happy, but if he thought something was important, that she wasn't quite telling the truth or allowing herself to see the truth, he would go silent. No matter how much he knew what she wanted to hear.

"Do you think she'll die?"

And he says the thing she needs to hear, which she knows he believes, because he doesn't say what he does not think is the truth.

"No, I don't think she'll die," he says. "You won't let her."

Travelers

When you have decided that you will die —
which is a different thing from knowing that you
want to die and different, too, from the idea that
you no longer want to live — when you've come
to that point, nothing is difficult. You are in love
with your own lightness. You grow radiant to
yourself. Transparent. You can take in anything
and nothing can be taken from you.
  This is who and what I am.

★ ★ ★

This is who and what Pearl Meyers believes she is, who and what she is to herself. But what is she to us? A twenty-year-
old woman. A woman who is starving, a
woman chained to the flagpole in front of
the American embassy in Dublin, Ireland.
A woman who is lying on the ground.

But who am I? you may be asking.

Think of me this way: midwife, present
at the birth. Or perhaps this: godfather,
present at the christening. Although of the
three people with whom we are concerned,
perhaps the most important, Pearl herself,
was never christened. If not the chris-

tening, then, perhaps the naming. Present at the naming. At the speaking of the most important word.

Perhaps you cannot bleach a certain criminal association from the word *godfather*. But I would ask you to consider that, for two of the people with whom we are concerned, the word *godfather* signified the protector of the child from the world, the flesh, the devil, long before Marlon Brando changed its meaning for people like you and me.

I would, if I could, protect them, all of them, but I have learned that I cannot.

Let's get back to Pearl. The Irish government does not want to be seen using force against an American. The American government does not want force used against one of their own. The police could cut through Pearl's chains. It would not be easy, she's made sure of that, but it could be done. She has handcuffed herself, looped one medium-width chain through the handcuffs, looped a thick bicycle chain through that and around the American embassy's flagpole on a tile pavement a few feet below street level on the Aylesbury Road. They are giving her a chance to free herself; for the moment they are only speaking to her. They will try other methods: unlocking the cuffs with their keys and, if that doesn't work, cutting through them with something like gardening shears. The chances of hurting her, of wounding the delicate flesh of the underside of her wrists, is great if she resists.

Pearl is, thus far, resisting. When the police have approached her she has thrashed and kicked. So for a while they are only talking to her. The Irish are a civilized people; the Dublin police are known to be humane. And she is on embassy ground; the embassy staff has been in charge. Doctors have been consulted, experts in the field, people who have had experience with this sort of thing. This is, after all, Ireland, and hunger strikers are not unknown.

What is she doing here? is a question people keep asking. You may be asking it yourself. *What are you doing here?* Isn't this always a hostile question? Doesn't it always imply, *You have no right to be here, you should be somewhere else?* It would be very easy to say that both these sentences are true in relation to Pearl Meyers. Only, she is American. The embassy is technically her country, although it is in Ireland. You could say she has no right to chain herself to the flagpole on pavement that dips down a few feet from the high embassy ground. And if you said to her, *You should be somewhere else,* she would deny it. She would say, *I am where I belong.*

★ ★ ★

There are reasons. You may not believe there is any reason for a young woman like this to want to die. By which you would mean any good reason, a reason that would be good enough for you to understand. You may never have wanted death yourself. But Pearl experienced the desire for it as a kind of thirst. Do you remember, as a child, waking thirsty in the middle of the night? Getting up, walking into the kitchen, the air cool against your arms and legs, exposed except for the thin cotton of summer pajamas. Filling a glass from the faucet, carefully, right to the brim. The water running out of the spigot with a *swoosh,* tasting sweet. Because you were so thirsty. It was strange, wasn't it? It was exciting, drinking water in the dark room. Strange to be drinking water in the darkness all alone.

Her thirst for death has been like that, like the imagination of that water. As she began to starve herself, her weakness had a sweetness, her exhaustion was as desirable as the slaking of a thirst. To fail to live. To fail to live up to things. Simply to fail. A sweet exhaustion, like a bluish gas or a white fog. No longer to base your life on a series of actions, but to say that one action, in its absolute visibility, its absolute meaningfulness, is worth your life. The giving up of which is nothing but a lovely handing over. The delight of giving over, of giving up. To lie down in the snow or in the woods. In darkness. No longer to go on.

But what, you ask me, could have been the source of such a thirst? She is a fortunate girl, you are telling me: beautiful, healthy, American.

Perhaps we should begin with the document on the ground beside her. It is in a clear plastic envelope, transparent, secured by a device: a cardboard red circle, around which is looped a white string. Let's call it a document, or perhaps it would be better to call it a statement. I don't know what it really should be called. In any case, I offer it to you exactly as she wrote it. These are her words:

I have not eaten in six weeks; I have drunk nothing in several days. I have decided to do this, to chain myself here, because of my conviction that the only important thing I can do with my life is to offer it in witness. I am doing this here, in Ireland, on what is officially American soil, because what I am doing is connected to the history of Ireland, even my method, and yet I am not part of the history of Ireland. I am American, and so I find it proper to do what I must do here on what is legally American soil. To be American is to be paid attention to.

First and most important, I am giving my life in witness to the death of Stephen Donegan and to the goodness and importance of his life. Second, to show my support, my admiration for the peace agreement, and those who have worked toward it. Third, to mark the human will to harm.

I am, in part, responsible for Stephen Donegan's death. This is because in being caught up in an idea, I forgot a living person. He became, to me, invisible. This made it easy, even natural, for me to insult him. This insult was a form of violence. They said he died because of an automobile accident, but he died as a result of my insult. The death of Stephen Donegan was an event in history, a loss to the world.

My insult was a private act, an act of private violence, and yet its source was the Troubles of Ireland. Stephen Donegan was a victim of the Troubles, but he is not being mourned as that. I insist by my death that he be mourned as a victim of the Troubles. And so, because I believe that nothing I could do with my life can be as powerful as the power of my death, I give my life in witness to the goodness of Stephen Donegan, and to the goodness of the peace agreement, and to protest the evil of continued violence.

The idea of the peace agreement and its reality will bring about a cessation of some death. I know it to be true that the diminishment of the possibility of violent deaths is an entirely good thing. I know too that the peace process is in danger because of those who love violence and death more than peace. I understand this impulse to violence because of the violence of insult I committed against Stephen Donegan. And I see this impulse — in myself and in those who would put the peace process in danger — as part of a larger impulse, which is true, I believe, of human beings: they possess the will to harm. And my witness to this impulse, my desire to mark its strength, is the third reason for my decision to be here as I am.

I believe it is a good thing to offer my life in witness to these things I know to be true. My death will be a far more powerful witness than my life or anything that could be accomplished by a life such as mine. I act in perfect freedom and in certainty that what I am doing is right. No one has influenced me in this choice.

Pearl Meyers

In the large transparent envelope, along with the document, there were two smaller, ordinary envelopes, one addressed to her mother, one to Joseph. She addressed the one: *For my mother, Maria Meyers, Personal and Confidential.* And the other: *Mr. Joseph Kasperman, Personal and Confidential.* Was she aware that she used the intimate form for her mother, the official one for Joseph? Perhaps because there was no name for her relationship to him. Or perhaps because she could not think of Maria Meyers in any other way except: my mother.

Here are the letters. I call them letters, as opposed to the other words she wrote, which I call a statement, unsealed, unaddressed, its envelope transparent: inviting anyone's attention, everyone's. We might as well begin with her mother's. It doesn't matter, really, but a letter to one's mother would seem to take pride of place. This may not be correct, but it would seem most ordinary.

Mother:

Try to call on the values you have given me: a love of justice, a need to bear witness to the truth. I am doing this in the name of justice, in witness to the truth. I am marking a wrongful death, for which I was responsible, and other public wrongs that will lead to death and more death.

I have considered, of course, the sorrow this will cause you. Yet I know that you are a person of hope, a person at home in this world, and that you will go on. Try to understand that I am not a person of hope and I am not at home in this world, which I believe to be a place of harm. And though I am a person of no force, I have learned that I am capable of harming. This consideration has led me to believe that it is best that I remove myself from this life and my own life and become, rather, a witness. Also, having seen the possibility of harm within myself, I have become more convinced than ever that the darkness is stronger than the light. At least it is stronger than I am. I know what you would say: Focus on the light, focus on what can be changed. I believe that I can change nothing by my life, but that my death has the possibility at least of shedding some light. I have not said these things in the statement I have left on the ground here at the embassy. What I believe about the nature of the world is not for the eyes of the world but for yours and Joseph's. You will be witness to this thing that I believe. You, a person of greater force, can use your force, perhaps, in some way I cannot imagine.

I know that you love me. Please know that I have loved you. You may think I should live for you, to keep you from this sorrow, but I cannot. It is better that I am not in this life.

Please understand that this has nothing to do with you. There is nothing you could have done.

Your loving daughter Pearl

And here is what she wrote to Joseph:

Joseph:

I believe that of all people you will understand this best, will comprehend most fully the decisions I have made. A boy died because of me. Because I rendered him as nothing in my self-righteous blindness in the name of an idea. I made a thing of him. I stole his faith and hope.

I know about some things that you and my mother never told me: faith, hope, and love. I have never been naturally a person of hope. Nor, I believe, are you. I have lost my faith in the goodness of life. Replacing that belief: a belief in malignity. In the will to harm. And the dismay that this impulse is in myself.

Still, I know some things are better than others. The peace agreement will lead to things better than endless violence. I give my life, however ludicrous it seems, in witness to this. And in witness to the commonality of the impulse to harm.

Take care of my mother and yourself.

Thank you for years of love and care.

You have done nothing but good to me. When I think that there might be one person in the world free of the impulse to harm, it is you. For this, I honor you.

I know you understand what I am doing. You have always understood me. This has been a gift I am more grateful for than I can say.

Take care of my mother and yourself.

Your loving
Pearl

Now what do these explain — the statement, the letters? They sound rather different in some ways, don't you think, one from the other? The statement is quite cool; you may find it confusing in the way it mixes categories: terms. The letter to her mother is protective — or does she want to keep her mother at arm's length? I think she must have been farther along in the process of starvation when she wrote to Joseph. She repeats herself; she must have begun to lose control. What do these words tell you about this young woman with a thirst for death? You can see she is serious, intelligent, thoughtful, but tormented in her seriousness. She believes she has done wrong. She believes her life is nothing. This is what these words say: that her life is no use of itself, only as witness.

Do these words help you to understand

why a young woman, a healthy, fortunate American woman, would do what she has done: starved herself to the point of death and chained herself to a flagpole at the embassy?

I want you to understand that although you may think of her death as a suicide it is also more than that. She wanted to die to be out of this life, but she also wanted to use her death. Her death was the vessel of her hope. She could use her death as she could not use her life. Her death would be legible, audible. Her life, she believed, was dim and barely visible; her words feeble whispers, scratches at the door.

As she gave up eating, this sense of purpose, the joy of pure statement, pure act, took her over. She felt at rest. In emptying herself, she was turning from body to idea, the idea that a chosen death could serve as a marker for a wrongful death. The idea that, like the Irish hunger strikers of the 1920s and the 1980s, she was giving her life in witness to a good much larger than her own survival on the earth — where, living, she would make no mark.

And yet you will say she is different from the hunger strikers who went before her in Ireland. The hunger strikers hoped against hope that they would be stopped, that they could stop before their death. Pearl doesn't want to stop; she wants her death for its own sake, as a release from being overwhelmed. Her death is desirable to her: a glass of water in the darkness. This act is full of contradictions, you might say. What is it: suicide or hunger strike, private act or public statement?

She would say to you, proud of the economy of her death: It is all of these.

All right, all right, you might be saying to me. But what about Stephen Donegan? Who is this boy and what were the circumstances of *his* death?

You have to trust me: it will all come later.

Pearl isn't thinking about him now, and we must proceed as she proceeds. We must follow Pearl, follow the pattern of her mind. She is starving; she moves from clarity to blankness: there are moments of hallucination, flashes of what she thinks of as pure darkness, then pure comprehension.

Suppose we are standing on a pier. It is early morning; we are in some warm climate, maybe Florida. We are looking down from where we stand on the pier, down into the water. A school of fish swims by, smallish but colorful. Then, appearing as if from behind a cloud — but there are no clouds, only distance — a bird swoops down, sensing the far school of fish. He dives, lands in the water; the school of fish gives up form and cohesion, scatters. Dark gaps of water appear between clusters of fleeting color. The new form disappears into the darkness under the pier. If we wait, the form will re-cohere. Will it be the form we first saw or will it be a semblance of itself? No matter: it will be distinguishable to us as one cohesive whole.

This is how it is with Pearl. The beak, the wingspan of her anguish flies at her, scatters her thoughts, breaks up the center. First there is a cohesion, then descending wings, then clusters; then the clusters re-cohere. To understand now we must follow the new form: clusters that come together, and separate, and then come together again.

In her clear moments she sees faces — her witnesses, she calls them — hears voices telling her their stories, telling her she is right to do what she is doing. The faces come to her, hover in the air before her eyes, then fade and disappear. Faces in frames, faces surrounded by blue air. A blue that appeared when the darkness that surrounded her began to lighten, when she felt she was truly in the place of rest.

The faces and figures (they are torsos only; she never sees their hands) are cut out of bright air, as with a knife: cut with extreme precision and then pasted with the same precision back into the air. So they are at once separate from their background and a part of it. One shoulder perhaps shading off into a darkness only the width of a pencil line, the shadow of a greater darkness. The faces are illumined, particularly the air, by a light whose source she cannot see, a light that strains their eyes and makes them tighten their mouths. She begs them to stay until the time when she will understand.

We all like to believe that before death there is a moment of great clarity: what we call understanding. But suppose there isn't, only a series of shadings-off? A set of increasing vaguenesses, then darkness, and then nothing at all?

It is possible.

She doesn't see Stephen Donegan's face: Stephen Donegan, whom she calls Stevie. When she says his name, only a shape appears: dish-shaped, featureless, white. She sees other faces. Faces she thinks of as witnesses telling her that she is right to do what she is doing because it is too much for her to live with. Because the most truthful thing to be said about human beings, the most common thing about them, is that they will do harm. And she too has the will: what she has done to Stevie shows that she is one of them, one of the crowd with stretched lips, bloody eyes, the vacant patient stare that with its blankness can erase the world.

Perhaps you are thinking that if you knew more of Pearl's background you might understand why she is doing what she's doing, why she is where she is. But what do we mean by background? If we knew what we meant by background, would it help us to say more clearly what the nature of the foreground is? A painter might spend far more time considering the background of her work than what is nearest to the eye. Let's imagine we're looking at a Romantic painting. There is a blackish-purple sky, tall thin-leaved trees; through a gap in the trees a white full moon surrounded by a haze of cloud. In the front, three small figures stand, bent, their backs to us, looking at something on the ground, trying to see something in the moonlight, something that absorbs them but that we can't begin to discern. Of what use is it to say that the sky, the trees, the moon, must be known as the background? Would it mean that the figures are more important than the sky?

So what could I tell you about Pearl's background that would be of use in answering the question *What is this woman doing here?* By which you would mean starving, chained, lying on the ground in front of the American embassy in Dublin. If I told you that Pearl's grandfather was a Jewish convert to Catholicism, that her mother is the supervisor of several day-care centers in the Washington Heights section of New York City but had a history of involvement in radical politics during the Vietnam war, that her father was a Cambodian who disappeared into his own country before her birth, would that explain anything about why she is where she is on Christmas Day of 1998?

Perhaps you should know what she looks like. A beautiful girl, people have said, struck by looks that they almost always call unusual. Black Asian eyes but light brown hair, commonly called dirty blond. A wide forehead. Thick eyebrows, darker than her hair. Her body: long-legged, small-breasted, tall. A beautiful girl.

But what does any of this explain? How

46

do any of us explain why we are where we are? How do we retrace our route; what maps do we consult to follow our road backward; who is the native guide? Do we look in the coils of our heritage? For the surfeit or starvation of early love? How far back is it useful to go?

In Pearl's case, should we go back in the history of Ireland to the sixteenth century, the beginning of the English conquest? Or do we go back to Pearl's first days in Ireland, at the beginning of the year 1998?

Certainly it would be one way of answering the question of what she is doing here. If by *here* we mean Dublin, it might be truthful to say: *She was studying the Irish language at Trinity College. This is her year abroad.*

Let's see where that will lead.

But if we take this route you must understand it is one that Pearl is no longer capable of traveling. Her mind will not move in a straight line. It will not connect specific events of the present to specific events of the past. There is a face she needs, Stevie's face, but when she tries to call it up it is a blank, a dish shape, a featureless white plain.

There are other faces, other names: Finbar. Breeda. Mick. The names, the faces of her time in Ireland. Shall we go back to the beginning of that time? January 1998, when she arrived in Dublin, a student from Wesleyan University, Middletown, Connecticut, to study the Irish language at Trinity College.

We can go back to that. We are seeing what Pearl cannot see: a line.

But we are not starving; we are not cold or lying on the ground. So you can say to me — certainly you have a right to say to me — Tell me how she came to Ireland. And that, certainly, is something I can do.

• 3 •

Eleven months ago, Pearl Meyers saw the city of Dublin for the first time. Sharing a cab from the airport with Jessica Henderson, not exactly a friend but someone she liked well enough to sublet a flat with, twenty minutes' walk from Trinity, a neighborhood with no real name, between Fipsboro and Stonybatter, between the Corn Exchange and the Four Courts. A one-bedroom apartment in a modern complex: a series of four-story buildings around a central courtyard.

There'd been the excitement, first, of having her own apartment. Not her mother's, not a college dorm. She and Jessica, her not-quite friend, had shopped for posters, a tablecloth, agreed to share a hair dryer and a toaster, which the original tenant seemed not to own or had taken with her. They were just settling in, and what didn't work in the flat was a joke at first: the washing machine that turned out to be unusable, because the water didn't drain and so they had to empty it into the toilet; the doorbell that didn't sound; the telephone whose wire fell out in the middle of every conversation. And then one night Jessica developed a high fever. She phoned her mother in Pennsylvania. Her mother told them to call the head of the program. It was four in the morning. They waited till eight. The head of the program said she would meet them at the hospital. In time, it was determined Jessica had encephalitis. She was kept in the hospital ten days until she was pronounced fit to travel. Then she was sent home to recuperate. Her parents, grateful to Pearl for nursing their daughter and prosperous in any case, agreed to go on paying her half of the rent for the rest of the year.

What had seemed a joke with the energetic Jessica now seemed an oppression. Like the number 137 bus, which stopped or didn't stop at the place the sign indicated, causing Pearl to jump into the middle of the street to hail it; sometimes drivers would stop, sometimes not. Once when she asked a driver if the bus officially stopped there, he shrugged and said nothing.

In the morning, it was still dark at eight. She would sit in the armchair by the window, a mole-colored chair covered in velveteen with a pattern of unnameable leaves and flowers. The too-new bricks on the adjacent buildings sank her heart: an attempt at variegation: some rust-colored, some mustard, some a powder beige. The stone tiles of the pavement were already discolored from moisture. A metal door on the storage building reminded her of a prison, and the lights, still on in the transitional moment between dawn and light, spoke to her of surveillance, as if, walking into the courtyard, she would set off a siren. The heels of early workers clicked in the damp air.

Pearl didn't know what to do with herself in the week before classes started. She would sit in the student canteen, eating her grilled cheese sandwiches, too shy to speak. Pub life seemed beyond her; she'd had no experience of a social life built around drinking. She tried to walk the city but didn't know what she was looking for. She remembered a saying her mother lived by: You must be sure that you enjoy one thing every day. Most days, for her, it was the colors of the doors or the painted surfaces of the buildings, bright blue, candy yellow, festive in the dim air. And the voices of the people, and their good manners, which made her hungrier, as they suggested a warmth she felt herself a

51

failure to be unable to take advantage of.

It wasn't any better when classes started. She was shy, and no one seemed anxious to include her in their conversation. She was taking classes in the Irish language. It was her Irish teacher who suggested to the class that even though they were beginners they should go to meetings of the Gaelic Club, just to hear the language spoken. That was where she met Finbar, whom she probably wouldn't have talked to in the United States. At home she would have found him an embarrassment: shoulder-length hair, army greatcoat, tie-dyed shirt, overlarge boots. But Finbar talked to *her*. And it seemed to her that she hadn't had a conversation in the two weeks since Jessica had left. She let him buy her a drink. They discovered they both had a facility for languages.

★ ★ ★

Perhaps you would feel more sympathy for Pearl if you could say she did what she did for love. That she had met a young man, loved him, given herself to his cause. But it didn't happen like that. For Pearl, it was more an affair of the mind than the heart, more a thing of words than of the body. Also, she was very lonely. She was alone in a strange city. It was winter. The sky darkened early. She didn't know how to make things work: the buses, the telephones. And there was the accident of her roommate's getting sick and having to go home. How much of what happed to Pearl is traceable to a microbe? To the weak sun? To the failure of the Dublin buses?

But no, you will say to me, that can't be it; there must be more than that, more than the sun, the washing machine, the buses. Of course there is. But that is the beginning.

It would not be right to say she fell in love, but after she met Finbar she felt happier, not so alone. Finbar McDonagh. He had a circle of friends, boys who dressed like he did, who wore their hair to their shoulders, who collected in his flat to talk about politics. Because of Finbar and his friends, Pearl had to learn a whole new set of terms. Republican is not the party of Ronald Reagan and George Bush; to be Republican means you believe in a United Ireland, an Ireland healed after the split that occurred in 1922, when the six counties of the North were declared not part of Ireland but of Britain. Then, if you learned the word *Republican,* you needed to learn many new names: Michael Collins, Éamon de Valera, Pádraig Pearse. And then you had to learn that the opposite of Republican is Unionist, or sometimes Loyalist: names for the Northern Protestants who want to keep the North a colony of England. Names for the enemies.

Everything Finbar and his friends did was connected to the Republican cause. They studied the Irish language because it was the language of the Republic; they played Irish football because it was the proper game for people with their politics. There was only one worthy endeavor and only one vision: a united Ireland free of any English taint.

She was fascinated. It was a new kind of being political, different from that of her mother and her mother's friends, who went to meetings to stop the construction of buildings too tall for the neighborhood or to start the construction of vest-pocket parks, who worked on school board elections and traveled to Albany to lobby state senators about universal pre-K education. The language of this new politics was large; history was invoked, in poetry and song: colonialism, oppression, the true spirit of the Irish land. Heroes were called *martyrs*. Her spine thrilled when she heard the word; she'd discovered it secretly, on her own, as other children might discover the term *sadist* or *coprophilia*. She had never heard the word *martyr* spoken aloud.

But her mother had heard the word and spoken it; it was a word her mother was born knowing. So would you say that it was part of Pearl's background even if it was silenced, rendered invisible? Maria Meyers was raised Catholic, but she was determined that her child would not be.

The most venerated martyr of them all was Bobby Sands. Bobby Sands, a hunger striker, dead by self-starvation in November 1982, when Pearl was almost four years old. She saw his smiling face first over the mantel in Finbar's apartment, a place of honor that in other Dublin apartments, the kind of apartment she would never see, would be reserved for a picture of the Sacred Heart, Christ with hair the same length as Bobby's but not smiling, no, not smiling at all.

Pearl first saw the picture of Bobby Sands framed in Finbar's flat and then, later, enlarged, huge, on the wall of the room where the Cumman na Gael, the Gaelic Club, held its meetings. She enjoyed it there, enjoyed hearing Irish spoken, listening to the songs, moving on to the pub, and then to other meetings where the face of Bobby Sands was also on the wall. And she heard stories of great cruelties on the part of the British: torture, discrimination, civil rights denied; the innocent murdered, the guilty set free. She was excited because she felt that this, finally, was life, the life she dreamed of, where things were serious and people knew what was important and would say it. In Ireland, Pearl felt for the first time that she was a part of history. In America, history had no meaning for her. She could never see herself as part of American history: the founding fathers, with their pigtails and their faith in human goodness. It was in Ireland, beginning with Bobby Sands and his faith in the power of suffering, that she began to take her place. A place where people talked in large terms and sang songs about life and death and sacrifice, plaintive songs that seemed not about violence but about the loss of the hills, the mother, the beloved brave young man.

Finbar's first gift to Pearl was the complete writings of Bobby Sands. Bobby Sands described himself as an ordinary young Belfast boy, a boy who loved playing games, particularly Irish football, who loved walking in the mountains, who was particularly interested in birds. He did not begin by being political. He even played football on a Protestant team. He worked as a kind of mechanic for a company that repaired buses. And then the Unionists destroyed his neighborhood, setting fire to streets he'd lived on all his life, and evicting his family from their home for nothing, for being Catholic. He was eighteen years old. He said he joined the Irish Republican Army not because he loved violence but to protect his home and those he loved. He was arrested for participating in a demonstration that turned bloody, put into prison, set free; arrested again, found with a gun in his car. Put in a nightmare prison, a prison that became a synonym for inhumanity: Long Kesh, the H Block.

At first when he was imprisoned, he and his comrades were classified as political prisoners and therefore not required to wear uniforms or to engage in ordinary penal work. They were permitted to meet together, to study, to consult. These privileges were revoked by Margaret Thatcher. The imprisoned IRA men were reclassified as ordinary criminals, no different from murderers or rapists. They were required to wear ordinary uniforms. This they would not do. They stripped themselves naked, wrapped themselves in blankets, and took the name of Blanket Men. The guards became truly sadistic; Pearl read Bobby Sands's stories of having his testicles squeezed and his anus violated; having his toilet privileges denied, his food pissed in, his shit not emptied from the pot they gave him; given food that crawled with maggots. The kind of detail her mother would have read of the martyrs to the Romans, the Communists. But her mother would have read them triumphantly; Pearl had to force herself to go on.

★ ★ ★

In protest against their filthy conditions, the prisoners treated the wardens with some of their own. They refused to wash; they wiped their shit on the walls of their cells. They called this the Dirty Protest, but these words were inadequate for Pearl. Blanket Men. Dirty Protests: she felt the cold, the filth, the wafer-thin foam mattresses soaked in urine, the plastic pen refill Bobby Sands hid up his rectum so he could pull it out and write on scraps of toilet paper the poems that were in his head, that he was denied permission to write. Pearl could not help noticing: the poems weren't very good. Then she despised herself for such a thought. What did it matter if the language was clichéd if you hid the means of writing it up your ass, if you risked being beaten senseless to write it at all? You had to think of poetry in a new way, she told herself; you had to think of everything in a new way if someone was willing to give up so much.

There were some things she didn't understand. It seems that Bobby Sands and his comrades went on hunger strikes to protest being classified as ordinary prisoners. Margaret Thatcher stood firm: Bobby Sands and his kind were criminals, and criminals they would be called. She stood by as Bobby Sands starved himself to death. Eight weeks it took: he suffered horrible stomach cramps; he went blind; he lapsed into a coma. Then, as the world watched, he died. He was twenty-eight years old.

Margaret Thatcher let Bobby Sands die — and nine others who followed him — because the force of their deaths was less strong than the force of her determination not to be defied. Some commentators thought her being a woman made it even more important to her that she appear strong. In the end, those deaths were strong enough to turn the head of the world; not strong enough for one woman to give up her terror of appearing to be weak and allow these men to call themselves political prisoners, a name she thought incorrect.

Sometimes Pearl asked herself, Did Bobby Sands die for an issue of language? And if so, what did that mean about language's power? And the power of his ideas, which frightened her: peace at the end of a gun? The words didn't make sense to her. But she knew they must be made to make sense because someone died for them. It was the first time the thought came to her: the strength of offering up your life.

Pearl couldn't get enough of Bobby Sands, but that was true of many people, in and out of Ireland. She took herself to the Sinn Féin bookstore to buy everything they had about him: posters and books and CDs of songs recorded by his fellow prisoners, songs about him, songs that yearned for the hills and the trees and the birds, songs about monsters of imperialism, one about the British occupiers called "Strangers, Devils, and Thieves." She was drawn most not to the image of the smiling boy with the rebellious, playful, counterculture hair but to the bearded figure, whom she would not have thought of the way natives of Catholic Ireland would have: as a figure of the suffering Savior,

Christ on the road to Calvary beneath his cross.

Bobby Sands pictures, tapes, bumper stickers, T-shirts, key chains, ashtrays, scarves. The artifacts of veneration. It didn't occur to Pearl, but if Joseph had seen the Sinn Féin bookstore he would have understood that they were both in the same business: the business of religious articles. He would, perhaps, have been tempted to give them advice. On the layout of the store. On the fact that it wasn't a good idea to take customers down to the smelly basement to get access to the credit card machine. He might have told them to think about investing in new lighting. It would, he might have said, be good for business. Because that is his business; he is president of a company founded by Maria's father: Panis Angelicus, Inc.

This is the sort of thing Joseph knows: what's good for business. He is a successful businessman. He makes money for himself, for Maria, and for Pearl, so that when Pearl wanted to spend a year in Ireland, studying the Irish language, which she had come to love because of the poetry, he could say, "What a good idea; of course." Perhaps it would have been better if he hadn't been able to say it. But he did say it, and she did go to Ireland: for poetry, for the rich language. That was what she thought. That was what everybody thought.

And in the end, that was right; everything did have its roots in her love of language. They really were happy together, she and Finbar, when they were studying. Finbar was proficient in the Irish language. He'd studied it since he was a child; he'd gone to Irish language camp on the Aran Islands to polish his skills. Thrilled that a woman, and a beautiful one, was impressed with him at last, he helped Pearl with the parts of her studies she found difficult. He explained the different uses of the verb *to be:* two forms, one denoting equivalence, one descriptive. The examples he chose interested her: "My father is a doctor"; "My father is playing golf." The words for *is* were different, he said. He didn't hear himself mentioning the things about his doctor father he believed that he despised: his profession, his prosperity. He told her that, in old Irish, they used the form that denoted equivalence to speak of color. "The stone is gray." But so deep was the equivalence that the words for the object and its color were the same. The word for *stone* was the same as the word for *gray*. More exciting to her: the word for *yellow* was the same as the word for *noble*. The word for *brightness* and *wisdom* was the same as the word for *white*.

She could almost, but not quite, convince herself that she loved him then. And his body moved her by its suggestion of unhealth, as if it were the body of a student in a Russian novel, starving himself for books. They were happy, sitting in his flat and studying Irish, she showing him the bits of Cambodian she knew, going over some Latin (she was the more proficient), throwing each other words like arcs of grain. Yes, there were times they were happy.

At first she didn't understand that her relationship to the languages she'd studied — Spanish, French, Latin, Cambodian — was different from Finbar's relationship to Irish. She loved studying language as a thing removed from human beings, like a mathematical theorem. She came to study Irish because it was difficult and complicated. But she would have been quite happy with a series of abstract sounds.

For Finbar, the Irish language was the vehicle that could transport him and transform him into the man he longed to be. He was a well-bred boy and he hated that, as he hated so many things about himself: the well-mannered son of well-mannered parents, both doctors. He hated his house in Dun Laoghaire with the high windows whose glass seemed thicker than American glass, more like water with a few drops of darkness in it, so that the leaves seen through it wavered, wobbled in the air that always seemed silvery in that garden, as if his parents' prosperity had saturated the light that surrounded their house. He hated it that his parents liked Pearl, that she liked his parents. He took her home only twice and wouldn't take her again; he wanted to show her off and then he wanted to deprive them of her. He begrudged them every ounce of pride and pleasure they could take in him. Finbar, the least successful son of a spectacularly successful family: the smallest boy, always the smallest boy, the clumsy boy, pale, with red hair and brown eyes so that he always looked a bit anemic, his skin bluish like skim milk. Believing always, though he could never admit it, that boys like his brothers and his brothers' friends, whose skins were penetrated by the sun, boys who could catch balls and throw them and shout to one another in an easy way, as if words were not precious, as if words counted for nothing: those were the right kind of boys to be. Boys like his brother Seamus, his brother Rory, who could run and run and never get tired and joke with people, who were always glad to see them, and tease their mother out of giving them a punishment: Seamus, a doctor like his parents; Rory, making his way up in the bank. Finbar couldn't catch or throw or run or joke, but he could put his mind to words. Pearl did not love him, but she loved what he could do with words, how he could catch words like coins; no boy could catch words like Finbar. He believed at the same time that words were the most important thing in the world (he despised people for their slowness or carelessness with language), that his mind was the finest thing on earth, and at the same time, helplessly, he despised himself for not throwing and catching and running and joking, for not having a skin that absorbed the sun.

She had never seen anyone so clumsy. If there was a table to bump into, he'd bump into it. What he did to a piece of fruit with a knife was terrible to watch. And she didn't know whether it was just the light in his bedroom, the naked lightbulb in the room without windows, but the hair around his cock always looked yellowish, like the leaves of the plant he got from his aunt. The plant he always overwatered. The plant he kicked over with his heavy boot when she told him he was overwatering it. Then, when she swept up the dirt and tried to repot it, saying to her, "Well, aren't you the fucking lovely little housewife."

He was often bad-tempered, but they were happy together for a while, particularly when they studied. And she was even happy for a time among his friends: Wendy to his Peter Pan, the prize among the loser boys in their tie-dyed shirts and ponytails, all of them wanting to be other people in another time, wanting to be IRA soldiers in the great days of the seventies and eighties, a time when events and situations were given names that became part of the language. And one of them not a boy but a man, Mick Winthrop, and then his son Stevie, Stephen Donegan, whose name you have already heard, whose death Pearl feels responsible for, whose death she is giving up her life in witness to.

One night, February 13, 1998, when she went to the meeting of the Gaelic Club, she met Mick Winthrop, Michael Revere Winthrop, another American, older than the boys, of their fathers' generation, yet one of them in his desire for a connection to a more heroic time, a more heroic identity. I understand now, and you can understand it too: if she hadn't learned about Bobby Sands, if she hadn't met Mick Winthrop, father of the bastard son Stevie, she would not be where she is now, lying on the frozen ground, chained to the flagpole of the American embassy. You and I can see it, and she may even be seeing it too; she did not see it then. She was excited to be learning new things, meeting new people. She had friends. She was no longer feeling so alone.

Was it just another symptom of homesickness that Pearl was susceptible to Mick Winthrop for so long? It did seem wonderful at first: Mick, so American, so healthy, with skin that looked like it absorbed what little sun there was in the dark climate and took in the good of it and used it to manufacture health. As if he were a tycoon of health, had made his fortune on it, and would spread its benefits wherever he might be. His gray hair was cropped short. His face was always — well, not tan — a kind of russet color, like a healthy apple just off the tree. His clothes fit him as if the cloth had been woven with him in mind. It was a pleasure to watch him walk. He could walk miles over mountains and play the game of hurling with boys half his age. He could build things, fix things; his hands were comfortable with tools; they were short and broad and the hair on them was dark and fine. He ate as if the goodness of food were no surprise to him, as if he'd never had to worry about having enough or getting fat. She'd never seen a man eat like Mick ate. When he was passed something — a basket of bread, a platter of meat — he took it, almost smiling at it, as if it were an old trusted servant or a faithful animal, just the right amount, not too much, not too little, consuming it happily, readily, with no sense of hesitation or of shame. When Joseph was passed a dish of something he would always hesitate, look to be sure there was enough for everyone, and calculate the amount he considered his due. Finbar shoveled food onto his plate as if he were afraid someone would beat him to it if he weren't desperately fast.

Oh, there were many reasons it took Pearl so long to come to the understanding that she finally did of Mick. Some you may be sympathetic with, some not. Bear in mind she was a fatherless girl; she hadn't known many men. The fathers of her friends tended to be fatigued or brash, kind or aloof, but none of them had the animal vitality of Michael Revere Winthrop. She'd never heard a man sing as he did; none of the fathers of her friends sang, and she'd never heard Joseph sing. All this combined with a set of maternal gestures, upon which was layered a habit of seductiveness — surely he walked barefoot in the house because he knew his feet were beautiful; surely he noticed the way Pearl's eyes followed his unbuttoning of his long-sleeved shirt, rolling up his sleeves to reveal the silky black hair that covered his forearms. Surely he understood that it would mean something to her when he bought her little presents: books, mainly, but then a scarf, a pin, a traditional Irish cookbook. He would not have known that it hadn't happened to her before, a man, not a boy, giving presents in homage to her as a woman. She liked his gratitude when she'd bring him a cup of tea; she was pleased when he said "Outstanding" when she made brown bread from the recipe in the cookbook he'd given her. She was comforted when he cooked for her, Irish oatmeal, which took nearly an hour, ethnic dishes with lots of garlic — the smell of which had always permeated her mother's kitchen but which she'd got no hint of since she'd been in Ireland. "I want to enact the cuisine of diversity," he said. "If there's anything valuable about America, it's diversity." He said he'd made friends with lots of different people by asking them to teach him to cook their favorite dish from home. She was impressed by that: Joseph had never cooked; none of her friends' fathers cooked.

At first it seemed to her that she had finally met a man who was the way men were supposed to be. Who looked like he'd always had all the citrus fruit he needed, all the sports equipment he wanted, whose accent was like hers, who could recite *Make Way for Ducklings* and *Goodnight Moon.*

And then it stopped — the presents, the cooking — when she began to suspect that his ideas were not the ones she wanted to go along with. No one had ever censored her reading, but when she read a history of Ireland he didn't approve of he told her to "put down that counterrevolutionary crap." She was entirely shocked; in her whole life no one had ever told her to put down a book.

He could tell, she knew it, that her mind

wandered when he began to talk about his big ideas. He was American, so he loved big ideas. He had big ideas about himself and Ireland; he mixed ideas with magic, or really it was superstition: he was always meant to be here, his parents had kept him from his roots, never told him he'd had an Irish great-grandmother. It wasn't just an accident that he'd met his IRA friends when he was looking for his ancestors in county Tyrone. He'd always known his roots weren't just American; he'd felt himself part of the Irish soil the minute he'd stepped onto it. And then to meet, right away, the brother of Reg Donegan! It had to have been meant to be.

Mick had a theater company based in Roxbury, in Boston. Street theater, he called it, guerrilla theater, people's theater. Scenes played out in what he called "public spaces" — supermarket parking lots, in front of abandoned buildings. Actors improvising, actors in masks, actors with painted faces and bodies: everything connected to what Mick called "the life of the people, the life of the street."

When Pearl heard him talk about this work she was embarrassed; it was an old idea, one that had been seen not to work, a reminder of a past that hadn't kept its promise. He said he was into the idea of life as performance and performance as life. He said that people talked about performance artists, but what you needed was life artists, people who made an art form of their lives. Finbar and his friends lapped it up, but Pearl resisted. She didn't say what she thought: that art was not life because the material of life is unrevisable. That at the end of a work of art there is another work of art. At the end of life there is death. She wanted to say, Surely you see the difference. But she said nothing.

There was no one she could speak to about her misgivings. It's too bad she didn't think of speaking to her mother. I believe things might have turned out very differently if at a certain moment Pearl had called Maria. But if she'd spoken to her mother, she would not be the person she is, in the place she is now, chained to the flagpole of the American embassy in Dublin, Ireland, where she came for the first time in January, less than a year ago.

• 4 •

We will leave Pearl for a little while, because this is not her story only but the story of three people, and we have not attended to Joseph and Maria for quite some time.

Maria is in the first-class cabin of Aer Lingus Flight 865, New York to Dublin with a stopover at Shannon, hoping she is in time to save her daughter's life. She is trying to understand why her daughter is where she is, why she has done what she has done. She is terrified.

But she must stop being terrified. She has six hours in the air, six hours in which there is no possible action she can take to help her daughter.

The plane takes off into a black sky. She is nowhere; the sky turns from black to greenish, a thick weaving over of cloud. Useless to note the number of miles piling up, the figures on the screen in front of her. The pilot, who is Irish, says, "Keep your seat belts fastened, we may be experiencing some light chop." Light chop, what does that mean? she asks herself. She wishes someone she knew were sitting beside her so she could laugh at the pilot's language. But she's afraid the fattish blond man beside her would take it as encouragement if she laughed. He might think she wants to talk. She does not want to talk, to him or anyone else. She does not want to explain why she is traveling to Dublin first class, the day after Christmas. What could she say when there is nothing that she understands?

She would like to use this time well, or at least not badly. She would like to begin to understand what her daughter is doing, what she has said.

Witness. Against what? For what?

And why?

There is only one thing she knows, one thing she would tell her daughter: *Nothing is worth your life. You are my child. Nothing is worth your life.*

Would she say that first? Or would she say kindly — or angrily — *Why are you doing this?* What has happened means she does not know her daughter. Which means she does not know herself. Which means she is a different person from the one she was twenty-four hours ago.

The prospect of her daughter's dying is a burning place she cannot stand on, must

74

run from, but must return to, just in case — in case being there might stop the fire. In case she can think of something. But it is impossible; simply to form the thought is impossible. Pearl could die. It is unendurable. She is drawn back to the place and then must run from it; no stillness is possible, no stable plane. Fire and avalanche and flood: she cannot catch her breath and yet she must, for it will only make things worse if she can't catch her breath, if she can't find the piece of ground that will support her weight, that will allow her to take the first step. She has always believed in the first step: that taking it is better than not taking it. But she is on an airplane. Her scope of movement is radically small. There is nowhere for her to go.

What did I do wrong, what did I do wrong? she keeps asking herself, seeing Pearl's face, the high forehead she put her lips to when she checked her child for fever, the beautifully cut nostrils, the dark eyes that demanded, always, that nothing be kept back.

She hears Lynne Craig's words, *witness, politics,* thinking of Pearl lying on the freezing ground chained to a flagpole, seeing chains around her wrists, hearing her say, "Mother . . . Mama . . . Mommy

. . . Mom," but she isn't calling her; her mother was not the one she called. And why not? Why didn't her daughter call her if she needed help? What has she done wrong? Was she too indulgent? Not indulgent enough? Was she too much the animal mother, thinking all her child needed was warmth and food and a place under her arm, near the warmth of her side, that licks and nips and hugs would take the place of something else, something she needed more, some kind of knowledge, some kind of discernment or attention? Had she had too much faith that this overwhelming, drowning love, as natural as breathing, as sleeping, was the thing that would get her daughter through? Or was she not enough the animal mother; was she too judgmental, not accepting enough, did she fail to cook enough, did she assert her own opinion too vehemently, too often? Did she spend too much time at work? Should she have only worked part time, should she have been more available? Or was she too intrusive, not giving her daughter enough distance, not keeping the space between them inviolate, pristine? Does she think I don't love her? Maria wonders. Isn't my love enough to keep my child alive? What did I do wrong, *what did I do wrong?* What else can she say? Because it is impossible, of course it is, for a mother not to blame herself if something has gone wrong with her child.

It is always complicated, it is always difficult to raise a child. But I would say it was a particularly complicated project, a particularly new endeavor, to have led a life like Maria's and to be the kind of mother she wanted to be to Pearl. Maria wanted to protect her child; at the same time she wanted to give her freedom.

Perhaps if you knew more about Maria you would understand how the questions she has asked herself might begin to be answered. So as there is not much to say about Maria in the present, not much action on an airplane flight unless there's an emergency (and this is a perfectly normal flight), I will use the time to tell you about her past, to sketch in her background.

I want to set the story of three people in its time. I want to tell their stories as a part of history. Because sometimes a story is not just a tale but a chronicle: "In the reign of A, B begat C, D, E, F, G, H, I, and J."

I'm now going to take up the form of the chronicle. To talk about a time in history, a person in history, focusing on particular

77

years rather than on an individual.

Maria Meyers was born to Seymour and Pearl Meyers in Larchmont, New York, on November 14, 1948. When she was two, her mother died of ovarian cancer. A priest found Seymour Meyers a housekeeper, Marie Kasperman, who came with her son, Joseph. The four of them lived in a house in one of the wealthier suburbs of New York City.

Although the chronicle centers on Maria's life, to understand things properly we must go back to the years before her birth, to the youth of Maria's father, Seymour Meyers, a young Jewish man who in 1938 received his PhD in art history from Columbia University, where he had completed his undergraduate education three years earlier.

The year is important: 1938. An important year for Jews. The year of Kristallnacht, the night of broken glass. Synagogues and Jewish businesses smashed, the sound of breakage in the streets largely unheard. That sound traveled to New York, where Seymour Meyers, rather than fearing for his people, rather than hearing in the air the sound of broken glass, hears something else, a tone that is in the localized air around Columbia University, something heard clearly by the kind of young man moved by the example of the conversion of Thomas Merton. Something that pulls a certain kind of young man to a vision of the past formed by the philosophy of Thomas Aquinas, the poetry of Dante, the music of Gregorian chant. Conversions become — I do not want to say fashionable, but there is a sort of — what shall I say? — *trend* toward conversion to Catholicism in those years among intellectuals of a certain — do I want to say nondemocratic bent? No, that would be too strong. Let's just say of a certain nondemotic, nonpopulist bent. So Seymour Meyers does not hear the sound of boots marching in Germany, of glass breaking on the streets, but the sound of *Tantum Ergo*, a hymn written by Thomas Aquinas himself. A question that could be asked: Did he not hear the marching, the falling glass, or did he turn to music to drown those noises out? I will not answer for Seymour Meyers; it is not a question he ever asked himself, and he is now among the dead.

Hearing the sounds he does, he believes he has no choice; his immortal soul is at stake: eternal damnation. In November of

1938, he is baptized in the same church where Thomas Merton was welcomed into the Mystical Body of Christ. Seymour's family, irreligious, had made money in the fur business. At his baptism, they not only cut him off without a penny, they sit shiva for him; they declare him dead. He declares this tolerable. All this time he has lightly courted Pearl Robbins, whom he has known since childhood: an orphan, brought up by an aunt. He persuades her to convert; having no family to sit shiva, it is not quite as difficult for her. He is what she has that is of value; he is luminous and her past is drab, confining: not much to give up.

To support his wife, to use his gifts for nourishment of the Mystical Body of which he is now a member, Seymour Meyers starts a business in religious art. He is determined to take a stand against the vulgar taste of immigrants and their instinct to display the most gross of what the religious imagination of Europe has reproduced, rejecting the finely wrought, the austere line, the demanding countenance. Their cloying taste for sentimental pieties, which he thought they often confused with food: girly haired Sacred Hearts pointing to their chests at something the shape of a pimento, fat-faced Madonnas on clouds that looked as if they had been carved from marzipan. Statues of the Infant of Prague, dressed by women like dolls whose costumes they changed with the season: green for Pentecost, white for Easter, purple for Lent. The faithful were starved for beauty; he would feed them with the bread of angels. He named his company Panis Angelicus, Inc. He specialized at first in Eric Gill woodcuts, Dürer engravings, birthday cards of Fra Angelico's annunciation: the shy Madonna, the angel strong in his news-bearing, his wings a striped marmoreal construction: green, red, peach, white, yellow. Oh, but the faithful did not want his food, so he convinced himself that he must train their appetite slowly: gradually, over the years. He included in his stock Carlo Dolci and Guido Reni, and then miraculous medals and then holy-water fonts in the shape of a lamb (glowing in the dark), rulers with the Ten Commandments printed on them, planters in the form of the Virgin's head (a slot in the back of the neck for soil and philodendra). But in his mind he was the purveyor of the work of the great masters of religious art; when the time came to stock Christmas cards of Sister Corita's penmanship and ones with a flower saying *War is not healthy for children and other living things,* Seymour Meyers filled the order forms, pretending he was not, casting his eye on the Byzantine image of Christ Pancreator, suitable for framing, 8 by 10, or laminated, 2 by 3, perfect for wallet or purse. Later, when the church, probably because of birth control, was losing its share of the consumer market (people didn't parade their Catholicism as they used to, either in decoration, jewelry, sacred images for hallway or living room, or birthday and anniversary gifts; fewer Catholics had their children baptized or confirmed), the business did not go under. A commercial crisis might have undone Panis Angelicus, Inc., as it had undone others, had not Joseph, in the seventies, eighties, and now the nineties, branched out into less sectarian realms, adding to his stock Serenity Prayer mugs, angel pins, Velcro hearts that said I'M SPECIAL CHRIST DIED FOR ME, and chip clips (available to match the colors of Dorito bags) with the name JESUS embossed on the plastic in white script.

But enough about the business. We'll get on with the story. With one of the stories. For now we again take up the chronicle.

Maria Meyers grew up a wealthy Catholic

child in the suburbs of New York City in the 1950s, a successful and triumphalist period for both the United States of America and the Catholic Church, no longer adversaries but linked in their determined hatred of Russian communism.

You must understand something of the history of that time, of the intersection in those years between the United States of America and the Roman Catholic Church, to understand Maria and Joseph and Pearl.

You will remember that both Maria and her father and Joseph and his mother lived in Seymour Meyers's house in Larchmont. The 1950s were famous for unexcitement. Maria and Joseph are good children, good students, and do not make public trouble; Maria and Joseph's mother dislike each other to the point of silent hatred, but these are years in which such secrets are not made public but are feverishly kept.

Then it is 1958: John XXIII is elected to the papacy; and 1960: John F. Kennedy is elected to the U.S. presidency.

In the fall of 1961, Maria became the special pet of Sister Berchmans, to whom she confided everything. In those years, there was great glamour in being the pet of a particular nun, especially if she was considered demanding or difficult. And in those years, there was a particular strictness, a particular anxiety, about the chastity of young girls in the world at large, but in a special way in the world presided over by priests like Father John Lynch and nuns like Sister Berchmans, of Sts. Cosmos and Damian Church and School.

Maria trusted Sister Berchmans and wanted to please her. To please her and to entertain her. To bring her the sweets of the outside world. Oh, they knew how to get you, did nuns like Sister Berchmans. They encouraged you to tell them everything and made you feel you were safe because you were special to them. They gave you little privileges: a visit to the nuns' private chapel; a holy card with their signature on the back, in perfect blue-black script, the name preceded by a cross. They encouraged you to chatter. Sister Berchmans was fascinated by Maria's father. For that kind of nun or priest in those days, a Jewish convert was a particular prize. "Your father is a very distinguished man," she said. "It's a high standard to live up to. But with God's help" or "with the dear Lord's blessing . . ."

It's certainly possible that Maria enjoyed the suspicion that her father made Sister Berchmans feel a little worried about herself, maybe a tiny bit inadequate. If her father could do that and she was his daughter — that was a sentence she was afraid to finish for herself, even in the silence of her own vain heart. Oh, I must tell you that in those days she was very vain. The incomparable vanity of the pious adolescent. But they bred it in girls like Maria.

It was an impulse born of the diction of saints' lives that made her say to Sister Berchmans, "Oh, but you know my father can be a lot of fun too." She blames herself for wanting to tell the nun stories. She believes everything that followed sprang from that: the impulse to entertain, to impress the nun with tales, in the shape of the Lives of the Saints. Because she forgot herself; she lost herself in the story, not remembering that with nuns and priests you always had to be on the alert, because at any minute the gate could come down and the person you'd just been chattering with could bring into the room the whole authority of Rome. The Holy Roman Empire. Just when you'd been eating chocolate chip cookies or talking about *My Fair Lady* or a hat you'd seen in a store window or the Dodgers winning the World Series or your favorite shade of blue or the flowers that bloom in the spring.

Sister Berchmans loved the story about Dr. Meyers and Joseph and Maria in Rumpelmayer's. Maria described the room; it was like a doll's room, pink and white and ribboned, a room that looked like you could eat the whole thing up. "My father ordered cream puffs and hot chocolate for us. He put on his very serious face. 'It is important,' he said, 'to know exactly how to eat a cream puff. When I was in Paris, very great ladies would say to me, *C'est de la plus grand importance savoir manger un cream puff comme il faut.'*" She told Sister Berchmans how he kept his pretend-serious face on and cut into one cream puff deliberately, carving up pieces with the right mixture of pastry and cream, then popping them into his mouth like Charlie Chaplin. "My dear children," he said. "It takes a lot of practice. You must eat many, many cream puffs before you can truly say you know how to eat them comme il faut."

She told how he ordered one cream puff for each of them and then said, "That's good, that's good; you're getting the idea but I don't think it's quite yet comme il faut." And he kept his serious face on, almost an angry face, and ordered another for them, and another, and then when he saw they were completely stuffed he said, "Ah, I think you're getting there. You're learning the fine art of eating cream puffs comme il faut."

Oh, she was really getting into her saint's-life narrative, saying, "He takes us to Laurel and Hardy movies, Three Stooges movies, and he laughs so hard we have to pound him on the back." And, letting her know his tender side, "He's very kind when I'm sick or anything," painting her a domestic scene by Chardin of the time she and Joseph had had scarlet fever and had to stay at home for a week. "One night, we couldn't sleep because we'd slept so much during the day," she said to Sister Berchmans. All her life, she has been able to recall that feeling of feverish wakefulness, her eyes pressing out past the bones of her skull, pushed out as if on stalks, her hot restless body longing for sleep yet excited by its own overalertness; frightened too by the numbers on the thermometer going up, up, up.

She tells Sister Berchmans her father let her and Joseph lie on his bed. "He read us *Ivanhoe* by Sir Walter Scott." Purposely naming the author: with nuns you could at any moment come upon a pocket of virtuous ignorance. She didn't admit that

Ivanhoe bored her; it is a famous book, an important book, and Joseph and her father like it, so she will not allow herself to understand that she is bored with it; she tells herself that what she's feeling isn't boredom but something else, something whose name she doesn't know, because books are never boring and if her father and Joseph are interested it must be interesting, and what she is feeling is not important or not real but has to do with the fever.

"You and Joseph were lying on the bed together?"

Her alarm, then, seeing the nun thinks it's wrong, realizing she should have known it.

"It was my father's bed. Joseph's and my rooms are next to each other and my father's is across the hall. He could hear we were awake."

"Your rooms are next to each other?"

A knife falls down between them.

"Your father has been very kind to Joseph and his mother. I'm sure they're very grateful."

"They're like our family."

She said that because she thought it was something the nun could understand, and she was hoping it would make her forget that there was something bad about her and Joseph lying on her father's bed. But the minute Sister Berchmans asked the question — "Your rooms are next to each other?" — Maria knew it was wrong, although it wasn't wrong before, so it was wrong but it *wasn't* wrong, and for the first time in her life Maria experienced moral confusion. So she said, "Joseph is like a brother to me, we're like brother and sister," and Sister Berchmans said, "I'm sure."

Maria saw the light glint off her rimless glasses and took in for the first time that the nun had some darkish hairs on her upper lip. And she knew that she and Joseph were in danger, and she had put them there.

It wasn't long after that conversation with Sister Berchmans that Maria's father took Joseph to the city, just the two of them.

When they came home, her father looked a little flushed and Joseph looked sick. He went right up to his room. When she knocked on the door, he said he was busy. Then she realized he was crying. When she went into her own room, she could hear his sobs through the wall. Joseph rarely cried, even as a child, and when he did his tears were modest, reluctant, whereas Maria's were loud and violent.

Joseph still looked punished when he came down for dinner. Maria's father tapped his water glass with a knife, as if demanding silence. But no one had been saying anything.

"I have an exciting announcement. Joseph and I had a marvelous adventure today. Today we met Brother Raphael, the head of Portsmouth Priory. Starting in September, Joseph will have the privilege of studying with the brothers at the finest boys' school in America."

Maria jumped up and stood close to her father, closer than he liked. "Joseph will be going away to school?"

"Yes."

"Why are you doing this?" she shouted at her father.

"It's a great opportunity for Joseph."

And then she knew he was a liar, and she hated liars, and she saw his cruelty, and the cruelty of Sister Berchmans and Father Lynch, the cruelty of a whole way of life, a way that believed in purity and punishment, and she understood that this was happening because people, starting with Sister Berchmans, thought it was wrong that they were a boy and girl not related living in the same house. And this had happened because she trusted Sister Berchmans, who was unworthy of trust. She would never forgive them, any of them.

And she never has.

★ ★ ★

These were the Kennedy years, when people of Maria's age dreamed of going into the Peace Corps, dreamed of facing down Bull Connor's dogs and Lester Maddox's hatchets. Maria saw Joseph's being sent away as an injustice she must stand up against. If her father could be untruthful, she could, in the name of justice, be the same. If Joseph was being banished, she would see that she was banished too. She told her father it wasn't fair: if Joseph was being given the opportunity for the finest education in the world for young men, she should be given the opportunity to have the finest Catholic education available to young women. She presented him with brochures for the Sacred Heart School in Noroton, Connecticut. She had chosen that school particularly because she knew it would appeal to her father's Europhilic fantasies: the madames of the Sacred Heart, a French order (she didn't know that almost all the nuns were Irish), with holidays called congés and four years of compulsory Latin.

Her father was in no position to refuse her. And so he lost her, and she lost her childhood faith in her father's word. She believes she gave up her old love for him in the name of justice, in the name of standing beside Joseph. But none of this would have happened if the times were not as they were, in the reign of John F. Kennedy and John XXIII, when the glamorous dreams were of tipping the scales of justice but the chastity of young girls was considered fragile and beyond price.

★ ★ ★

Now we are in September 1962. Maria starts school at Noroton. For the first time she has friends, friends who are girls. For the first time she thinks of herself as one among many. These are the years for this, when many people think of *we* as opposed to *they,* whom *we* shall overcome.

Maria learns the joy of having friends, a joy she will never lose. She and her friends try to copy Joan Baez. They sing "I Am a Maid of Constant Sorrow," "I Was Born in East Virginia," and "Long Black Veil" and iron their hair so it will look like Joan Baez's (it never does), but only on the weekends when they go to someone's house, because the nuns won't allow hair ironing. Maria and her friends form a folk group, The Poor Girls, because to perform they wear herringbone skirts and poor-boy sweaters, short-sleeved ribbed sweaters that are the rage. Maria is happy wearing something that is the rage, happy shopping at Orbach's and B. Altman on the weekends with her friends, sometimes even at Bloomingdale's.

Maria and her girlfriends sail through stores like heiresses, buying their too-short skirts — or skirts the older nuns think are too short. But not their champion, Mother Dulcissima, who does not accuse them of anything and encourages The Poor Girls to sing at folk masses, which are allowed once a month. They make up liturgical words to Peter, Paul, and Mary songs: "Take this bread and take this wine and take our hearts and take our minds." They sing this to the tune of "500 Miles." Maria's father abhors all liturgical reform and, most of all, folk masses. He travels to the city every Sunday for a Latin mass.

Her life is her friends. They think of their lives as a wonderful movie, perhaps a musical; at least a film with a great sound track.

Then it is November 1963. The president is shot. The palette of the world darkens. The music is silence; silence goes around the world, or if there is sound it is the sound of taps or bagpipes. For months, everyone moves as if they'd been the victims of a crippling blow. The world is not as they had thought, but still they think they can change it.

Maria and her friends are the heads of everything, presidents of everything. They have the solos in the glee club; they are the stars of the plays, the captains of the debate team and the basketball team and the volleyball team. They believe that one of them will be president of the United States, one will cure cancer, one will be the female Picasso. Maria, since she is thought of as a poet, will be the female e. e. cummings. They mention their femaleness in their plans for themselves; they know it is a factor, but they don't know how, only that they don't want to be boys and yet everyone they think is important is a man.

They rarely see boys, sometimes to debate in debate club or to sing with in glee club; there are dances, longed for, dreamed over, always disappointing. The boys are sweaty in their herringbone jackets; they spill punch, they drop potato chips and crush

94

them into the floor with the soles of their desert boots. Their jokes are stupid. Everyone is in love with one or two of them, but they have girlfriends, girls who have no time for other girls. Maria and her friends dream of sex, but only as an accompaniment to their dreams of the great world. Their dreams of sex are mainly about kissing or about the moments after sex. Their images of themselves as great lovers are taken from the book in Mother Dulcissima's homeroom, *The Family of Man*. In their dreams, they are not themselves, they are the black woman in the photograph in the book, gripping a lover's back with strong red fingernails; they are the Parisian woman in the raincoat and high heels being kissed on the Champs-Élysées. They don't know what the Champs-Élysées looks like, but it sounds like the right place to be kissed in Paris. Or they are Cathy Earnshaw, and Heathcliff is on a motorcycle. Or they are the girl at the edge of the sea in *Portrait of the Artist as a Young Man*; they are Holly Golightly, but only on the fire escape in the rain; or Jackie Kennedy, but only at the grave. They are Franny in *Franny and Zooey*. They are ancient peasant women surrounded by grandchildren who kiss their gnarled hands.

Everything is extreme. They can't imagine it being any other way. When they think of weather, it's blazing hot or freezing cold. Some days all they do is sleep. The way they sleep! Sleep seems to fall on them hard, like a safe falling from a cartoon sky. *So tired,* they say to themselves, *just exhausted.* They drop down to filthy sleep; their dreams are perverse, murderous; they wake and say they had terrible dreams but they don't remember them. On weekends, the nuns won't let them sleep enough. The girls who live close enough go home to their mothers on weekends just to sleep. They sleep and sleep. In their dreams they beg people to allow them to sleep, not to force them to wake up. To allow them to wake at two in the afternoon to roam a mother's spotless kitchen and make combinations of sweet foods, followed by salty ones, then savory, then back to sweet. They crave sweets and sometimes take them from the kitchen back to their beds.

Maria does not go home. She does not have a kitchen stocked with sweets by a mother who would allow her to sleep until two in the afternoon. Her kitchen is spotless but is presided over by Joseph's mother, and there are no snacks there:

Maria's father does not believe in snacks, as he doesn't believe in sleeping late. So she doesn't go home much; she goes to her friends' houses, where their mothers are kind since she is motherless (not knowing she is punishing her father by being with them), and where they sleep and sleep and then take the commuter train into New York City and go to the Village and talk their way into bars and talk to men who frighten them, but they go home with one another and tremble a little on the train at what they might have done. They hear Ravi Shankar play the sitar; they listen to Allen Ginsberg chant his poetry. They love Monet's *Water Lilies* and Shakespeare, but only performed outside where the poor can see it.

They love everyone, they hate everyone; their school is heaven, is a prison; Mother Perpetua is a mental case and Mother Emmanuel is a saint; and they adore and envy Mother Dulcissima because of the berry color of her full lips and because she went to Selma and their parents wouldn't let them. She is the nun they all want to be. Except that they would like to marry. Someone like Bobby Kennedy or Harry Belafonte. They imagine what their parents would say if they came home with

Harry Belafonte. They are not afraid of their parents. Mother, Father, they would say, this is my fiancé, Harry Belafonte. Harry, don't worry about my parents or race prejudice. Everything will be fine because we are very much in love.

They, of course, know they have no race prejudice. The two black girls in the class are the same as everyone else, Maria and her friends are sure of that. When do Maria and her friends start calling them black? They cannot imagine a time when they used the word Negro. One of the black girls, Barbara, is a little prickly, a little unfriendly, but they know it has nothing to do with being black. She must know they are on her side. They are Democrats and anti-Communists. They will be virgins on their wedding night. None of them has had her breasts touched. They know they will love being pregnant. They will each have many children. They will all live together. They will raise their many children together on a sheep farm in New Zealand. First, though, they will teach children in Harlem, like Mother Dulcissima in the summers.

Except that then the boys in their sweaty jackets do things to them, make the girls want them; when the girls leave them they want to take their nightgowns off, take the sheets off their mattresses to feel the rough ticking on their skins, they want the boys' hands, they can't stop thinking of them, they are restless in their dormitories, they would like to climb out windows and meet boys in the dark. They would like to give over their bodies, which they are afraid to look at and yet guess somehow are beautiful. That is why they run outside in thunderstorms or jump into Cassie Maguire's pool at three in the morning. There is something abroad that is dark, something not nice, not kind and benevolent, like the world they easily inhabited six months earlier. Their bodies are pulling them into the world. They see the beautiful white face of Mother Dulcissima and believe, because of what happened when the boys in sweaty jackets touched their breasts (none of them would let any boy, as they said, "go further"), that for the first time there are things they know that she does not. Will never. And so their admiration for her becomes mixed with pity and they understand soon that they need not call it admiration anymore.

They still believe that they will change the world. Rumblings come to them from Southeast Asia, but vaguely, indistinctly. Soon they will hear only that, and they will be able to believe in nothing.

In 1965, the weather changes from high summer to sick dog days; the air is filled with smoke and the sun is never healthy; everything it falls on becomes livid, ill. Everyone is afraid but they don't say that; they say that they are angry. Anger is the weather of the day. Anger is most often in those days called rage. The president's face is diabolical; Maria and her friends understand it is the face of all the men who want to hurt them, who they will never allow to touch them, who they would never marry. The president lifts his dog up by the ears; he shows the world the scar on his hairy stomach. He sends children to their deaths, he will send their friends to their deaths; he says he is doing it for them, for Maria and her friends and girls like them. The newspapers are full of death, not the heraldic death of John Kennedy, to the accompaniment of bagpipes, but the deaths of strangers continents away, people who do not look like Maria and her friends, and there is fire in the cities and fear the cities will burn down and perhaps — who knows? — in the name of justice they ought to. Boys their age are dead, buried in pits with hundreds of others. Asian children run in flame.

In 1967, Maria disappoints the nuns, choosing Radcliffe over Manhattanville. She goes to demonstrations. She loses her virginity.

★ ★ ★

Then it is 1968. It is the spring of the terrible deaths, King and another Kennedy, and there is no hope, only more rage, more fear, more death. What should be done? Fight or smoke till nothing matters? Turn on, drop out, or forgive nothing? Armed or stoned, which are you? Certainly nothing you thought you were, not the nice girl you thought you were, the loving girl, the hopeful girl. It isn't so long ago that you were a hopeful girl, maybe only five years, October of 1963.

Maria and her friends have to learn new words: *napalm, friendly fire*. Death is surrounded by lies. They do not know what to believe. The men they thought of as, if not their fathers, then something like their fathers, are lying to them again and again, and people like them, boys like them — or not like them, poorer boys, but boys their age — are dying because of those lies, and if they believe the lies they are with those men in the party of death. The men they thought of as their fathers, men like their fathers, Robert McNamara, McGeorge Bundy, cannot be believed. No one can be believed. Maria knows her father cannot be believed. He keeps using the word *communism*. She keeps telling him he doesn't understand communism. The North Vietnamese, Mao and the Chinese he leads, she says, are agrarian idealists, heroes. In years to come, Maria and her friends will discover that they were wrong about the North Vietnamese and the Chinese, but their fathers were wrong too, and their inability to determine who was more wrong will hobble their minds — the parts of their minds that think about the larger world — for years and years.

Colored lights cut through the sickish air. They dance till they fall on their backs, fall in a group embrace; they sing, "Looking for fun and feeling groovy," and a minute later they see a child running in napalm fire; and *Sergeant Pepper's Lonely Hearts Club Band* is the same time as the March on the Pentagon, where people like Maria and her friends for the first time cannot breathe because the police, who four years earlier they thought of as their friends, are not their friends; they tear-gas people like Maria, who then call them motherfuckers, although Maria and her friends had never heard the word three years before when the weather was different. So which is it, which is real, which is the truth: "I Get By with a Little Help from My Friends" or bayoneted children?

I am not a good enough historian to say whether or not there were other periods in history like those ten years, eleven maybe, 1962 to 1973, the year before the death of John Kennedy to the year of Watergate, years in which so easily, so quickly, you became a person you would not have recognized. The Maria of 1962 would not have recognized the Maria of 1968. The Maria of 1962 was a hopeful girl; the Maria of 1968 was not. Perhaps this uncertainty marks my failure as a chronicler. Nevertheless, this is the way I must tell the story of those times.

It is May 1970: Kent State. The girl, kneeling, outraged, shocked, beside her dead friend. Students like Maria and her friends, shot by the Ohio National Guard. People like Maria and her friends who did not believe that people in American uniforms would shoot people like them. People in uniform were their fathers in the good war. But not Maria's father. Too frail. His eyesight.

A week after Kent State, Maria's father calls her and asks her to come home. He says he's been a bit ill but he didn't want to worry her; she has seemed so absorbed in her studies.

She has not been absorbed in her studies. She sleeps through her classes. Everything important happens at night: she goes to meetings all night, night after night; that semester everything is pass/fail and nearly everybody passes everything doing the absolute minimum, one night spent doing a term's work, another all-nighter after months of all-night meetings, shouting, raising their fists. They turn their attention to metaphysical poetry, the sonata form. They pass through the university, the university which, they think, perhaps should be burnt down because it can exist only if it takes money from defense contractors. Wasn't napalm invented at a university, doesn't the company that invented it support the university?

Yes, Papa, she says, I've been very absorbed in my work. Lying to her parents like everyone does in those days. I've been very busy. She must spare him. He has been ill.

It is difficult for her to call him Papa, her childhood name for him, given the facts of her life (the filthy room, the filthy dishes, the sheets that don't fit the mattress, the new knowledge that men like her father are murderers, the smell of Ortho-Gynol jelly that clings to her clothing). But she can only call him Papa. What else can she call him? Not only is she frightened of the evil of the world, the death machine, she is frightened of the weakness of her father's body. She does not want to be his treasure, but she is. His treasure, the rest of which is made up of things that her boyfriend, William, says are produced by the death machine. But because her father has said to the world: Preserve, preserve my treasure, she has always felt that, whatever else happens, she will be preserved.

Her father says he needs an operation, that his heart has a little squeak and needs to be fixed: not an emergency but something that must be dealt with. He's set a day for the operation. Will she be there beside him?

Of course, Papa, she says. She doesn't know what she will say to William Ogilvie, who shares the mattress and the greasy sheets, William, who may be hiding guns in the basement. Violence is the only language they understand, he says. You know that, don't you? And she says, Yes, of course I understand. She understands because he's said that if she doesn't agree with him it's her weakness. But she will not give in to her weakness, and she will refuse her privilege. She believes what he says, partly because it makes her afraid, and she knows she must get over fear; that is the only way to be strong; she must love truth more than comfort, justice more than mercy; she must cast her lot with those who will give their lives to end injustice and oppression. She is afraid all the time, but she thinks it's right to be afraid, it's the only honest thing, because the times are evil and in the presence of evil the honest are afraid.

What will William Ogilvie say if there's an important meeting or an important demonstration on the day she's said she'll be at her father's side at the hospital? She tells him she has to go somewhere, but she can't give him the details. She hints that she's going away with another man, thinks he will admire her for that, call it independence, but in fact he barely notices that she's gone; he is busy smashing the war machine, he is busy with the revolution.

William Ogilvie — Billy — knows nothing about her father.

The night before her father checks into

the hospital, Joseph and Maria and he have a peaceful, harmonious, enjoyable dinner. For the first time in years they don't argue about politics.

Joseph and Maria wait six hours in the hospital while Dr. Meyers is operated on. Even while her father's chest is an open cavity, she listens to the news; when the doctors speak of invasive surgery she hears the word *invasive* and thinks of the invasion of Cambodia; even while she is worried that her father is at the door of death, she reads the newspaper, she traces the location of the troops.

The operation is successful. She sees her father, pale in his white bed. She holds his beautiful fine hand. She stays with him a week; she misses classes, but it is the year of Cambodia, the year of Kent State, after all, and regular attendance no longer seems important.

When she gets back to Cambridge, she is met with the end of everything. The filthy house is empty and, in its emptiness, no less squalid. While she was away, the FBI came in the night and found boxes of guns in the basement and material for making bombs. Billy has been arrested; he is in jail with some of the other people who were staying in the house, people whom she'd met but whose real names she was not allowed to know.

She tells the police she should be in jail; she lived in the house too. The police say there's no evidence she was involved; she's registered in the Radcliffe dormitories, and there is no record of her presence in that house. She insists she is guilty; they insist she is not. Go home, honey, they say, go home to your father; you've got friends in high places, take advantage of it. Go while the going's good. But the going is not good, and she cannot make it good, and she cannot make them arrest her.

It is true, I suppose, that she could have done something to make them arrest her. Thrown a bottle through the police station window. Chained herself to something, as her daughter would later do. It is strange that she only railed; Maria did not act, as her daughter is now acting, Maria, whose enduring belief is in the liberating force of action.

All she did was shout at the police and beg Billy to believe that she didn't know what was happening. He doesn't believe her. He doesn't want anything to do with her. He goes to jail for six months only, because he is a Harvard student, a PhD candidate in microbiology, and the guns and explosives had not been used.

She begins to be suspicious. "Go home to your father . . . friends in high places." The name of the FBI agent on the case is Ryan. She remembers that her father's very good friend, Monsignor Ryan from the chancery, has a brother in the FBI.

She doesn't care that her father is weak, that he has just been operated on. She borrows a car and drives, at top speed, to Larchmont. She throws open her father's bedroom door. Her father is in bed but she knows that whatever else he's done, he won't tell an outright lie.

She says, "Did you know my friends were going to be arrested? Did you arrange to have the operation so I would be with you when it happened?"

White, his white face against the white pillow, his white hands holding a black rosary, sign of the church. Monsignor Ryan's church, Maria thinks, church of the FBI.

"Say it, say you trapped me. Admit you lied to me!"

"I never lied to you."

"Spare me your Jesuitical machinations."

Even in her rage, she does not use, with her father, the diction of her friends. She doesn't say "Jesuitical bullshit," which is what comes to her mind; she says

"Jesuitical machinations."

And those are the last words she says to her father.

Pearl knows nothing of all this. Would it be better if she had known? If she had known about her mother's past, her mother's anguish and confusion when she was the same age, might she have gone to her in her own time of anguish? It doesn't matter. Pearl didn't know. She never went to her mother. She never thought of her mother as someone with a life in history. As a character in a chronicle. Does any child?

• 5 •

We will leave Maria now in her first-class seat. A woman who has always been in love with movement, now in terror for her child, trapped in a severely circumscribed place.

Joseph, on the other hand, is on the streets of Rome. We have been talking about history, so it would seem appropriate to follow him, in this city where more of the history of the West is centered than in any other place: the history of the West, the history of the Roman Catholic Church, from which, after all, Joseph makes his living. A strange phrase, that, *making a living.* As if living were something that could be made.

Joseph leaves his hotel, the Santa Chiara in Piazza Minerva, a few feet away from the Church of Santa Maria Sopra Minerva, where, atop Bernini's elephant with its heaving saddle, stands an obelisk, found in the church's garden and preserved by learned monks, a monument to the Egyptian goddess Isis. Santa Maria Sopra Minerva: the Virgin mother atop the Roman

111

goddess of wisdom and, on top of that, the Egyptian goddess of fertility. A mishmash, a mix-up, no pure statement possible; contradictions stacked one on top of the other, no structure, no hierarchy: just a pile. A pile of history, a pile of understandings. Chockablock.

Maria called with the news of Pearl at 6 a.m. Joseph knew he couldn't book a flight till ten and he couldn't bear waiting in his hotel, so he went out into the street. Now he walks from the Piazza Minerva to the Campo de' Fiori. He is terrified. He walks stiffly, as if any wrong step could bring about disaster.

Two days earlier, Christmas eve, Joseph took the same walk, under a Roman sky that suggested nothing of the implacability of northern winter. The sky was frothy, like the bay before a storm; it made you think of water more than air, its movement more textured than air and less abstract. The night sky was white, and everywhere he went there seemed to be the scent of carnations and mimosas, of peeled oranges, of celery, apples, violets, discarded Christmas roses like stains or blood against the gray cobblestones.

He walked to the Piazza Navona, festooned with tinsel strung from palazzo to palazzo (this too for tourists). He was killing time until he could return to the Campo. Killing time (as he is now), looking at Bernini's great male gods who obviously cared nothing about the birth of a baby in a stable. What he wanted to see was the cleanup of the Campo, the moment of transformation, of transition from color and activity and bustle to the matte palette of black cobblestone and whitish marble, the harsh puritanical figure of Giordano Bruno. Joseph wondered, every time he entered the Campo, what Bruno made of it all: the fruit, the flowers, the cheap toys and plastic buckets, the machine-knit woolen hats, the numbers called out: cheerfully? mendaciously? What can he be thinking? Joseph would wonder, looking up at the hooded statue, its face invisible, Bruno burnt by the church for insisting on our right to tell the truth. Was this, Joseph wondered, Bruno's last punishment, to be placed amid this friendly chaos, the amorality of easily satisfied appetite?

How happy Joseph had been — was it only two days earlier? — watching the peddlers pick up, put away, sweep up. He was there when it happened. He saw it. He made note of it: the end of bustle and tumult, the return of calm, the pale moon barely visible in the whitish sky, the harsher yellow-white of the electric streetlights.

He cannot be happy now. The sellers are putting out their wares, their colorful fish and fruits and vegetables. But what he wants this morning isn't there. He walks behind the Campo to the Piazza Farnese. He is surrounded by palazzi that suggest judgment cruelly or carelessly meted out. He wonders if Pearl will be judged by official forces. She has broken the law, chained herself to a government building. He looks at the harsh palazzi of the Piazza Farnese. At the streetlamps, too bright when illuminated, as if placed there for interrogation. Will Pearl be interrogated? Is she protecting someone? Is she someone's pawn? Is there vital information she will not give up? He wonders where these questions have come from, how they have entered his brain. Whether they've come from some book, a boy's book, an adventure he would have thought had nothing to do with his life, the kind of book he'd never liked, not even as a child.

He loves the beautiful streets of Rome; nothing in his life has brought him more joy than the contemplation of beautiful things. But he can't concentrate on anything, his eye can stay on nothing; his mind can only go to Pearl. She is in danger. He sees her on a stretcher, white and flat, her eyes closed. He cannot banish this image. He can't do what Maria would do. Don't think of it, she would say. I can't help it, he would answer. Or no, he would say nothing. But he would be unable to do as she said.

And when his mind makes the image of Pearl, lying flat and white, it cannot banish another image that rises up alongside it — as if his mind were a book and on one side there was the image of Pearl and on the other side: Ilaria del Carretto, the fifteenth-century white marble figure on the top of a sarcophagus he had seen in Lucca.

He had made a special trip to Tuscany to see the figure. He had come across a description of it by Ruskin in a biography he had picked up for $2.50 from a table on Broadway at 72nd Street. The book was beside *Low Fat Cooking for One*, an anthology of Russian poetry, and Frantz Fanon's *The Wretched of the Earth*.

It was one of the things he liked best about New York, the surprise encounter, the odd juxtaposition, coming upon a book he really wanted to read when he thought he was out shopping for his dinner: a trip to Fairway for a salmon steak, a head of broccoli, two whole wheat rolls, a carton of raspberry sorbet. And then this book, which he calculated would be perfect for his upcoming trip to Italy. He always took one large paperback with him, an experienced traveler's strategy he's proud of. A serious book, a book he wanted to read but might not get around to in his ordinary life. So that he could mark each journey not only by a business trip successfully completed but by a book satisfactorily read.

He hadn't thought about Ruskin since college. He had been an art history major and had very much liked Ruskin's embellished descriptions, his exact, perhaps obsessive prose. Poor Ruskin, father of art history, patron saint of careful looking. If you ask the average man about him he will say he's someone who went berserk on his wedding night because he discovered women are not statues and have pubic hair. No. If you ask the average man about him, he will never have heard of him. Yet it is possible that no one in the history of the world has known better how to *look* than this man. Madman, eunuch, genius eye.

Reading Ruskin's description of the

figure of Ilaria del Carretto, Joseph had decided to take a day trip from Rome to Lucca. Why not? He had planned enough time so that he could do his work — buying vestments, clerical linens, chalices, and ciboria from the stores surrounding the Piazza Minerva — and still have the kind of holiday he liked. Why not? No one was waiting for him in New York; he was president of the company. He could please himself.

And he had pleased himself in the quiet, orderly Tuscan city, following Ruskin's lead to the tomb of Ilaria. There he fell in love with the white, peaceful girl, so comfortable on her marble pillow — her elegantly carved curls, her small breasts, her narrow waist, her slender folded hands perfect in a beauty that would never change. Ilaria would not grow old or thick or coarse. Ilaria would remain perfect.

It distresses him to think of Ilaria as he thinks of Pearl. Pearl is alive; Pearl will remain alive. She must. It is only art that finds a beautiful stillness in death. Pearl must not die. With Pearl dead, there would be nothing in the world worth seeing. Today, thinking of her, his eye can take in nothing. His eye is useless; no images on the streets — that only yesterday brought him such joy — can penetrate his mind. No image can banish the one of Pearl: white, flat, on the stretcher, close to death.

He feels his spine has been hollowed out. A glass tube has replaced solid bone; inside it, thick, black, electric, a wire thrums at the thought of her image: pale, stretched out, no longer alive. He doesn't understand. He imagines she thinks he understands. His failure to understand shames him; mixes the terror with a thicker, duller residue. He must walk; there is nothing else to do. It's seven-thirty. The ticket office won't open till ten. He walks, seeing nothing, understanding nothing, saying to no one whose face he can imagine: *Please, please keep her alive.* The closed eyes of Ilaria come to him, and he wills them away. And then the words again: *Keep her alive.*

★ ★ ★

As a child, there was a face he might have imagined responding to such a request. He would have called it prayer. Then he would have prayed simply; now he cannot. Some things of the child have, of course, endured in the man, but not this habit, not this ability to call up a prayable face.

What kind of child was Joseph? A good child. A grateful child. A child who was

118

told with his every breath, "You must be very grateful."

He has never been without this sense of obligation. He knew, always, who he was: a servant's son. A servant's son who had been plucked out of the gray dead world he'd been born into, plucked by shapely fingers and cradled in the fine white palm of Seymour Meyers, given what had not been his birthright: education and access to the highest things men have created, treasured, prized.

This is Joseph's story. Is it part of the chronicle? Joseph has never been representative of his time as Maria was. Never has he asked himself the question so important to his generation: What will make me happy? Instead, he has asked himself, What should I be doing now?

"You are a lucky boy," his mother told him repeatedly. By *lucky* she meant the recipient of good luck. If good luck is nothing but the benevolent hand of chance, we'd have to say it was a series of lucky chances that brought Joseph and his mother to the house of Seymour Meyers in the spring of 1951. And if we place these lucky chances in the cup of history, Joseph's story is part of the chronicle not of the sixties but of the thirties and the forties: the history of the Second World War.

It wasn't until he was in his thirties that Joseph learned the story of his parents' marriage. During a period when he was desperately trying to find out about his father, he tracked down his mother's cousin, a machinist living near Rochester. "I know this sheds a bad light on your mother's family, but don't think of it that way. Think of the times." The suggestion, by a decent man, of the details of an indecent act.

Adam Kasperzkowski, Joseph's father, was a distant cousin of Marie Wolinski, Joseph's mother, from the same town in Galicia as her parents. Poor farmers. They feared the Communists. The Communists were devils. Adam needed to be sent to America to keep his faith.

And who was Adam, in America, to the Americans? A young man who became Marie Wolinski's husband. A young man who had been starving in postwar Poland. Adam Kasperzkowski, changing his name in New York at the suggestion of the Wolinski family — so difficult, those z's, don't show yourself too foreign — to Adam Kasperman. Adam, the first man. Brought to America. Bought by America. And how was this bargain made? "Marry this woman, this unmarriageable because unbeautiful woman, and you will buy yourself prosperity."

They married and moved to Detroit. Adam got a job in a Ford automotive plant. Joseph was conceived. Joseph was born. And then, while he was still an infant, the cliché line: Adam said he was just going out for a pack of cigarettes; Adam was never seen again. He disappeared into the fog of America.

Father Lipinski, an uncle of Adam Kasperman, was the chaplain in a home for blind children in the Bronx. He hired Marie as a cook: the workings of the fostering, manipulative hand of Holy Mother Church, a wise and practical housewife, keeping her children alive and healthy. And then another manipulation: a colleague of Father Lipinski, Monsignor Ryan, friend of Dr. Seymour Meyers (such a fine man, such a tragedy, his wife's death to cancer, the two-year-old child). Seymour Meyers needed a housekeeper. Marie Kasperman was put to work for the grief-stricken Seymour Meyers, in need of someone to watch his house and care for his two-year-old daughter, nearly the same age as Marie Kasperman's fatherless son, Joseph.

His mother, a servant. Marie Wolinski

Kasperman, a girl born in western New York State to Polish farmers, raised on an ungenerous soil. Dirt poor, she liked to say, though we had our self-respect; we always kept ourselves clean. Her battle a fight to the death with dirt and disorder. Wasn't there something admirable in that? But there was no love bestowed on what dirt was kept from. Only enmity. Only a confusion between dirt and life.

He remembers there were some things she liked. A teacup: white, thin, with red roses. She liked her needlepoint hassock, on which she would rest her aching, tired feet. He wished he could have been the kind of boy who took tired feet in loving hands and said, "Mother, let me rub your feet. What can I do for you, Mother?" Instead of always the recoil from her presence, the polite, abashed, always guilt-ridden dutifulness, the self-hate born of unease around her body. Who do you think you are, he would ask himself, that your flesh crawls at the nearness of your mother's flesh? Do you think you're something better? No, he knew that he was not. If he is his mother's son, he must be her. Whenever he began to think that he might be something else, he didn't know how to name it, so he decided it was impossible.

Beauty and fineness. "Your father had looks, I'll give him that." This was said reluctantly, as if she'd take away his father's visibility if she could, as she had tried to do by cutting his face out of photographs. Instead of his father's face, an empty oval.

Joseph has often wondered what his life would have been like if he had not been set down by some merciful and tender hand into the palm of Seymour Meyers, devoted to the beautiful, the fine. How could he fail to be grateful? He was a child abandoned by his father, a gifted child born to an ungifted mother and introduced to a greater world. An introduction that meant he would always place himself at an uneasy distance from his mother.

He sometimes wonders if he ever loved her. He cannot remember feeling for his mother anything like what he felt for people whom he later said he loved. He hopes for a merciful, preconscious Eden, a time before memory when he was drawn to her out of sheer animal need, a time before distinctions could be made, when her body was the body he needed, to which nothing else had to be compared.

He has no idea how old he was when the difference between coarseness and fineness entered his mind. Knowing his mother was one and not the other, that the Meyerses were the other and not the one. He has tried to be fair to his mother, stopping himself when he said to himself, She had no sense of beauty. She cared about cleanliness. Americans believe there is no beauty without cleanliness. But this, he learned, was not something all the peoples of the world believe. The treasuring of cleanliness above all, which made her buy the chair covered in olive leatherette (*I can wipe it with a sponge; it'll last forever*), never an ornament (*They're dust collectors*). You must believe me: Joseph has tried terribly hard not to be unfair to his mother. He told himself that she was tired. That she worked too hard. That she worried about money. That she had no reason to prize beauty when her own lack of it was the cause of her sorrow. He tried very hard to call up times when he was not unhappy to be near her. He would remember that sometimes they enjoyed playing cards. But the meagerness of that sentence — We enjoyed playing cards — would cause him to feel something like despair and then self-pity, and like Maria he believes that of all emotions self-pity is the least acceptable.

Lately he has begun to wonder: If he had never met the Meyerses, could he have been happy with his mother? He could be a blue-collar worker in Detroit, married to a nice Polish girl, taking their many children to a church called St. Kasimir or St. Stanislaus, his patient, kind, ungifted wife caring for his mother in their ranch house rather than leaving her to the care of strangers at Regina Caeli Home for the Aged. The last time he visited her there, she said, "You're a nice young man, do I know you?" "Mother, I'm your son." "I don't remember having a son." If his mother does not know him, how can he be loved? And is her love something he deserves?

He has often asked himself, Is it possible that a child who never loved his mother is capable of love? Is what he has called love only a form of misapprehension? Perhaps he isn't capable of love, only of attachment to a creature formed from his own imagination. He asks himself quite often if he is really an idolator — a failed idolator, for his imaginations have disappointed him.

I must tell you, Joseph often thinks of himself as a disappointed man. And yet what, he has asked himself, is disappointment? He has come to many conclusions. He has reckoned that disappointment isn't one of the great states of mind. Nothing glamorous — like ruin — only a gradual diminishment, a gradual nibbling away of bounty, until what is left is cramped and meager, adequate for livelihood but every luxury, every amplitude, begrudged. At fifty, he has taken stock of himself and found a failed idolator, a disappointed man.

Joseph isn't thinking of these things now. He isn't thinking of his past. He walks blindly; his mind can't settle; his eye falls on things but he cannot be said to be seeing them properly. He is walking, praying, to no face that he can see, *"Just keep her alive."*

He remembers walks with Pearl in Central Park, walks downtown to look at architecture or just have lunch. The time in the museum when he took her to see some Cambodian sculptures. Both of them silent before the faceless goddesses, not Madonnas, their round hard breasts impossible to think of as a food source, their secret smiles, the girlish narrowness of their shoulders.

He can't remember one word he and Pearl said to each other. And he wonders, with a kind of desperation, if it would be of help to her if he could remember some of the things she said. He tries and tries; he cannot call up a single word. But he believes, he tells himself that he is right to believe, that they were happy. In all the times with her, he believes he was never disappointed. Except when she chose, for her diary, a purple plastic notebook with a laminated picture of a unicorn on the front. He never told her, though; he paid for it without a word. But he was glad to notice that at some point she had given it up, choosing, instead, a black leather journal with unlined pages.

Now he walks to Piazza Mattei, where just a few days before he saw a FOR SALE sign in the window of a flat. Right there, in one of his favorite squares in Rome, VENDERSI, the stone of the building just the right shade of sunburnt yellow, the trailing ivy just the right mix of ornament and camouflage. It is the district, historically, of woodworkers. On the wall of one of the buildings in the square is a sign listing the craftsmen represented in the woodworkers union of 1624: makers of barrels, casks, tambourines, cabinets, drums, whips, boxes, chairs, and clogs; inlayers; sawyers; lathe turners. Only a few days ago, he imagined himself protected by those skilled, industrious ghosts, so near to the playful seductive bronze boys who stand below the tortoises of the Fontana delle Tartarughe. Why not? Why not wait till a few days after Christmas and call the number and see how much the flat costs? He has a house worth $750,000 in Larchmont, a house he doesn't want. A house whose old trees and leaded windows and deep lawns would be free of resonance for someone else.

He is aware that it is winter, but the cold doesn't press on his limbs or cause him to think about going inside. Why not walk all night, why not walk until dawn? What would it matter if he were murdered by some large-featured boy from a painting by Caravaggio, murdered on the Via Giulia or one of the streets that leads from it, one that turns and turns and may lead nowhere?

It had given him a feeling of great luxury, of leisure, to know that it was no longer necessary to prevent himself from being murdered. It meant that no place was closed to him. He could go wherever he wanted, but it wasn't any specific action or activity that interested him, only the possibility of wandering anywhere with no need to check in. No place to which it was necessary that he report back.

Certainly not the staff of the hotel Santa Chiara, who had known him for many years and might be pleasantly surprised if he didn't return one night to sleep in his bed, assuming, as Italians always do, some amorous situation. Or perhaps they didn't think him capable of it.

He had been happy, alone and uninvolved in the holiday activity, the festivities that all the life of the streets prepared for. He wondered who would believe him if he told them he was happy. He thought it might sound pathetic, like something a girl might say who hadn't been invited to a dance, trying to convince you that she'd had her opportunities but she preferred to stay at home and wash her hair. But in his case it was true. He did have invitations. He had lied (this was unlike him) to get out of them. He could have taken a short train trip to a house in the *campagna*, to warm hearths, large tables, rooms full of firelight, children with dark eyes and cheeks red from the fire, young, thin, fashionable mothers without the unease of American mothers toward their young. Or he could have gone skiing in Zermatt and eaten Christmas dinner at midnight, the moon a blue disk on the frozen snow, with a private mass in the morning said by a bishop, also the guest of his excellent hosts, who would not be displeased to see Joseph attentive to their plain, shy, intellectual daughter of whom he was fond and about whom (they were not wrong) he occasionally speculated, but entirely without desire, considering the possibilities of a quiet, decorous, but not unstylish Roman life.

Joseph was a widower, you see, understood to be Catholic and to have sufficient money. For someone like him, invitations would never be lacking.

He had lied to several groups of friends, suggesting a Christmas spiritual in its overtones, perhaps spent in a monastery, perhaps turning to God for consolation in his grief over the loss of his wife. In fact, he was not feeling grief. He was, after two years, unable to describe the nature of his feelings. Perhaps because he believed he wasn't grieving. Simply, he wanted to be alone.

Now, alone, he walks near the Tortoise Fountain in Piazza Mattei, thinking of his mother, in the Regina Caeli Home for the Aged on the West Side of New York City. She has been there for six years.

Her days are a fog. What will she do on

this day after Christmas, after she eats her breakfast? Will she wear a Santa Claus pin on one of her polyester shirts? Polyester is required in the Regina Caeli Home: all patients' garments must be able to withstand laundering in large machines that shrink, fade, and eat up natural fabrics. Are her lips still stained red and green from Christmas candy? Does she have a Santa Claus hat? Do the nurses? He pictures the dining room with everyone wearing a Santa Claus hat: the aged nodding, openmouthed, or sitting with their eyes closed, or trying to make conversation, the nurses passing out food, wiping mouths, chins, wheeling patients toward their tables and then away from them, back to bed.

Each day, Marie Kasperman makes herself a pirate's hat out of a paper towel. She smiles more than formerly; it is not a false smile. Joseph wonders if, for the first time in her fog, his mother is happy.

Why not, then, he'd thought on that earlier day when he'd walked to the Fountain of the Tortoises, move to Rome? He could do everything he needed for the business by fax and e-mail and on the Internet. He could be someone who woke every morning to the prospect of a silence nourishing as manna, living for what his eye would fall on, in high rooms, nearly empty, in a flat that was only his. The sheen of the marble floor, the white and yellow light on the red roofs. He could plan his days around what he would see. One beautiful thing in the center of each day, easy in a city where you had only to turn a corner to see a beautiful and unexpected sight.

He could become a man without close human connections, only acquaintances, Europeans who would be happy to speak of what they'd seen that day without the unseemly American avidity for personal details. Most days, he would speak to no one. Most days he would be silent. He's imagined the silence, liquid, seeping down to the dryness of what he would once have called his soul, a word he now refuses to use, even for want of something better, because he is sick to death of the endless call-up of false terms, the hunger for the food of the pseudo-sacred, the word *spiritual* as much a staple of the TV talk show as the words *child abuse* or *drug addiction*.

His mother is wrapped in silence now, but it is not the beautiful silence he dreams of and craves. The silence that surrounds his mother is heavy, blank. After Marie Kasperman eats, she puts her hands over her stomach, which is more huge than ever, suggesting not self-indulgence but disease. But Marie Kasperman has no disease in her. "The dear soul is, thankfully, very healthy," says Sister Theresa, the pastoral counselor at the home. Sister Theresa is eternally grateful for the plastic statuettes Joseph regularly brings her by the gross. "Mr. Kasperman, you are always in my prayers." Sister Theresa assured him it was all right for him to leave his mother for a Roman holiday. "Mr. Kasperman, she wouldn't know Christmas from the Fourth of July."

So why not leave for good? Why not leave her to the nuns who care for her, the nurses who answer her for the hundredth time when she says, "Did I ever have any children?" Why not leave all that for the clear dimensions of the Piazza Navona, the Piazza Farnese, the Piazza Mattei?

But that was his past life. What Pearl has done has divided his life inexorably. He is not the same man he was yesterday. His past has no importance to him, and the future is something he dares not contemplate. He walks in the present, in a present as foggy as his mother's, in this city of clear light, this city of history in which he now feels no part.

Joseph goes back to the Santa Chiara.

He stays at this hotel, as Dr. Meyers stayed there before him, not for the Pantheon or the synchronistic evidence of Santa Maria Sopra Minerva, but because it is in the district where religious articles are sold. Unlike the windows of other piazzas (those shrines to minor commercial gods, windows filled with beautifully wrapped chocolates, beautifully tailored suits, gloves in every shade), the windows of the streets leading from the Piazza Minerva are filled with vestments and sacred vessels with singular, evocative names taken from their ancient use: chalice, pyx, ciborium, monstrance, censer, thurifer. And the sad clothing shops for nuns: mannequins in veils, mannequins meant to be unalluring, so unlike other mannequins with their prominent nipples. The nun mannequins are overlarge and wear neutral-colored nightgowns — white, gray, baby blue — bed jackets and booties testifying to the graying of the religious population and their need for clerical garments suitable for life in an invalid's bed. This morning, as every morning when he leaves his hotel, he looks away from the windows full of ten-foot-tall statues of Pope John Paul II, averting his eyes until he comes to the window of vestments: silk embroideries and embossments, rose, green, white, purple. Some ugly, but not all. There is so much in his business he cannot look at. But he does his work well; he makes money, not only for himself but for Maria and Pearl, who have never had to worry about what anything costs because, at Maria's father's request, Joseph took up the business.

He phones the ticket agent from his room and discovers that there is only one flight a day from Rome to Dublin. It leaves at 8 a.m.; he has already missed it. But he tells himself this is all for the best. It would not be a good thing for him to arrive first. Maria is, after all, Pearl's mother; they are tied by blood, bound in the law. The ties that bind. He is free of ties. He is bound to no one (except his mother); there is no name for what he is to Pearl. Therefore, whatever it is — this love he has for her, this love he has had since the moment of her birth — it is a thing unrecognized by the world and therefore a thing of no force.

The airline schedule dictates that he has another day in Rome. He will take a longer walk: he knows where he wants to end up: a place of rest, of contemplation, a cloister in Trastevere known to him and few others, concealed in the center of a building that suggests nothing of its hidden treasure. You press a bell that says SPOSINI, and a reluctant watchman lets you in to the cloister of the Order of St. John Hospitalers.

It is winter and nothing will be in flower; it is the quiet, the enclosure, the geometric rightness of the space that he craves.

He sits, hearing the plashing of the fountain that refreshes nothing. Dusty bushes eat up light; some hardy winter birds swoop lightly for a drink. He allows his mind to remain a blank. He tries not to think of Pearl, or to allow only a kind of thought that rockets straight past credibility: she will be all right, she will be all right. The weak sun warms the top of his head; the stone begins to chill his spine. He will move on.

• 6 •

Pearl hears someone saying her name, softly, in an Irish accent. She opens her eyes. A man and a woman, faces without features, kneel down, put their featureless faces next to hers. They are holding something, a cup of something. Something hangs over the edge: oh, she thinks, a straw. The straw brushes her lips. "Just take a sip of this," the woman says, in a voice that is pretending to be kind. Pearl clamps her jaws down, thrashes her head. And then the voice no longer even pretends kindness. "If you think you're a bloody martyr, little girl, you don't even know you're born."

What would Maria Meyers think if she had to consider at this moment, as her child is lying on the ground and she is flying first class on Aer Lingus 865, that Pearl knew many of the things she'd kept from her. Knew saints' lives, the lives of martyrs, because she'd found her mother's childhood book, *A Girl's First Book of Saints*, by Jerome Lowery, OSB, the letters cut in gold into the purple spine. Reading her mother's book, she had to understand that some deaths were said to be a good thing. It went against everything else in her life to think that a death might be what your life was leading up to all along. She had never had the slightest hint that death might be a good thing. What would Maria say if she knew Pearl's first thought about the death she is pursuing now came to her from a book with Maria's childhood signature on the flyleaf, girlish loops and curlicues Maria excised from her adult signature, a sign, treasured by Pearl, that her mother had also once been a child, reading this same book?

What Pearl could not know was that the child that was her mother did not read the book in the same way, not in the same way at all. Maria, a Catholic child of ten in 1958, would have read the book as if her life were at stake. And not just her life but what she would have found it very easy to call her immortal soul. She read not from curiosity but as a model her salvation depended on. She read the lives of the martyrs and believed with all her heart that she had to pray for a martyr's death. She would say to Joseph, "Let's think of what we'll do, exactly, if the Communists put a gun to our heads and tell us they'll shoot us unless we say God doesn't exist." And he would say OK and let her talk.

In Joseph's mind were terrifying images of men in brown coats, their faces distorted by hatred until they were hardly faces anymore, stretched mouths, pig stubs of noses, blood-red eyes. He knew they wanted to kill him. He felt the terror in his flesh; he imagined himself reneging at the last minute, saying, "All right, God doesn't exist," and then having to live a shamed life. Maria, on the other hand, always imagined herself glorious, triumphant, welcomed in paradise by throngs of fellow martyrs. So Maria savored the gruesome details of the deaths of virgin martyrs: St. Lucy with her eyes gouged out; St. Anastasia with her breasts chopped off; St. Apollonia, her teeth pulled out by rusty Roman pliers.

How could Maria have imagined that her daughter would be in Dublin reading *One Day in My Life* by Bobby Sands, which her group thought of as one of the Lives of the Saints? That they followed the weeks of his death by starvation, the cramps, the coma, as their parents and their grandparents followed the Way of the Cross?

Are you surprised at the gaps of knowledge that exist between this mother and daughter? You shouldn't be. If you asked Maria what she wanted for Pearl, she would have said, "I just want her to be happy." And what did Pearl want? She would have said she wanted to live in her own way. And Maria would have said, "Of course, that's exactly what I want for you; we want the same thing, you see." And Pearl would have said, like many daughters, "My mother doesn't have a clue." But what clues was she given? What cues did she fail to take?

Perhaps you would like some clues from Pearl's childhood to help you unravel the mystery of why she is doing what she is doing now. Would it help you to know what kind of child Pearl was? Or — a related but not identical question — what kind of childhood she had? If we say, What kind of childhood did she have? and use the verb we have chosen, don't we have to ask another question, What kind of childhood was she given? But given by whom, her mother? The world?

I suppose the first and truest thing to say about Pearl as a child was that she was very quiet. She seemed almost afraid of excessive noise. Her mother once took her to a Thanksgiving parade, and the noise of the marching bands terrified her. She liked to look at books, to draw; she liked to sew. She very much liked animals. As a matter of fact, some of the most important things she treasured were connected to dogs. By which I do not mean the ordinary doggy lessons of fidelity and joy in life.

She may not have been given the right kind of childhood for the child she was. Perhaps this is because her mother gave her the kind of childhood she would have wanted for herself. Maria had hated the surveillance of her own childhood, the privileged enclosure, being kept from the world as if she were a fragile and precious object. She detested what she knew about her father's feelings for her: that she was a work of art, always in progress, always potentially revisable. Her father watched her with the tyrannical eye of the camera or the iconographer: waiting to freeze the moment, preserve it, make it stand not as itself but as a type of something. Like the time she tried on her First Communion dress. She could see he was disappointed at the crinoline, the lace. "A bit ornate, wouldn't you say?" And then his revision on the day of the ceremony: "My Goya Infanta." So by his naming her a type of something, she could be his again.

There was a right way of doing everything, tied to eternal reward. A right way of turning a page, of walking across the room, of saying thank you, of holding a rosary, of lighting a blessed candle, of curtseying (particularly to priests), of thinking about Europe versus America, the past versus the present, the cheap happiness of the present as opposed to future gold. She felt she was constantly being watched and was often a disappointment. She loved running, swimming, braving thunderstorms, hailstorms, blizzards, high waves, long jumps, deep drops down into nothing. Her father wanted her at his side. At his feet.

She would not do that to Pearl: make her feel she was being looked at. She felt she had grown up in a rifle sight. Sometimes you remembered and that was all right: you knew you were being watched, you did what was required. But sometimes you forgot, you were running somewhere, singing something, and — *blam!* — the gun went off, the shot right to the heart. She would not do that to her child.

It might be possible to say that, refusing to keep her eye on her daughter as an eye was kept on her, she wasn't looking closely enough. Or that, believing she was looking at her daughter, she was really looking at herself. But the way she thought was this: surveillance was entrapment. She had no impulse to trap her daughter: she felt no need to catch her out. She believed in her daughter's goodness. She believed in her daughter's essential safety in the world. But her daughter did not feel safe. Does the fact that Maria never knew that, or never allowed herself to believe it, mean she wasn't paying attention, and so her daughter was more unsafe than she might otherwise have been? Doubly unsafe? Is Pearl where she is because her mother wasn't looking closely enough? Or looking at an image of her child that was her own reflection? You may draw these conclusions if you like. I think Maria was trying to bring her child up as a child of hope. That she did not succeed is not, I think, her fault.

Maria wanted a life of freedom and openness for her daughter; she wanted a life that denied the power of privilege or at least denied its scope. So she chose to live with Pearl in a racially mixed neighborhood among the working poor. And she chose to educate her daughter first in the Washington Heights day-care centers where she worked. She could have Pearl with her every day, and Pearl would grow up knowing everyone was not just like her, wasn't blessed with her blessings. And she wanted Pearl to grow in her own way, at her own pace, not checked on every minute, questioned, tested.

I will not say that all these things were mistakes. Pearl was never snobbish or exclusive. In the day-care center, which was sometimes a torment to her (she was not a scrapper and found it hard to fight for a place), she met, when she was four years old, her best friend, Luisa Ramirez, whom she has loved from that day to this. She learned Spanish at three; her love of languages was fostered without effort, without the hideous self-conscious deliberateness of her neighbors forty blocks to the south, taking little Amanda, little Oliver, to lessons at the Lycée Français to impress the admissions office of Dalton, Chapin, Horace Mann. But Pearl was often afraid, often overwhelmed, often guilty, because she knew she and her mother had more money than the other families and could do things the others could not, or avoid things the others had to do. Perhaps this story, which I would like to tell you now, will give you a better sense of things. This is the story of the beginning of Pearl's and Luisa's friendship.

Pearl is four years old, the only one in the day-care center with blond hair. There is another little girl there; Mariposa is her name: Butterfly. She wants to touch Pearl's hair. That's what she wants to do all day: touch the blond hair. She walks into the room, throws off her coat and her backpack, runs over to Pearl, touches her hair. Plays with it. Every day she brings in barrettes and hair elastics, so she can put them in Pearl's hair. Pearl doesn't like it, but she thinks that if Mariposa wants to do it so much, she has to let her. So many people seem to know what they want better than she does, so she lets them have her things; their wanting something so much makes her feel exhausted, defeated. Are you surprised that a prosperous, loved four-year-old should feel exhausted, defeated? We don't like to think of those words in relation to young children. But I think perhaps we should.

Pearl allows Mariposa to touch her hair.

This is how Pearl and Luisa become friends. Luisa knocks Mariposa to the ground one day and says, "Leave her fucking hair alone, you fucking little freak." The director takes the three children into her office and asks Pearl if she minds Mariposa playing with her hair, and Pearl says, "It doesn't matter," which makes Luisa furious all over again. The director, Maria's boss (who she thinks is an idiot), suggests that Luisa needs to learn other choices than inappropriate language and might need a time-out.

That night, Pearl cuts her hair off, liking the sound the scissors make, liking her hair in a pile on the floor, more pleased with it there than on her head. And her mother comes into the room, begins to cry, stops herself, holds Pearl's head against her breast. "My poor little lamb," she says. "My poor shorn lamb."

★ ★ ★

Perhaps Maria might have made wiser choices. Seen to it, for example, that Pearl had some experiences — if only in the summer — of the wilderness, the woods. A garden of her own. Maria told herself that Pearl was quiet and reserved and did not demand from her (this was a mercy) a more outgoing approach to classroom life. But she didn't see, until Pearl was eleven, that her daughter might have done better in a smaller, quieter classroom, where little Amanda and little Oliver might inflict spiritual harm but probably spoke in lower tones and might not be so prone to pocket loose change or desirable accessories. It took Maria a while to give up her dream of public school education, but when Pearl was twelve she did see, finally, that her daughter wasn't thriving and arranged for her to take the test for the Watson School, a private girls school on the Upper East Side. They were eager to have her. Maria arranged for Luisa to be tested too. She was accepted on scholarship. Maria could therefore convince herself that she had bleached the experience of the stain of privilege. Pearl never imagined that the stain was lighter than it was, and Luisa, who flourished at Watson, resented it as well and rails to this day (from her Harvard dormitory room) about the fucking white girls and the fucking old-maid teachers who taught her the Latin she adores and majors in, picketing the administration building in support of the creation of a major (good for others but not herself) in ethnic studies.

Luisa Ramirez, who loves Pearl fiercely, felt her always in need of protection. She did not like Maria, hated that Maria believed she understood Luisa's parents, thought it a sacrilege that Maria should even speak of an experience she had no knowledge of. Maria and Luisa: similar in nature, forceful, loving Pearl, who from childhood had disliked and feared even the idea of force. Feeling herself a person of no force, except, now, in this one act: her forceful death.

Things would happen to Pearl that gave her an inkling of a kind of life she knew she was protected from, but which, she feared, was truer than the version created by her mother. These things all involved random malignity, so it is possible to say that as a child she was distressed by a pattern she inchoately perceived, which she believes now has come together in a truth that makes room for no other. That demands her death. But she was very young when she began to be distressed by things she saw, so distressed that she believed the floor of the world was breaking through. She would feel herself falling. Then the world, or her mother, would catch her. Now nothing has broken her fall. But the experience of falling: this is something she has known for as long as she can remember.

Pearl saw things in the apartment building where she lived all her life. She knew that it was a very nice apartment building, a fortunate apartment building, and that the people in it were very nice. So the fact that terrible things could happen there made her even more distressed. For example, what happened to Miss Alice Stevenson, the year Pearl was six.

I am going to tell you the story of Miss Alice Stevenson to explain what Pearl calls her witnesses; it is their faces that appear behind her eyes, cut out against cold blue, telling her she is right to do what she is doing. That is why I tell these stories: so you can see the faces Pearl is seeing.

Miss Alice lived in the same building as Maria and Pearl. She took in typing. Pearl and Maria met Miss Alice when Maria gave Miss Alice her thesis to type when Pearl was three. She always called herself Miss Alice, and that's what she wanted to be called. She loved Maria and Maria found her interesting. Maria was always saying she liked people on the edge; she said they had imagination. Often these people frightened Pearl. She thought her mother didn't see their desperation, and this frightened her too: what her mother didn't or wouldn't see. When she was older and had the words for what had been a feeling, she wanted to say to her mother, What you call lively I call chaotic. But she never did, because she knew how much it would cause her mother to give up.

Miss Alice always wore identical short-sleeved striped knit dresses, with the zipper down the front, the handle of the zipper a small metal circle that just begged to be humiliatingly pulled down. She never wore stockings, even in winter. And never shoes or boots, only sneakers — Keds — white or black. She had a dog named Clancy. Both had underbites. Both of them had hair that was curly and unkempt. They really did look alike.

Miss Alice walked Clancy six or seven times a day. He peed every two or three feet. You didn't like thinking about his penis, but you couldn't help it.

On her kitchen wall, Miss Alice had pasted pictures of movie stars cut out of Sunday supplements. Next to the pictures were letters she'd typed and signed.

Dear Miss Alice, thank you for the wonderful typing. Elizabeth Taylor.

Dear Miss Alice, it's always such a pleasure working with you. Charlton Heston.

Dear Miss Alice, you saved my life this time. Woody Allen.

Miss Alice was never separated from her dog. She made the dog crazy. It wasn't that Clancy was vicious. It was simply that he did not know rest. She wouldn't let him alone. If he was lying down, trying to sleep, she'd rattle a box of Milk-Bones till he barked, and then she'd break one of the Milk-Bones in six pieces and throw them and he'd catch them in his mouth: one, two, three, four, five, six catches for each little chunk. Sometimes he'd bark for no reason. Then Miss Alice would give him a Milk-Bone. Then she'd complain about his barking. Maria would say, "Don't give him a treat when he barks; you'll encourage him." Miss Alice liked Maria, but she didn't listen to her; she didn't listen to anyone about Clancy. She'd say, "Oh, he's used to it by now, it's our game."

As Clancy got older, he started peeing in the hall. Just a few drops, but Miss Alice never cleaned it up. This infuriated one of the other tenants, a German woman, Mrs. Habermas. She was a very tidy woman, Mrs. Habermas. She often looked furious. Have you noticed how that is with very tidy people? At Christmastime, she'd bring Maria and Pearl cookies, but Pearl was always afraid to eat them.

When Clancy peed in the hall, Mrs. Habermas would knock furiously on Miss Alice's door. Pearl could hear her knocking, shouting, complaining about the dog. "Filthy, filthy!" she would shout. Pearl was frightened. Maria would say, "They'll get tired of it," but Pearl knew they wouldn't. Or Mrs. Habermas wouldn't. And, in fact, Pearl was right.

Miss Alice shouted back at Mrs. Habermas through the apartment door. She kept calling Mrs. Habermas a Nazi and saying she had no intention of going into a concentration camp. One night, Mrs. Habermas knocked on the Meyerses' door. "She's making our beautiful building filthy, filthy." When Mrs. Habermas said the word *filthy* her face changed shape; she wanted to hurt Miss Alice. Maria wanted Mrs. Habermas to know she would not allow it. Maria told Mrs. Habermas to leave; Miss Alice was an unfortunate soul and needed help, not persecution. From then on, Mrs. Habermas counted the Meyerses among her enemies. She divided the building up into allies and enemies. It was war. And Miss Alice did have her enemies, because of Clancy. He did bark all the time, and he did pee in the hall.

Everyone knew it was Mrs. Habermas who called the IRS. It seems that Miss Alice never paid income tax. How did Mrs. Habermas find that out, the cunning of the hunter? Maybe she just took a chance. She reported Miss Alice for conducting a business from her apartment.

Miss Alice wouldn't open the door for the IRS. She screamed at them like she screamed at Mrs. Habermas. Pearl was very frightened. She was only six when all this happened.

Miss Alice had had a little something once, and she lost it. It was taken from her. Pearl could see she had become a hunted person. Soon after the IRS came, Clancy died. I don't know if that was Mrs. Habermas's fault. I don't know how she could have made it happen; Miss Alice never let Clancy out of her sight. Pearl didn't know whether Mrs. Habermas was responsible for Clancy's death, but she knew that the kind of hate Mrs. Habermas felt could result in death, even if she didn't know how, and this frightened her. She thought her mother didn't understand; she knew she couldn't ask her mother if Mrs. Habermas's hate had made Clancy die, because her mother would say, Of course not, don't think that way, don't think of things like that; let's just think of something to do for Miss Alice to make her feel better. But Pearl knew that Miss Alice had lost everything she once had, and because her mother didn't understand that, she no longer felt as safe with her mother as she did before.

Pearl was eight when the incident with Janet Morehouse and the super happened, another incident in the building.

Janet and Maria met while Maria was pregnant. Janet had always wanted a baby but believed she didn't have the strength to raise a child on her own. Maria incorporated her into her project — the project first of having Pearl on her own, then raising her. Maria believed it would be good for everyone. Perhaps it was.

Janet designed and made clothes. She liked clothes with very special details — French seams, covered buttons — that no one she knew well could afford. So she made ends meet doing upholstery and slipcovers and sometimes just altering clothing and making hems. The apartment was always full of fabrics, and sometimes Pearl enjoyed that, losing herself in colors and textures for whole afternoons. But sometimes Janet's apartment just upset her. There were too many things, things in the wrong places. When you sat on her couch, pins stuck out of the burgundy velvet cushions. There were lots of ashtrays with dirty tissues in them, though Janet didn't smoke.

Pennies, turning green, were stuck to the glass top of the coffee table. A withered balloon on a long stick was shoved into a dusty blue glass vase.

One day, Pearl and Janet were dancing. Pearl was still quite young; I think she must have been five. Janet had made a cape of magenta silk for Pearl and a violet one for herself. She had bought Pearl Hawaiian Punch as a special treat; it was the sort of small transgression she allowed herself. Maria didn't approve of drinks with such a high sugar concentration, but Janet knew Pearl liked the color, and she liked to think of herself as a naughty aunt. She put some music on, maybe Palestrina, and they were dancing, twirling their capes. And then Janet knocked over the glass of Hawaiian Punch with the corner of her cape. It spilled onto a stack of paper and made a magenta-colored pool that didn't seep into the stack. The two of them stood looking at it for a while, unable to think what to do. Then Pearl began to wipe at it with the corner of her cape (which was the same color as the Hawaiian Punch — that was part of the fun), but Janet said, "No, that's no good," and Pearl knew she was right nothing was any good, nothing they could think of would do the slightest bit of good.

What did they do then? Maybe just stood there and waited for Maria.

The super hated Janet. He wanted to hurt her. He was a terrible man, everyone knew that. He was a drunk and he lived alone in the basement. He could have fixed anything if he wanted to — but he often didn't. On the nights he dressed up to go out, he'd put on a lot of heavy gold jewelry and a blond Beatles wig (he was bald without it) and then he'd drive his Cadillac, loud, up the street.

He liked Maria but, as I said, he hated Janet. He'd never do anything for her. Or if he did, he made it worse than before. Her toilet never worked right. You always had to flush it three or four times. He tried to convince her it was her fault, saying she must be "putting something funny down there." For a few minutes she'd try to convince him that it wasn't her fault, but then she'd give up. If Pearl was in the apartment, he was a little better. Janet tried to get the super to come when Pearl was there because she knew he didn't want Maria to know he'd acted badly. Pearl heard Maria telling Janet once that she always let him think she might just make her way to the basement for a little smooch.

She said she had to keep that possibility in mind, but make him believe it was pretty unlikely. That's the kind of line Maria always seemed able to walk. It was the kind of thing that frightened Pearl. Suppose her mother couldn't get away from Mr. Murcherson? Suppose he took her to the basement and she couldn't get away?

One night, Janet was doing her laundry in the basement. Usually the super locked the laundry room at ten, but that night he wanted to lock up at nine-thirty and Janet wasn't finished. She told him she had another half hour. He told her she'd leave when he said she'd leave. When she stood her ground, he turned the lights off and locked the door. Janet was locked in the dark cold room all night. She banged and banged on the door and no one heard her. Or maybe the super heard her and he didn't care. Maybe he was glad.

At six the next morning, he unlocked the door but didn't open it. Pearl had a cold the next day and couldn't go to school, and when Maria took her down to stay with Janet, Janet was sitting on the couch in a daze, like she'd been beaten.

Pearl saw her mother moving very fast, the way Janet never could. She called the center and said she'd be half an hour late, and told her assistant ten things to do. Then she ran down to the super's apartment in the basement and made him apologize to Janet. This frightened Janet; she felt she'd pay for it in the long run. Maria said of course she wouldn't.

Nothing really changed, but Maria felt something *had* changed, that she'd made something happen. Pearl felt her mother didn't understand. She knew something her mother didn't know: that some things were hopeless. There were some things no one could do anything about. The super would always want to hurt Janet, because he could, just as Mrs. Habermas called the IRS on Miss Alice because she could.

All her life, after these two stories, fourteen years of life in the case of Miss Alice, twelve in the case of Janet, these stories have come to Pearl when she's been tired or discouraged or just sad, and when they came they suggested to her that they were the truest things about the world. But although she always knew they were there in the background, she was capable of being newly shocked, as she was when her mother told her John Lennon had been killed by someone who was jealous of him. From the time she was a baby, her mother would dance with her to the Beatles. "All

You Need Is Love." Her mother would lift her up, the two of them laughing, Pearl and Maria both singing at the top of their voices: *"Love is all you need!"* But sometimes her mother would spin her too fast, and she got dizzy and the moons came in front of her eyes; stripes of light crisscrossed each other and she wanted to say, Stop, Mama, stop, the floor's going upside down. But sometimes she liked the moons and the crisscrossed lights and wanted the floor to go upside down.

One day, when Pearl was nine, she and Maria were dancing to the Beatles, dancing as partners now: Maria could no longer, would no longer, spin Pearl off the floor. It was a clear cold day in December; the light fell on the wooden floor in thin hard bars. Maria started crying because it was the anniversary of John Lennon's death and told her about Mark David Chapman. Pearl was only nine but her mother thought she believed in not keeping things from her, although in fact she kept many important things from her daughter. But she did not keep from Pearl the story of John Lennon and Mark David Chapman. Mark David Chapman, unloved, ungifted, reading *The Catcher in the Rye* alone, wanting to erase the loved face so his face would be, as it has become, unerasable.

I don't want to suggest that Pearl was miserable all the time. Many things gave her great joy. Her dog, Lucky, rescued from the pound, part yellow Lab, part something unidentifiable: her boon companion, absorber of dread, tears, anguish, and, later, mother-directed rage. She and Maria and Lucky would run in Riverside Park, and then, when Pearl became a better runner than her mother (this happened when she was thirteen and Maria forty-three), she and the dog would run from 120th Street far, far downtown and back. Run along the river, the light enchanting in all seasons — metallic or powdery or a fall of silver — and her breath and the dog's breath going in, going out, their hearts pounding and relaxing in the New York air. Maria and Joseph and Devorah rented cottages at the sea: on Cape Cod, at the Jersey shore. Pearl loved swimming with her dog, with her mother, with Luisa, because most years Luisa was invited along. The two of them would take long, tiring swims that folded into sweet restoring afternoon sleeps on screened porches or in white beds where the sun fell straight onto the pillows, warming their cold cheeks, their still wettish hair. For many years Maria and Pearl shared a vivid joy in bodily life, and Maria was good at thinking up treats: going for ice cream could become an event, a trip onto the roof of a summer evening. Their bodies enjoyed many of the same things: running, swimming, eating, dancing. Pearl had no important friends other than Luisa but their connection was constant, electric. They studied together; they discussed the world, their souls: who they were, who they were in the process of becoming. Pearl had boyfriends — brutes or dolts, they would be called in retrospect — and in their senior year she and Luisa decided they should lose their virginity before college, which they unceremoniously did, primarily in order to discuss it with each other. She had, properly speaking, never been in love.

★ ★ ★

This is the kind of child Pearl was. Does it help you understand why she is where she is?

Now she is lying on the freezing ground. She has felt the cold more keenly ever since she gave up eating, but she is not feeling it now. For six weeks she has eaten no solid food. She is an intelligent girl, a modern girl; she has researched the details of starvation in libraries and on the Internet. She has understood, rightly, that

161

the great threat to life is not starvation but dehydration — or a combination of the two. She has taken nothing to drink for six days. She knows it is much easier to rescue a person from death by starvation than from death by dehydration. She planned it so that she would reach the irrevocable point of death from dehydration on Christmas Day: the day she would be most legible. This is what she has told herself to do: to make a sentence of herself, to make of her life one sentence that she knows to be true. She is, after all, a student of language. She has often thought that in the place on her passport where country of origin is written she should put: *language*.

She would be closer to death now except for a miscalculation: she miscalculated her own health: the power of her youth, her fine nutrition, a strong body trained and disciplined (she was, in high school, a cross-country runner; she swam the quarter mile). It was not mentioned in the data she found that if you were fortunate and disciplined and gifted it would be more difficult for you to die. I cannot but think that we are all grateful for this error. I cannot but think that some of us would call it not an error but grace.

• 7 •

Maria can't think of anything but Pearl; she wishes something else could absorb her mind, just for a little while, and then she castigates herself for the thought. As if, by relinquishing vigilance for a moment, she would place her child in danger. How can it even be imagined that she would watch a movie, read a book? She must keep the image of her child before her. How can someone think she should be watching a movie about an e-mail romance between Meg Ryan and Tom Hanks? When the flight attendant offers her a magazine, she would like to throw it back. *How could you imagine that I can read a magazine while my daughter is dying?* It is the first time in her life she's ever traveled without a book. But no, that isn't right; she does have a book with her, but not really to read. She slipped into her purse a small edition of George Herbert's poems that Devorah had given her for her twenty-first birthday. She brought it as a talisman. So she would have the protection of the beloved dead.

She wants to see Devorah's handwriting, her name in Devorah's handwriting, as if she could, by touching the page that Devorah touched, absorb the magic of the dead. She sees her name in a handwriting still childish; at twenty-one, Devorah was not yet her adult self. Pearl is only twenty. What does that make her? And what was I? she wonders, trying to remember this girl who thought she might write poetry in the manner of George Herbert, parson of Bemerton, living a hidden life, a quiet life, devoted to perfection of the form. But she could not do that when Asian children ran in flames, when men like her father were bombing Cambodia. The sound of buzzing wires that was the undertone of every moment in those years, the sound that was quieted when Pearl was born, begins again. It has begun, only she hadn't recognized it, had not named it for what it was. Buzzing wires. And before her eyes the image she cannot quite form of her daughter, chained, lying on the cold ground. She flips through the book. Stops at a poem that had never been her favorite, "The Collar." She remembers: it is a poem about restriction, about a rebellious thrashing and then a succumbing to the discipline of the Divine. The poet gives up his struggle when he hears God address him as "Child." Well, there had been nothing like that for her, would never be. The collar. She feels trapped, caged in this enclosed space where she can barely move. She allows herself to look at the poem, hoping her lapse of attention will not bring her child harm. There is the word *cage,* which has just been in her mind. "Forsake thy cage, thy rope of sands." Rope of sands. A wonderful image; she can feel it on her skin, the chafing, the restriction.

Collar. She thinks of a collar she had used to train Pearl's dog, Lucky, whom they had rescued from a pound. Lucky had become aggressive when he saw black men. Clearly, that was not acceptable. But if they sent him back to the pound he would be destroyed. The vet suggested a shock collar. Every time Lucky snarled at a black man, Maria pressed a button and a shock was delivered to his neck. He never knew where it came from. Now she knows what the dog felt. It is what she feels in her body, a series of shocks, every time she thinks that Pearl might die. The shock lodges first in the deep organs, travels through the blood along the muscles, then spreads its way through the skin, which has become a network of electrified strings, each one thrumming, bearing heat upward to the neck's bones and then the skull. When the shock subsides an irritation is left, like a rash spreading across the skin, following the path of the strings that had, a moment earlier, borne heat. Irritation, then: a rope of sand. Until the next shock, and the process starts again.

Lucky had changed as the result of a series of shocks whose source he could not determine. How will she be changed? The collar. Shocks, and the chafing of restriction. Her situation is unbearable: she is in the air, unable to get to her daughter, who may be dying. Her mind spins with fatigue. She is very tired, but she dares not sleep.

In the confusion brought about by her fatigue, it takes her a while to determine that the noise her brain is trying to respond to is the sound of a child crying. It is in economy; there are no babies visible in first class. She wonders if babies aren't allowed in first class and is prepared to be outraged by that. She has no evidence that babies aren't allowed in first class, only what she knows of the world from working for twenty years with children. The false claims of allegiance to the young and the real failures to provide for them make her think it's possible that babies are excluded from first class; thinking it's possible, she quickly moves to believing it is really the case. Outrage is strikable in her: a flint always ready to catch fire, and the actual, potential, or remembered treatment of children is always able to inspire her outrage. *Our children,* people say, but she knows they mean only their own, only the ones who live in their houses or similar ones.

My treasure, her father had called her; it made her bristle. Treasure to be protected, hidden, like his fourteenth-century French ivories, his icons of the Madonna dark against their backgrounds of burnished gold. When she was a teenager, seventeen perhaps, she said to him, "I want a world where everyone's children are as important as our own." And her father had said, "That's impossible. It's against the Natural Law."

The Natural Law. It was something Seymour Meyers invoked, she'd come to see, to justify all kinds of tyrannies. But now, flying to her daughter who is at the edge of death, she knows he was right. If someone said to her, Choose, you must choose now, right this moment; we will sacrifice a hundred children to keep your child alive, what would she say? She knows what she would say, and she knows what it means about her. She has cast her lot with those who say *my own* and mean something connected to themselves, the radius of the circle that surrounds their own bodies: nothing larger, nothing as large as the whole world.

The baby's cry breaks up these thoughts, and she's grateful for the breakage, or there would only be a solid wall that she must beat her head against until her brains were bloodied. Nothing is worth your life, she wants to say to Pearl, thousands of miles away from her, inaccessible as she flies through the green-black air.

Maria moves her mind to the sound of the baby's crying, more frantic now. She stands up, shakes herself like a wet dog, bursts through the curtains separating first class from business and then the curtains separating business class from coach. She pushes the curtains aside like a great actress in a tragic play: she is Clytemnestra, Hecuba, Phaedra. No, not Phaedra. Phaedra was not a mother.

Her eyes fall on the frantic baby. The mother is young and overwhelmed. She has two other children. Maria, an expert, calculates their ages: three and four. They are tugging at their mother, trying to crawl on her as she tries, futilely, to comfort the infant. Maria sees that the mother is not much older than Pearl, and she is filled with the kind of desperate tenderness that often comes over her in the course of her work at the sight of a young mother in despair.

She makes a quick calculation: how can she offer help without suggesting to the mother that she is a failure at the thing all successful women are born knowing how to do.

She touches the young woman's shoulder. The young woman jerks her head toward Maria, ready to defend herself, ready for a rebuke.

"Hello," Maria says. "I don't mean to intrude, but you seem to have your hands full and I'm bored out of my skull. I run a day care and I'm used to crying children. Why don't you let me walk the baby up and down the aisle, and you can pay attention to the other kids and get a little break yourself?"

The mother — Maria is right, she is very young — begins to cry.

"I couldn't ask you," she says. Maria hears that she is Irish.

"Believe me, you'd be doing me a favor. I

love babies and I hate sitting still."

The woman hands the baby over, along with a bottle and a blanket and a rattle that makes a jingling noise. The baby, Maria calculates, is six months old. She doesn't know its name or sex: it is simply a child, a child in distress. Maria clasps the baby to her. And the long drowning that began when she first held Pearl, the remembered swoon that comes over her when she holds a baby, is now hers. She puts her mouth to the baby's skull and breathes in the milky salt.

Walking the baby, feeling its dampish warmth at the front of her body, its heaviness against her chest, she thinks of Pearl's babyhood, of the day of her birth, after the mess and blood and shouting and pushing were over, and she heard, "It's a girl," and thought, Thank God. She hadn't wanted to admit that she was afraid of having a boy, afraid of bringing up a boy without a father. But she was not thinking of Pearl's father at that moment: only of the two of them. Her baby. *Mine.*

When she was in the recovery room with her clean wrapped baby, alone with her for the first time, she knew that never in her life would she need anyone as she needed Pearl.

Alone with her. Her baby. *Mine.*

Nothing had ever been so quiet, nothing had ever been so purely sufficient to itself. A perfect circle. A circle as pure and powerful as the white Host.

Miraculous, mysterious, common as dirt. She knew in that moment she had more in common with any woman who had just given birth — with the most venal Hollywood starlet, with the wife of the Grand Dragon of the Ku Klux Klan — than she did with her closest friend. Tentatively, Pearl put her mouth to her mother's breast, both of them inexpert. Only later would the urgency of real hunger strike. For now they were alone and silent. Hello, my own, Maria said to Pearl. She has been saying that to her with every sentence since that moment, believing (what Pearl does not believe) that no one will ever know her so well and she will never be known so well. *I am the beloved and the beloved is mine.* The ellipse of the most ecstatic sex is ragged, partial, next to this. This moment of knowing. *Knowing I am known.*

You may be curious about the details of Pearl's conception.

Well, to understand Pearl's conception we must go back and take up our chronicle once again, go back some years before her birth, to 1971, the year of Maria's graduation from college, the year after her break with her father.

She told her father there would be no conversation between them; she seemed not to notice that he paid her last year's tuition. She tried to get Billy Ogilvie to forgive her; she tried to get the police to arrest her; she would not go home; she worked as a waitress in a café on Massachusetts Avenue that summer; she finished at Radcliffe with her class. Maria was always someone who liked finishing what she started. She did not, however, attend her own graduation; nor, of course, did her father.

A month later she took a plane to Guatemala, where she worked in a clinic. She helped deliver babies; she bathed the sick; she bound their wounds. She was, however, not very good at it.

She didn't like the care of broken bodies, but she found she was very good at teaching children. She was often impatient with the mothers who gave their babies rice water instead of milk, but she was rarely impatient with the children, who seemed beautiful to her, their small hard dirty hands, their reedy voices sounding the letters of the alphabet, their lively songs, their colorful drawings. She was touched when she walked into the room and they cried out, proud of their one English sentence, "We lof ar titcher."

And she *did* love them back, so it was easy for her to tell them the same thing again and again, to tell them any number of ways until they got it. But some of them never got it, and those were the ones she did not love, the ones whose eyes were dead. Perhaps that meant she did not love the ones most in need of loving, the ones for whom nothing could be done. But she didn't think that way. She focused on the ones for whom she could do something: no sense, she told herself, worrying about the ones she couldn't reach. And no sense regretting that she couldn't help the sick, that she couldn't be patient with her children's mothers, who beat them, or their fathers, who beat both the children and their mothers. They seemed hopeless. Maria couldn't love anyone who made her feel they were hopeless. Perhaps no one can.

The news of her father's death came to her in Guatemala. Her father died without asking for her. When Joseph called Guatemala to tell her the news she could not weep, would not, because she knew if she allowed herself to grieve she would become a mourner, which would dilute her sense of righteousness, her sense of acting in the name of justice.

The children wanted her to grieve and the parents wanted her to grieve, so eventually she left Guatemala because she had become unknowable to the people she was working among. They couldn't understand a daughter who did not grieve for her father, a daughter who was dry-eyed at his death. They didn't understand that she had replaced filial love, which she believed to be inferior and cheap, with a love of justice. In those days she called up the words of the psalms but changed them for her own needs. *Take this heart of flesh, give me a heart of stone,* she prayed. But she did not use the word *prayer;* rather, she sent up into the galaxy a wish she sealed with all the strength of her intention to stand for justice. "Give me a heart of stone." And she has kept it all these years. In the place where there was love for her father: stone.

If you ask your father for bread, you will not be given stone. And if you ask for a stone, will it not be given you?

You want to know about Pearl's birth. The line of Pearl's birth isn't a straight line but a series of intersecting circles.

It is 1973, Watergate. The evil face of Richard Nixon, the mad face, is known by everyone to be evil, mad. The bad guys are visibly bad; you can see their badness by the way they look, especially their hair.

One day on the 72nd Street subway platform, Maria, staying with Joseph and Devorah while she tries to figure out what to do after Guatemala, meets two old friends from Cambridge. They invite her to dinner. Jeanne is working on her PhD in history; she is writing on Queen Elizabeth. Rosemarie is an assistant at *Ms.* magazine.

Rosemarie and Jeanne introduce Maria to women who work at hopeful jobs: legal aid, social work, clinic medicine. No one has money; everyone eats together: large plates of spaghetti, which is not yet called pasta. Some women are part of female couples; some speak apologetically (but not so apologetically as they would have the year before) about planning to get married. Maria has no impulse to be mated: not at all, she says. During one dinner she dramatically proclaims that she'd rather have her labia sewn together than get married.

In those years, for people like Maria, life moved very fast. Everything was rapid. Rapid, rapids: white water. Boulders. Some boats were overturned and wrecked. Many were not. For those who felt the goodness of the ride, it was exciting to get together in fragile boats. It was a cataract-filled rush, but there was a thrill in it compared to the dead stink of the swamp, the distorting light, the choking vines, perfect for camouflage. How the light seemed to clear when the swamp had been left behind! And if, to keep their crafts light, they had to throw out some things that were of value, some things they didn't realize couldn't be recovered? Well, they would say, that was sad. But there was the exhilaration of being set free.

One of the women in Maria's consciousness-raising group decides to move to California and offers Maria her job, assistant at the Independent Organization for Refugees, a human rights organization. She is paid almost nothing; she types and files and is told she is saving lives by placing the right piece of paper in the right folder. Her friend who gave up the job no longer believes this. She says the work depresses her, the endless need to protect the innocent from mindless evil. She wants to move to California and make pottery in the mountains, a plan for which Maria has contempt. The word *burnout,* you see, is not yet current.

The Independent Organization for Refugees was founded and run by Clelia Roberts, an old-style Yankee idealist in her sixties with hair on top of her head in a Gibson girl knot, a navy blue suit, a series of identical light blue blouses that tie at the throat, flesh-colored stockings, and Hush Puppies that lace. She travels to the terrible places of the earth, comes home and writes about what she has seen, and sends it to newspapers and to powerful men: friends of her family. She raises money for heroic people to take back to their own countries. And then, for two months every year, she retreats to her family's camp in Maine to look at the sea and pick blueberries.

Clelia likes Maria and Maria likes Clelia. Born an aristocrat, Clelia has no trouble showing her favoritism. She admires Maria's speed and decisiveness and the style of her prose; soon she has Maria writing important reports. Maria doesn't mind Clelia's sharp tongue; when Clelia is rude, Maria tells her so and Celia is instantly abashed, shocked at her own behavior. In the five years Maria works for Clelia, ten other assistants come and go. Clelia keeps promoting Maria, but the raises in salary that accompany the promotions are quite small. Clelia doesn't notice and Maria doesn't mind because she doesn't need much. A bohemian girl from the twenties, Clelia invites Maria to Maine and to badly cooked dinners in her town house in the Village. The two share the unease of knowing themselves as favored daughters, but they would never dream of speaking of it.

Day after day, Maria looks at photographs; she reads reports of terrible atrocities. She hears of the worst things human beings can do to one another. She wants to travel with Clelia and see for herself, but Clelia always needs her at home to run the office. One day, Clelia says. I promise. But it never happens.

On July 6, 1977, Maria meets Ya-Katey, who has come from Cambodia to the United States to get help for his people, trying to make the full horror of his country known.

Do we remember Cambodia, its names and places, or have they blurred for us in the fog of atrocities, other sites of mass murder, other killing fields: Bosnia, Rwanda, Kurdistan? We search our memory; we call up names: Pol Pot, the Khmer Rouge. The people's army of Kampuchea. Do we remember 1975, when Pol Pot took over the city of Phnom Penh? Do we remember what Pol Pot stood for, what his ideas were? A Marxist-agrarian idealist, violently nationalist, violently antitechnology and anti-intellectual, he murdered one in four of his people. In the years 1975 to 1979 the odds against any Cambodian dying a natural death were two to one.

Maria learns all this in 1977 from Ya-Katey, as she takes him to churches and to the homes of the wealthy to raise money for medical supplies. This is his focus; he has trained as a doctor in Paris. One statistic he presents is this: as a result of Pol Pot's executions the number of doctors in Cambodia has fallen in two years from 270 to 40. Ya-Katey was imprisoned in a special jail set up for doctors, a former hospital. Each morning, one doctor was shot in front of the others. Each morning, they were told there was no more need for doctors. On one of the mornings, the soldier holding the rifle made an imaginary cutting motion with an imaginary knife across his stomach. "If someone needs to have their intestines removed, I will do it."

Forty doctors for a country of eight million people. Imagine, he says, having only forty doctors in the city of New York.

He tries to make these wealthy well-meaning Americans understand Phnom Penh in 1975, when Pol Pot took over. "Imagine your city, New York, evacuated in one day like Phnom Penh was because the Khmer didn't believe in cities; cities were dangerous. Imagine someone saying that all pure Americans were country people: that city people were a dangerous pustule on the healthy body of the nation." He reminds them that Pol Pot wants a pure Cambodia, a peasant ideal he believes he experienced when he was in hiding in the north of his country. Try to imagine, he says, everyone you know being marched at gunpoint to the countryside to work as slaves — that is, those who are allowed to survive. You must remember, he says, that people are killed for anything, for almost nothing: for having an education or technical skills, for knowing French, even for wearing glasses. "Our school is the farm, the land is our paper, we will write by plowing," Ya-Katey heard a soldier say before he shot a group of teachers.

There is no possible private life: children are buried alive for refusing to report on their parents, people are beheaded and their heads put on pikes for mourning the dead too publicly or too long.

You must try to imagine the madness of a country in the grip of a murderous madman, he tells the safe Americans. To illustrate his point, in every speech he describes an orphanage he passed by as he was being led out of the city at gunpoint. The workers had been ordered to leave by soldiers who had convinced themselves that babies in cradles were enemies, counterrevolutionaries, didn't deserve care. Some of the workers at the orphanage had refused to leave and were shot. "I heard the babies crying and I broke away. The soldiers followed me. I saw the bodies of the dead workers on the floor. Their bodies were rotting, and some babies were crawling around beside them. There were forty-eight cradles; forty-eight babies trapped in their cradles with literally no one looking after them. Some of them of course were already dead. There were twins in one cradle; one was alive, the other dead. Some babies tried to cry, but only a horrible sound came from their throats as they gasped for breath. Some people had sneaked in during the night and left cans of water and rice on banana leaves for the children on the floor. One of the children who had managed to crawl out of his crib was sitting on the floor, eating. His stomach was bloated and he looked dazed, but he couldn't stop eating. A dead baby lay nearby."

Ya-Katey told the soldiers he wouldn't leave the children in this condition. He was hit in the head with a rifle butt and beaten to insensibility.

When he woke up, he was in prison in the countryside. Then the camp was attacked by the North Vietnamese. In the chaos, he escaped: over the Thai border and finally here, to America.

Every evening Maria drives him to the places he will speak; she introduces him in the name of Clelia's organization. Clelia is very taken by him and tells Maria to show him around New York. In the mornings, in the afternoons, he wants to see things; he wants to eat well, particularly French food. He says he wants to store up images, images of beauty and of things beautifully done, so they will be a bank of hope for him to draw on in hopeless times. That is how he can order *escargots, agneau sanglante, haricots verts, tarte aux pommes;* return an unsatisfactory wine; accept, graciously, the apologies of the sommelier. How he can lose himself in the watery landscape of the Corot at the Frick, delight in the daub of red that is the boatman's hat. "Pol Pot would have me killed for desiring *angneau sanglante,* and Corot," he said, "because he says it is part of the corruption of Cambodian purity, an imperialist corruption. I fear purity; I fear it very much; it is a dangerous idea. I am a scientist, and I know that nothing alive is pure. To be pure is to be impervious to change, to mixture. Change and mixture is our lot, our lot as living things."

And one night, delighting in her body, he says, "If we should have a child it would be very very impure: Jewish, Russian, Cambodian, Catholic, Buddhist. A real mess. I am in love with the idea of mess. The mess is our only hope against the tyranny of the pure."

When he speaks about purity, he is thinking of murder. When she thinks of it, she thinks of surveillance. The kind of purity he fears is revolutionary purity. The kind she fears, the kind her experience has provided, is sexual. The purity that flew under the banner of virginity. The purity of the untouched body. The purity of the child. In her childhood, impurity meant only one thing: sexual defilement. Even to touch your body was a sin of impurity. She refuses a definition of virtue that insists she be either untouched or a child. But she feels that her ideas of purity are childish compared to his, and she is embarrassed to speak of them. When she asks him once why the idea of purity — of which there is no model, as he had often said, in nature — seems to have such a hold on the human imagination, he says, "It seems greatly desirable to be only one thing. To be, to do one thing fully, with no contradictions. To be a closed circle, impenetrable, impermeable. This, I believe, makes people feel safe."

When he says *a closed circle, impenetrable, impermeable,* she thinks of the White Circle of the Host and of her First Communion when she was six. She does not want to admit to him that it was a wonderful feeling, a day when she had felt entirely pure. Her father had told her once that Napoleon had said his First Communion was the happiest day of his life. She didn't know how her father knew this, but it was the kind of thing her father knew.

At twenty-nine, the age she is when she is with Ya-Katey, Maria hopes there will be happier days in her future. She would never have admitted, feeling as she does about her father and what her father stood for, that her First Communion was the happiest day of her life. If the thought entered her mind, she would banish it, annihilate it: a dangerous insurgent that must be blasted upon sight. As she has banished, every time it came to her, the thought that it was a wonderful feeling, the feeling of purity, of being whole, of being entirely one thing, and that thing only.

She wants to tell Ya-Katey about her First Communion, but it embarrasses her to be thinking of it, to be granting it any importance, when he is thinking about the horrors he has seen and the horrors that are going on in his homeland while he is here. Compared to that, her First Communion is ridiculous; she tells herself it would be blasphemous, even, to mention it to him. But the memory is vivid, and when he speaks of the dangers of purity, against her will the image of herself in her white dress enters her mind.

She remembers waking up on the day of her First Communion. Even the light coming in her window seemed sanctified; not drinking water that morning (although water was allowed), bathing herself in silence, dressing herself in silence, everything touching her body pure white, the living perfection of the form. A spotless girl child in white, with a bride's white veil. If you died on the way home from your

185

First Communion, one of the nuns had told them, it would be a perfect death. Were you supposed to pray for the grace of this perfect death, to pray for the favor of being run down by a car on the street at age six?

Inside her body: the Host, an illuminated circle; her ribs incandescent; the bones of the crucified Jesus visible to her through the stretched skin of his torso, ribs like her own incandescent ribs, illumined by the Host. She was glorified, transfigured, shining like the whitest snow. In her heart, an oval flamed, like the light of a lamp in a dark room, and she knew of course she would be one of the children willing to die in the name of this, this thing that was only one thing, the body of Christ, the thing she too had become: illumined, without blemish, without contradictions. Of course it would be easy to die. Only she could not pray for it. She did not want to die. Knowing she didn't want to die, she feared herself imperfect, impure. But she very much wanted the perfection of the form, her sense of her life as shining and complete.

Maria is afraid of the connection between her childhood vision of beauty and the murder from which Ya-Katey has fled, perhaps only temporarily. She feels she has no right to speak. So she doesn't tell him much about her life; she considers it far less important than his; she wants to give him pleasure and refreshment before he has to go back to horror, to what will probably be death.

"Must you go back?" she asks him once, and he says, "Yes, I can't be safe here in this dream while my people are living a nightmare."

So she creates a dream for him: a dream of pleasure. They laugh together; he teases her, calling her his luxury: *Ma Luxe, pas calme, mais voluptueuse.* He calls her his Jewish princess, and she tries to explain what that means in New York. He quotes the Song of Solomon: *Thy breasts are like two young roes that are twins, which feed among the lilies.* And his body, slight to her, and light, almost as if a girl were above her, a girl with a man's force but without the crushing mountainous feel that a heavy man's body would provide.

Is it that they are exotics to each other? Certainly they are that. Is that why their bodies please each other so? Does it matter? They desire each other, they admire each other. They both know it won't be for long. They don't say much about what they feel, only that they enjoy each other. And for both of them, that seems enough; it seems a very good thing.

Almost by accident, they discover they aren't entirely foreign to each other. She is driving down Fifth Avenue in front of St. Patrick's, and there is a terrible traffic jam. "What the hell is this?" she says. "It's the middle of the week, the middle of summer, August fifteenth, for God's sake." And then both of them say, at the same second, "August fifteenth: Assumption Day!" The Feast of the Assumption.

They laugh very hard. They have both been to Catholic school. He has been educated by the Jesuits, sent to their school in Paris. His father had been Buddhist but, enamored of French civilization, had converted. They are astonished to find in each other bits of a history that intersects. One night, a little drunk, they sing Salve Regina to each other. Then Pange Lingua: Sing, my tongue. They are a little obscene about that one. You can imagine. He hadn't liked Catholicism; he felt he'd been robbed of his heritage. He is a stranger to Buddhism. When he saw the desecration of the temples by the Khmer Rouge, he grieved for what he had not been allowed to know. He asks Maria if she's felt robbed of her heritage. "I don't think about it much," she says. And even Ya-Katey knows there is no sense in saying more. I'm not sure what he thinks, because he leaves soon afterward. He plans to sneak back into the country as he'd left: through the Thai jungle. He knows he probably will not survive.

Maria never hears from him. The organization cannot track him down. And then she discovers she is pregnant with his child. She didn't mean for it to happen; her diaphragm failed. She had known him little more than a month. And so she had, as her model of what a man to whom she could attach herself should be, a ghost: someone against whom all other men she met would be found wanting. It is possible to say that this suited her very well. She never said to herself that even with this man, this model for her of what attachment had once been and would never be again, she had not felt free to say what she was thinking. She felt under surveillance; that she herself was in charge of the operation did not change the essential shape. She doesn't admit to herself that she has always divided the men she has known into the ones who made her feel, if not unworthy or insignificant, at least not up to scratch, and the others, for whom she felt, if not contempt, a bored impatience, a desire to flee. She tells herself only that she is better off alone. But not alone: she has her child.

Why did she decide to have the child when she discovered she was pregnant? She believed in abortion, she had marched for it; most of her friends had had at least one. She had not thought before of having a child; when Ya-Katey spoke of the child that would be theirs, "a real mess," she had laughed with him; it was only a joke. But when she found out she was pregnant, she had no hesitation. Having a child seemed simple; not having the child of a hero seemed strange; refusing to have a child in the name of hope seemed wrong. The noise that had filled her ears, the sound of the world since 1965, the sound of death and lies and wicked incomprehension, the crackle, the buzz, the wires' hum, was covered over, muffled, for the first time.

It has occurred to me that sometimes a story is more a tone than a tale. This is true of the story of Maria's motherhood. She decided she would have the child, and in this way Ya-Katey would not be silenced forever. She would have this child, Ya-Katey's child, in the name of hope. She would live her life hopefully now. And with that decision, the tone of the world changes. The light that had begun to darken with the death of John Kennedy and turned murderous in the murderous days of Vietnam and the horrors of race war and the burning of the cities, the light that had fallen on her and her father, that had distorted his face till it became the nightmare face she had run from, the siren tone of danger and distress: all this is gone. She and her child will begin a new history, a history where good will not be defined by impossible heroics and enforced by impossible surveillance, impossible purity, the amputation of everything human. She has learned from Ya-Katey the horrors of the impulse to purification. She and her child will simply live: alone, together, in the larger world.

The greatest passion of her life seizes her when she first holds her baby. It is not gentle, not at all; it is a violent, predatory bird with a strong sharp beak that lifts her, exhilarated, over treetops, swirls her dangerously, dangles her, turns her over and over, sometimes allowing her to soar in the plain ecstasy of sheer flight. The predator bird: mother love. She cannot explain it to anyone, this power and danger, the danger of being taken up entirely, whirled who knows where, then dropped, just anywhere at all.

Why, she wonders, do people think that mother love is peaceful? The soaring and the drowning, the terror, the exaltation, the sharp bites of the beak in the soft skin at the back of the neck: it has not claimed its proper language. The mystic, her skin melted by the touch of God, the lover set aflame at the sight of the beloved — these are nothing compared to her flight in the beak of this predatory bird. My own, my own: you had to say it, you could not keep from saying it. And yet children are not your own. For a while you think they are, as you clasp them safe. And then — how does it happen? — they have somehow wriggled free and *they* are riding on the bird's back now, and the direction of the flight is in their hands. They ride, unreachable by you, heads in the clouds, while you are dangled, while the beak bites harder now into your neck. You can't get me! they shout, intoxicated by the height, their hair windblown, their cheeks burnished, unaware of the danger you can see from your lower position, closer to the ground. "I am not yours," they say, and then the beak shakes you, turns you over, shows you how far, how devastatingly it would be possible to fall.

Nothing has ever been more powerful, nothing has ever been more dangerous. And it takes her entirely by surprise. She hadn't been one of those girls who played with dolls, who dreamed of hordes of children. She hadn't even meant to get pregnant. But she is never happier in her life than when Pearl is a baby, a small child: the exhaustion, the boredom, the cub's lapses — these are nothing compared to the drowning joy.

The baby's mother comes behind Maria, taps her on the shoulder.

"I can't thank you enough," she says.

Maria hands over the sleeping infant. The front of her body feels cold now; without the weight of the child she feels insubstantial and quite lonely.

She wants to weep or cry out, to bellow like a cow who calls for a missing or endangered calf. What has happened to my child? she wants to scream. She tries to imagine what Pearl looks like now. Always the sight of Pearl has been the sight she has most longed for. Now she fears it.

"You're a lifesaver," the baby's mother says.

A lifesaver, she thinks. That's what I must figure out now: how to save my own child's life. She says goodbye to the mother, who is gingerly trying to get back into her seat. The other two children have fallen asleep too. She imagines that the lucky mother will sleep now with the baby in her arms.

She thinks maybe she will take the pill her doctor friend prescribed: Halcyon. She is amused for a moment at the lavish outcome promised by the name.

• 8 •

Pearl is lying on the freezing ground. Around her they have set up a series of propane lamps: six-foot-high columns, two feet around. At the top of each column, a dishlike shape, made of black metal, from which a flame flares up; it looks like a torch on top of a tree. In the darkness, she cannot see the base: only the flame shooting up, seemingly out of nowhere. The lamps were in the basement of the embassy. One of the staff who had once worked in a restaurant in Big Sur had ordered the lamps from California. The weather in Dublin was often unseasonally cold for outdoor receptions; the lamps had come in handy, and the staff was grateful for them now. No one wanted to force the girl; they would only use force if it became absolutely necessary. For the meantime, they would keep her warm.

The flaming torches cast a livid light on the cold stone where Pearl is lying. They make her think she is in a jungle, in a movie about a jungle. The sound of traffic on the road comes to her like drums, or like a wind blowing itself up into a typhoon, a tornado. The voices of people buzz around her. It seems strange to her, very strange: the flickering of the torches, the buzz of the voices, the moon a fingernail in the gray, starless winter sky. She is thinking of blue. The blue of the sky, of the sea, a blue that is an idea of blue, a cold color, desirable in its coldness. The color of emptiness. She has worked at emptying herself. The work of emptying, of getting to the essence. Of making of her life only the essential sentence, the one she can know to be the truth. The framed figures that she sees seem to her essential; the rest, which she considers unessential, comes to her as blocks of darkness.

★ ★ ★

She is lying on the ground; she is chained; she is starving; she is warmed by propane torches; blankets have been placed on her by the embassy staff. She thrashes them off; someone replaces them; she thrashes them off; they are not put back again.

"If she wants to freeze to death on top of everything, it's her funeral," a woman says.

"Nice choice of words, Mulcahy," a man says, and the others, two or three of them, begin to laugh.

• 9 •

Joseph crosses the Tiber at the Ponte Fabricio, not looking at the heads carved into the white stone of the parapet. His eye is on the synagogue: an Eastern-looking glass-roofed building that overlooks the river. Is this the place, he wonders, that he should go, if not to pray, at least to think about what is happening to Pearl? All the people he has said he loved — excepting his mother, whom he is not sure he loved — have been Jews. What does Pearl think about her Jewishness? Maria had seen to it that Jewishness was no part of who Pearl knew herself to be — or, rather, has failed to help her come to terms with it. What is a Jew? What is it not to be a Jew? Dr. Meyers, Maria, Pearl, Devorah. All among the chosen people. He has always known himself to be unchosen, not among them.

The feeling of being unchosen in this way came to him first on Yom Kippur in the year 1960, when he was twelve years old: the Day of Atonement. Pearl is giving her life in atonement for something whose lines none of them yet know. She would not have the word *atonement* in her vocabulary. But why, he wonders, would anyone have imagined that an impulse so deep, so ancient, would evaporate because it had not been nourished by the proper word?

He is in Rome, it is December 1998, he is waiting to travel to a girl who may be dying in atonement for something he doesn't understand. He travels from that place of terror, of incomprehension, thirty-eight years back. To Yom Kippur of 1960. Falling late that year, October. He and Maria are twelve.

Maria had decided she must go to synagogue for Yom Kippur. She had been talking about it to Max Diamond, who ran the candy store near Sts. Cosmos and Damian School. Maria was Max's favorite customer; they often talked about religion. She had tried to explain to him her desire to be a contemplative nun. So she told him about the two orders of nuns she thought of joining: the Good Shepherds and the Carmelites, both of whom she had written, saying she would be with them after she graduated from high school. During that period, it was all she thought of: her religious vocation. She talked about nuns endlessly to Max Diamond; at that point, she didn't have many friends her own age to talk to — most of the girls in her class found her too competitive, too intense, and boys didn't easily talk to girls about serious things.

"You see, Max," she would say, "what I like about the Good Shepherds is, they're cloistered but they do good for the world. People — you know, like judges and policemen — send wayward girls to them, girls who stay with them in the convent for a while till they can get their lives under control. They send them there instead of prison."

"So that's what you want, darling," Max said, "to put yourself in a prison? A beautiful young girl like you? Excuse me, but I don't get it."

"You must lose your life in order to gain it, Max," she said to him. I don't know what he said. He might have just made her another egg cream.

It was after one of her conversations with Max that she first talked to Joseph about wanting to go to Yom Kippur services at Max's synagogue. She needed him to go with her. He told her he didn't think he could; it might be a sin.

She invoked Pope John XXIII and opening the windows of the church.

"It's a very important day, the Day of Atonement," she said. "Of course maybe it's not important to you. You can feel free to say it's not important, but I can't. I mean it doesn't happen to be your heritage."

"I didn't say it wasn't important," Joseph said.

"If it's important, we have to do it," Maria said. "Think of Anne Frank." She was obsessed with *The Diary of a Young Girl*. She carried it with her everywhere. She underlined it in the turquoise ink she liked that year.

Max got them two tickets to the synagogue. Maria said people wouldn't understand, so they couldn't tell anyone, not her father, not Sister Berchmans or Father Lynch. She knew they wouldn't have liked it, though those were the years when ecumenism was in, even if they'd invoked Pope John XXIII. That year the word *ecumenism* was as fashionable as Jackie Kennedy's pillbox hats: there were interfaith services all over America, perhaps all over the world. What had been considered a sin months before — entering a Protestant church, a synagogue — was suddenly encouraged, accompanied by an exchange of baked goods. Maria was inspired by all that.

I don't know why Max failed to tell her that she'd have to sit upstairs with the women, separated from him and Joseph. I can tell you, though, that she was quite unhappy.

Downstairs with the men, Joseph was not. He loved the music of lament, of sorrow for sin that was rooted in the sinning flesh, not like the music he knew, which must be rooted in the dreams of angels. He loved the long elaborated lists of sins, each named, each dwelt upon in its particularity, loved the rocking, the beating of breasts, the drone of the prayers, the incomprehensible words. He wanted to sway with the men, cover his head and shoulders with a shawl as they did. But of course, he didn't know what to do; he didn't know any of the words. So he just stood and sat when Max did and was thankful to be there.

Then the usher came up to him and said his friend had gotten sick and needed to be taken home. And there was Maria, pretending to be sick: not really sick, he could tell, but furious.

"We've got to go home," she said. He didn't ask her why, in case it might be something female, mortifying.

When they got a block away from the

synagogue she said, "I don't ever want to talk about it. Let's just forget we went."

She gave him her hat, a black straw pillbox, and he had to carry it all the way home, because she wanted to run, she needed to run, she said, and she couldn't run holding the hat. He prayed nobody in his class would see him, walking on the street on a Saturday morning carrying a girl's hat.

And they didn't ever talk about it again.

If he had asked Maria what happened to her at the Yom Kippur service, if he had asked anytime in the nearly forty years since they were there, would she have told him the truth, that she was going through what we would now call some kind of panic attack? At the time we would have said that she got very nervous, she had always been *high-strung*. A few years later, we would have said she *freaked out*.

★ ★ ★

Maria had been full of herself as Anne Frank's alter ego and convinced — oh, I don't know what she was convinced of, maybe that she'd have some experience that would connect her to Anne Frank while creating no problems in her life. But suddenly she began to fear that she was putting her immortal soul in danger. In the middle of the service, she saw herself in confession having to tell Father Lynch what she'd done.

She was sitting beside Max's wife, who clearly didn't approve of her being there. None of the girls or women talked to her. She tried to follow in the prayer books, but she was completely lost. She just read some prayers in English, having no idea if she was at the same place as the cantor.

But even reading along in the prayer book, the extent and variety of sins overwhelmed her. The Catholic confiteor was brief and general; in the prayers of Yom Kippur, all the particulars of human failure were named. Some scared her because she was afraid of the standard they implied: a strictness that could not be predicted or guarded against: "the sin that we have sinned before you in the matter of extending a hand, and for the sin that we have sinned before you in confusion of the heart." But wasn't it good to extend a hand? And her heart seemed so often to be confused. She tried to find a connection between the Hebrew letters and the sounds. She could not follow the music, or she would not follow where it led her. The music at mass was light and high and elevating: pure. This music was pulling her to the center of the earth, the center of accusation and lament, where she would see the face of God, a face in the whirlwind, not the face of Jesus holding children in his lap. This was a face that said a child could be carried up, thrown out of the whirlwind, lost.

In the middle of the service it occurred to her that her father had listened to that music as a child, and she felt ashamed of him for having left it. Her father had denied his people. He had abandoned Anne Frank. He never talked about the concentration camps, or Hitler, or the Jewish dead. At that moment, she was ashamed of her father but also frightened of being ashamed of a man she knew was much finer, much purer, than she could ever be. She longed for the cool disembodied air of Sts. Cosmos and Damian Church, where she could forget she was of a people who, fifteen years earlier, had been nearly destroyed.

The Jewish people. She was one of them; Joseph was not. She became ashamed about that: that she could, if she chose, claim her place in the synagogue and Joseph could not. So she convinced herself it was for Joseph's sake she had to leave. For the sake of justice. But I must tell you: it wasn't justice, it was terror.

She ran away into the October air. She ran and ran until she got home, and then she lay on her bed and closed her eyes and made herself think of something else. Of herself as a contemplative nun. And she never spoke to anyone about it.

Afterward, she has always told herself, with pride in her restraint (a rare pride in a nature not often given to restraint), that she refuses the false alliance with Jewish suffering. That she isn't a Jew because she hasn't suffered as a Jew. If anyone asks her, she says, "Ethnically I am a Jew. My parents were Jewish. But Jewish culture has made no mark on me." She will not claim more kinship than that. And Pearl? Maria, of course, told Pearl that she was half Jewish and half Cambodian. But she said those sorts of things weren't very important to her. Pearl could explore them on her own if she wanted, but as for herself, she wouldn't claim attachment to things that didn't attach her. She did not say to her daughter, I am who I name myself to be. But she lived as if this were something they both understood.

Joseph will not go inside the synagogue. In all the times he has passed it, he has never once gone in. He hasn't been inside any synagogue since the time he went with Maria. No doubt this is because, of the Jews in Joseph's life, not one was observant. Of course when he met Devorah, his late wife, Devorah, she was practicing. A strictly observant, strictly Orthodox girl. It occurs to him that when he married Devorah she was twenty, the same age Pearl is now. He thinks of her white skin. The white marble of the statue of Ilaria. And Pearl, flat, white, stretched out. About to be carried off. To death? Don't even think it, he tells himself. Maria, he knows, is able to stop herself from thinking of something that is too difficult. But he cannot. He must contemplate the possibility that Pearl might take her place alongside his wife, Devorah. Her place among the dead.

★ ★ ★

It is not surprising, is it, that the face of his dead wife should come to Joseph now as he passes the synagogue? The white skin, green eyes, red hair of his late beloved wife. For a while, twenty years perhaps, he thought the story of his life was a love story, a great romance. But lately he has begun to think it was a tragedy, even a crime, that Devorah ran into Maria and him, that she became Maria's roommate and friend, and then his girlfriend and his wife. How can a story change form so radically? How did he come in the end to understand that his wife, whom he thought rare and extraordinary, was quite a conventional person? Now he believes that she ended up being the kind of conventional person she was always meant to be, only in the process she suffered and caused a great deal of suffering, to say nothing of upheaval.

He often wonders: if she'd never met him and Maria, if she'd never talked about her love of Bach with anyone, her need of Bach, or only talked about it with people of her own kind — who would have advised her to sit tight and it would pass, like a fever — she very well might have ended up with children and a husband who had no desire for her to be anything but a simple wife. People in the Orthodox community would have discouraged her. He knows people like Maria are used to believing that burying a gift is the wrong thing. They forget the price paid for exposing it to the harsh winds, the torrential flooding, and they forget that some lights are extinguished by a force that is, after all, greater than themselves. Quite often now, he believes that his late wife would have been better off if she'd never met him. He does not allow himself to say that perhaps he too would have been better off.

But what constitutes a proper judgment of something like that? Could you not say that Devorah Blum Kasperman made a journey, learned things, and for a while loved deeply and was loved in return; that for twenty years Joseph Kasperman was a happy man because he believed in his wife's gift for music and believed in the absolute rightness of the way he lived his life, so that the gift could be honored, preserved, amplified? It is certainly possible to say they would have been better off if they'd never met. But what I have just said is also possible. I must tell you I believe both are possible, therefore both are true.

★ ★ ★

Let us go back to September 1967. For many years, Joseph believed that the story of his life began in September 1967, when he met Devorah, and that his life up till then was only preparation for this great event. It is proper for me to begin telling this story using the strong tones of romance.

September 1967. Dr. Meyers drives Maria and Joseph to Cambridge, their trunks in a station wagon he's borrowed from some priest. People are arriving in jeans with guitars, in pin-striped suits, in tweeds; with long hair or crew cuts; in penny loafers, in desert boots. All frightened, all with their special brands of fear, Joseph with the fear of the scholarship boy, in a herringbone jacket bought for him by Dr. Meyers at Brooks Brothers. It is too warm for a proper September day, and he is sweating; he is sure he stinks.

Only Maria does not seem afraid. She wears a long flower-printed dress and shoes that look like a child's, with a strap, a round toe, and a flat heel. They are introduced to their roommates — his a mathematician from Georgia, Maria's a music major from Worcester, Massachusetts: Devorah Blum. And so Devorah and Joseph meet that first day, and he is drawn at once to her shock of flame-colored hair, pulled back, as though she could contain a fire. If the story of Joseph and Devorah's life together were a tale: simple, consistent, beginning "Once upon a time" and ending "And they lived happily ever after," this would be a good place to begin it. But I haven't begun it here, as you see. I began it earlier. I began it so you would know, from the beginning, that it would end not happily, not well.

Soon the three of them are having dinner

together all the time. Devorah explains the rules of kosher eating and Maria says to Devorah, "You see, I'm a Jew, but not a Jew." She is still going to mass — folk masses, they are called — still singing "Kumbaya" at the Sanctus.

Joseph is miserable. His roommate never speaks to him. He doesn't know how to make friends. Maria seems to belong everywhere: the third day after they arrive, she signs up to tutor ghetto children; by the end of the first week, she's made twenty friends. She begins wearing a wooden pendant in the shape of a peace symbol, given to her by a boy from Choate with hair down to his shoulders. They play their guitars and sing till all hours, "The Times They Are a Changin'," sung like a battle cry, over and over again.

One night, Maria gets drunk on beer and phones Joseph and he helps her when she gets sick in the bushes in front of her dorm, Cosgrove. She doesn't want Devorah to know she got drunk, in the same way she doesn't want her boyfriend from Choate to know she lost her virginity to him. Joseph doesn't want to know, he doesn't want her to tell him the details, any more than he wants his mother to tell him the details of her constipation, or her disgust at finding Maria's hair in the bathtub drain or a thread of shit along the seam of Dr. Meyers's underwear. But Maria wants to tell, just as his mother wanted to tell. And so he has to listen. She wants Joseph to know everything, needs him to listen to her regretful weeping because her boyfriend from Choate doesn't love her, but she shouldn't be crying, she knows better; you don't need to be in love to have sex. Then she forgets him, begins to go to SDS meetings, hangs on her wall a quote from George Sand she'd hand-lettered: HUMANITY IS OUTRAGED IN ME AND WITH ME. WE MUST NOT DISSIMULATE NOR TRY TO FORGET THIS INDIGNATION WHICH IS ONE OF THE MOST PASSIONATE FORMS OF LOVE. It suits her very well, this connection of love with indignation. On his wall, Joseph has hung the Eric Gill woodcut of the Madonna that Dr. Meyers had had framed for him. (He'd had a Gill crucifixion framed for Maria, but she'd hidden it in her closet.)

Devorah is thrilled and a bit frightened by the George Sand poster on Maria's side of the room. On her wall she has a Chagall print of musicians in the shtetl and van Gogh's sunflowers. Devorah feels so lucky to have found Maria. Maria gives her a more exciting life than she's ever known.

211

This is something you should know about Maria: she has often made people feel lucky to be with her.

Because Devorah is always with Maria, she is often with Joseph. He is in love with her quietness, her smallness, her white skin, and her flame-colored hair. But he doesn't let her know. At night in his bed he burns with desire for her white skin and the patch of flame between her legs. He confesses, he confesses each week, and the priest says, "Don't sweat it; why don't you go out for crew or track?" As though the only acceptable form of sweat is a particularly athletic one, not one induced by guilt or dread. But he does sweat it. He sweats it for fear of his body's nature, and he is happy only in art history, where he studies the Cycladic forms he loves because he feels they have nothing, absolutely nothing, to do with him.

He still wears a jacket and tie everywhere. When the Buddhist monks set themselves on fire to protest the war in Vietnam, he can't sleep for nights. He sees the flames. He feels the flames. He does not protest. He feels he is a coward; he is frightened for his scholarship. Maria is involved in protest after protest but never rebukes him, never says a word. For which he is grateful, for which he is abashed.

He likes working late at the library. Sometimes Maria and Devorah come by at ten o'clock and tease him, call him a grind. Once Devorah comes up behind him, puts her cool white hands in front of his eyes, and says, "Guess who?" and he is aroused and full of self-hate for his arousal. He says to himself, "She's only a girl, and if she had any idea she'd be appalled." He can't speak to her for a minute without getting an erection; he thanks God, to whom he still prays, that she has no idea how he dreams of the flame-colored patch between her legs. He works into the night. He does a paper on Thomas Aquinas and his teacher is floored. Maria regularly cuts classes for political activities and does her papers by staying up all night; sometimes she is praised for brilliance, sometimes caught up short for carelessness.

Maria goes to Washington on the Pentagon march, but Devorah and Joseph don't. They are both afraid, he of being arrested and losing his scholarship, Devorah because, as an Orthodox girl, going to a demonstration is so far from anything she can imagine for herself it isn't even a temptation. Maria comes back and tells them about tear gas and about how she had to take her earrings off because "the pigs rip the earrings out of girls' ears just for the fun of it."

Devorah speaks to him about her religious crisis, which it is not fashionable to be having in the bloody smoke-filled autumn of 1968. Martin Luther King has been shot, Robert Kennedy has been shot, Vietnam is on fire, the ghettoes are burning; who can be thinking about religious crises? So Devorah tells her secret to Joseph, not to Maria, her best friend, who is busy with the war and the ghetto.

Her secret is this. She is a highly intelligent girl from an Orthodox Jewish family in Worcester, Massachusetts. Her mother supported her in her struggle with her father, with the community, to go to college. Her mother said, "She must honor her God-given gifts." Nights of weeping, pleading, before permission is granted, reluctantly, tentatively: she is allowed to go to Radcliffe (close enough for them to keep an eye on her) to study music, so that later she will return and teach music to the children of the community, and they will be able to present her credentials as proof that their children are getting the best. She would teach the girls; the boys only below a certain age. The community convinced itself, as the brothers at Portsmouth Priory had done, that sending one of their own into the large, dangerous world would be proof of their great strength.

But something happened to Devorah that split her soul, like a tree struck by lightning: she listened, in her history of music course, to the choral music of Bach. She attended a performance of the St. Matthew Passion. She didn't ask the rabbi whether this was allowed; she simply went, knowing she risked transgression. And she was seized. Seized with a desire, not only to hear the music, which would have been permissible — certainly she could listen to it on the radio or the phonograph — but also to sing it. She felt that those notes needed to come from her throat. She tells Joseph that the notes of Bach are burning a hole in her windpipe, that every morning she wakes feeling she can't breathe. No one would understand but Joseph, she says. She knows what Maria would say: You have to march to your own drummer. But she is thinking of her dark-eyed, severe father, her abashed, overawed mother who supported her in her ambition, the teachers who believe in her, the millions killed by Hitler only twenty-five years ago. Yet every morning she wakes feeling she can't breathe.

Joseph looks at her and knows himself a failure. Every word she says makes him more in love with her. Being in love with her makes him desire her, and he knows it is impossible; his body is not his friend, although Father Martin at the Newman Center says, "Of course it is. But it is a friend that must be reasoned with." Joseph cannot control his body by his reason; he is in love with Devorah, he longs for her with all his mind and soul and heart, the way he has been told — but never experienced — that he was meant to long for God.

He understands that Devorah is frightened. She studies in the library with him and Maria, listening in the music collection to the powerful notes of Bach, which are dangerous to her, eating holes in her windpipe like acid. Or are they an angel's hand, strangling her? Every Friday she goes home to her family and comes back Sunday morning with bags full of kosher food. Every Sunday night, she cannot sleep. Every Monday morning he sees olive-colored pouches beneath her large light-green eyes.

Joseph has no idea how to help her; when she speaks to him, he is mostly silent. (Later she says his silence was the best thing; when she was with him she felt, for the first time in her life, not alone.)

In her distress, she becomes more beautiful to him; her skin grows more translucent; he can see the bluish veins under her skin, the color of milk standing in shadow, the blue veins of her white hands. Her hands are very small, perfectly formed. Her nails are beautifully shaped; Joseph is fascinated by the white moons above her cuticles. He wants to kiss her hands. He wants to take her fingers in his mouth. Her green eyes burn and deepen with her suffering, and he can't help her. He wants to say, I would give my life for you, do you understand? He wants to take her in his arms, but he believes it would be a violation, though afterward (his joy in those first days of rushed confession! The crescendo section of the romance, if it were a romance, would begin right here) she says she had longed for him to take her in his arms, but he'd been right to hold back; it would have frightened her; it was only his silence that allowed her the courage to love him.

But he has always known that, left to his silence, she might never have made her move. It is Maria, a wind rushing, who gives her the confidence.

Devorah talks to him about hearing

Bach's Magnificat. She is embarrassed; it seems like something out of the nineteenth century (they were juniors by then and they'd studied the great novels of the nineteenth century). And it certainly doesn't seem like the thing to be talking about when their friends are marching in the streets shouting, "Hey, hey, LBJ, how many kids did you kill today?"

He knew what had happened to her when she'd heard the Magnificat. Maria was sitting next to her; Maria was the one who had to sit with her on the steps and bring her water; Maria has always been great in a physical emergency.

Walking the streets of Rome, along the Tiber, past the synagogue, he thinks of Devorah listening to the Magnificat. *Beautiful girl, my beautiful beautiful girl.* Dead now, under the ground. The terrifying thought: Pearl might join her. Pearl, too, is a beautiful girl. The beautiful should not be allowed to be among the dead. He remembers a line of Virgil that he had copied down while he was still in college. "Among the dead there are so many thousands of the beautiful." He was struck by the word *thousands;* what a negligible number after Hitler's and Stalin's millions. Now the wire that is his spine tingles with shock.

He knows he was the first to tell Devorah of her beauty, which, until he told her, she didn't know about. She'd been brought up like a princess in a tower, the tower of Orthodoxy: serious and devout and, in all that time, all the time of her girlhood, because no one had told her she was lovely, she hadn't looked at herself with pleasure. She had dressed herself for modesty; she had combed and braided her remarkable hair as another task; she'd washed her beautiful face with the same utilitarian attention she'd given to brushing her teeth.

When Joseph thinks of that time, it is always autumn; they are sitting under trees in full gold, trees that flame like her brilliant hair, trees that the light struck so that the leaves were platefuls of light; even their veins were illuminated. Some stories shape themselves around an image, and if Joseph's story shaped itself this way it would be around this: the gold leaves of the sugar maple under which they sat in Harvard Yard.

She tells him that she would go down to the river with the music of Bach, stand by the water, and sing her heart out, Latin words, German words, words spoken easily, she knew, treasured by those who had destroyed her people twenty-five years earlier. But the words come out of her throat, she says, like those ribbons of words formed from the mouths of angels in a medieval painting. She signs up for voice lessons; she tells Joseph this while Maria is in Washington being teargassed. Telling him how frightened she is but that she has to be part of it, and it has to be just that, just that music, or she will die, literally die of strangulation. And she knows that to be part of it she will have to leave everything she has, everything she is.

Joseph hadn't understood — it wasn't common knowledge, of course — that it was impossible for her, keeping her faith, to sing in public. Orthodox women, women as observant as she was brought up to be, are not allowed to sing in front of men. She could have sung in private. But not the music she desired, the great choral music of Bach, the music she said was irreplaceable.

The fifty-year-old Joseph would have urged her to find another music she could call irreplaceable. The fifty-year-old Joseph would have told her, Train, of course, train with a woman teacher, but choose, for example, Schubert's Lieder as the irreplaceable music. Sing in private, sing by the river or in your room, sing with other women, sing in front of young girls, but do not shape your life as if beauty can sustain you, because in the end you are not one of the rare ones and it will not.

But the twenty-year-old Joseph is silent when the twenty-year-old Devorah says that what she is in the service of — that music — is important and beautiful and true forever. If this story were a tale, this might be true. But it is not a tale, it is more complex; the form changes quite near the end. And so the fifty-year-old Joseph can no longer be sure that anything is true forever.

Over the years he has been tormented by questions about his wife. Not of infidelity, no, nothing like that. He has been tormented by the question of whether Devorah was drawn to something she called beauty, something she believed was important and true forever, in order to be far away from her own people, from their misfortunes and the suffering they'd borne. Was that music important in the camps that were exterminating her people? Many of them were run by men who believed Bach's music to be eternally important and beautiful and true. Was what she called beauty just a liberation from the fate of the

Jews, which she was terrified to be part of?

Joseph is right that if Devorah hadn't spoken to Maria, but had spoken only to him, she wouldn't have done what she did. He had never heard her sing; she couldn't sing for him without automatically throwing everything away. Singing for Joseph would have made everything irrevocable. But she could sing for Maria and still, she believed, leave room for choice.

Maria falls on her and says, "You have no choice. You have a gift. The gift that it is death to hide." Maria is in love with the seventeenth century. "Devorah, we are not of the party of death, we are of the party of truth."

Devorah adores Maria. She loves it when Maria explains the Magnificat to her. "Oh, yeah, the Magnificat, oh, sure. My soul doth magnify the Lord, and my spirit hath rejoiced in God my Savior." Easy for Maria to rattle off, as if she were saying the pledge of allegiance. Easy for people with her kind of Catholic education to impress people with a knowledge of medieval or Renaissance iconography when it was something they'd learned by third grade, like the names of presidents: St. Lucy is holding eyes on a plate, because her eyes were gouged out by the Romans; you prayed to her when you had conjunctivitis. St. Apollonia's teeth were pulled out by those same Romans; you prayed to her before you went to the dentist. "Oh, sure, the Magnificat," Maria says. "Mary is saying, 'I'm a big deal, but not really; it's not really me, it's really God. I'm not the important one, it's only what I make larger, what I reflect.' " Joseph has often thought that of himself, but he never told Devorah that the piece of music that was so important in her history told the story of his life.

Maria goes with Devorah to audition for the chorus. Maria sits with her afterward in the dormitory bathroom while she vomits. Maria says, "You see? They knew when they heard you that you were extraordinary." Maria gets the money from her father for special voice lessons recommended by Devorah's teacher, who says Devorah has gone beyond her and suggests somebody in Boston.

It happens so quickly, as things do in romance. Joseph and Devorah begin spending more and more time together. Maria is entirely absorbed in politics; she is almost never in their room; Devorah doesn't even know where she is on the nights she isn't in the bed her father paid for. How does it happen that one day he gets the courage to take her hand, to kiss her, to hold her in his arms? He doesn't even remember which came first, the decision to tell her parents she has to sing the choral music of Bach or his assurance that if they disown her he will take her as his wife. They are twenty years old; the whole thing seems entirely straightforward.

They decide that Devorah must, as Maria said, "confront her parents." Her parents tell her she cannot devote herself to singing, in public, the choral music of Bach, music that was written in the language of the murderers of her people, music that insists that the Jews killed Christ, and furthermore she cannot sing in public, in front of men, and still be their daughter. She says she will no longer be their daughter, she will be Joseph's wife. Joseph, a non-Jew. They sit shiva for her; they declare her dead.

It all happens in a matter of three months. They wait until they are both twenty-one. Seymour Meyers, unexpectedly romantic, becomes their protector; he agrees to pay Devorah's tuition. As Joseph's wife, Devorah is not under the authority of her parents; they are given space in married-student housing. They are no longer children of a family (although Joseph had never thought of himself as the child of a family); they are on their own. On their own to devote themselves to Devorah's gift.

Seymour Meyers tells Joseph that the honoring of Devorah's gift — which he believes very great — will require money. He offers Joseph a place in his business after graduation. Instantly, Joseph gives up his dream of studying the art of the Middle Ages. He had, in his first year, attracted the notice of Professor Stivic, a Polish émigré (pleased that the gifted young man was also of Polish ancestry) whose specialty was reliquaries. There was something about Joseph as a young man that made older men want to train him, to groom him, to imagine him in their place after their death.

Joseph loved the idea of reliquaries, the elaborate casing for the proof of corruption: bone, tooth, sliver of nail, scrap of bloody cloth. Jewels, gold, silver, then the window: peekaboo, the proof — all flesh is grass. No, worse, the saint is nothing but a bone, a tooth, a nail, a scrap of cloth. The embellishment is all.

He does not acknowledge his own disappointment; this is drowned in his new love. Rather, he regrets that he has to disappoint

Professor Stivic. He could disappoint either Professor Stivic or Dr. Meyers and Devorah. And what had Professor Stivic done for him? Had he rescued him and his mother from starvation? Had he given Joseph his intact body, left his family, offered him love unto death? There is no question. He must be able to earn money to support Devorah's gift, which he believes is far, far greater than his own. In doing this, he will also be repaying Dr. Meyers. It was only later that he wondered. Did Seymour Meyers become their protector because he saw that in doing so he would be buying an excellent steward for his business and his fortune, thus ensuring the welfare of his daughter, who had no interest in the business and thought money was an evil thing, having no idea what it provided in the way of the good things of this world?

★ ★ ★

Joseph has also often wondered: If Devorah had only spoken to him and not to Maria, what would have happened? Perhaps she would have seen her situation as sad and impossible and stayed with her people. He would never have held her in his arms. He would not have devoted his life to her and her gift; perhaps she would still be alive, the mother of children. He had thought she wasn't very interested in children. She never seemed attached to Pearl; she was mainly worried that Pearl might be carrying germs, exposing her to sore throats. When Maria and Pearl came to visit, it was Maria who interested Devorah. It was one of the reasons he had spent so much time with Pearl: to free Maria and Devorah for what they called *ladies' lunches* or *girls' night out*. He hadn't minded. On the contrary, when he looks back, the days he spent alone with Pearl are of the greatest value. What will be lost to him if she is no longer in this world! His Pearl of great price. But not really his. There is no name for what they are to each other, no tie of blood or law. That does not mean the bond is not of gold. Only that there is no name for it.

Quite early in their marriage, Joseph and Devorah agreed they would not have children — because of her work. And then, later, when she told him she had made a mistake, how could he believe her? How could he understand that she had always wanted to be the mother of children but had suppressed it, in favor of the music that she loved? He told himself that Pearl was enough, more than enough; he couldn't imagine having a child he would love more than Pearl. He couldn't imagine, given his heritage, his unlovely mother, his deserter father, fathering a child who could in any way come up to Pearl.

Everyone acknowledged that Devorah gave up everything she came from to sing the music she considered irreplaceable. No one ever considered: What had Joseph given up?

So Joseph and Devorah married. They lived in Cambridge, then New York. They devoted both their lives to her gift. She studied voice; she performed the music she loved. Then she came to believe it was too hard a life; she wanted something easier.

Perhaps in the end her gift was rather small, too small for all Joseph's devotion. Too small a vessel for the amount of love he poured into it. Or is it not that the gift was too small but that the price it exacted was too high for her to pay?

She told him one day in 1994 that she was unwilling to martyr herself any longer. "I just want a life," she said. Joseph wanted to say to her, What do you think you're having? What is this thing that you call life that you think you haven't got, or that you have to hoard?

Was he wrong? Was she? Must the world

be divided between martyrs and misers? What would be the appropriate reply to someone who said, as Devorah said to Joseph, only two years before she died at forty-eight, "My life is all I have." She said it, as most people would, as if it were self-evident, as if they were saying, "The universe is all there is." Devorah didn't say it this way, but what people usually say is, "You have only the one life," using the pronoun *you* and the definite article *the*. *You have only the one life.*

But do you? Well, of course, in one sense yes, in that you don't get more than one. In that the universe is, of course, all there is. But isn't it possible to say, "You have your life, and the idea of your life, and what your life stands for"? Stands for. Stands where?

Pearl believes she is standing somewhere. Right now she believes that the idea of her life is more important than her life itself. Of course we do not agree with her. But because we do not agree, does it follow, then, that there is nothing worth dying for? Or against? And if there is nothing worth dying for, what is worth living for? This is the kind of question that has led Pearl to where she is now, chained, lying on the freezing pavement in front of the American embassy, while the police wait to decide the right thing for them to do and Pearl waits for the death that she has summoned, planned.

But when Devorah said she was unwilling to martyr herself any longer, she didn't mean she'd been planning to die. What had she been martyring, her desire for comfort, for ease? Earlier, if she'd given up her desire to sing, she would have had to martyr her ambition. These would, of course, have been little deaths. Joseph has often wondered if she shouldn't have martyred her ambition, her desire to sing. But he believed it wasn't even that. She would have had to martyr her desire to be heard, her desire for performance. And he wondered: Was that such a very great thing, that desire, that it should have been honored at the expense of her family's happiness and peace? Is it greater than a person's duty toward her people? And was her desire for ease and comfort so important that it should have killed his dream of her?

★ ★ ★

In 1967, 1968, the idea of not using your gift was considered a betrayal of the highest sort. In those years, you did not give up your gift to satisfy your parents —

certainly not if you were someone like Maria. Joseph always knew that something terribly important had been lost. But if he had said that, he would not have had a certain kind of joy, the joy of loving a woman he considered gifted and miraculous, and she would not have had a certain kind of joy — a joy that is irreplaceable — the joy of performance.

He has never understood it very well, the impulse to perform. He doesn't have much sense of his own visibility. The impression he makes on people is something he has to screw himself up to a pitch of unnatural attention to think of; he does it only for business. He has never understood the desire to be seen; he's always supposed it was part of the artistic process. But he wishes it wasn't. He wishes there could be, at least somewhere in the world, at least one artist who doesn't care if anybody sees his work.

So after twenty-five years of devoting herself to her music, when Devorah said she was giving up her dream of being the kind of singer she had always wanted to be, that she was content to have the occasional private student and teach voice at Westchester Community College, that she just wanted to be happy, he felt terribly let down. Does this mean he never really wanted her to be happy?

He had thought he understood her. He thought she was the woman he loved, the great love of his life. He thinks he will not love another woman in that way; he is past that kind of belief.

He believed she would shape her life so it was devoted to the gift of her voice: the pure gift of a pure voice. She had an extraordinary voice; he knows he was right in that. He wasn't the only person who thought so. Teachers, coaches — even some critics — praised Devorah's voice. What he didn't understand at first, what she might not have understood at first but came to understand long before Joseph, is that many people are greatly gifted. It's not as unusual as we might think. Oh, it's unusual, of course, or we wouldn't notice it at all, but it's not unusual enough. There are, particularly now, at the end of the century — I should say at the end of the millennium — simply not enough places so that all the people in the world who are gifted in singing the serious music of the eighteenth and nineteenth centuries can be listened to with the kind of attention they crave. The kind of attention that makes all the effort worth it.

It is a difficult life. A great deal must be

given up. Joseph was perfectly willing to assume his share of the difficulties: to watch out for his wife's voice, to be silent for days, to be alert to drafts and changes in temperature, to pay large sums for lessons with great teachers, to put up with lousy accommodations in lousy hotels in third-rate cities, to have her away from him for weeks at a time, to have her refuse to answer him on the day of her performance when he asked if she'd bought any jam. Of course, she had to endure much more, he knew that: the anguish of believing she hadn't got it right, she hadn't done it well enough. For an hour, two hours, three hours of being responded to? It's not enough, she said. No, he wanted to tell her, you're not doing it for the response. You're doing it to bear witness to the greatness of your gift and the greatness of the music.

After twenty years of what she called martyrdom, Devorah felt it was no longer worth it. Afterward, he believed he should have seen it coming when she wanted to move into the Larchmont house that had been rented out for twenty years, the house Dr. Meyers had left to him and not to Maria: Dr. Meyers and Maria were estranged at the time of his death. He should have seen it coming when Devorah began talking about a garden.

"Why a garden all of a sudden, why now?" he asked her.

And she said — it may have been the first time she really hurt him — "I've always been interested, but I knew you wouldn't approve. You wouldn't think it was serious."

He was hurt because she'd kept something from him, possibly for years, and because he got a hint for the first time that his love might be something of a burden to her.

But he wanted her to be happy. And if she said a house and garden would make her happy, she was too old for the apartment on the air shaft, she wanted space and light, it would be good for her voice — well, how could he refuse her?

One thing, of course, led to another. She spent time in the garden. She became interested in redoing the house. Then she had to learn how to cook all the vegetables in the vegetable garden and how to use all the herbs in the herb garden, and to how make beautiful arrangements of the flowers in the flower garden. Joseph hated that garden. She was right: he didn't think it was serious. He didn't believe there was greatness in gardening. A garden didn't stand for anything. Oh, it might be a source of inspiration for a poet or a painter, Marvell or Herrick or Monet. But he believed that a poem about a garden or a painting of a garden was greater than a garden itself. If Devorah had sung about a rose, he believed that would have been greater than growing an actual rose. She knew what he believed, and it hurt them both.

He did not know, although Maria did, that she got back in touch with her family. Maria went with her on her first tentative visit but did not go back again; she wasn't needed. She called Devorah's brother when Devorah died.

Joseph wasn't there when it happened, when Devorah, standing at the top of the stairs, caught her heel in the hem of her long skirt and fell. He came home to find her. It was six o'clock but still a summer afternoon. The light was beautiful when he walked into the house. He called his wife's name. And then he saw her, lying at the bottom of the stairs, her face in the dirt of the ficus plant she'd been carrying, smashed beside her.

He called the police. His next-door neighbor, whom he hardly knew, came when he saw the police car. A doctor whom he'd never met came by. He said Devorah had died instantly. There was no pain. He was grateful for that.

He phoned Maria. Maria wasn't home so he told Pearl, and Pearl came up on the train. He met her at the station. They did not embrace. They sat quietly, and the sun bled out of the day and then it was dark. She made some sandwiches.

When he thinks of Pearl that day, he remembers that everything she did was perfect. She was quiet; every gesture she made was a comfort; there were no abrasions. Her voice had a kind of elegant maternal quality, a quattrocento Madonna of the time of Ruskin's Ilaria.

He was almost sorry when Maria came, Maria with her loud weeping, her cries of "I can't believe it! It can't be!" Calling Devorah's brother, so that then her parents, who were still living, phoned — he had never spoken to them, not once in twenty-five years — and asked if they could have her body to bury in a Jewish grave. He felt that, having taken so much from them, he had no right to refuse.

★ ★ ★

Two years later, on the Via Arenula, Joseph would like to go into the synagogue

236

and — do what? — not say a prayer but perhaps think for a moment of his dead wife. But he feels he has no right. He is not one of the chosen. And he does not know how to mourn a wife whom he will always have to suspect of ceasing to be his before the day that she was — the words come so easily to people's lips — taken from him.

Now I must tell you about a strange episode in Joseph's life. It may be more common than we think for a quiet man, a man who lives his life reasonably and honorably, to have a period of irrational obsession. Joseph had several months in which he believed the history of the Jews was a burden he must carry in his living flesh, to expiate the history coiled in the snail shell of his genetic makeup.

He began to be terrified that he had more connection to the sufferings of the Jewish people than simply marrying one of their daughters. He became convinced that his father, of whose face he had no knowledge, who had left no trace in his life, had been a torturer.

His obsession with his father's role in the Holocaust took shape in 1993, when Joseph was forty-five years old. It began when he read the newspaper articles about Ivan the

Terrible, the Nazi guard who'd been hiding out as an autoworker in Chicago. In his face, Joseph saw something of his own: the widely spaced eyes, the arching of the brows, the ears, the forehead. John Demjanjuk, Ivan the Terrible, was born the same year as Adam Kasperzkowski, Joseph's father. The same date as his father's date of birth on Joseph's birth certificate. He became convinced that John Demjanjuk, Ivan the Terrible, was his father. Or that was the first step. It was a multistep operation, a gradual delusion, a split-level obsession.

His father was born in Gdansk in 1919. So was John Demjanjuk. He saw his eyes in the eyes in the grainy newspaper photograph; he would stand next to the mirror looking from his own features to the newspaper clipping; calibrating the width of forehead, the shape of the nose. Why couldn't it be his father? His father, who had acted barbarously, walking out — "Just going for a pack of cigarettes" — on the infant Joseph and his mother. Why should he have been an exception, one of the few who did not rush to torture the Jews?

How do we trace the roots of this strange flowering? How do we explain this sort of thing in a man we would have said was normal in every other way? A successful businessman. A loving husband. For three years at least, Joseph believed himself to be the son of a war criminal. He told himself that someone like his father would surround himself with edifice after edifice of lies. By the time Ivan the Terrible had hit the newspapers, Joseph's mother had disappeared into the fog of her senility.

Was it that if Joseph imagined his father a torturer he would have been able to describe abandonment by him as a lucky break? Better to have been abandoned by a torturer than to have been brought up by him. How lucky: the torturer left him, so he could be taken up by the fine hand of Seymour Meyers. What a lucky boy. How wrong his mother's cry: "Both of us have always been unfortunate."

And then the fever broke. There was no more reason for its breaking than for its onset. One day, he realized he wasn't thinking about Ivan the Terrible anymore. Wasn't looking at himself in the mirror, comparing his features with the pictures in the papers. It was over. He stuffed his newspaper clippings into a large green plastic bag and tied it shut with the yellow tie that came in the same box. It was over.

He never spoke to anyone about it; he's grateful at least for that. What took its place? Simply a mistrust of stories, a desire that history be made up not of stories and not of the personal but of large forces: like the Pantheon, the music of Bach.

It is eight o'clock, the Roman time for dinner. Then it will be time for him to head back to the hotel and check out, as he must leave very early the next morning, bid goodbye to the clerk (who will pretend to look forward to his return), and ask that he book, for five-thirty (Joseph is always early at the airport), a taxi to Termini Station. Termini. The end. He is traveling to something whose end he cannot imagine. Or perhaps he doesn't want to. He is a different person from the person who took a cab from that station ten days before. He may be a different person yet again when he returns.

And who is Pearl? He must believe she is still one of the living. He will travel to a living woman; he will not allow the possibility that he is traveling to the country of the dead.

· 10 ·

A policeman kneels on the ground beside her. "We'll try all of these, see if any of them works," he says, to someone Pearl cannot see. He is holding a huge ring of small keys. He keeps trying to unlock her cuffs. She thrashes. Another policeman holds her down. "It would be better if you'd cooperate," he says. She closes her eyes. The policeman with the keys keeps trying to find one that will fit, but he cannot. The handcuffs are Japanese; none of the available keys will work. Pearl didn't do that purposely; she simply bought the most expensive pair available at a sex shop not far from where she lived.

"Should we go for the cutters?" one policeman says to the one with the key ring.

"Not until the doctor gives her approval. This is an American we're dealing with, remember. Lawsuits are their middle name. If we should hurt her, we'd be the ones to blame. . . . I don't suppose there's a chance you'd give us the key," he says to

Pearl, almost pleasantly.

His pleasantness makes her want to be pleasant. She would like to say, I swallowed it, which she did, and laugh with him. Because it is funny, she thinks, isn't it, that the only thing she's swallowed for a rather long time is a key? But she keeps her eyes closed. She will not smile or laugh.

"If you do it the hard way, we'll have to cut the cuffs open. You could be injured. We'd rather not do you any harm."

She keeps her eyes closed. Harm, she wants to say. Yes, I know about that.

But she says nothing, and the policemen walk away.

• 11 •

The flight attendant removes Maria's tray: so different, she thinks, from what's being served in economy. She was given fresh squeezed grapefruit juice, yogurt and black-berries, a warm croissant. Maria hadn't eaten since she'd heard the news of Pearl: almost twenty hours without food. She'd cleared her plate quickly. "You enjoyed your meal, I'd say," the flight attendant says, and Maria feels ashamed. How can she be eating when her daughter is starving herself? How can she fill herself when her daughter is empty?

How can her daughter be doing this to her body now? And why? Starvation: a female tactic of self-punishment, Maria thinks, and then, more desperately: What does she think she needs to be punished for? She thought she had protected Pearl from the idea of punishment, the presence so pervasive in her early life: punishing surveillance. Who is my daughter now? she asks herself. I thought I knew. She is tormented by the false security of her former false understanding.

Perhaps all mothers think they know their daughters better than they do. And perhaps (this would be like her) Maria was too hopeful about the ability of the human species to absorb quick change. Is it possible that, in one generation, centuries of a way of thinking can be wiped out? The idea of chastity, the purity Maria was brought up believing she embodied and must defend with her life — could it have disappeared from the human mind in thirty years? She doesn't think of her daughter as having a meaningful category in her imagination under the heading Purity. Because of her history and the history of Ya-Katey, she has seen to that. She imagines that Pearl has been spared more, perhaps, than she has. She doesn't know for instance (and a good thing too) that at one time Pearl was obsessed with hatred for her mother's body. Was it born of hatred for her own? And what is the source? We can blame the world, but that would not be of much use. Whatever the source, Pearl Meyers, at twelve, hated her mother's body.

Something happens to some girls at a certain age, a kind of madness, as if their own bodies were too powerful or too busy or too changeable; they are appalled. They indulge peculiar hungers; they want to stick their noses, their tongues into the filth of the world, maybe to reassure themselves that it doesn't all come from themselves.

That year, Pearl would come home from school and eat horribly sweet things, things whose sweetness had no goodness in them, sweetness that turned to acid, cakes with frosting made entirely of chemicals, neon-colored icing, cream fillings white as toothpaste. Half-liquid fats: melted cheese, margarine out of the tub. Orange drinks with a touch of blue in them, chips whose coatings made her fingers looked diseased. Afternoons hating the company of her own body, wanting only to get into her unmade bed, where she'd explore what she believed were the disgusting parts of her own body: conjuring sights of huge-breasted women being pierced by men whose hungers were insatiable, who spoke humiliating orders: put this in your mouth, put that over your face. That year she went through all her mother's clothes, wanting to touch them so they'd be defiled. That year she found, in her mother's underwear drawer, the "adultery diary," a notebook with sentences she read over and over as she fingered her mother's lingerie. The sentences she can't forget: *I thought of myself as a poet. Now I'm someone who reaches into her pocket and finds a pair of underpants, taken off in a taxi so I can be finger-fucked.*

That was her punishment, that knowing. Maria doesn't know what Pearl knows, what her daughter read in the diary she thought was always hidden. Pearl reading her mother, who would have said she was committed to the sisterhood of women, calling another woman *the walking vulva,* talking about wanting to take all the clothes out of the woman's closet — the closet that was next to the bed where she had sex with the woman's husband — and burn them in the driveway. Saying of her lover, Jack Rappaport, that it was *nothing but sex.* A sentence that Pearl hated, yet that thrilled her as if she were being shown into the real life women lived: *When he traces the curve of my breast, I feel in the league of women who've done stupid things for what they call love, but what they mean is sex.* Excited when she read: *There is no man whom I admire as I admire P., no one whose company satisfies me entirely as hers does.* So her mother loved her best. Then, cast down, having to understand there were times she passed out of her mother's sight:

I think of P. and that she is not with me and that I do not miss her.

Her mother's body, loved a year before, now horrifying. As her own, ignored a year before, becomes the site of revulsion.

Maria had believed that because of the way she'd brought Pearl up, and because of the way the world had changed, Pearl had been spared a sense of the hatefulness of the female body. And she shivers now, in anguish that she had been so wrong!

Of the malignities Maria traces to her upbringing, among the most heinous is the habit of thinking herself impure by virtue of femaleness. The female: insufficiently fine. The female: overfleshed.

There was nothing in her life to suggest that the female body was anything but something to be overcome. Who was there to say otherwise? She was a girl without a mother. Pearl Meyers, the first Pearl Meyers, dead at thirty-one of ovarian cancer, diagnosed a year after she had given birth.

The only other female in the house, Marie Kasperman, Joseph's mother, revolted her: the thick greasy curls under the thin hairnet, the visible pores of her perpetually reddish, perpetually shining nose, the hands that always reminded Maria of raw meat. There was no time Maria didn't flinch from her touch, and she knew Marie Kasperman understood and hated her for it. When she brushed Maria's hair and braided it, Maria wanted to be sick. It was bad, this thing between the two females in the house. Perhaps Seymour Meyers should have seen it, should have stopped it. But he was a man. Even if he'd seen it, he wouldn't have known how to name what he'd seen. Perhaps no man would.

And besides, Maria tried to keep it from him, because she'd endure anything rather than lose Joseph. She was proud of her silence, like one of the martyrs: Isaac Jogues refusing to deny Christ even when the Indians pulled out his fingernails. She was particularly afraid of having her fingernails pulled out or having bamboo stuck under them, which Catholic children in the fifties were often told was something regularly done to priests by Chinese Communists. Later, when she read in the lives of the saints about what were called *silent martyrdoms,* she saw herself. Like St. Thérèse of Lisieux putting up with the nun who deliberately splashed muddy water on her when they were scrubbing the floor on their knees side by side. She thought there could be no greater mortification than not flinching when Marie Kasperman braided her hair. Sister Berchmans encouraged her in this habit of mind with one of the catchphrases she could so easily reach for — all the nuns could, as if it were candy or a holy card at the bottom of the enormous pockets of their habits — and hinting at her own experience (thrilling for any girl: the sense of being given an encoded glimpse of convent life): "Quiet martyrdoms are the most trying." The cult of martyrs. Maria remembers now: *martyr* means witness in Greek. Pearl says she is a witness. Does she think she is a martyr? Maria can't imagine where she would get such an idea.

Maria couldn't learn about being female from the nuns, their bodies hidden, praying to be delivered from the heaviness of the flesh. She could learn only from Marie Kasperman, both of them trapped in their interlocking hatred of the other.

Forty-two years later, Marie Kasperman afog in dementia, Maria Meyers, on a plane to save her daughter's life, still hears the word *filthy*.

"Filthy," Marie Kasperman would say, picking Maria's underwear up off the floor, holding it away from her with two fingers.

Maria had loved her body, but there were so many voices telling her this was wrong; it was a danger and could, by its very nature, hurt itself and hurt the world. Corrupting and corrupt. So she considered the joy that she took in her body's life a mystery: and a victory over all the forces she would keep her own child far away from. But she has kept her child from nothing. Her child wants to die.

★ ★ ★

Maria's eyes fall on the woman in the seat across from her. The woman stretches, raises her hands above her head, intertwines her fingers, circles her neck three times, puts her arms down, refolds her hands in her lap. As tired as she is, Maria feels the woman's pull. The woman stands in the aisle and raises her arms again; her breasts are lifted, and her skirt reveals just a little of the flesh above her ruby-colored boots. Her hair is copper curls, her sweater — soft cobalt wool — shapes the curves of her breast and waist, and the skirt, light gray, has a slit up the back, perhaps (but Maria suspects not) set there for easy walking. The men's eyes fall upon her because they want her; the women's because they want to *be* her. I was once the one, Maria thinks. I could stand up, raise my arms above my head, show the red inside of my mouth in a fine yawn, and pull them toward me, everyone, the eyes of everyone: I knew I could make them fall on me. Not anymore, she thinks. I am no longer young.

She thinks of all the bodies she has had: the little girl's body, the desiring and desirable body, the childbearing body, the body that moved through space, that swam and danced and ran and ran, and now the aging body, feeling the first bites of the inevitable bad news. None of the bodies lost, all contained in the same envelope, reliving their histories, sometimes insistently, sometimes muted for long periods, dormant but not quite asleep.

Now she remembers, in her discomfort in the closed space of the plane, how as a child she would run and run, for the plain joy of running; she would make Joseph race — he never wanted to — and she would always beat him. She loved her boyish body then. It never occurred to her that her body was different from his. She loved the pumping of her blood against stretched ribs, loved that her legs would slice through space, sail over roads. And she wanted to win; she couldn't bear not winning. She would have died trying to win. Afterward, after she'd won, she loved lying on the ground, flat on her back, dizzy with the aftermath of effort, loved her fast breath, her breath matching Joseph's, and the sky wheeling above her, the hint of moon in a sky still glazed with daylight, loved chewing blades of grass or leaves, the harsh, unfleshly taste. For a long time she believed that if something was growing and it looked good, it would be good to eat: it would taste like what it looked like. She ate an iris once; she thought it would be sweet and crisp with a soft, confectionery coating; she imagined the yellow centers would taste of cinnamon. She was shocked when the flower hurt her throat. After that she no longer ate plants.

When she and Joseph ran, they were a pair of running animals. Then she'd put on the final push and he wouldn't. She knew he wasn't trying, but she couldn't stop. He could have beaten her if he'd wanted to. Later, when they were grown, she asked him why he never did. He said, "You wanted it so much. I could never want it as much as you." She was touched by that — ashamed, a bit — but she didn't dwell on it for long.

Maria hasn't had a lover in more than a year. The long adulterous affair with Jack Rappaport, judge of family court, came to an end when his wife died and Maria perceived that he thought of her as a potential replacement. She liked adultery; even the accoutrements amused her: phone calls from public booths at freezing hours, fake accents, *Can't talk to you now.* She could see that as an adventure. But she has never wanted to be married; she dreaded the stasis, the old feeling of being fixed in a rifle sight, right in the middle of the cross-hairs. Trapped. What she told the young mother of the crying baby was the truth: she can't stand being still. The stillness of marriage felt to her like incarceration, incarceration under the name of protection. So now she is fifty years old, unmated. All the years of a desiring body, the intoxicating longing, foolish headlong yearning muted now. She wonders sometimes if it is possible that she will never be a man's lover again.

The woman with the copper-colored curls is slipping now into her seat and buckling her seat belt. The trick, Maria thinks, not for the first time, of the female body. Here it is, the prize above all others prized, only you must hide it, call it dangerous or something worse.

She wonders what the state of Pearl's

body is now. She thinks of all the ways she's known that body, all the bodies it has been (as her own has been many bodies), none so loved as the earliest, the infant's; then the child's skin, desired to the point of swooning, the point of exhaustion, a tenderness far more complete, more heartbreaking than the love for any man. Then the child's body taking on its competence, charming, comic with the comedy of animals. The fear, then: I send this body on its way (because I cannot stop it) into a world on whose hard surfaces these beautiful feet, barely articulate in their new bones, must walk. Then the body more the world's than mine: rounded breasts, lengthened limbs. To be a mother is to be perpetually stolen from.

The starved body of her child. The shock of the word *starved:* the dry hard single syllable, formed at the roof of the mouth.

If she could see Pearl's body now, unclothed, she would be shocked. There is a sprinkling on her arms and legs and breasts of a fine coating of light hair — lanugo, it is called — the starved body's protection, the same hair grown by babies. Pearl's teeth now are too big for her face; her hair is dull and brittle, her nails broken, her skin tinged yellow-green. Maria doesn't know any of this, but she knows enough to be afraid of seeing her daughter now, the sight of whom was always the most desirable thing she could imagine.

The copper-colored beauty, bored, looks in a mirror she takes from a bag at her feet. She plays with a comb, rearranging her lush hair. *Devorah,* Maria thinks, remembering the red curls of her beloved friend, now dead. Grotesquely dead, catching the heel of her shoe in the hem of her skirt, facedown in the dirt of a ficus plant. Copper hair. Red hair. Devorah's.

My friend is dead, my friend is dead, my daughter wants to die, she thinks, over and over, pressing the heels of her hands against her eyes. Surely this is something she should be allowed to weep for. She searches in the seat pocket for the sleeping mask. Does it matter, she wonders, if someone sees tears dripping below a mask? My friend is dead. My daughter is dying. I am alone.

Surely she can be allowed to pray to Devorah. What is prayer, after all, but asking for help, any kind of help you want, saying anything that comes to your mind?

That was what she did with Devorah all the time; they helped each other, they told each other everything. They understood each other completely. Neither of them ever judged the other; always, they took the other's side. Why can she not do that now, talk to Devorah as she always talked to her, ask her for help as she always did? If that was prayer, it must be a permissible kind, even when you are not a believer, when you've staked your life on having left belief, in the name of justice, in the name of truth. And who will know she is praying to Devorah? Who will censure her, punish her if she prays for her child who wants to die to the friend of her youth?

But what is the language of prayer for someone like herself who has staked her life against all that prayer stands for? She thinks of her favorite poem, Herbert's "Prayer." She has Herbert with her. Her copy with Devorah's handwriting: *To Maria on her twenty-first birthday. With all my love.*

She no longer believes in prayer, but it is still her favorite poem. Learned by heart. Yet her heart has proved inadequate, because she doesn't in fact remember the whole thing, only phrases, disconnected from the whole: "A kind of tune, which all things hear and fear . . . the milky way, the bird of Paradise . . . the land of spices; something understood." She had memorized it once, as a Christmas gift to her father: Christmas 1966. She'd learned it in Mother Emmanuel's class and loved the speed of it, each phrase a whole world, each phrase a complete vision of the desirable. "Heaven in ordinary, man well drest, the milky way, the bird of Paradise." She had thought it wonderful, the jump from the plain words *ordinary* and *well drest* to the extravagant world of stars and feathers. Proudly, she had recited it to her father on Christmas morning in his library. He tapped his fingers together. "Very fine," he said, "but without, I think, the spiritual complexity of Hopkins." She realized she hadn't pleased him, and immediately she knew why. She had offered him something outside the protectorate of the church. Herbert was an Anglican; therefore he must be named inferior, somehow lacking. He must be condescended to. Did her father feel his response had been inadequate? Did he regret dashing his daughter's joy? I don't think so; he would always have seen before his eyes the beacon of his duty, the singular vision, one way and one way only of right being in the world. She excused herself from her father's study and went up to her room, not to cry but to be alone with the dryness in her heart. There had been a lively warm place where the flame of excitement at the idea of pleasing her father lapped and climbed. Now there were only ashes in an empty and cold grate.

And yet it hadn't made her love the poem less. She doesn't believe in anything on the other side of prayer, but she believes in the language of that poem, the potential of language for transformation, the forcing of the miraculous, for comprehension of all that seems to be incomprehensible, a place of rest at last. Surely it is all right to go to your friend, your dead friend, with your wish for the miraculous, your wish for consolation. Surely, at a moment like this, you can speak as you like. She closes her eyes, hoping no one sees her folding her hands, and speaks to her dead friend in what she knows is the language of prayer: the speech of perfect freedom, pure desire. There can't be anything wrong with it. She presses her head against the cool plastic surface of the window and looks out into the sky, which is beginning to lighten; it is nearly 6 a.m. She will talk to her friend. She will say whatever she wants, as she always did.

Devorah, help me.

Where are you now? We are both in the sky but I can't see you. Are you part of something now, something that makes sense of everything?

How can this have happened? I loved her so much.

And now she's saying that her life is worth giving up. All I want to say to her is, "Nothing is worth your life."

I will stop it. Help me, Devorah. Help me to stop it.

I will stop her.

I will stop her death.

I will make her live.

Help me.

The voice of the pilot interrupts her.

"About to make our descent into Dublin," says the Irish voice.

And now, Maria thinks, it will begin.

· 12 ·

"I'm Dr. Morrisey. I'm in charge here. We've got to get her to a hospital. We can't wait any longer."

A man's voice responds, one of the policemen. "So you come on a white horse, riding to the rescue, and she gets her fifteen minutes of fame."

Pearl looks up. She sees men and women in uniforms and then one woman, not in uniform, wearing a camel-colored coat. She leans down, takes Pearl's wrist. "I'm Dr. Morrisey. I'm going to take you to hospital. It would be easier if you'd cooperate."

Pearl has expected this. They will tell her to cooperate; she will resist. Civil disobedience. Gandhi and Martin Luther King. She will say nothing; if they hold her she will kick and thrash. Not to hurt anyone but to protect herself.

She sees the doctor's face. Older than she but young, still a young woman. Glasses. Not on a white horse at all. And not coming to her rescue. Perhaps she believes she is, but Pearl knows she has planned well and rescue is impossible. It is much too late. She is proud of this.

The two policemen are holding what looks like gardening shears. The handles are red but the blades, curved down toward her now, are silver. She hasn't been afraid until now. The shears are so large. She hadn't thought they'd be so large. They could pierce her skin; they could cause her to shed blood. She is afraid of the sight of her own blood. They aren't kind, the faces of the men who hold the shears. It wasn't kind, what one of them just said to the doctor about her fifteen minutes of fame.

She could almost laugh at the idea of fame.

She thrashes as they approach her, but they are no longer patient. One takes her head in a tight grip. Others grab her legs and arms. They come near her with the shears. Will they put out her eyes? She closes them. "No, no, no," she says.

"Too late for that, my girl," one of them says. Too late for what? she wants to ask them.

"I don't want her hurt. Take it easy," the doctor says.

"She didn't make it easy for us," a policeman says. "There's not much space between the cuffs and her skin. And she's doing this limp trick. If she's cut, it's on her head, not mine."

"Just be careful," the doctor says.

She can't move. One policeman is holding her legs, one her arms, and a third has her head tucked between his elbow and his side.

"Let me do it," the doctor says.

"I think we can handle it, doctor," the policeman says.

"I've done surgery in war conditions, officer. I think I'm qualified."

The doctor leans over her. She can't see her face; her head has been immobilized; she can't look down. She hears the sound of a snap — no, a snip.

"All right, then," the doctor says.

Her chains have been cut. Her skin has not been pierced. She is being lifted, then put down. Something soft is against her back. A bed. A stretcher. She is being carried across the pavement. She looks at the people gathered. She has the impulse to wave, but she stops herself. From the corner of her eye, she sees a face she knows. Finbar. Finbar has come to see what she has done.

It isn't Finbar's face she wants to see, but Stevie's. She closes her eyes, closes out the glimpse of Finbar so Stevie will appear. But Stevie will not come. She calls him: Stevie, I need to see you now. I need to see your face. You were my friend.

My friend, he was my friend, Pearl says, over and over in her mind. She will not think about the doctor or the shears or the policemen with their unkind words. She will try, instead, to remember how she and Stevie became friends. Perhaps this will bring his face to her. Seeing his face will bring her courage, the courage to resist. But when she tries to think of how their friendship began she sees not his face but the body of a horse. "So you come on a white horse, riding to the rescue." No, not that horse. No one is riding the horse she sees; the horse is dead, hanging upside down.

That was how she became friends with Stevie: when they saw the dead horse.

She called for the image of Stevie's face, but another has come to her: the image of a dead horse.

She's right, Pearl is. She and Stevie became friends in Mayo, and it happened at the time they saw the horse.

I will tell you the story of Stevie and the

horse. I will tell you everything that happened to Pearl in Ireland, everything since we last spoke of her, everything that led up to the place she is now, as long as you understand that at this moment she is not capable of such a sustained narrative; she has only an image: the image of a dead horse, hanging upside down, at the top of a hill in the county of Mayo. But I will tell you the whole story.

Now you will learn about Stevie Donegan, his life and death.

★ ★ ★

It was the tenth of March, the beginning of lighter days, of spring, a stretch of a few days of unseasonably warm weather. Things were still pleasant in Finbar's apartment; Pearl was enjoying her life with him and his friends, even if she'd begun to grow suspicious of Mick Winthrop. Mick invited Pearl and Finbar to stay for a few days at his place in Mayo. Mick's son Stevie would come along. She'd hardly spoken to Stevie, she didn't even know for sure how old he was; on one of their walks he told her he was fifteen. It was the horse's death and burial that made them friends. She cannot call up Stevie's face, but she can remember the horse. She feels that at least this is something to have of Stevie.

Finbar and the other boys thought Mick was wonderful, a wonderful father to recognize his bastard son, to support him, to come over to Ireland several weeks a year to be with him. Stevie is of a noble line, they all said, the nephew of Reg Donegan, an IRA hero. In 1982, Reg Donegan had been convicted, with two other IRA soldiers, of leaving a bomb in a suitcase in the Leeds railroad station, a protest against Margaret Thatcher's treatment of Bobby Sands and the other hunger strikers. Two people were killed, one a commuter, a mother of three, one a Pakistani workman. Fifteen more were wounded. Mick and the boys never saw those bodies when they talked of Reg and his heroism; those bodies were erased for them by the pressure of the word *hero*. "Your father was a hero," Maria always said to her, but Pearl didn't have to erase any bodies because of the pressure of that word. She couldn't erase the bodies when she heard Reg's name; she wondered about the dead, the two of them, and the injured, wondered if they'd recovered or if they'd lived maimed and imprisoned all those years. Stevie's uncle Reg had been in an English jail for sixteen years: Brixton prison, among the most notorious.

Pearl could see that Stevie was a disappointment, an embarrassment to Mick. Stevie was slow; his eyes were weak and pale behind thick glasses; his lips were full and girlish; there was a mole the size of a dime below his left eye. He couldn't catch a ball; no one around Mick, except for Pearl, seemed able to catch or throw, and when Mick threw a ball to Pearl she sometimes felt his surprise — or was it chagrin? — when she caught it. When Mick kept saying that Stevie came from a noble line, she could see he was trying to make something up to himself.

She was so happy to be in the country. The trees along the road leaned toward one another, friendly, sheltering, forming a kind of airy roof, making up for the starkness of the Dublin streets. In the morning, the mist would rise up and she would look at the vagueness and think that she was, in that vagueness, entirely happy. And the color: a smoky whiteness, then a silver, then the pink pressing up beneath it and then all at once a blueness — or blue grayness on the mornings when it rained. It is called a burning off, what happened to the fog, but nothing so violent as flame seemed part of it. It often rained, but by noon the rain would stop and the sky would be rinsed and pure and it was wonderful simply to breathe.

★ ★ ★

Mick called his house a shack, but it wasn't a shack, it was a house with white stuccoed walls, two bedrooms whose walls were also white stucco, a kitchen painted yellow, and a bathroom with hot running water. There was a wild garden, junglelike, lush and overgrown, and a vicious-looking patch of raspberries said to be wonderful in June. Down the road from the house there was a working farm, and Stevie and Pearl walked down there the first morning they were at the house. They said good morning to the farmer. He was very old, and he didn't really run the farm anymore; his son and his grandsons ran it. But he wasn't speaking to them. He'd built himself a little house on the edge of the property and had isolated himself almost completely. He went to church and to the pub; no one ever came to visit.

Mick learned from the son that the old man had fought with them over the treatment of the hay. The farmer would never have talked about it. Once he said the way hay was being treated now was "diabolical" but made no mention of his son's role in the devil's work.

I will explain the dispute about the hay as far as I understand it. For as long as anyone could remember, hay had been stored in stacks; they'd been a feature of the landscape. But in the past few years, the farmers had taken to covering the haystacks with black plastic. It was much more efficient; it kept the hay from rotting, so you weren't at the mercy of the weather. But Pearl thought the old man was right when he said that covering the hay was diabolical. It looked evil: malevolent black lumps sitting in the fields. Mick said it was just feudalism, just tourism, to want to keep the hay in the old way; it was progress to put it under plastic. It was a good thing and only someone who wanted to keep the people picturesque for the tourists rather than prosperous would oppose it. What about the ecological impact of all that plastic? Pearl asked Mick. She'd passed the point where she accepted everything he said as true. "Look," he said, "that's an elitist issue. If the farms disappear entirely, it will have a much worse ecological impact long term. What about the ecological impact of tourism? Fat-assed Floridians bringing their tour buses, their litter, their state-of-the-art hotels. To say nothing of the political and psychological aspects.

Complete poison. Look, these guys can't survive, competitively, unless they take up modern methods. I've talked to them, not to some 'ecological expert,' some Trinity don who hasn't worked the land but only reads about it. I know what's what for these people; I'm on the ground with them."

She wanted to tell Mick he was in Mayo only about ten days a year total and had no right to speak for anybody but himself, but she knew that would upset Stevie. She saw, spending time with Stevie, that any sign of discord distressed him. It pained him that the old farmer thought one thing about the hay in plastic, which was what Pearl thought, and that his father thought another. He loved his father and didn't want to think of him as being wrong. Also, he wanted to please his father, though he knew he rarely did, so it was important at least never to displease him, and he knew Mick would be displeased if his son didn't agree with him. Pearl was growing fond of Stevie; she liked their times together, slow-moving, nearly silent. She didn't want to distress him. So she stopped arguing about the black plastic, even though she knew she was right, because she also knew that Mick would argue in such a way that, even though she was right, she would appear to be wrong.

The old man had a dog and a cat and an old horse that used to pull a hay wagon, but she was only up to eating grass when Pearl and Stevie met her. The horse — or mare, as she should be called — cropped the grass, very gently. Pearl and Stevie would stand by the fence looking at her, not saying anything. Pearl felt a rightness in the world with that horse, whose name was Queenie, looking out at things. Looking out for things. The old man would say a few words to them; none of them said much really. Eventually, the man would offer them cigarettes, and she could tell that Stevie felt he ought to take one, but that when Pearl said no he was relieved because he could say no too.

One day the horse got sick, agonizingly sick. She'd eaten some grass that had gone moldy, her guts had twisted up, and she was in agony. She kicked the walls of the stall right down. The old man had to get his son to shoot her. Then he needed the son's modern machinery to deal with the horse's body and to bury her.

Pearl and Stevie didn't know the horse had died; they went over in the morning, as they always did, and what they saw was terrible. The mare's body had bloated to a grotesque size, or her belly had (her legs looked fragile and spindly, although in the ordinary way they were far from fragile; she was a cart horse, a workhorse, not a thoroughbred). The son and grandsons attached a pulley to the tractor so they could lift the horse with chains; her legs stuck straight up into the air, so they wouldn't break, and her head had rolled back. The horse hung upside down: huge, precarious, her legs useless, and the weight of her, even though she was suspended, made them all feel crushed. The old man just stood to the side; he was so taken up with sadness that Pearl and Stevie were afraid to talk to him. Pearl thought a grief like the old man's should not be exposed to the light of day. The son, who seemed like a very nice man, a man in his forties, the father of the family, with thin blondish hair and a very red face, said they were going to bury her at the top of the hill. Pearl asked if she and Stevie could come along. The old man nodded.

The son and the grandsons had used the tractor to dig the grave earlier that morning. Pearl imagined it nearly killed the old man to ask for the help of their machines when those machines stood for everything he hated. But he had no choice. In some ways, she thought, that was the most terrible.

They hauled the horse up the hill. Pearl was afraid the chains would break and the horse would fall and splatter on the ground. *Dead weight,* Pearl thought, as she saw the horse being hauled. She had never seen anything dead before, and for the first time she understood that death also meant deadness: heaviness and absence, mass attached to nothing but itself. She kept her eye on the deadness all the time that the tractor did its work, slowly, steadily, inching up the hill, till Queenie was lowered into the grave. And then the dirt was spread over her, and the old man walked away. Pearl and Stevie walked away too.

They left Mayo soon after that; they never saw the old man again. But Stevie and Pearl were friends because they had seen that thing, that terrible thing, that thing with so many terrible parts to it. Because, although they never spoke of it, they knew they could.

She is seeing it now: the huge mare suspended in the air, her eyes rolled back, her teeth visible. But she cannot see Stevie's face.

They were friends after they came back from Mayo. It was the middle of March and there was warmth in the air; in the garden of Finbar's parents, primroses were pushing up, and crocuses. Pearl mentioned this to Finbar and he sneered. *Why don't you just fucking move in with my parents and their fucking garden if you love it so much?* She doesn't listen; she waits till they are home in his flat, till he is the boy she likes again and they can be the people she likes, sitting across from each other, under the inadequate standing lamps that distort the print they both love, throwing words to each other: Irish words, Cambodian words, quick-quick or in long arcs: words like grain from the hand of a figure in a painting from the nineteenth century. Now she can see Finbar's face. She has no interest in Finbar. She is trying to see Stevie's face.

Think, think of the things we did, she tells herself, trying to calm her panic. She must not die without seeing Stevie's face.

When they got back to Dublin, Pearl began spending time with Stevie and found out that he didn't know how to read. She asked her mother for advice. Maria advised her to have Stevie (whose name and situation she did not know) dictate stories to her. Pearl typed them up and printed them out, and Stevie began learning to read his own words.

Stevie's stories were all about a mare from the country who escapes to Dublin and gets a job carrying people from place to place. She learns to read the street signs, although reading is hard for her. She races buses and beats them. She can beat the fastest car. People want to take her to a racetrack but she won't go because she likes living with a boy who lives in a big house and keeps her in the garden. There are a lot of details about what the horse likes to eat — mainly sweets — although there is the occasional healthful meal of oats and hay. The horse and the boy and his mother have dinner at a table in the garden; the boy and his mother eat theirs off trays. The garden is full of flowers, and the mother and the son pick them and weave them into wreaths for the horse's neck. The horse is called Princess.

Pearl thought she was teaching a boy to read. She didn't think what she was doing was about politics or would lead to death. Anyone would have said that what she was doing — helping a dyslexic boy to learn to read — was innocent; what could it be called if not that?

But what do we mean by *innocent?* Presumed innocent. Presumed by whom? And why? Who is the presumer, who the judge? Is it possible for us, ever, to give up the idea of a judge on high, even if we no longer believe in a real presence there? *Real presence.* These words would have a religious meaning for Joseph and Maria — and for Breeda, Stevie's mother, Reg Donegan's sister. For Pearl it had none. Yet *innocence* did mean something to her, something important. Where did the idea come from, what was its source, the idea of the purity for which she longed, of which she dreamed, which she sought in and by her death? You may think I can tell you, that my saying I can't is a willful holding back, but you must believe me: it isn't. I can't tell you because I don't know. I do know she was right to believe in her own innocence. She was doing one thing, and it was a good thing, although in the end it led to a death. So after Stevie died she was afraid to do anything, to have any contact, because potential contact was dangerous and she herself was therefore a vessel of danger.

How did Pearl become friends with Stevie's mother, Breeda? She can remember the incident of the horse and trace her friendship with Stevie to that vivid moment: the image stays with her now as she is being carried on the stretcher. She knows that she and Breeda were friends, and that Breeda does not think of her as a friend any longer. Breeda's face? Oh, she can call that up, all right, all too easily.

Breeda's face: not a face, really; a face implies something composed for the world to see. The face Pearl sees now had given up all composure; it was a face that cared nothing for what people made of it. A mask of grief, of outrage: primitive, unself-regarding. Pushing her way into the room, Breeda, who had lived a life of not making her presence felt, was knocking over furniture. "His blood is on your hands, the lot of yez, but especially on yours —" pointing at Pearl. Breeda's son was dead. She had no care for what the world thought of her.

But before that, the eyes behind the glasses, swimmy blue, almost overlarge, those eyes, almost too much expression. So sometimes, depending on your mood, you wanted to look and look and sometimes you only wanted to look away. Breeda Donegan, known to Finbar and his friends as the sister of Reg Donegan. Thought of that way by Mick Winthrop, was her body penetrated for that reason? Or was it because she was young and slender and compliant? Could everything that happened have been predicted, was it so predictable as to be almost a cliché? That was Stevie's genesis — a child fathered by an admirer of the brother via (almost accidentally) the body of the *hero*'s sister. And so Breeda was thought of as someone's sister, someone's mother, a body without a name, a pair of relationships (sister, mother) and what would be called *herself* an empty circle, a container for those other things (sisterhood, motherhood). She was faceless to them (as Stevie has no face to Pearl now). Breeda, who was her friend, who said to her, "His blood is on your hands."

But it was not like that at first. I can tell you what it was like at first, those late afternoons in Breeda and Stevie's flat in Fatima Mansions. And I must tell you what Fatima Mansions were: four-story blocks of flats built in the Stonybatter section of Dublin in the 1930s, built hopefully, very hopefully. Slum clearance, they were called. Flats without central heating, even in the year 1998. Considered a failure now, an urban disaster, a breeding ground for crime and drug use and depression.

Pearl had been working with Stevie for a

couple of weeks, having him write stories as her mother had advised, when Breeda sent a message with Stevie. "My mam wonders if you'd come to our place for tea."

It is more difficult to trace the course of a friendship than a love affair, a friendship that consisted of drinking tea and telling things about themselves, quiet stories, details of childhood. What is the critical mass, the point at which the thin material thickens so that a solid has been formed, and you can call it, without overstating anything, a friendship? That is what they had.

The first shy afternoon: three shy people, Pearl, Breeda, Stevie, drinking tea, talking about cookies — biscuits, they were called. "Mrs. Reilley told me these were on sale and as I knew you loved them I bought five packets of them. I think they'll be good in the freezer." "That's a great thing, mam," and they really did seem happy about the purchase; they went on talking about it for what seemed to Pearl an excessive amount of time, but she would learn it was not excessive. Their life was made up of small events, small triumphs like that: packets of biscuits gone on sale, the opportunity seized, the memory hoarded, as were the biscuits, for future delectation.

Pearl and Breeda were drawn to each other by a net of likenesses and differences. They were both shy, they both liked to be quiet, they both looked more than they spoke. And yet Pearl felt she'd never known anyone like Breeda, someone who thought of herself as so much in the hands of fate, someone to whom things happened, rather than someone who made things happen. She wondered if that was what it was to be American, that you thought of yourself as someone not in the hands of fate. Certainly, the people she had known in America, her friends, her mother's friends, but most especially her mother, had thought of themselves that way. She and Joseph had been unusual among the people who surrounded them because they watched others moving rather than move themselves. When she was with Breeda she felt the same sort of peacefulness drop on her that she felt when she was with Joseph, when they would walk or go to museums, often for long periods in silence.

They didn't speak about things that were important to them at first. For a while, there were patches of silence that were not comforting but uneasy, broken, perhaps by talking about Stevie's stories, almost as if the stories were a guest that had been invited for his social skills, his ability to start a conversation. Then Breeda would let something drop — "I miss my friends fiercely since I've come to Dublin" — and ask Pearl about *her* friends. And Pearl would say something without much detail, and Breeda would say something with a little more detail; they built the edifice of their friendship slowly, bit by bit, as if they were building a stone wall, each stone chosen deliberately, carefully, for its shape and size. So that when Pearl had heard some stories about Breeda's friend Paulie and his sister Rosalie who won dancing competitions, Pearl told her about Luisa and Luisa's family and how her aunts could dance no matter how old they were (but not about Uncle Ramón), and Breeda told her about her Uncle Joe who liked to dress up as Elvis for family parties (but not about Uncle Tom, who'd been shot by the RUC, the Royal Ulster Constabulary, or Uncle Will, who'd been interned without trial). So they made, at first, a pastel-colored world of each other's childhoods, and then soon they understood that as children they had both been, quite often, afraid and ashamed of that among others around them who seemed never to be afraid: in

Pearl's case, her mother and Luisa; in Breeda's, nearly everyone she knew. They didn't tell each other the things that had really frightened them, they didn't need to, perhaps; it was enough that each knew the other had been frightened by things that most people didn't think were frightening.

It was easy for Pearl to understand why Breeda had been frightened; she'd been brought up in a time and place of violence. She'd been one year old in the year of Bloody Sunday 1972, the killing of thirteen unarmed civilians in Belfast by British troops, and had no memory of a life before the Troubles. Breeda, though, didn't understand why Pearl would have been frightened. She didn't understand Pearl's relationship to her mother, who seemed so strong and so energetic. When Pearl finally told Breeda the story of Luisa's Uncle Ramón (after they'd begun to darken the pastel palette of their memories of childhood and tell each other the details of what had frightened them), Breeda didn't understand why Pearl wasn't grateful to her mother, why she was so angry at what her mother did much later, when Pearl was well out of danger, when she'd been safe for years.

"My mother has no idea that some

things aren't hers to tell; she has almost no sense of privacy. She'll sing at the top of her lungs right on the street." Breeda wanted to ask why that was so bad, but she didn't want to seem not to understand. It was then that Pearl told the story of Uncle Ramón. She'd told Breeda all about Luisa, that they'd been friends since they were three; that she loved going to Luisa's house, because there were always so many people there, and Luisa's mother was so kind and liked to cook and dance, and that her mother liked to come, too, and cook and dance with Mrs. Ramirez. But that Luisa didn't like Maria, because she thought Maria had no right to think she understood Luisa's parents, when she'd never been poor. Luisa, who was never frightened and often angry (just like my friend Eileen, Breeda said), and always had the courage to do or say exactly what she wanted — which was why, Pearl told Breeda, the situation with Uncle Ramón was so hard for her.

Uncle Ramón lived with the Ramirezes for months. He slept on the living room couch. Every night he drank quarts of Corona beer and got drunk, and all day he slept in his stained underwear and snored with a noise that Pearl and Luisa knew meant nothing good. Those snores, that underwear, his hairy legs, his black socks with the holes: Luisa and Pearl knew they would never go near that kind of man.

"He kept calling me Chiquita Rubia, Little Blondie. Little Blondie, he'd say, almost growling it. I was eleven years old. Whenever he saw me he would find some excuse to brush against me, saying Rubia, rubia, Chiquita Rubia, and whenever Luisa went to the bathroom he would stand behind me and rub himself against me, and when I tried to get away, he'd say, What's the matter with you, blondie, little chink blondie, you think you're too good for me, with your Jew mama? You're nothing but a little chink Jew. Then he would rub up against me and say Rubia, Chiquita Rubia."

For some time, Pearl told Breeda, she didn't think there was anything she could do about it. She was afraid of embarrassing Luisa's mother. Afraid if Luisa got embarrassed she'd get mad and then she might not be her friend. She began having nightmares, and one night she told her mother. Maria understood everything — why Pearl felt afraid to say something — and said Leave it to her; she'd take care of it.

"And she did take care of it. She had a

friend, a guy who worked in one of her day-care centers. Great with kids but scary-looking. Leshawn was really huge. She told him what Uncle Ramón was doing. She waited with him by the apartment house till Ramón came out. Leshawn went over to him. He twisted Ramón's arm and took him to the back of the building, shoved him against the wall, and told him if he ever went near Pearl Meyers again he'd be wearing his balls for a bow tie. Uncle Ramón went back to Santo Domingo the next day."

Pearl told Breeda she found out about it only a year ago when Leshawn died of a heart attack. "He was only forty. My mother told the story at his memorial service. And when she used his words, 'You'll be wearing your balls for a bow tie,' everybody laughed. I was furious at her. It wasn't her story to tell. My mother will do almost anything for a good story. She had no sense that she'd invaded my privacy. And if I told her, she would have said, 'You have to have a sense of humor about things. It's the only way to live with them.' "

Breeda would have liked to say, Well, a sense of humor is a great thing, in the same way that she would liked to have said that what Maria had done was a great thing. But she knew she mustn't, because she didn't understand Pearl and her mother, not the first thing. Why had Pearl gone so far away from Maria, to study? This seemed unthinkable to Breeda, who would never have left Belfast if her mother had still been alive. Her mother, who loved her but was disappointed in her, though she tried not to show it, her mother a staunch Republican, never afraid, embarrassed, almost, by her fearful daughter, whom she tried to shelter. Breeda, the youngest of the family, the only one young after the Troubles began: small, nearsighted, asthmatic. Her mother wanting to protect her but afraid for her, so sometimes she would be harsh, her fear turned to impatience. "You'll have to learn to be a bit tougher, Breeda pet. This is a war we're living through." So that Breeda knew her mother was a bit ashamed of having a daughter who needed to be sheltered; she would have liked Breeda to be like her sisters, her cousins, a warrior, hardening her eyes and tightening her lips when she passed a Protestant on the street, singing along at family parties instead of sitting silent, as she did when the family sang the song, laughing themselves silly, to the tune of "Catch a Falling Star," a Perry Como song from the fifties.

Catch a falling bomb and put it in your
     pocket,
Never let it fade away.
Catch a falling bomb and put it in your
     pocket,
Keep it for the IRA.
For a peeler may come and tap you on
     the shoulder
Some starry night,
And just in case he's getting any bolder,
You'll have a pocket full of gelignite.

Pearl said it was amazing, she never talked to anyone about being frightened of songs as a child; no one she'd ever known before Breeda would have understood. Breeda was thrilled with this distinction. Pearl told Breeda about the song that had scared *her*. It was on a record her mother liked to sing to, her voice higher than usual, strange, as if she thought no one was listening to her or didn't care. "Mary Hamilton" was the name of the song. Pearl told Breeda it was about a servant girl who'd had a baby by the king and killed it; she sang the words that had scared her:

286

I put her in a tiny boat
And set her out to sea,
That she might sink
Or she might swim
But she'd never return to me.

And Breeda confessed (it did seem like a confession) that she was scared by a song the girls would sing on the street:

Wallflower, wallflower, growing up so
    high,
All the little children are all going to
    die.
All except for Breeda Donegan, for
    she's the only one,
She can dance, she can sing,
She can show her wedding ring.

Breeda said it made her scared either way. When it was her name put in, that she was the one who could dance and sing and show her wedding ring and live, she was afraid she'd be the only one left alive; when her name was not put in she was afraid of dying when still a child. And they both remembered they'd been terrified by the end of "Molly Malone," when she dies of a fever and no one can save her, and her ghost wheels her barrow through streets broad and narrow.

Breeda never told Pearl the relief she felt at being able to speak just as she liked, to tell stories the way she wanted to, not strung together by events but by the look of a thing, a smell, snatches of a song. She knew that sort of thing wouldn't be admired among the people who raised her. Until she met Pearl, Breeda had never felt admired. Perhaps we forget that admiration is something large numbers of people never feel but yearn for without being able to name. Admiration is a luxury, a big-ticket item. And yet it can't be bought or even asked for. It must be bestowed. Pearl bestowed admiration on Breeda, and Breeda felt its richness; suddenly she was, to herself, a person of wealth.

Breeda knew her mother loved her but did not admire her. She was pretty sure no one she had ever known admired her, except for her body: slender, high-breasted. Mick Winthrop had admired her body and wanted it, for itself but also, as it was the body of the sister of a hero, so he could engender a hero son upon it. To his disappointment, Stevie was not a hero. Stevie was a tender boy.

Breeda was often afraid, ashamed; she felt herself inadequate. Who do we blame for that? Do we say she was just born at the wrong time and place for someone of her nature? But can't eggs be laid in the wrong nest? Breeda, brought up in a family devoted to violence, was appalled by violence, frightened by it. Shouldn't someone have seen that, shouldn't someone have been looking out for her? It simply wasn't possible, among those people, at that time, at that place. She had an older brother who might have done this, but he thought of himself as a soldier, on active duty in a time of war. How could he look out for his little sister when he was placing bombs in railway stations? And her mother? Her mother thought of herself as the mother of a soldier in a time of war, and in times of war, sacrifices had to be made. So the offering of Breeda's young, desirable body to a rich American who could pay for Reg's legal defense — it seemed like the kind of thing the mother of a soldier son should go along with. Shouldn't Breeda have been glad to offer herself as a sacrificial victim for the ancient cause? But I will not call her a victim. There is more to Breeda than that: she has her ways of getting through; she can surprise us. Simply, I will say: I wish there had been someone to look out for her.

At least her mother stood by her when Stevie was born. But her mother had also stood by when they gave her to Mick, as payment for the American dollars he raised for Reg's legal fund. Breeda didn't like to think of that. She loved her mother. If you loved someone, you didn't think anything bad about them. She didn't understand Pearl, criticizing her mother all the time: My mother's a control freak; my mother thinks she wants people to make up their own minds, but really she wants everyone to agree with her. Breeda didn't understand why Pearl was so angry. Maria had seemed very good, bringing Pearl up on her own as she did, which couldn't have been easy. So there were, between Breeda and Pearl, areas of silence, tactfully observed, as if they were two diplomats creating a new state. A state where men were excluded, except for Stevie. And Pearl's mother was excluded. As long as these exclusions were honored, it was a livable state, a state that nurtured its people.

They didn't talk about Finbar or Mick. Pearl knew she had never before met a woman whose life had been so critically shaped by doing what men wanted without saying "This is what I want" or "I don't want that." Breeda had been made pregnant by Mick Winthrop when she was sixteen. Pearl knew that, but she didn't know what Breeda really considered her greatest shame: that she was given to Mick Winthrop, sold by her family, for her brother's sake. She tried not to think of that. She told herself that she'd been flattered by Mick's attentions, proud that such a man, handsome, well educated, from America, would want someone like her. And he'd been a good father to Stevie. Many people say that; that I don't quite believe it, and that Pearl didn't — I suppose we are in a minority. Breeda wouldn't allow herself, for a very long time, to question whether or not Mick was a very good father, in the same way she didn't allow herself to understand how cleverly she'd seen to his doing what he did for Stevie: keeping Mick in touch with the people in her family whose politics would excite him, so that there was that ring of violent men behind her, exciting to Mick, who he was just enough afraid of that if he reneged on his obligations to their nephew he might be worried for himself, or at least worried about losing their regard. Like Pearl, I admire Breeda. She was reared in difficult circumstances, but she saw to it that she had some things of her own: her son, her own flat where they could live in peace, free from fear and violence. That she lost nearly everything is another matter. The point is, she made some things happen. There are many who cannot do this, not once in a whole life.

Pearl may not have understood how Breeda got herself and her son out of a place where she was frightened and ashamed to a place where she felt proud and on her own. Pearl only knows that Breeda came to Dublin because some man brought her and then went away. She doesn't know that Breeda attached herself to Dan Callahan partly because she knew he had plans to move south and she couldn't bear the northern life, the violence, the danger. And then, when he left, because he didn't like living with Stevie — Dan felt Breeda wasn't giving him enough attention, and Stevie was an embarrassment to him — Breeda didn't really mind. She wouldn't have been able to make the move south herself, but now the move had been made. So I think you'll see it's possible to say she got what she wanted. But Breeda suspected Pearl wouldn't like the way she went about it, so she was careful not to put Pearl's admiration in danger. She knew how elusive it was, how fragile, how precious, how easily lost.

Occasionally, Pearl was taken up short,

almost shocked, by the things Breeda didn't know. When she told Breeda that her friend Jessica had had to go home because of encephalitis, but that they were lucky because it was viral rather than bacterial, she understood that Breeda didn't know there was a difference between a virus and a bacterium. When she got a postcard from a friend taking a year in Brazil, speaking of the oddness that in February she was tormented by the heat, she came to see that Breeda didn't know that in the southern hemisphere the seasons were the reverse of those in the north. And once, when they rented *The English Patient* to watch together, a film chosen by Pearl (she wouldn't make that mistake again, forgetting Stevie and Breeda in her desire to see a film interesting to her), she was shocked that Breeda didn't understand that the invalid in the bandages was the dashing pilot who had tried to find his lover in the cave. She was careful after that to choose only films that they could easily all like: older films, musicals, *My Fair Lady. Oklahoma!* They would sing along. They would talk about how much they liked the songs. Favorite lines: "I have often walked down this street before/but the pavement always stayed beneath my feet before."

Slowly, in snatches of stories, Breeda began to reveal the true terror of her childhood: her street set on fire; her family forced to move three times, at gunpoint, in the middle of the night. Their neighbor Mrs. Fitzpatrick running away in a melee caused by who knows which side, blinded by plastic bullets from the guns of British soldiers, bullets that were called humane in Northern Ireland but forbidden in England as inhumane. Breeda had been afraid of Mrs. Fitzpatrick, afraid of the look in her new glass eyes and ashamed of her own fear, ashamed that she'd walk around the block to avoid seeing her, that she'd look away when her mother made her take Mrs. Fitzpatrick a plate of biscuits, a freshly baked cake. She was afraid of their soldiers in their camouflage and berets, their faces charcoaled with black stripes, afraid of the Loyalists who would grab her arm and twist it behind her back — she was a teenager; it was just after her brother was taken to jail — and say to her, "We can kill you anytime we like. We can do anything we want with you anytime we like." And then they would laugh and push her away. "We weren't people to them, we were things," she said to Pearl. So that Pearl, who hadn't understood the taste for violence, could taste it now, the appeal of it: to defend people like Breeda from people who did things to her *because they could*. She understood for the first time the desire to raise your voice, your hand, to defend the innocent, to protect the weak. Breeda and Stevie were innocents; they were weak. Pearl could imagine herself bringing an iron bar down on the head, the body, of someone who would try to hurt them.

Gradually, Breeda told Pearl her secret: she was in favor of the peace process. She would vote for it, among other things, because it was possible that if the peace agreement went through, the British would set her brother free. There'd be an amnesty for all Republican prisoners, he would come back home, she would see him again, and he would have his life back. Her father said, Don't fall for that, don't be so stupid, so she didn't talk about it anymore. No one knew she was in favor of the peace agreement and would vote for it — no one except Pearl, who told no one. Breeda trusted her, and in that, at least, Pearl knows she has been worthy of trust.

You might find it hard to believe that a thirty-one-year-old woman, from a family of ten, brought up in the same streets her family had lived in for a century, had never said to a human soul what she really felt. It took her until she was thirty-one to say what she believed: that nothing was worth all that death. She said it to Pearl. She told Pearl to keep her secret. She hated the violence, she wanted peace, but she knew everyone who loved her would see that as a betrayal.

How did it come to her, this frightened woman, this woman whose ideas of the world came from images and stories and songs, who could not follow an argument or even a complicated narrative, whose ignorance of the physical world was monumental? How did she come to believe she knew better than the people whom she loved; that they were wrong? She came to this idea in shame, because she knew what they would say: that she was thinking like a child; only a child would say what she said, believe what she believed. What are you, they would have said, if you're not willing to give your life for a great idea, the idea of a united Ireland? She would have liked to say: Peace is a great idea; forgiveness is a great idea. And they would say: What did the dead die for, what has your brother given his youth for? She would have said, "Nothing is worth all that death." They would, perhaps, have spat on the ground in their contempt for her. She would never have done anything like that, spat on the ground, slammed the door of a room. Yet she believed that they were wrong: that nothing was worth all that death.

Yet it didn't make her love them less. It made her doubt herself, of course, but gradually, tentatively, she began to believe she could be right. She told Pearl things she had heard, things she was afraid to have said before: that her own side had done terrible things too. Like what they'd done to the man who worked in the British army commissary. They kidnapped him with his family, the family was tied to a tree, and the man was told they would be killed unless he made himself a human bomb, walked into the army commissary with explosives strapped to his body, and blew himself up. He died, five British soldiers were killed, and then the family was killed anyway, so they wouldn't tell. And as soon as she said that, horrors from the other side: the Unionists who broke in on a Halloween dance and said *Trick or treat* before they threw a bomb into the middle of the dance floor, killing thirty-five, running away, laughing, it was said. Horror upon horror; all she could see was endless horror unless someone stopped it. It must be a good thing simply to say, *Stop, stop for a moment.* The word *stop* seemed to her a blessed word. If you went back far enough, back through blood, through centuries of killing, Breeda's family was right; they were fighting for justice, the English should not have taken over their land, the Protestants should not have denied the Catholics jobs and civil rights. But you could not go back, and if there was any other way to live rather than tying a family to a tree or throwing a bomb and saying *Trick or treat,* wasn't that better? Wasn't it better to stop living in a way that allowed people to believe it was right to do such things, in the name of justice, or of goodness, or of history or ancient right?

Her family hated Gerry Adams, for having been an IRA soldier who turned to politics, who negotiated the peace treaty, who worked with his enemies for what they believed was a pusillanimous surrender. They thought he had betrayed his history, the blood of the past. Breeda admired Gerry Adams. "They used to call him 'the big lad,'" she told Pearl, "and then suddenly he was the lowest of the low." But she believed in him. When he said, "No more violence," she felt, for the first time in her life, a little hope. Hearing his voice, seeing his face on the television, she confessed to Pearl that she was going to do it. She was going to vote in favor of the peace agreement like Gerry Adams said. Her family would never know. She would live with the knowledge that if they knew they would think she had betrayed her brother and the blood of all the brothers that had been shed down the years.

We forget that there are moments, public moments, what could be called moments in history that change a life. By *we* I mean those of us who have been brought up, as Pearl had been, in safety and prosperity, whose lives have been shaped by private moments, private acts. We forget, or believe it distantly, as we believe in the orbiting of the planets, the working of DNA. Pearl saw that the peace agreement vote was a moment like that for Breeda. She was doing the first thing she'd ever done that would make her family angry. That they would never know was neither here nor there. Breeda knew it, and she knew herself cut off, for good, or cut away from something. And the cutting away gave her, for the first time, a sense of her own strength. And she was not alone: she could talk to Pearl about it. Pearl admired her for it, and Breeda loved feeling admired by her beautiful intelligent kind friend from America, whom she did not quite understand, but who wanted to listen to her and thought that what she said was important.

Pearl admired Breeda because Breeda had lived in the world, in history, through history; she had no choice but to think about important things that were not just about herself. And so Pearl felt Breeda would help her think about important things. And she could say to Breeda, "I don't understand, I just don't understand who is right, who is wrong, what is right, what is wrong," and Breeda would say, "I don't understand either," and they would talk and talk and try to understand the world, the world that was not just their lives but a part of history.

Good Friday 1998: a crucial day in Irish history. A good Friday, it is believed by many, but not by all. Two elections are held simultaneously, one in the north, one in the south. Both elections ratify the treaty. Breeda and Pearl toast the victory; they buy champagne, which neither of them has ever drunk much; they toast "the big fella" and John Hume, a liberal, a pacifist, once Gerry Adams's enemy and then his colleague in the architecture of the peace agreement, who, not being handsome, they have no nickname for.

Finbar and Mick and the boys toast nothing; they believe they have been betrayed. Mick understands from Pearl's silence during the rants of betrayal and sellout that Pearl does not agree with them, though she never says so. He begins to be critical of her, to make snide comments on her seriousness, her lack of imagination. And then he asks if Joseph and her mother ever "played doctor" when they were growing up.

And what was Stevie doing when his mother and his friend sat by the TV and talked and talked? He did not talk with them. He listened. He was confused. Pearl and his mother (whom he loved) thought one thing; his father and Finbar and the lads (whom he admired, whom he thought exciting, who included him in their drinks and games and jokes and made him feel alive, part of the world) thought the opposite. His mother called Gerry Adams a wonderful fella and his father called him a motherfucker. He knew you could not be both. He was confused. His confusion caused him to suffer. And he suffered, too, as the women spoke more and more to each other as Good Friday and the election approached; talks that did not include him. Pearl seemed not to want to work so much on his stories as to talk to his mother. When the three of them watched movies, the women hardly got through them without talking about the peace agreement. When his father and the boys talked, they shouted, they raised their fists, they lit cigarettes and poured beer into glasses and threw things on the floor and walked around in heavy boots and sang loud songs. They laughed loudly, through cigarette smoke (except for his father, who didn't smoke), they slapped each other on the back to stop themselves from choking with laughter; their laughter heated the air in the room, seemed to tear a hole in something thick and gray. Pearl and his mother rarely seemed to laugh; they would laugh quietly and shake their heads, but their laughter tore through nothing, made no mark. He would visit his father at Finbar's, play cards, walk home in the dark, late, to his mother, to the room that was too warm in places, too cold in others, ashamed of the origami birds he'd made, ashamed of the stories about horses and farm animals, and saw they weren't quite so interested in him anymore, not as interested as they were in each other's talk or what was going on in the world. And when his mother would say to him, Would you have more tea, pet, would you have another biscuit? he felt she was tearing herself away from something, that for the first time in his life he was not the focus of her attention (though she wouldn't have put it like that; she would have said, "the apple of my eye").

When they talked about being afraid, his mother and Pearl, he felt more like them. But he didn't want to be more like them, he wanted to be like the lads, who never mentioned fear, who mentioned struggle and comrades and the glory of the fight. There was no one he loved as he loved his mother, but he knew he couldn't stay with her. The world was frightening, but he had to take his place in it. He loved his mother; he loved Pearl. But he admired his father and the lads. He wanted to be like them.

In June it was time for Mick to go back home; he had a summer theater on Deer Island, Maine, where he'd always summered as a boy. In July they'd be doing *Marat/Sade* and *Waiting for Lefty* in repertory.

Pearl and Finbar were finishing up their term and studying hard together; he made love to her in a new way now, like a tired workman looking for release at the end of a long shift. They were happier than they'd ever been. They got on much better without Mick, and Breeda liked making supper for Pearl and Finbar and Stevie and herself, telling them they were too busy to think of cooking for themselves; it was her pleasure after all they'd done for Stevie.

Maria spoke of coming to Ireland for a visit. Pearl didn't want that. She didn't want to see Maria's look of disappointment at the sight of Finbar; she didn't want to have to explain that Stevie and Breeda's living arrangements suited them, even though they didn't have central heating; they didn't need the kind of flat Maria would have thought essential. She didn't want Maria's searching gaze on her: she liked her life; she didn't want it picked apart by her mother. So when Joseph wrote and told her he was going to Italy in mid-July, just after her term finished, Pearl suggested that the three of them meet up in Rome.

It had been twenty-five years since Maria and Joseph had been in Rome together. Pearl had been to Paris and London and the south of Spain with her mother, but she'd never been abroad with Joseph. Shared vacations had been in rentals on Cape Cod or at the Jersey shore.

Joseph was happy to introduce Pearl to Rome, glad to show her the hotel Santa Chiara, where he had stayed first with Dr. Meyers, then with Maria and Devorah, and later, as a widower, by himself. He enjoyed taking them to his favorite restaurant near the Pantheon, and to the one near the Tritone, and to the little workman's café, nearly impossible to find, behind the boys' school in Trastevere. And he was happy to introduce Pearl to the Puglises, colleagues of her grandfather, and to reacquaint Maria with them after nearly forty years. He was proud to be walking with Pearl and Maria down the Via Nomentana, where the Puglises lived. Pearl wore a long flowered skirt and stiff white blouse that made the angles of her shoulders seem heartbreakingly inexpert. How could shoulders like that get through the world? She needed protection; he felt able to provide it. Never had she seemed more like his daughter than when she stood in the doorway of the Puglises' apartment and he saw the pleased, tender look in their eyes.

Was it his fault that he hadn't realized how the Puglises had changed over the years? Was it his fault that the night Maria and Pearl came for dinner all they wanted to do was talk about the appearance of the

Virgin in Yugoslavia and how a client of Signor Puglise had had a pair of silver rosary beads that turned to gold when he came near the site of the apparition? Certainly, Joseph's disappointment was disproportionate; he felt as though, not realizing who the Puglises really were, he had stolen from Pearl the vision of Europe that had been, for him, such a vivid, irradiating dream. He didn't know that Pearl had had no expectations of the Puglises so she could not be disappointed, only saddened because she could see how disappointed Joseph was. And irritated with her mother when she said, speaking much too loudly, Pearl thought, on the street where they tried to hail a cab, "And this is what my father thought of as the real deal, the real European deal we were all supposed to go down on our knees for? Give me Elvis Presley any day."

Pearl didn't understand how her mother could fail to see the pain Joseph was in. The two of them sat very still in the cab; Joseph declined Maria's offer of a drink and Pearl said she too was tired. She pretended to be asleep while her mother, lying in the twin bed five feet from hers, spoke to her assistant in New York, gave orders, listened to what had gone wrong in her absence, cried out "Shit!" and "Jesus, fuck."

She was glad to be leaving her mother the next day; glad to be leaving Joseph too, because she felt she had failed to comfort him, and she felt him very much in need of comfort; glad to go back to Finbar's flat and to plain, uninspired Irish food, to the TV and the VCR and the hanging origami birds in Breeda's small living room, and to the demanding grammar of the Irish language.

Then came August 15, 1998, one of those days that marks a cleft in the rock of the world — it did so, certainly, for the Irish nation — the day of the Omagh bombing. A bomb placed in a car on a shopping street in a small city in county Fermanagh, a border county in Northern Ireland, exploded on a Saturday morning, the busiest shopping day of the week. Twenty-nine were killed; hundreds were injured.

Pearl and Breeda were coming back from shopping; they'd bought some lovely pears at an open-air market and decided to make a tart. They were walking into Fatima Mansions when a friend of Breeda's, Loretta Shaunessey, came running up with tears in her eyes — "Have ye heard about the bomb?" — so they ran into Shaunesseys' and watched the television for a while, and then they went back to Breeda's flat and sat and watched some more. They did what we all do at the moment of a large disaster — sat hypnotized, watching the details over and over. They learned that five hundred pounds of explosives had been placed in the trunk of the car, detonated from long distance. The day the bombers had chosen — August 15 — made it likely that the majority of the victims would be women and children; it was a prime day for back-to-school shopping. Many Catholic children would, that day, be fitted for their uniforms. It was a Holy Day of Obligation for Catholics: the Feast of the Assumption of the Virgin.

As the hours pass, Breeda and Pearl watch, transfixed; they can scarcely do anything else. They tell themselves they should move away from the set; they tell themselves how awful it is: TV newsmen and women saying to those who have just lost husbands, wives, children, *Tell us what happened, tell us how you feel.* Simultaneously wanting to say to the newscasters, *Leave them alone; for God's sake leave them alone!* and yet avid to know the details of the dead.

Over the days and weeks, Pearl collected

images. Faces. James Barker, who was twelve, and Sean McLaughlin, his friend, both killed. Philomena Skelton, killed, and her daughter, who lived but whose face would be permanently scarred. Lorraine Wilson, seventeen, who died beside her best friend, Samantha McFarland; they were both volunteering at the Oxfam shop. The Omagh dead, not the heroic dead of the Greek friezes, but pathetic in their ordinariness, with their squints and lantern jaws and double chins.

The stories of the survivors. The sister whose last words with the sister who'd been torn to pieces by the bomb had been a fight over taking too long in the shower. The mother who'd encouraged her son to go out to the stores because he seemed unaccountably depressed that morning and she thought just hanging around would make it worse. "I feel so lucky he came back all in one piece. That was more than some others had," the mother said.

The stories of the wounded: the twenty-year-old girl who looked over to see her leg on the street ten feet away from her, the man who heard a child in a wheelchair screaming, the woman who saw a little girl running with no hands. "No one was talking to the child," she said. "Everyone was afraid to look at her." And Pearl thought, Yes, that is what we do: we are afraid to look. And so she would make herself look — past her fear. Make herself hold on to images: The broken main that streamed water so that body parts came sluicing down the street. Downed electric wires sizzling beside the bodies of the dead. The RUC officer who turned over a young woman to find the naked body of an infant underneath her, the baby's arms crossed in front of its chest as if it knew the formal pose for death. The officer's words: "I pronounced extinction on her and, as it turns out, on her mother. When I look at my own daughter's face, I see their faces." *Pronounced extinction.* Pearl thought those were terrible words to use. And then she thought, But what are the good words?

She and Breeda didn't want to talk to anyone. She couldn't bear hearing what Finbar might say. Breeda, who knew Omagh and its shops because she had a cousin who lived there — thank God she hadn't been in town that day — Breeda said, "They knew it would be the day for mothers and children shopping; they knew it and they did it deliberately. It was a diabolical thing."

Diabolical: the word the farmer in Mayo

had used about the plastic covering the hay. But Pearl did not believe in the devil; she kept trying to understand. What could they have had in mind, the planters of the bomb: the Real IRA, as they called themselves, the ones against the peace process, the ones feeling betrayed?

She tried to understand the politics. One reporter suggested that Omagh was chosen precisely because it was a Sinn Féin success story. Sinn Féin, she'd come to learn, was the political wing of the IRA, as distinguished from the military. The injustice of the old jerrymandered districts had been corrected in Omagh: it was a 60 percent Nationalist town with a Sinn Féin–dominated town council. She tried to understand: the Real IRA thought the regular IRA, represented by Gerry Adams, and especially Sinn Féin, was the enemy for having supported the peace agreement. She could understand that. But then what happened to their minds? What could they possibly have been thinking? Who could they be punishing or warning by the death of twenty-nine Protestants and Catholics, mostly women and children, rich and poor?

When Pearl learned that one of the movers behind the bombing was Bobby

Sands's sister Bernadette, she understood that the sister thought she was doing something to mark her brother's death. It was entirely comprehensible, the desire to mark a death. But then other marks would have to be made for other deaths, more and more marks till the surface of the world was pocked with them: marks made for the dead.

She couldn't know what was in their minds; in hers — she cannot banish them, or won't — were the First Communion picture of Sean, the photo of James with his dog, the wedding pictures of Philomena, a policeman's description of an old woman, water streaming over her corpse, a corpse that was only a torso: "I thought it was a dressmaker's dummy at first." The flashing wires, the roof tiles floating along with parts of brains, hands, feet. What could it mean about a person that he or she could imagine such a thing to be in the service of the good?

Her inability to understand, her relentless replaying in her own mind of the images, the faces, made Pearl feel she had lost her grip on the world. She called her mother, and Maria said, Oh, darling, how awful, tell me about it, tell me everything, do you want to come home? But Pearl could tell that in America, the meaning of Omagh was dilute. Her mother was of no help, and Finbar's response appalled her: "It fucks our side but good; it makes us look completely in the wrong."

She only wanted to sit with Breeda, the two of them going over and over the details with each other, saying over and over, "I just don't understand."

And then, in early September, Mick came back, his summer season over, a great triumph theatrically. "People are wrong," he said, "to think summer theater has to be brain candy. They loved *Marat/Sade*. They loved *Waiting for Lefty*. We really raised some consciousness."

Which, he thought, needed to be done about Omagh. He blamed not the bombers but the police; they were given warnings. The warnings were misleading, Pearl tells him, another part of the nightmare: the bombers told the media the bomb would be in front of the courthouse, and it wasn't. The police led the people away from the courthouse, unwittingly to the center of the bomb's radius.

"You believe that shit?" he said. "It's just part of the history of the failure to listen on the part of the Brits and the Unionists.

I don't believe a goddamn word. I believe they were given plenty of warning, but they decided not to respond to it because this would blacken the revolution's name."

Finbar agreed with Mick; all his friends agreed with him. She couldn't bear to be in the same room with any of them. She spent time with Breeda or alone in the flat that she had rented, months before, with Jessica, who e-mailed her from Colorado, where she was hiking with her boyfriend, saying that she was feeling great, all better now, the Rockies were awesome, she never wanted to leave Colorado.

Why didn't Pearl go home then? The semester at Wesleyan had already started; she'd signed up for her courses at Trinity. But it was more than that. She felt she and Breeda needed to work on understanding things together, quietly, slowly; they needed to talk about things, say the same things over and over, try to figure out what had happened. It was not her land, but she couldn't go back to America, where Omagh was just another name of horror, worth, perhaps, thirty seconds for two days on the seven o'clock news. She must stay in Ireland; she must try to understand.

Afterward, Pearl blamed herself for what

happened to Stevie, for not paying attention to him in the way he needed, in the way she and Breeda always did. The country of Ireland would have gone on exactly as it had if they hadn't been paying attention to it, but the boy, if they'd paid attention to him, would still be alive. This is what she tells herself. Because blame is a solid platform we can stand on, a still place in the whirlwind. It tells us: this happened because of that; it could have been avoided. Whereas the unbearable possibility is that nothing can be avoided, the wind bloweth where it listeth and becomes a whirlwind that takes everything up: indiscriminate, violent, incapable of turning or slowing down because of any human word.

So Pearl blames herself for Stevie's spending more time with his father and being susceptible to his puerile ideas, for wanting to regain the attention his mother had always given him, and Pearl had started giving him, by doing something that he thought would make him a man.

At last you will hear the story of Stevie. The story of his death.

I suppose it began like this. One day, Mick and the boys had had too many beers. They were very downcast in the aftermath of the bombing; they felt their side had been discredited. It would be difficult for the Real IRA to recover.

Mick was talking about his theories of theater. The resistance to the Real IRA was a solid wall that had to be blasted through; some explosive gesture was needed to balance the effect of the Omagh explosion. Then he started talking about the explosive power of laughter, how laughter could break up tragedy, blast a hole in it so you could walk through to something else: to revolutionary transformation. How could they get people to see that the dead of Omagh were the victims of the police and not the revolutionaries?

They'd had a lot to drink. None of them were heavy drinkers; the boys were young and Mick was always concerned about his fitness: proud of his flat stomach, his ability to run like any of the boys and better than most. But that day they kept on drinking, and that was when the idea came to them: they'd do guerrilla theater.

Mick brought up a precedent from the history of the Troubles. Around 1910, a group of women factory workers in Belfast had been forbidden to laugh or sing at their jobs. In response, they created something called the "Laughing Protest"; they kept laughing and laughing, forcing themselves to laugh until they drove the overseers round the bend and the absurdity of the ban on laughing was made public. He told them about seeing Jerry Rubin dressed up as Uncle Sam and as Paul Revere, to appear before the House Committee on Un-American Activities. "That's people's theater," Mick said, thumping the table so hard the empty beer cans fell to the floor.

Then he came up with the idea. They would do something to change the focus from the Real IRA to the police, show that the deaths should be laid at their door.

They went out, a pack of them, Mick and five of the boys, to a sex shop that was open late. They bought (charged to Mick's platinum Visa) a set of ten assorted dildoes. They tied them together with a ribbon they'd bought on the way and attached to the bouquet of dildoes a note: *A bunch of cocks as a tribute to the Gardai cockups of Omagh who are responsible for the deaths of twenty-nine.*

How did it fall to Stevie to deliver the package to the Gardai station? The six of them, sitting around the table, had been delighting themselves with the details of the plan. "One of us has to leave the package and get out in a hurry," Mick said. And Stevie, who'd also been drinking more than he'd ever drunk in his life, said, "I'll do it."

"It's brilliant," Mick said, proud of his son for the first time, slapping him on the back to show he was one of the boys: the bravest boy, the most heroic. "Because of Stevie's age, if he gets caught they'll be easy with him."

"Brilliant," everybody said, opening another can of beer and handing it to Stevie, toasting one another and him for their act, which would explode the wall of misunderstanding and resistance and make way for a new world.

★ ★ ★

They phoned the Gardai station, saying there was to be a bomb planted sometime that night. Stevie set off; he was meant to leave the package and run away but he was paralyzed. He set the package down and moved only a few feet from it. Immediately, he was seized by Gardai. Specially trained dogs approached. The package was determined not to be a bomb and was opened in secret.

Breeda and Pearl went to the station together. They made a case for Stevie's innocence; in his confusion, Stevie became even more inarticulate. The police were kind; they didn't tell Breeda what was in the package, and she was too upset to press them. Pearl went along with the line she took.

The police told reporters that the package was the confused work of a feebleminded boy who responded to the Omagh bombing by making a package of sex toys. The newspapers noted that Stevie was the nephew of Reg Donegan, and the headline of the small story read THE BLOOD RUNS THIN.

The explanation of what was really in the box was left to Mick and the boys, and the explosion that occurred was not caused by laughter breaking through the wall of Irish resistance to revolutionary necessity. No one laughed at the package. It was seen as an annoyance, a pathetic act by a near-idiot. The explosion happened in Pearl's mind. She lost her temper.

What is lost when we say *she lost her temper?* Pearl lost her temperateness; she became a body, no longer at body temperature but a boiling thing, a thing on fire. That was what she felt: something inside her had been set aflame, or a flame had touched her somewhere, starting, perhaps, at the soles of her feet, and her blood, her insides, boiled. Whatever its source, the heat of rage took her over. If she could have seen herself, her own aspect might have frightened her. She seemed to swell and grow, her face grew very white, and her eyebrows — which were always noteworthy, being so much darker than her hair — looked exaggerated now against her whitened skin, as if they'd been drawn on with charcoal. She shouted at Stevie. Her mouth was very small but her voice, which he'd always heard as a soft voice, and kindly, was no longer kindly. It was the voice of accusation. It was the voice of rage. He had heard accusation before, heard rage, but he had never expected it in Pearl, with whom he had always felt entirely safe. She looked right at him, and her black eyes were terrible. "How could you have been so stupid, stupid, stupid!" These were the words she said. She said the word *stupid* three times, the word he feared above all others, the word that was to him most terrible. She might have meant it for all of them, but he knew she meant it only for him. And his face lost all its features: went flat, white, like a plate.

Breeda grabbed her son and said she was taking him home. Mick said everyone should cool off; he gave Breeda the keys to "the shack" in Mayo and told her to lie low with Stevie for a while. And then there was the accident.

Stevie was alone, so no one but the driver saw what happened. It was a foggy night. Stevie was standing in the middle of the road. It was not intelligent, to be standing in the middle of the road, but we will never know: was Stevie standing in the middle of the road because he wanted to die? Pearl believes she made him want to die because she had called him stupid. It was what so many people had called him, the thing he feared about himself, the thing she had told him was not true about him: he was gifted, special, of great worth. And then she said it to him just like everybody else.

The driver said he honked his horn but Stevie appeared not to hear. He tried to brake; it was too late. Stevie was dead when the ambulance arrived; it had to come all the way from Castlebar, a twenty-minute drive, but probably it didn't matter. He was killed right away.

Breeda breaks into Finbar's apartment, shouting, her face not a face but a mask, twisted, desperate. Her eyes don't focus. She knocks over furniture, she who'd been afraid to knock too loudly on a door; she turns her uncomposed gaze on them, particularly on Pearl, as Pearl had turned her gaze particularly on Stevie, and says, "His blood is on your hands, the lot of yez, but especially" — she points to Pearl — "on yours!"

The world explodes; the cover is blown off. Pearl sees that all the time underneath this cover — a cover that is fragile, thinner than anyone would have imagined — there is another world, the real world. Exposed now like the rubble of the buildings and the roads of Omagh, the real world: a pit with shouting men, red eyes, open mouths, the twisting faces of the watchers in the paintings of Goya, of van der Goes. And she is one of them. She turned on Stevie. She didn't turn on Mick or Finbar, who were in the room at the same time. She turned on the weakest, the one who would be most harmed. Automatically, as if she had been bred for it. The will to harm.

Afterward, Pearl was tempted to say, embarrassed at the cliché but unable to let go of it immediately, *I don't know what came over me.* As if a net had dropped and she had to thrash and strike out for her own escape. Or as if a fiery rash had come over her skin and she had to scratch herself bloody. But no, she knew quite soon after hearing in her own mind the words *I don't know what came over me* that the cliché was wrong. Nothing came over her. Something came *out of* her, something that had been inside her all along. Was it a snake that traveled from the belly, where it had lain coiled and hidden — since when? Perhaps since birth, uncoiling only now, and traveling like lightning to the brain, biting at the roof of the mouth, the tongue, the jaw's hinge, till it forced the mouth open and then hit its mark. No, that was not it either. It wasn't something other than herself, that could be removed, coaxed out, entrapped, struck to the heart, and buried. What had made her say the words was nothing *but* herself, immovable, flesh of her flesh, embedded in the deepest part of her, and you could hack and hack, think you'd got it, but you would never get the whole thing, there would always be more, and it would always be there, always ready to uncoil and strike.

But what had made it come to life? This snake whose name was insult, this wild biting at the brain, until the words that wanted to annihilate, erase, were out at last: the words insisting *You are nothing, you are nothing; you are much, much less than anything I am.* Because, among the other things, insult is at least this: a release of pressure, a relief.

She saw what Mick and the boys had done as a defilement. They had taken the idea of peace, the images of the Omagh dead, and made a joke of them. Her impulse had been to strike at the sight of defilement. Moses and the brazen snake. The golden calf.

But why had she struck out at Stevie? Why him and not Mick or Finbar? Why at the weakest? That was part of it, that she had struck out at the weakest. Because that was what was done by creatures, of whom she was one. By her kind.

★ ★ ★

"All right, fellas, this is it."

Pearl is surrounded now. She is being lifted again, slowly taken down steps. She sees the whirling blue light of an ambulance. Hears the crackle and buzz of radios clipped to the policemen's belts, like animals riding on their hips, making dangerous noises: grumbles, pops, then words, conveying nothing to her as they lift her — steady, then — they are talking to each other, not to her. The prick in her arm, what was shot into her, has stolen all her clarity. But she is glad to be cut off from their words; she retreats from them to a world of quite small compass: her own skull. She knows that nothing they do now can have meaning. She has planned it well; whatever they think, she knows she is too far gone. *Far gone,* she thinks. But where? Away from them. On her way out of life.

She passes the embassy gates; looks at the round building, remembers being there when something important happened, but she doesn't remember what.

But I can tell you. She came upon something there, you could say it was by accident, but it triggered something. It could have been almost anything. How do we ever trace the charge that unearths the buried — I don't want to call it treasure; let us call it ore. What detonates, and when and where, so that we move in one direction or another, or move at all when we are paralyzed? How does anything, ever, come to be?

★ ★ ★

It was October 10. Pearl had come to the embassy to have her passport renewed. She was waiting in the lobby and picked up *Time* magazine. It was two weeks after Stevie's death.

After Stevie's death and Breeda's accusation she'd felt only shock, as if she'd been given a blow to the head. She couldn't formulate a thought or concentrate on anything. There always was a ringing in her ears, like the after vibration of a siren. It was as if a sheet of slate had been pressed down on her body and her mind; her life was a dull constriction; she found it hard to breathe, eat, and sleep; she kept seeing Breeda's face and hearing her words: *His blood is on your hands.* She would wake up in the midst of a fitful sleep and run to turn on the light to be sure her hands weren't covered in blood, that her eyes were eyes and not sockets covered over with skin. She knew Breeda was right. She had insulted Stevie, taken the heart out of him, so that he cared so little about living he was careless of his life. He'd learned the carelessness from her. *How could you be so stupid!* A sentence spat out in an anger that erased him, to a boy who all his life had feared precisely that sentence. And it came not from an enemy but from her, whom he had trusted. Hers was the mouth.

Her heart was a stone; she could hardly move. Her limbs had lost their nimbleness; her feet feared every step as if the surface of the world might easily, at any moment, give way. She could only tense her body against something, some kind of falling through that she feared but could not yet name.

And then, in the embassy, her eye fell on an article about a seven year-old girl who had been raped and killed in a Las Vegas casino, a resort that advertised itself as "a place for the whole family." The girl had been found dead, her neck broken, sitting on a toilet seat in a restroom of the family-friendly casino. She'd been raped and murdered around four o'clock on a Sunday morning while her father was losing money at the craps table where he'd been gambling all night.

Security officers had found the child wandering alone through the casino at one-thirty on the morning she died. They'd paged her father and turned his daughter over to him with a warning not to violate rules by allowing her to enter the gambling portion of the casino. He apologized, said it wouldn't happen again, led his daughter back to the almost deserted "family fun" section — a video arcade next to the slot machines — and hurried back to the craps table. Alone and bored, the little girl wandered off again.

The rapist and murderer was an eighteen-year-old, a wealthy boy, good-looking, with a history of spending a lot of time in child-porn chat rooms. This brilliant young man, an honors student in his California high school, had often confided to his Net friends a desire to have sex with a child. He enticed the bored little girl into playing a game with the bright orange plastic cones set in a small part of the casino in the predawn hours to indicate danger from wet floors. She had not seen the danger. She followed the handsome boy into the bathroom, into a toilet stall. He raped her there and then broke her neck. He said he broke her neck "to take her out of her misery." He said he knew he'd killed her when he heard the snap. He didn't know all this was recorded on a casino surveillance camera. But it was too late; when the security guards got to the restroom, the child was dead.

Later, officials of the family-friendly casino reported that when they informed the child's father of her death, he proposed a deal. He wouldn't sue the casino if he was given a night of unlimited chips, unlimited beer, an airline ticket to LA, and expenses for his child's funeral.

But there was more. A witness was discovered. The security cameras revealed that a friend of the murderer, who was with him just before the murder, had followed him and the little girl into the restroom and stood on a toilet seat in an adjacent stall to see what his friend was doing with the child. The witness, an honors student at Berkeley, was called the Bad Samaritan. There were calls in the days that followed the murder for the Bad Samaritan to be arrested too. But Nevada law did not demand that a witness stop a killing in progress or even report it.

The young man from Berkeley complained, "Now I'll be known as a witness to a murder, not as an outstanding science student." He said he couldn't understand why some fellow students refused to speak to him on campus or why he was barred from attending his prom. But he expressed satisfaction with offers from television, newspapers, and magazines to tell his story.

He said, "I have a lot of remorse toward the girl's family. They lost a loved one, and that's a tragic event. But the simple fact remains that I do not know this little girl. I don't know people that die of disease in Egypt, I don't know dying children in Panama. The only person I knew in this event was my friend, and I'm sad that I lost my best friend."

She read this article and everything

came together for her. Once again, she felt alive.

She felt it all: the young girl alone at four a.m. wandering in a casino, alone in her final terror. She was with her in everything, her body took in everything. It was one of those moments when a cliché becomes lived out in the body. Pearl, too, heard a snap: she felt the snap of the girl's neck and was snapped out of her paralysis. "I did it to take her out of her misery," the child's killer had said. The words took Pearl out of her own dull misery, into something else, something she wasn't ready yet to name.

And then the other story: *There was a witness.* A sidebar in the magazine, a discussion in the legal community: Does a person have a legal responsibility, if not to stop a crime at least to say what he has seen? Is one compelled, morally, to witness? Is a legal compulsion the next logical step?

Witness. The word spun around in her head, images from who knows what movie, what TV show: the raised hand on the Bible: *Do you swear to tell the truth, the whole truth, and nothing but the truth, so help you God?*

I do.

She felt herself rise up from under the packed earth. The stone slab that had pressed her down below the level of life was thrown up with the force of her new rising.

Witness. The whole truth. Say what you have seen.

And it came to her, everything she had not known she had been seeing in the weeks after Stevie's death. All the faces that had kept coming to her, randomly, now collected in an order that told her what she now knew to be the truth. The human will to harm, in all its shapes, all its varieties. Stories, faces, coming to her in the lobby of the American embassy. Witnesses that what had happened to Stevie — no, what she had done to Stevie — what had happened at Omagh, were not just isolated incidents, they were a proof of the true shape of the world: a world where the desire to harm was the most true thing that could be said about it.

The faces spun toward her: Miss Alice Stevenson and Janet Morehouse, John Lennon and Mark David Chapman. The faces of the Omagh dead. And a voice — only one — the voice of the judge: her voice, hers. *Call the next witness.* And after a while, no need to call them; they came readily, unbidden, spinning against the background of unliving blue, the blue that is in the background, now, of everything she sees. The blue behind her witnesses. And she would be, for her part, judge, jury, and witness herself: witness to the larger world of the crimes her witnesses had reported and the judgments she had made.

She would give her life; she would become a witness. And what is the strongest possible witness? The witness unto death.

When Pearl decided what she would do — that is to say, when she decided she would die — she wondered why it took her so long to think of it, to plan how she'd accomplish it. She wondered why, with all her books of Bobby Sands's writings, and stories about Bobby Sands, and the pictures in the drawer of her flat and all around the apartment, she hadn't thought of him sooner. Bobby Sands, whose name and face are famous all over Ireland. The strong witness. The strong death.

But she would be an even purer witness. She had no demands. Nothing could stop her, nothing anyone could say or give. A strong death. In life she was overwhelmed, weak. In the purity of her death, a death no one can stop once she has set it in motion, she will be strong. Stronger than life.

Stronger than this harmful life in which she too has a part, because she too has been harmful. Harmful unto death.

The back of the ambulance is open, waiting for her. The men with the crackling, buzzing gadgets hooked to their waists lower her, then slide her in. Someone else, not one of them, gets in the ambulance beside her. The door is shut with a bang. Pearl is enclosed now in the hard shell of the ambulance. The faces of her witnesses come to her, as they came in the time when she was deciding what she would do with her life; as they have come again and again since that day in the American embassy. When she decided that she would make a death of it. *Tell the truth, the whole truth, and nothing but the truth. So help you God.* God, like Stevie, a name without a face.

Looking up a few inches only (the only space she has), she sees on the white inside roof of the ambulance, projected (but from where?) as if on a screen, Miss Alice Stevenson and Janet, and the Omagh dead — and one, not silent — John Lennon and Mark David Chapman, and she hears the music, and the words over and over, "All You Need Is Love." *Love is all you need.*

Now she wants to tell her mother that was wrong. Love is not all you need. She remembers, learning in her research on starvation, that in a starving person the heart shrinks so that on an X-ray it is nearly invisible. She wonders if she has a shrunken heart. Perhaps that is why love is not all she needs, not what she needs at all.

She has never doubted that she was greatly loved. But it was not enough to let her to live in a world where her witnesses tell her there is nothing stronger than the will to harm: harm in all its varieties: harm done because it is easy, because someone has something, because someone does not have something; harm done out of carelessness or envy or fatigue, or the hunger for ascendancy, or for the sheer pleasure of lowering the fist. She had not desired to lower her fist, but her fist lowered and a young boy died. And for a long time she felt very weak; her head spun; her limbs would not move. Until she got her idea, right here in the embassy, from the article on the girl killed in the casino. The idea of witness. Witness by starvation.

The strong death.

One of the young men in uniform, encased in the ambulance shell beside her, takes her arm. "IV fluids," she hears. They keep punching the inside of her arm, light shallow punches. "Make a fist, Miss Meyers; can you make a fist for us?" But she will not. Make a fist? The idea seems so ludicrous it makes her smile. "Almost impossible to find a vein," the man is saying. "This level of dehydration." He opens the door. *"Get Morrisey!"* she hears.

Somebody else takes his place beside her. Ties a tube around her arm below the elbow. Then the shallow punches once again. And then a piercing, hot and sharp, and someone says, Bravo.

"It's all those years with neonates," the woman says, the doctor, what was her name? Pearl does remember *neonates*. What does that mean? Oh, yes, Pearl thinks: newborns. She wants to laugh: but I am nearly newly *dead*. The woman pops out, fast. "Quick as you can." The car bounces once, twice, as she gets out and the man gets in. An engine starts up. In front of her eyes, the faces of her witnesses are framed, with their stories, against cold blue. She is being driven now. She smiles, because they think they are doing something that will save her, and she knows it is much too late.

Dubliners

· 13 ·

They are wheeling Pearl down a corridor. The lights shine in her eyes. She is still happy; they are too late. They lay her in a bed; they take her clothes off.

They dress her in what feels like paper. One of them holds down her hands. Another tells her to open her mouth. She refuses. They open it against her will. They shove a hard tube, the width of a pencil, into her nose and down her throat. She begins to retch. "Steady now. If you fight, you'll make it worse." How can she fail to fight? They are trying to steal what she has worked so hard to accomplish. A needle pierces the inside of her elbow. A tube is attached to her arm. They speak. "Pray God we're not too late." And worse: "The mother's been contacted. She's on her way."

Don't, she tries to say, but she knows that because of the tube she cannot be understood.

A young man stands beside the bed. "I'm Tom," he says. "I'm a medical student. I have to be keeping an eye on you, me or one of my mates, to make sure you won't be doing harm to yourself."

Harm, she wants to tell him, harm; yes, harm is something I know about.

"What were you trying to say? I'll try to help," he says.

"Not my mother," she says.

"You don't want to see your mother?"

She shakes her head as hard as she can: no mother. "Tell the doctor not to let my mother in. Tell the doctor: Joseph won't make me."

"Joseph?"

She doesn't answer. She has drifted away.

· 14 ·

Maria is finding it difficult to pull herself up from sleep. She has dropped down or has been dropped — by her friend's Halcyon pill — yet it seems to her that she has willed it, as if she had jumped through a hoop, like a show dog or a showgirl, but not triumphantly, not to applause, but to silence, deep snow, darkness. And because she has dropped down so far, it is a struggle for her to respond to the flight attendant's voice. "We're landing in Dublin."

Dublin. Pearl. Pearl is in Dublin, trying to make herself die. Maria is here to stop it.

She must get to her instantly. Every step of the way is a torment: passport, customs. She wants to scream, Don't you know that this is an *emergency!* Why hasn't someone from the embassy cleared her way? Why is no one here to help her?

She gets through customs. Walks down a hall and through a series of doors. Sees the sign, in Irish and in English: WELCOME TO DUBLIN. She was never tempted to travel

341

to Ireland; she'd had too much to do with too many Irish priests, been irritated by their provincialism, their puritanism. Dublin in her mind was a city whose life finished in 1922, the year of *Ulysses*. A city in literature, in history. Her daughter, maybe, is becoming a part of history. She hears the words from *The Wizard of Oz*: "You'll be history. You'll be history. You'll be hiss, you'll be hiss, you'll be history." Munchkin voices, mad-sounding, frantic. The words wheel and circle in her brain. Then another voice, calmer: "One by one we are all becoming shades." "The Dead," her favorite story, from the collection named for the city she's about to enter. That was the point, wasn't it, that the living were turning into the dead? All right, but not her daughter. It doesn't help to think like that. That was why she gave up that kind of reading. It won't help her daughter now for her to have visions of souls whirling in snow. It probably isn't even snowing.

★ ★ ★

Maria hails a taxi to the embassy. It takes her to an area that is beginning to look suburban, and she thinks the driver must be mistaken. "Are we going to the American embassy?" she asks, and he says, "We

342

are so," and she wonders if he resents her lack of faith. He stops the car in front of a building that is not what she imagined any embassy could be. No grandeur here, no imperial display, no suggestion of men in elegantly cut suits making decisions that could reinvent the globe. This is a building badly thought up, an ill-digested, circular misunderstanding of the modern. She has expected crowds: spectators, policemen, surrounding Pearl. But the area around the entrance is empty; there are the usual guards but no throng of onlookers. Pearl isn't there. She runs up the shallow stairs. Should she ask the guards? What would it be, polite? "Excuse me, my daughter was chained to the flagpole here; would you happen to know what's become of her?" Or frantic? "If my daughter is dead, you must tell me instantly."

A guard asks her business. She tells him she is here to see Caroline Wolf, the woman for whom she was told to ask. She gives her name and is told to wait.

She wants to rush at the guard and say, I cannot wait! I need to know this instant if my daughter is alive! But she sits down, sweating with the effort of inaction. Breathe in, breathe out. Hope for the best. Believe the best. Believe that she is not among the dead.

She trains her eye on the double glass doors, as if fixity of focus can make something happen. A woman in a red knit suit with brass buttons and hard-sprayed blond hair approaches.

"Ms. Meyers? Caroline Wolf."

Another southern accent. Maria doesn't at the moment have the impulse to overcome regional prejudices. Or to make small talk or ordinary polite exchanges.

"Where's my daughter? Is she all right?"

"She's been taken to the hospital. She's in good hands. Would you like to come into my office?"

"I want to see my daughter."

"Please come into my office. I have some information for you."

Maria would like to scream, *Just tell me which hospital. Don't waste my time!* She digs her nails into her palms, ordering herself to be obedient, something she hasn't had to do in thirty years. Obedience was something she gave up when she left the world of the Catholic Church for the secular universe. Now it's a skill she must reemploy. Is it something you never forget, like riding a bicycle? Walk slowly. Keep your mouth shut. Do exactly as she says.

Maria follows her into a small bare office. A minor diplomat. Where is the ambassador?

Then she remembers: it's Sunday, two days after Christmas: skeleton staff. She sees a skeleton staff. She sees a skeleton. She wills herself to stop seeing it.

"We're very lucky in our ambassador. She's a mom herself, you know."

Maria wants to say, Of course I know, do you think I've been on Pluto? Jean Kennedy Smith, sister of the more famous brothers. She thinks, The ambassador will understand me. She wants the ambassador. The 1960 pull. The Kennedys are on our side. And therefore we shall overcome.

"The ambassador has seen to it that criminal charges aren't being pressed against your daughter. It was a wonderful thing for her to do."

"I'm very grateful," Maria says, barely able to stop herself from lunging across the desk and grabbing the papers in Caroline Wolf's hands, shuffling them wildly, throwing them around the room till she finds the doctor's name, the hospital. She understands that Caroline Wolf has no sympathy for Pearl, whom she thinks of as a girl who has spoiled her holiday.

"The ambassador would have been well within bounds to allow criminal proceedings. I can think of many another ambassador in her position who would have dealt

345

with it as a criminal matter. After all, your daughter was trespassing on United States property. But the ambassador's not that sort of person. And it was quite a scene: the police having to cut the chain, carry her out. It's a shame the media got hold of it, but I guess that's what she wanted, your daughter. I think our people here are going to be able to softball it. I mean, everyone seems pretty committed to keeping it pretty low key."

"Thank you," Maria says again.

"This was on the ground next to your daughter. A sort of statement." She hands Maria a piece of typewritten paper in a plastic see-through envelope, also two regular envelopes: one with Maria's name on it, one with Joseph's. Maria begins to read the statement; she will not open the envelope addressed to her in front of this woman.

You and I already know what the statement says; we have already read it, but it is new to Maria and the effort to understand strikes her like a speeding truck, like a boulder rolling toward her from the top of a mountain, like a roaring fire that consumes her mind. How can she understand what these words say? Her daughter wants to mark the death of a boy she has never heard of? Her daughter wants to die for a peace agreement she hadn't given a thought to ten months earlier? Her daughter wants to die because human beings want to harm one another? Her daughter is insane? Is a fool? Is speaking the truth? Which is the right interpretation: insanity, folly, or the truth? But what does her understanding matter? The thing is, she must get to Pearl, and she must use the power of the American government to do it. She must use Caroline Wolf.

"May I have this, please?" she asks, holding Pearl's statement.

"You may have a copy of it. We're keeping the original for our file."

"Thank you," Maria says, wondering what the file is. Will it do Pearl future harm? She does not consider what you and I might think: If she has a future. She does not allow herself that thought.

Caroline Wolf goes into another office and comes out a minute later with a copy of the page for Maria.

"On our end here, we've pretty much signed off on this. We've written a report that pretty much gives our position. You're welcome to read it. It should be viable in a day or two."

"Thank you."

"Right now it's the hospital's issue. Your daughter is in the psychiatric ward. I don't know the doctor in charge, but here's her name; I'm turning you over to her at the hospital." She hands Maria a piece of paper with a phone number.

Over and out, Maria wants to say, but simply says *thank you* again. It's occurred to her that she hasn't said *thank you* so frequently in this short a space of time in her whole life.

"May I use the phone?" Maria asks.

Caroline Wolf gestures but makes no move to leave the room.

Maria dials the number. "Dr. Morrisey is unable to speak to you until this afternoon," the secretary says. "She's expecting your call. She'll certainly get back to you."

"I'll just come to the hospital."

"The doctor will be unavailable until this afternoon. Please settle in and try her again then."

Caroline Wolf has been listening. "Why not check into the hotel we've booked for you? You don't want to carry your luggage around all day. Everything possible is being done for your daughter. There's nothing for you to do."

There is a dotted line of rage at the top of Maria's skull, as if someone were stitching a line in black thread. There is nothing for her to do because no one will let her do anything. No one will let her see her daughter. They are keeping Maria in chains. Her daughter, they told her, has been in chains. Pearl's chains have been cut; hers have not. She must calculate; she must keep everyone's goodwill in case, somewhere down the road, she needs their help. She refuses even to contemplate the possibility that there will not be a road on which to need help.

But she will go to the hotel. Joseph said he'd meet her there; he may be there already. Yes, this is the best thing to do. She knows it is the best thing and hates that the best thing to do is to do nothing except wait. Waiting is penitential to her, a hair shirt. Penance for what? What sin? She has no choice.

Maria doesn't want to be grateful to Caroline Wolf for anything, but she's glad someone has booked her a hotel. And called her a cab.

As soon as the cab takes off, Maria opens the envelope and reads the letter addressed to her. She reads it as if it were on fire, as if the words would disappear if she didn't absorb them with terrific speed.

What does Pearl mean? That she knows she was loved, but that it didn't matter. That she wants to die because she has no hope, but that she knows her mother to be more hopeful than she? How can it be, that her daughter is a person of no hope? She has failed, she has failed in the most important thing a mother can do for a child: to give her hope in life. How can she understand this? She leans her cheek against the cold window of the taxi; she closes her eyes.

Her hotel, the driver tells her, is "on the key side." On the key side of what? she wants to ask, and then realizes she is very tired. She cannot make a picture from these words until she reads the word *quay* on a sign attached to the wall, pronounces it first *kway,* then reminds herself that the sound is not long *a* but long *e.* Quay: a word she has never in her life spoken, only read.

Tall gray buildings that seem to have no windows loom along treeless streets. Practical. Censorious. Structures bereft of comfort, of forgiveness. Always there is so much to be forgiven, so much to forgive. She castigates herself for sentimental phrasing. She has nothing to forgive Pearl for. She has committed no offense. As for her own offenses — well, she won't think of them right now. I did what I could, she says to the slate-colored water, to the stones drained of light. I did my best.

She wonders what, to Pearl, seems unforgivable.

Do we agree with Maria, that she did her best and Pearl needs no forgiveness? Are we tempted to say that Pearl needs to be forgiven for failing to appreciate the gift of her life, for putting her mother through this terror, perhaps even for dramatizing her own suffering in a world where suffering is the norm? It doesn't matter what we think. Maria believes her daughter is in no need of forgiveness. She always has. Maria, so quick to judgment, so quick to cut off, to condemn, has never felt it necessary to accuse her daughter. Her daughter has seemed to her entirely innocent, entirely good. So it would not occur to her now, for the first time, to think of Pearl as someone who needs to be forgiven.

And yet this is not quite the case. There were times when, although she never doubted that she loved Pearl, she didn't really like her. There were even times when her presence was repellent: the years when Pearl would sleep nearly all day on the weekends and then sit in filthy pajamas eating junk food in front of the television, not rousing herself till the sun went down. When she wanted to say to her, You're not even quite clean; don't you know you need a shower, your hair is dirty, you smell bad? Days of monosyllabic answers to the questions: How's it going? What's up? Everything all right in school? Days when their eyes never met and she thought, My daughter is lazy, my daughter has no imagination; at her age I was up, out, doing things all the time, with lots of friends. Not just one. Not just Luisa, whom Maria admired but felt had too much power over Pearl. The sight of them, eating cereal out of the box or leaving their dishes, three quarters full of milk, with flakes or o's floating on the top, wiping their mouths with the backs of their hands on the way into the living room to watch more MTV, could put her into a rage. Did she think these were things that needed to be forgiven? No, she wasn't thinking that then, and certainly not now.

As her for idea that she has done her best, we know Pearl does not think that. But do we take the mother's or the daughter's side? It depends, I guess, upon whether we see ourselves in the position of parent or child.

The taxi leaves Maria at the Tara Arms

Hotel. The desk clerk is a young girl whose hair will not lie flat and yet cannot come up to the ambitious height the girl is trying for. It's awkward hair, Maria thinks, a girl's hair masquerading as a woman's, hair that wants to run down the girl's back like water, but she won't let it; she has set it in stiff rollers; she has sprayed it to a fare-thee-well. What does that mean? Maria wonders. What would it mean to spray something to a fare-thee-well?

The girl says, "Terribly sorry, but your room isn't available quite yet."

Maria puts down her bag and says, "I see," but tears come to her eyes, because she cannot bear her luggage anymore, cannot bear her upright skeleton, and cannot, simply cannot, contemplate calling the hospital from a public booth, standing with her luggage, fumbling with unfamiliar coins (she has none anyway, only paper money).

The young girl, catching her eye, is merciful. "Sit here in the lobby. We'll bring you a cup of coffee and get your room for you as quickly as we can." A generic mercy, perhaps; she may be a girl who would be merciful to anyone she encountered. She cannot possibly know Maria's situation — that it is dire, that her daughter is on the edge of becoming one of the dead, that it is up to Maria to persuade her daughter to live. Hold on, she must say to Pearl, but in exactly the right way; her words must be the right life preserver to throw to her daughter. So that she can preserve her life. But now all she can do is wait. The girl knows none of this. She is simply merciful.

Maria drinks weak coffee (instant?) in the lobby of the Tara Arms Hotel. The colors of the carpet hurt her eyes. A background of electric blue, acidic, acrid, on which there are imposed designs (an urn? a series of urns?) the color of fresh blood. Green leaves that remind her of the Pine-Sol or Lestoil (*There's less toil with Lestoil*) that sat in the bottom of Marie Kasperman's bucket like the signs of eventual corruption: the proof of original sin. On the carpet, a border of lighter blue. She thinks of an aftershave one of her high school boyfriends used: Aqua Velva. The words of the advertisement come to her: *There's something about an Aqua Velva Man.* When she needs to think of exactly the right words to save her daughter's life, why are these jingles for cleaning products and aftershave the only thing her mind will settle on?

Nothing in the lobby is pleasing to the eye except the flames that rise up from the fireplace. The hearth is cream-colored false brick; the mantel is surrounded by imitation stone embedded in the pseudo-wood of the reception desk in an abstract pattern in what appears to be stained glass but is really plastic. Joseph will hate this room, she thinks, and the idea of his disappointed face makes her angry because she knows him, and the first thing registering on his face will be aesthetic displeasure — before sympathy, grief, or a willingness to help. So that the first sight of him will be of no comfort to her. She blames her father for bequeathing to Joseph this curse of relentless aesthetic judgment, as automatic now as sensitivity to heat or cold, that trumps the living humors in their messy flow of grief or pleasure, joy or hate. Some of the best people she knows do not have what her father called "the seeing eye." But she has the legacy as well; she can't be indifferent to her surroundings. The lobby of the Tara Arms Hotel can't help but bring her discomfort.

She walks over to the table where the newspapers are piled. It is impossible for her to refrain from looking. Pearl is not on the front page. On page three there's a headline, US STUDENT CHAINS SELF TO EMBASSY FLAGPOLE, and, in smaller print, *Hunger Striker Supports Peace Agreement*. A photograph of a limp white figure — it could be a corpse — being carried by the police.

We will read the story with her.

An American student claiming not to have eaten in six weeks is under suicide watch at St. Giles Hospital after chaining herself to the flagpole at the American embassy here to protest "the human will to do harm."

Police said they had forcefully cut through her chains after failing to convince the student to free herself voluntarily. They found a "manifesto" on the ground beside her saying that she was acting against the violence that had followed approval of the Good Friday agreement.

The twenty-year-old woman, Pearl Meyers, had been studying Irish at Trinity since arriving in Dublin last January. Mentioned in her manifesto, police said, was Stephen Donegan, nephew of Reg Donegan, the IRA bomber who is serving a thirty-year term in Brixton prison for his role in a car bomb attack in Leeds in May 1982 that killed two people and injured fifteen others.

The police said they had briefly detained Stephen Donegan three months ago in connection with what was described as a prank involving sex toys at Central Gardai Station. Two weeks after the incident, young Donegan was killed in an auto accident in Mayo.

But Miss Meyers insisted in her "manifesto" that he be "mourned as a victim of the Troubles." She said she had some responsibility for his death and was offering her life "in witness" to his goodness and to the goodness of the peace agreement and to protest the evil of continued violence.

Maria's first response is outrage: How do they know she is under suicide watch and I don't? How have they gotten to speak to the police, the doctors, and I have not? She wants to call the newspaper and demand an explanation. But as she is planning how to do that, the girl behind the desk, the helpful girl, says in her merciful voice, "Your room is ready now."

She will phone the newspaper and the doctor from her room. She goes up in the elevator, which is barely large enough for her, the bellboy, and her bag. The boy opens the door to her room. As in the lobby, the light wood looks ersatz and there is another assaultive carpet, but the pattern of this one is different: gray on darker gray. The matching curtains and spread, a floral paisley type chosen by every inexpensive hotel chain in the world, are of a thickness to keep out light but not substantial enough for warmth or comfort. She does not unpack her bag. Instead, she goes back down to the lobby. She is hungry; she will make her calls after breakfast, which the helpful girl says is still being served. Her badge says her name is ORLA; she is standing next to a girl whose badge says TRAINEE, and for a moment Maria thinks this, too, is a traditional Irish name. She wants to laugh at that, but there is no one to laugh with, and she is tired and afraid of what will happen to her mind if she begins to laugh alone.

She must try to make sense of Pearl's statement. But she tells herself to eat first. She will not repeat the error of the earlier coffee. She rejects the limp-looking fried eggs and bacon in favor of a boiled egg and toast. The toast comes in a metal rack; it is thin and cold and the egg is underdone, too runny for her taste. She'd asked for three minutes; this is two.

She reads both Pearl's statement and the newspaper article. Who is Stevie Donegan? And his imprisoned uncle Reg? What does Pearl have to do with the morass of Irish politics, she who had no interest in politics at all?

Maria's concentration is broken by an overloud American voice. "This is what they call scrambled eggs? It's rather like a poor omelet, I'd have thought."

She doesn't know about American tourists to Ireland. It is often not a pretty sight: Americans assuming, wrongly, a familiarity with a country they think of as a fifty-first state, digging for their roots like fool's gold.

She looks over at the speaker, a woman in loose-fitting navy blue sweat pants and matching jacket, a red turtleneck underneath. Maria recoils from the too-girlish laugh, the stolen English diction — "rather like a poor omelet" — put on for the benefit, Maria is sure, of the woman's companion, who actually is an Englishwoman, with a stiff English haircut and bad dentures.

"Not that I'd say anything to them directly about the eggs. I mean, I hate that kind of traveler. I've just been on one too many tours for that sort of thing. There's always one or two who spoil everything complaining about the food. You remember that time I said to that fellow — oh, what was his name, I can't remember — oh, yes, Thornton, that was his first name; I remembered it because of Thornton Wilder. I said to him, 'If you're going to do nothing but complain, just stay home.' Everyone was really grateful. People kept coming up to me and thanking me. They were all sick of his ruining every meal with his complaints, but I was the only one with the guts to speak up. Well, I always was that way. You know that, Margaret. I really settled his hash."

Why did you come here? Maria wants to ask. Why don't you go home? Why don't you shut up? The skin around her eyes is fragile from fatigue; she's afraid it will crack if she touches it. Still, she wants to cover her eyes and ears to block out these women and the blaring of the television set, elevated like a worshiped god. But if she could cut out the sensations coming to her from the outside, she would have only what was in her own mind, more seriously tormenting than the chatter of the women or the overbright TV commentators, speaking of the weather in the west.

If she banishes the stimulus of the outside world, she will have to say the words "Who is my daughter?" To come to terms with the strangeness of the idea that her daughter is someone she doesn't know — as you would have to recognize, lying on the side of the road on which you were being driven in an ambulance, a limb that had been cut off your own body.

Her daughter is doing things, saying things, the meaning of which she cannot even begin to understand. Her daughter is under a suicide watch. Her daughter is saying that because of the death of a young boy of whom Maria has never heard, because of the Irish peace process, in which Maria has only marginal interest, because of the nature of human beings to do harm, she is ready to die. But who has harmed you? she wants to say to Pearl, shaking her by the shoulders impatiently, a prosecutor, not a comforter. Have I not kept you away from harm? If anyone had harmed you, couldn't you have come to me? The loud woman's words come to her mind: I would have *settled their hash*. She sees herself stirring up an enormous mountain of hash, and bringing her daughter to it by the hand, so she could watch her mother flattening it down, smoothing it with a shovel.

There is the terror that her daughter

could die; there is the grief that Pearl didn't confide in her. She knows nothing of what Pearl has been going through. Her daughter has been planning death and all the while Maria believed she was absorbed in following the contours of the Irish language, and if she had lost herself it was in that. Or because of some new boy who must be, like all Pearl's boys, a loser. Maria has always wished these boyfriends had been beautiful, like Pearl, or successful, or interesting and lively. But she has never said to her, Why are you with such a loser, why another loser, why again? And she has never said to herself, If these are losers, what is it that is being lost?

She knows herself to be the loser now. She may be losing her daughter; she has already lost access to her. She is frightened, as if she were walking down a dark corridor, aware that there are doors on each side, rows of them, all knobless, none of them responding to her touch. She knows there is a touch that is the right one, but she does not know what it is. Only that it is not hers. Her daughter is acting in a way she can't understand.

Once Pearl was in the world, Maria quickly understood she couldn't make her do what she wanted. She said to her daughter: Live only for yourself. What she really meant was, Live for yourself, but in a way that I approve of.

And now, with an urgency she'd never dreamed of: Simply live.

No, Maria thinks, I will not permit you to choose death. No longer the democrat, the rational respectful parent, she says in her heart what she would like to say to Pearl: I don't care what you want. You are my child. I will not allow you your own life if all you want to do is throw it away. Whatever you believe you want, I will keep you alive. I will press my mouth against yours and keep it there even if you resist my breath. I will breathe into you, with or without your consent. I will consume your wish to die. You cannot resist me. You won't win. Having once come from my body, you will bend to my superior, my far more ancient will — not only mine but every mother's throughout history. You will succumb and once again be more mine than your own.

"But I'd never go on another tour again. I'm so tired of those men buzzing around, those widowers. All they want is someone to cook and clean for them. Well, that's not the only thing; they think they have a last chance for some sex. Of course I like some male attention. I like a man to go to the theater and the opera with. But I wouldn't get married on a bet. I've had five proposals since I retired in 'eighty-nine. All five of them were impossible."

"I never get proposals," the other woman says.

"Well, you're the lucky one."

The idea that these women might soon be reading about Pearl fills Maria with outrage. What right have you to know anything about my child, of her and my trouble? Of her sorrow? Of her torment?

Trying to look casual, she picks up the newspapers and carries them out of the breakfast room that is, by night, a bar and always smells of beer. She will keep the newspaper from these two women. There is, at least for now, something she can do. Something she is able to prevent.

· 15 ·

"*Due ore in ritardo* — two hours' delay," the woman at the desk says. She pronounces *delay* delie, and for a moment Joseph thinks she is saying *two hours' delight,* and he wants to tell her he isn't interested. He tells her it's urgent that he get to Dublin, but all flights are delayed because of weather.

He has no interest in the drinks at the bar, the luxury goods for sale, even the coffee and snacks that are available. This is torment; this is entrapment: to be here in Leonardo da Vinci Airport when Pearl is in Dublin, perhaps near death. He walks up and down; then, feeling conspicuous, he sits down and tries to read his book, his biography of John Ruskin.

Ruskin, he reads, was so sensually starved as a child that he became obsessed with the pattern in the sitting room carpet. He tries to settle himself with the little boy, hungrily tracing the pattern in the carpet, but he cannot stop thinking, Where is Pearl? What condition is she in now?

He looks at the list of illustrations in his

book. She is there, Ilaria del Carretto, elegant in marble, elegant in her deadness. He would like to pray to her, but she is merely a dead young woman, not a saint. Can you pray to beauty, to the ideal of beauty that Ruskin gave his life for? No, you have to pray to a face. He cannot pray to Ilaria's face, a face without a story, so closed in its deadness. There is no face he can pray to. Not to Devorah, who was certainly not a saint, whom he suspects he no longer loved by the time she caught her heel in the hem of her gray wool skirt, carrying a ficus down the stairway; you cannot pray to someone who has disappointed you. Pearl has never disappointed him. His love for Devorah was diminished, like a sugar figure in the rain. His love for Pearl is not diminished; she has never disappointed him, not one bit. How can he pray to one who was less great for the safety of someone greater than herself?

He feels his heart like a lump of hard fat in the middle of his chest. He feels his terror like a bone caught in his throat. There is nothing to do. Swallow this terror, he tells himself, but he cannot cough it up as if it were a fish bone cutting off his breath.

There is nothing for him to do but wait.

In Rome, in the airport of Leonardo da Vinci, whom Ruskin taught us how to see.

He phones Maria to say his plane will be late. She isn't in her room; the clerk asks if he wants to have her paged.

No, thanks, he says. Just give her my message, please.

· 16 ·

Dr. Morrisey sits down in the chair beside
Pearl's bed. We have met her already, you
may remember. She was the one who cut
Pearl's chains; it was she who was able to
start the IV when the others couldn't. She is
youngish, blond, a short woman with a muscular body. Her eyes are gray, the eyes of a
candid boy, a boy adept at collection
(stamps, rocks) or the minor, nontheoretical
sciences (botany, taxonomy). Eyes that
would seem to have very little in them of animal warmth, no sign of instinct or of appetite. This is misleading; this is the effect of
her glasses, thick but not unfashionable.

"I'm Dr. Morrisey," she says. "I don't
know if you remember me from the time at
the embassy. I'll be in charge of your case.
I'd like to ask you some questions."

Pearl won't say a word.

"When's the last time you had something to drink?"

She turns her head away.

"I'm just going to check on some
things." The doctor moves the sheets back

so that Pearl's legs are exposed; touches her feet, presses them, pinches the skin on her hand. Pulls the sheets up again.

"You could die as a result of dehydration. We need to know when you drank last so that we can help you."

Help me? There is nothing you can do to help.

"We need to do some tests on you now you've had some fluids. Can you stand up at all?"

Pearl closes her eyes.

"I'm going to have to insist that you try to stand up."

Insist all you want, she thinks. There's nothing I will do for you.

"I would prefer not to do it this way, but I have no choice," the doctor says. She comes back with two nurses. They lift Pearl to her feet. She tries to collapse. They force her upright.

"We have to do postural vital signs," she says to the nurses. "Keep her that way, if you can."

The nurses hold her up; the doctor attaches a blood pressure cuff to her arm. Squeezes the bulb. The pressure on her arm, the force of being made to stand, the fear that they will steal her death are overwhelming her. She begins to cry. But she can only grimace. Tears will not come. She feels the sense of overflowing, but nothing flows from her eyes.

"You see, the dehydration is so bad she can't produce tears. I've seen tearlessness before, mostly in babies. It's a dangerous sign."

They lay her down, cuff her again, squeeze the bulb.

"The pressure's way different sitting and lying down. The signs both point to acute dehydration. This is very bad."

No, it's very good, Pearl thinks, and, closing her eyes, allows herself to smile. Tom, the medical student — the suicide watcher, as she thinks of him — comes back into the room. He sees she is smiling. She sees his worried face, and she is sorry for him. When she dies, when she achieves what she has worked for, he will have been seen to fail.

"I don't want my mother allowed in to see me," Pearl says, in a voice that is not a voice but a croak. "I won't cooperate unless you promise."

"She's flown all the way from America. She's in Dublin now," Dr. Morrisey says.

"I want her kept out," Pearl says. The tube in her throat makes it difficult for her to talk.

"I'll take it under advisement," the doctor says. "I won't do anything without consulting you. I promise there'll be no surprises."

I don't promise anything at all, Pearl thinks. I don't promise that I'll cooperate as I suggested; there are no questions of honor for me anymore, except to keep the promise of my death. She knows that, up to now, she has always been a person of her word. But now her words are precious; the only real ones are the words that make up the sentence of her death. Death sentence . . . the sentence of my death, she thinks, and smiles again, and worries once more that Tom, who watches her, is troubled by her smiling.

Hazel Morrisey is glad that at least she was able to make some connection with her patient, to offer something that might be the beginning of a bond. Even if it is only that she will prevent the mother from seeing her child, something which, as a mother herself, she finds disturbing.

But Pearl Meyers is her patient; Pearl is her concern. She can't allow herself to consider Pearl's mother's feelings or her own. She is a doctor; her job is to heal. In this case, to keep this girl alive.

Since she heard the first details of Pearl's case, she has known that creating any kind of relationship would be difficult. She is the doctor on call at the hospital. Her primary job is to keep her patient alive. In the best of cases, she will succeed and then pass her on to someone else for long-term care. How can she suggest that Pearl can trust her, can rely on her, when their relationship will be so short?

Hazel Morrisey is a psychiatrist who specializes in teenagers in acute distress,

distress unto death. But when she was Pearl's age and a medical student, she didn't imagine she would do this kind of work. She is an interesting woman, Hazel Morrisey, with an interesting history.

When she finished her degree, Dr. Morrisey traveled, like many Irish, to Somalia to work in the famine. She was overwhelmed by it, wasted body after wasted body. She would save a life, many lives, but it didn't seem to matter. There were so many who couldn't be helped. And even if she saved everyone she saw, there would be more and more. She would hear of shipments of food rotting in warehouses because of bureaucratic errors. She would think of the waste of food, good food in garbage bins behind restaurants, on the sidewalks of suburban towns. She envied people who turned these perceptions into solutions she found oversimple: that there were the greedy and the victims, and the greedy must be punished so the victims could have their share. These people were given an energy by their beliefs, as some of her brother's friends were given energy by siding with the IRA, but she couldn't do that either. Temperamentally, she liked to consider things carefully, from all sides, not rush into plans that could turn out to be disastrous. So she didn't know what could be done about her country, what could be done about the famine in Somalia. And she woke every morning, dead inside, to face dying body after dying body. A wave of them, endless to her.

She stayed her time; she knew that she did good, yet she left feeling a failure. She came home to her mother in Cork City and allowed herself to be cared for like a child. This went on for a month, six weeks. She decided she no longer wanted to treat sick bodies, to patch them up and send them on their way. The prospect of ailing bodies was dissatisfying to her imagination. In some ways it was impossible; in some ways it was too easy. She wanted a different relationship with death and body. Not just to treat a dying animal who would, whatever she did, somehow die of something. She would have a different relationship to illness. She would treat illness of the mind.

Dr. Morrisey retrained in psychiatry and found herself drawn to adolescents. Her time in Somalia had shown her the effects of hunger; it interested her that young people would choose death by hunger in places in the world where this could be a choice. She began treating anorexics, drawn to them in part by vanity, because most doctors didn't like treating them (for most they were an unsympathetic lot). She sympathized with anorexics. She would keep them alive. Observe and treat their desperation, the desperation of their hatred for their own flesh, which they would burn up, consume, with the avidity of the old saints. Feed them and wean them from an ideal of perfection, which was really the ideal of death.

Pearl is interesting to her. Hazel Morrisey understands her feelings of being overwhelmed by the world, her desire for purity. She is interested in this girl whose language is the body and yet not the body: who wants to use her body, use her death. But she may only say Pearl is an interesting case. Her job is to keep her alive with chemicals: nutriments, psychotropic drugs. To give her, for a little while, the sense that she is not alone. And then give the real work over to somebody else.

She worries, of course, that her identification with the patient will compromise her effectiveness as a doctor. This was not a problem she had to concern herself with when she specialized in internal medicine. But now she's a psychiatrist, and there is a word for the danger of overidentification:

it's called countertransference. She is the kind of psychiatrist who still believes in this sort of thing, this kind of language. There are others who would say their responsibility is to find the correct drug for the problem that seems to be in the patient's way, no different from trying to find the right chemotherapy for a cancer patient. She is young enough to have been trained in the usefulness of psychotropic drugs, but she is of a sufficiently complicated nature to believe there is more — that beyond the chemical soup there is something else. A self, a soul? She will not concern herself with the proper naming of this other thing, but she believes in the power of language, if not to cure at least to begin to heal. So how should she talk to Pearl Meyers? She cannot say, What you are doing is quite interesting, in some ways admirable. She cannot suggest a connection between them that will go on for more than a very short time. What she must do is try to make this tormented young woman feel less alone, less helpless — while understanding that, in thwarting Pearl's plan for her own death, she will have made her feel more helpless than before.

But she's made a beginning. She's said she'll respect Pearl's wish to keep her mother away. Or at least she'll consider it. That was something. Something is better than nothing. This is, perhaps, the most important thing her work has taught her.

· 18 ·

"There's a message for you, Ms. Meyers," Orla, the desk clerk, tells Maria, as she passes the desk on the way from the breakfast room to the elevator. Maria's heart beats hard. Has something happened to Pearl? She doesn't want to look. No, it is Joseph, only Joseph; his plane is delayed.

She goes up to her room to try the doctor's office again and is told, again, that the doctor will be unavailable until afternoon. There is no change in her daughter's condition. Is there any chance the doctor will be available before the afternoon? No chance, the secretary says. I'll try anyway, Maria says, warning the woman of her determination.

What can she do, alone, trapped in this room (she must not leave it, she must be by the phone), still with nothing to read except the papers she stole and the old copies of *The Economist* she borrowed from the lobby? She turns on the television: once again, they are speaking about the weather in the west. On another channel, politicians who mean nothing to her are discussing issues in which she has no interest. An episode of *Seinfeld*. She lets her eye fall on the familiar New York landscape but cannot concentrate; the laugh track irritates her, and she turns it off. She opens the newspaper. Reads about the Middle East. Puts the paper down. Why is the room so ugly? Its smallness, the ungenerous nature of its lines, makes her feel punished, and her punishment, she feels, with her daughter close to death, is already more than she can bear. And what is her sin? *Sin, punishment.* She thought she had given up those terms.

She turns off the light. Better to lie in darkness than have her eye fall upon the spirit-stealing curtains, the discouraging rug. She will enter a darkness in which she can compose herself. In which she can prepare a course of action. Arm herself. Against what? She must arm herself against assaults she cannot yet see or name. She must prepare a face and a voice that betray no uncertainty, a voice and a face like a fortress. Or turn herself into the tiger mother, using teeth and claws against the thick bureaucracy that keeps her from her cub. There is no one to help her; she must do it alone.

The air in the room is damp. The

artificial fabric of the spread insults her skin.

What is happening to Pearl? How can it be that somebody can keep her from her child at this her hour of danger? She is afraid to think of what might be happening to Pearl's body. *Just stay alive, just stay alive,* she whispers to her in the dark, pressing her nails into the palms of her hands.

She picks up the phone. Perhaps she'll call the embassy. But what would she say? She puts the receiver in its cradle. She looks at her watch. It's only twenty minutes since she's called the doctor. Five-forty-five a.m. in New York. It's Sunday; no one is awake; no offices are open. There is nothing for her to do but wait. She closes her eyes. Opens them. Turns the lights on. Pours herself a glass of lukewarm water from the sink. Drinks it. Starts the newspaper crossword puzzle. Puts it down. Turns the lights off again. The tiger mother. Caged.

• 19 •

"Just checking on a few things for a moment," says a young doctor, looking at the tubes coming from Pearl's arm, her throat, uncovering her legs, pinching the skin on her hands and feet. "Very good," he says.

She wonders what he means by that. What is the difference between good and bad? He turns away from her, toward Tom, who has not moved from his seat beside her bed.

"So you pulled the suicide watch? I guess that means you're one of Morrisey's fair-haired boys."

"It's fine. I can get my reading done."

"Don't screw up. If you get the rough side of Morrisey's tongue you might not live to tell the tale."

Suicide watch. So that is how they think of her: a suicide. In all the ways she has thought of what she is doing, she never thought of it as suicide. Suicide seems a private thing, a simple ending. She is making a sentence of her life, a sentence she wants others to read so that something can be learned. She's thought of herself, always, as a witness, never a suicide. Her anger at the violation of her body takes on a new tone. She has been misunderstood, misnamed. She understands for the first time the rage of Bobby Sands and his fellow prisoners at being misnamed — in their case, as criminals rather than political prisoners; in hers, as suicide rather than witness. There is a difference, she wants to tell them, using all her force, between a witness and a suicide. But what force has she now, attached to tubes, compelled against her will to take in nourishment? She would like to say to this young man, her watcher, "Don't you understand the difference between a witness and a suicide? Is it possible you will not understand my death?"

This possibility, which had at no time occurred to her, fills her with dread. As the idea of death itself has never, till this moment, done.

• 20 •

Joseph's plane left Rome two hours late. It is eleven-fifteen. Maria decides to wait till he arrives to call the doctor. The idea of sleep and the word *sleep* come together in her mind, so that the letters seem, each of them, full of meaning, distinct and at the same time indistinct, like writing against a whitish sky. Images form behind her eyes, geometric shapes that change and change again when what she most needs is the stability of lines and angles that are always only themselves. She allows her eyes to close. . . .

There is a knock on the door. "Yes?" Maria says, from the bed.

"It's me."

Foolish, of course, it's foolish to say, "It's me," the words revealing no fixed identity. But how dear the words are, assuming a familiarity, a singularity stronger than a name. "Me." The voice is enough, the sound of it; it is the dear voice, the voice that has always meant safety.

When Maria opens the door, Joseph is

shocked to see that she is no longer young. It isn't only that she's tired, jet-lagged, worried. It's that, since he last saw her, she has given up her youth. Under her eyes there are olive-colored pouches. Were they there before? Before Pearl did this thing that has changed their lives?

He will do what he has come for. He will provide her with comfort as false as the fibers of the bedspreads, the rug. But if she takes comfort from his attempt at comfort, is he right to call it false? I believe that he is not.

"Oh, God, Joe, I'm so tired," Maria says, laying her head against his chest. As if this were the problem he has flown here to address: her tiredness.

"You're all right now."

She believes him. Everything is no longer up to her. She is not alone, the tiger mother, grasping her daughter — but is she grasping Pearl with her jaws or with the jaws of some other? And whose jaws would they be, if not Pearl's own? She can't make an image now. The jaws of death. The jaws of life. Isn't there some machine used in car wrecks to extricate people called the jaws of life? She must be the jaws of life seizing her daughter from the jaws of death. And then, after she's done it, after she's succeeded in saving her child, Joseph will be the ground on which they both rest. Rest, she thinks, what a beautiful idea. Joseph has always been a man she could walk beside, unjudged, given the benefit of the doubt. When the world is a field where bullets whiz over her head, she has only to be near him to be safe. So when he tells her, "You're all right," she believes it.

"Have you had breakfast?" she asks.

"On the plane."

"Good. The breakfast room is a horror. The abomination of desolation."

He hears "the abomination of desolation" from the Gospel of one of the Sundays of Advent, and he is a boy in stormy November. The rain drips from the hems of everyone's coat onto the stone floors of Sts. Cosmos and Damian. The year galloping desperately, menacingly toward darkness. Advent, winter, the slice of lightlessness before the candles are lit, the time when everyone and everything can easily be lost. There are poisonous fires that cannot be seen from where you are, and rushing winds that have cast down buildings, and lights in the sky, greenblack, sulfurous, and we will all die, all of us, but especially he, Joseph Kasperman, unmourned and unlamented by the Avenging and Destroying Creator God.

That is the abomination of desolation. But Maria is using the words to describe the restaurant in the Tara Arms Hotel. She is describing a restaurant when her daughter is at the edge of death. Like so much in her speech, the gap between what is said and what is being described is enormous. His mind rejects her habit of exaggerating. And yet he knows that when he sees the room he'll say to himself, Oh, yes, the abomination of desolation. Her words can force him to believe something he knows to be untrue. And he resents it.

"Oh, God, Joe," Maria says again. "I feel so much safer with you here."

He wants to say, There's no reason for that. Instead, he simply says, "All right," and then, to avoid a cruelty, "I'm glad."

The abomination of desolation. The false words and the false colors of the carpets in her room both sicken his soul. Of the two, the carpets disturb him more profoundly. Seeing those carpets, and the dingy wallpaper with its pattern of olive-colored reeds, he feels despair for the world. And more: a sense of deep estrangement because he knows that the designers, the manufacturers, and the purchasers of this wallpaper and this carpet are people so different from himself that they could be another species. It cannot be good, he thinks, to feel less and less commonality with more and more of my kind.

"These were on the ground beside her," Maria says. "There's the statement, a letter to you, and one to me." She hands him all three.

Joseph reads the letter to him first, straining his eyes in the gravy-colored light. He reads the statement, then the letter to Maria. He wishes he could rush to Pearl and say, I understand exactly what you mean. Her feeling of powerlessness distresses him most of all. What she says makes perfect sense. And yet he can't bear the fact that she might die. She mustn't die. In this ugly room, the ersatz fabric of the spreads and curtains an irritation to every sense, he is anguished by his own powerlessness. There is nothing he can do. He can't imagine anything that would change anything. Would it help if he said Pearl, "I know exactly what you mean"? Or would she take that as a sign of his approval of her wish for death?

"It doesn't sound crazy," he says.

"Yes, it's that old Watson training. Lucid prose. Nice to see all those tuition dollars didn't go down the drain."

He knows she has no idea of how much the Watson tuition was. It was paid not out of Maria's salary but by the estate of Seymour Meyers, of which he is executor.

He shows Maria his letter from Pearl.

She begins to cry. "I just don't understand it. Has she always felt this way about the world? I never thought she was unhappy. Did she seem unhappy to you, Joseph?"

"I never thought of happiness in relation to Pearl. Or unhappiness. I thought she was serious. I never thought she was lighthearted. But I didn't think she was in torment. She seemed calm and stoical. Optimistic, no. But not tormented either. I would never have said that."

"You think she was pessimistic."

"She could get very upset by things."

"Not more than most kids, though. Do you think she got more upset by things than most kids? Was I just not seeing it?"

He doesn't want to say this is indeed what he believes. That she always sees only what she wants to see. He says instead, "You have a lot more experience with kids than I do."

"Well, adolescents tend to take things very hard."

He doesn't want to argue, he doesn't want to say, She always took things hard; it wasn't adolescence. And he doesn't want her to think she did something that led Pearl to where she is now. Because above all he wants to say to Maria, as Pearl said in her letter, "This has nothing to do with you." He believes that. He takes Pearl at her word. That she is acting as a witness, that she has seen what she has seen. He wonders who Stephen Donegan was and how he died.

"It's not that I don't understand," Maria says. "Who could have lived through the sixties and not understood?"

What Pearl has seen has nothing to do with a particular time in history, he wants to say. What she sees has always been there and always will be.

"There's a lot we don't know about her life here," he said. "Who her friends were. Whether she became politically involved. Who this person is, Stephen Donegan, whose death she says she's marking."

"She keeps so much to herself."

"Well, that was always the case."

"I always respected her for that. Her reticence. But now I feel I never knew her."

You never did, he wants to say. Instead he says, "What is it to know another person? Who knows anyone else?" He wants to say, I thought I knew my wife. But it is not the time to talk about himself.

• 21 •

They are stealing her lightness. They are making her doubt the truth. They are filling her with gravity. She will resist their force. They have held her down. They have put a tube the thickness of a pencil down her nose, her throat. She was sickened; they did not stop. She tried to resist; they were irresistible. They insist upon nourishing her. Did they do this to Bobby Sands, shove food down his throat? Did he resist? Pearl read nothing about his being force-fed. Why is she forced when he was not? Because they wanted him to die and they want her to live, so they insist that she be nourished.

As she is nourished, her despair returns. With the return of her despair she must not lose her will not to be part of it. Not to be a part: to be apart. She is interested at the similarity of those terms. She will not be a part of it. She will not be pulled down. They have forced things into her, but she will resist them once again. She will be exalted once again. And her lightness; she will rise again. She must wait for the moment.

She touches the tube that goes into her nose and down her throat. It is plastic, but inside her it feels like bone. A bone in the throat. She would like to reach into her throat and pull out the bone, as her mother did once when Lucky swallowed a chicken bone in the park: just reached into his mouth and down his throat and pulled it out. Her mother saved his life. Now Pearl must act to save her own death.

She touches the tube again. It isn't a bone, it's too thin for a bone. She imagines that if she could see inside her she would see a thick black straw, not a drinking straw but the straw animals eat or sleep on, a black straw, stuck, embedded in her flesh. She could put her fingers around it; she could pull it out. It would leave a gap, a wound, but she would have it once again, the thing she has worked so hard for. This strong death. They think this thing, this tube or bone or straw, is giving her back her strength. It is not; it is making her weak again, insisting on her weak life. She will resist its insistence. She will reach in, grab it, take it out, and in doing that take back her strength. Refusing her weak life; regaining her strong death, the death that makes a sentence of a life that everyone can understand: "This is the truth. Hear me."

The moment comes when Tom, the watcher, gets up and walks into the bathroom. She hears him close the door. She knows what she needs to do, and that she must do it quickly. Using all her strength, she pulls the tube, the hard thing, the bone, the straw, the thickness of a pencil. Violently she tugs. The pain is shocking. A needle to her brain. But it is done. Blood is coming out of her nose. It is streaming down her face. Blood, vivid and dark. How can such a dark thing come from a body she believed had grown so light?

The watcher comes back into the room. He shouts, "Oh, my God!" There is running. They wipe the blood from her face.

"Restraints," one of them says. "Get Dr. Morrisey!"

Her hands are tied to blocks of wood. Her arms are tied to the metal of the bed.

"Yes, just now, Dr. Morrisey . . . just for a fraction of a minute, just to go inside."

"Midazolam," the doctor says. "Two hundred fifty cc."

• 22 •

Joseph and Maria know nothing of this. They sit together on Maria's bed. "I'm going to call the doctor. They said this afternoon. It's two o'clock. I'm not waiting any longer."

It is a pleasant voice, a soothing voice, the voice of the doctor's receptionist, without judgment. But in a moment, the doctor's voice enters. A different tone: business, all business.

"Hazel Morrisey here. Your daughter's under my care. At the moment she's very weak and quite dehydrated, but we haven't given up hope of stabilization. She's been given IV fluids and nourishment and some tranquilizer. It's a dicey thing; we think she's had nothing but water for six weeks. We're fortunate she took water or we wouldn't be speaking now — or only in the past tense. I'd say she planned things carefully. She's a very intelligent woman; her statement shows that, doesn't it? But then it's often the very intelligent who'll do something like this."

"Something like what?" Maria asks.

"You can't tell me you've seen anything like this before."

"I'm a psychiatrist. I specialize in adolescents. My subspecialty is eating disorders. I've seen all sorts." She doesn't tell Maria that her field of expertise is suicide in the healthy young.

Maria hears the words *specialize, subspecialty, eating disorders.* She hears no tenderness in the doctor's voice, no tenderness toward her weak child, who is in need of tenderness. Is it possible to form from these words a safe place where she can leave her daughter? They seem so sharp, with edges, not like knives or scissors but like razors or box cutters. She feels her child is not safe alone with those words. But this doctor is her only hope; probably Pearl is alive because of her. A psychiatrist. She understands that the woman who has used the words *specialize, subspecialty,* and *eating disorders* must believe that a girl who is starving herself is insane. Surely there is a great deal wrong with this. Surely it's wrong to call what Pearl is doing an eating disorder. Surely this is a misuse of language, and in Pearl's name, Pearl to whom language is paramount. She must make note of this. Yet beyond words, beyond ideas, there is something that can properly be called life that can end because of lack of nourishment. This loss of life, than which nothing could be less abstract, is something it seems to be in Hazel Morrisey's power to prevent. But Hazel Morrisey cannot understand her daughter; she cannot provide her with a tenderness she doesn't feel. Pearl needs her mother for that.

"Is she going to die? When can I see her?"

"I can't promise you what you want. And I must tell you now: She doesn't want to see you. She refuses."

"How can she refuse? She doesn't know I'm here."

"She knew you'd be coming. She said she didn't want to see you. You need to know what she's done. She's pulled the feeding tube out of her nose and throat. Do you know how much will that takes? It's a very painful thing, what she did to herself."

Maria feels the pain in her throat; as always when she hears of Pearl's physical distress, she feels it in her own body. But she can't think about that now; she has to get to her.

Rage crawls over her skin like mites; it begins on her arms, then over her skull, settles at the nape of her neck, enters the soft spot there, liquifies, spreads, coats the skeleton. Do you like your power? she wants to shout to Hazel Morrisey, whom she now sees as the enemy. Do you like being able to say a mother must be kept away from her own daughter? Do you like saying *yes* and *no,* invoking the words *life* and *death* as if you had the key to them? My daughter's life is in this doctor's hands, she says to herself, trying to make an image of what a life might be if it were something to be held in one's hands.

"I want to see my daughter," Maria says, in her most unassailable voice, the voice that has always worked to get her what she wanted. And she has never wanted anything in her life as much as this.

But Hazel Morrisey isn't moved. She meets Maria, unassailable tone for unassailable tone.

"If I'm to have her trust, she must believe that I'll do as she says when it's essential to her."

"And it's essential to her that she not see me?"

"That's right."

"I'll come to the hospital in any case."

"Of course I can't prevent you. But I'd recommend against it. I won't allow you to see her. You can sit in the lobby, but it will accomplish nothing. She's safe with us. She's watched round the clock. I'm afraid there's nothing you can do for her but respect her wishes by staying away. I'll phone you regularly."

"I'm coming to the hospital. I've waited long enough."

"As you wish, but you won't get in to see her. I think you'll be more comfortable where you are."

"I don't think comfort is the point."

"No, your daughter's life is the point. It's in the best possible hands."

Why are your hands better than mine? she wants to say, but says instead, "Speaking of hands, I find your attitude quite high-handed."

"I can see that you would," the doctor says, "and I know how difficult this is. But right now you've no choice but to trust me."

"You've a hell of a bedside manner, doctor."

"It's not your bed I'm beside."

They don't say goodbye to each other before they hang up. Maria doesn't know whether or not it's a point in the doctor's favor, the unwillingness to paper over difficulties.

"Jesus Christ, that was some performance," Maria says.

Joseph thinks the same thing — that it was a performance, an extraordinary one — but he's only heard Maria's half of it. He would have to imagine what the doctor said, but he isn't willing to do that; it isn't his nature to imagine something that he knows may turn out to be wrong when by waiting he may learn the truth. Whereas if Maria had been listening to one side of the conversation, she'd have invented the other.

"She says Pearl doesn't want to see me."

He's never seen her so downcast, so without plans, alternatives.

"I just don't understand," she says, sitting down heavily on the man-made fabric of the bedcovers.

★ ★ ★

Joseph does understand. He understands perfectly why Pearl doesn't want to see her mother. He understands the press of Maria's relentless force: the sound of a running engine when all you can tolerate is silence; the assault of bright lights, noonday sun, when your abraded eyelids can stand only twilight or a neutral rain-gray sky. How often he has wanted to cover his ears and shield his eyes when he felt her rushing at him, heedless of her impact.

"This doctor, this shrink, she thinks she knows my daughter better than I do. She's known her — what, ten hours? — and she thinks she's the expert. Because eating disorders are her subspecialty. Subspecialty! What does that have to do with Pearl? She needs someone who knows her, she needs someone who loves her; that's what she needs. The doctor just wants to say she's crazy. Well, I don't think so. I don't know what to think, but I know the doctor's wrong."

Joseph understands that a psychiatrist would think what Pearl is doing is insane, because it is threatening her life. He understands that Pearl wants to die and that this desire must be thwarted. He doesn't want her to die; he's terrified at the thought of her death. Yet he refuses to disallow the value of her impulse to lay down her life. He can't understand this in himself. He thinks her giving up her life is a terrible idea, an idea that is unbearable, yet he understands its value. But as an idea to be lived out by someone else, not her. Not Pearl. Beloved. Irreplaceable.

He dislikes the doctor for automatically denying the possibility of value in an idea that ends in death. He understands that she is probably right to do so — he may even agree with her — and he is grateful to her because possibly, with her coldness, her science, her tubes, her withholding of permission, she will keep Pearl alive. But he won't grant the automatic rightness of her refusal to question the idea that life itself is the most important thing in life. Her insistence that what Pearl is doing is a sign of illness. Her determination to invoke the category *health.*

Perhaps you are impatient with Joseph's train of thought, believing that of course life is the most important thing in life and Pearl must be kept alive and to think in any other way is to be, in the language of Joseph and Maria's youth, not part of the solution but part of the problem. Perhaps you are more comfortable with Maria's way of proceeding: her desire to make something happen, get something done.

Joseph sees that Maria, in her insistence on casting the doctor as an enemy, is being Maria. But then he doesn't believe that anyone really changes. Pearl was always Pearl; her first words were deliberately chosen. He remembers her determination to climb a tree whose height terrified her, to run more laps when her heart was bursting, her stoicism when she stumbled into a hornets' nest on a porch in Connecticut and was stung, over and over, on the arms, the neck, the lips. She did not cry out. She was no more than ten years old.

And what do you believe? Which are you: fatalist or progressive? How much do you believe is over before we leave the womb, the crib, our mother's arms? Joseph would say, A great deal. Maria would say, Don't underestimate the power to change. What do you think? And which side, you may wonder, am I on? I am on both sides.

But let's get back to the room.

"This is intolerable, this behavior. This imperiousness. I'm her mother. She's not twenty-one yet. There must be legal issues here."

Maria is calling the embassy; she is phoning lawyer friends in New York. People are away for the holidays, but she's leaving messages on machines. Fiercely, she presses the buttons on the flimsy gray phone as if she were pushing buttons to activate bombs that would detonate, explode, and then destroy her enemy the doctor.

She is walking around the room, up and down the pebble-colored carpet, making a fist and grinding it into the palm of her other hand. Anything rather than be still.

It's Sunday, so her New York friends are not in their offices, and there is nothing for her to do but wait. He knows that waiting, of all things, is for her the most intolerable.

Her movements, her relentless pacing, are swallowing the room's air, already inadequate because of the curtains, the spread, the carpet. He coughs a few times, uselessly. But sometimes he too prefers a useless action. So he coughs again, lightly, shallowly, as if that would clear his lungs. She's making him feel tired. The prospect of his own darkened room, a little sleep, seems to him if not desirable then at least more bearable than being in the room with her.

He says he will go up to his room for a nap. She turns on him, one of her whirling motions.

"What for? You're not the one who's jet-lagged."

These words echo what she said on the day they went to Yom Kippur services, when she wanted to leave and he didn't. When he said he'd like to stay and she turned on him and said, "What for? It's not your religion."

Always asserting the primacy of her own experience, her own situation. And what does she want now? He knows she wants him to be in the room with her so she won't feel alone. Trapped, she wants to trap him too.

"Let me just go upstairs and take a shower," he says. "Why don't you lie down for ten minutes? You must be tired."

She nods her head. Permitting him, he thinks, to leave.

★ ★ ★

Once Maria is alone, there is nothing for her to do but wait. Why has no one ever told her that waiting is itself work? Well, someone must have told her, of course, one of the nuns, someone urging patience on her, but she never believed them or was never interested. If waiting was work, it was someone else's, not hers. She sees herself standing in front of a blackboard in a large, empty old-fashioned classroom, perhaps a Victorian one. Her hair is in a single plait. She is wearing a navy blue dress that has a white collar and reaches halfway down her calves; she is wearing black stockings and ankle boots. Perhaps it is a classroom in an orphanage, some harsh charitable institution funded by a philanthropist dedicated to the shaping, the reformation, of the ill-born young. Reformation. Reform school: perhaps it is a reform school; she is being punished for her crime — unnamed — by writing over and over, till her arms ache with fatigue, *There is nothing I can do. There is nothing I can do.* Is it an *I* she's writing, or is it a *you?* Is even the pretense of self-determination stripped, is she merely taking dictation? *There is nothing you can do.* Whose is the voice, who is the dictator? She hears it in her brain now. She doesn't know whether to turn the light on. Dark, the room takes on the aspect of a cell but, illuminated, the absolute wrongness of every line, form, color, and texture implies a prison of another sort: a modern one, meant to look rehabilitative but in fact as deadening as concrete walls and iron bars.

There is nothing you can do. She feels she must wait near the phone, just in case. In case the doctor summons her or Pearl changes her mind and will see her. In case Ambassador Smith has come back to Ireland and will give her an interview (after Maria reminds her how much the Kennedy family has always meant to her), and the two of them can storm through the barricades the doctor has set up. In case one of her friends gets home and has some plans or good advice to offer. In case of the worst. But she won't think about that now.

She has to stay in the room. Anything else is unthinkable.

"I just don't understand," she whispers in the dark, helpless. When something was incomprehensible, indecipherable, she has throughout her life felt a chafing, building from scorn to outrage at the knot the world has presented to her. Jack Rappaport, her lover, once told her, "You say 'I don't understand' as if you believe you were meant to." "Of course I believe I am meant to," she said, impatient with what she considered his perverse, pseudosophisticated neutrality. "Why else were we put on earth if not to understand, or try to?"

"What makes you think we were *put on earth?* By whom?" He liked to remind her — unkindly? — of what he called her "religious default setting."

"There doesn't have to be a first cause in order for us to believe in our obligation to understand. It's just another excuse for your laziness," she said.

Maria is often tempted to accuse other people of laziness because, in fact, she does work very hard, loves activity, is impatient with rest. So this enforced inactivity is more anguishing to her than it might be to another temperament. Jack was a man who enjoyed leisure, and she enjoyed herself with him a great deal. He could make anything a pleasure — lunch, a walk, choosing a melon, a tomato, not just sex — *the sex,* as she called it to herself and her friends, acknowledging how much she misses it. But she tells herself, she's told her friends, it wasn't worth it. When she was explaining to Devorah why her relationship with Jack was so unsatisfactory she said that when she would try to lean her spirit against him, she felt she was leaning on a cloud. And then he wanted to get married. Wanted that domestic life — "Time for a drink, darling. . . . When did you say dinner was? Maybe we'll walk around the block afterward. . . . And where will we go for vacation this year?" — which made her feel she was in a rifle sight, ready to be shot dead. She thinks how little good Jack Rappaport would do her now. What *would* be good for her now? What would be good for Pearl?

• 23 •

"Midazolam," the doctor says to the nurse. "It's best for the purpose. Takes away pain, induces amnesia. Sewing the tube to her nose will be quite a difficult procedure. She may remember something of it, but the memory, if any, will be vague."

A needle in her arm. Midazolam. Let us dazzle madame with Midazolam. Pearl smiles at the joke she's made.

Her lightness is returning. Nothing matters. "Not to be trusted," the doctor says. She is not be trusted? "Remarkable," the doctor says, "the strength, the determination. All used against herself." Myself, do you mean my life? Oh, that. "We can't have you pulling the feeding tubes out anymore," the doctor says. "You're very weak. You're very dehydrated. We're trying to keep you alive." Are you speaking to me? How odd that someone would be speaking to her. "That's why we're sewing this tube to your nose so you won't be able to pull it out."

The doctor must be joking. They could not do anything so funny. She used to sew.

You sew cloth to cloth; you might embroider. You did not sew things to noses. It was not a thing human beings did to other human beings, sewing things into their flesh. Yet they seem to be doing it. She understands it ought to be hurting, but it doesn't matter; it ought to hurt. A needle breaks through the skin of her nose. A sound like *crunch*. In and out the needle goes. A stitch in time saves nine. They are coming at her once again. Another tube, this time soft, like a piece of spaghetti. Why are they putting spaghetti in my nose? She feels she has become a cartoon character, a joke figure. Spaghetti in her nose, thread in and out. Well, noses are a funny part. Her lightness is back again. She swims above them; she sees herself on a bed, or what they think is her real self, the one they are sewing something into. But she knows she is above them. They are doing this thing to someone who is not the real her.

The amnesia will be a blessing, the doctor says. But Pearl knows there is no need for amnesia. There is nothing to remember, therefore nothing to forget.

Remembrance. Forgetting. The theory that pain is real only if it is remembered. This is a troubling paradox. Hazel Morrisey believes it, she has to believe it, or she wouldn't be able to do what she does. Sometimes she wonders about the connection between pain and memory. It is always said that if women remembered the pain of labor there would never be any second children born. Yet she remembers the pain of her labor. She has tried to determine the nature, the quality of her memory.

But we can ask the question: When the sufferer is suffering, isn't it an eternal present, like the mind of God? Would suffering be diminished if the sufferer were able to say, But I know I won't remember this, after all, so it must be all right?

Hazel Morrisey must believe that this drug, Midazolam, will make the pain nonexistent. That the eternal present will quite soon be nothing but a blur, an absence, the self gone from the self, the sufferer an empty vessel, without language and outside of time.

She makes herself see Pearl in ten years, coming back to Ireland, showing the doctor her beautiful children, saying, *Thank you for keeping me alive*. This is what she is thinking with the part of her brain that is not sticking a needle, threaded with catgut, into the nostril of this girl whose eyes are closed, who she has to believe is feeling nothing of what she does.

• 24 •

After his shower Joseph cleans, with a traveling nail brush, the immaculate space between the flesh of his fingers and his nails. He flosses his teeth. He picks up his coat and closes the door of his room behind him. He takes the stairs, rather than the elevator, down to Maria's room. He knocks lightly on the door. Once, twice, no answer. He uses the key, which isn't a key, just a plastic strip. He hears that she is in the shower. He answers the ringing phone, not really a ring but something between a buzz and a purr.

It's Caroline Wolf from the embassy. Her voice sounds neutral, pleasant. Nevertheless he asks, "Is anything wrong?"

Instead of answering, she asks, "Are you a family member?"

The question makes him feel exposed and he resents it, yet he is conscious of the paltriness of his answer.

"Not exactly. A close family friend."

There is only one legal member of his family now — his mother — with whom he has the connection that grants — what?

Access, the right to information, the right to exert your will. He had it once with Devorah: that was marriage, the law taking the place of blood. But he had very little real knowledge of her; he didn't understand the person she had come to be, he didn't know she'd gone back to her family. So what good did the force of the law do him? It meant he had the right to dispose of her dead body, but he had given it back to her parents; he had felt he had no moral claim. Certainly, Caroline Wolf would think he had no claim to Pearl, no authority. Friend of the family. Close family friend. Invited to dinners and ceremonial occasions. Counted on in times of emergency or distress.

Maria, wrapped in a towel, runs out of the bathroom toward him. He gives her the phone, saying to Caroline Wolf, puzzling her perhaps (who is this man in the hotel room?), "Here's Ms. Meyers now."

Caroline Wolf gets the full brunt of Maria's rage. He is sorry for her, but this is what she's trained for. She's a diplomat; she probably dreams of standing patiently while Yasir Arafat rages, or Ian Paisley. Maria is, after all, not much compared to them.

She is insisting on being given the names

of lawyers. The room is dim; only the bedside lamp is on. The lights are activated only from wall switches, and she can't turn them on from the phone.

"For God's sake, Joseph, get some light in here."

The lights are harsh, embittering the room's unnatural colors. She gestures to him, pointing to pencil and paper. She snaps her fingers. As if he were a servant. Like his mother.

He excuses her incivility. Would we excuse it in his place? Would we tell ourselves, like him, that she's upset, exhausted — that's why she pointed, snapped her fingers — she wouldn't behave like this under ordinary circumstances? In all the years he's known her, she's never snapped her fingers or pointed for him to do something, get something. Yet he knows the inclination has always been there: the impulse to give orders, to be served. As the impulse to serve is in him.

Joseph doesn't want to think what this means. It is for us, not him, to consider. But we don't like to think about it. Servants and masters: it seems an old idea, neatly disposed of, like a defunct factory once devoted to the manufacture of corsets. But Joseph knows his mother prepared the food that Maria and her father ate, washed the clothes they wore. He remembers her holding up a pair of Dr. Meyers's underwear, with a thin line of shit along the seam, and saying, "He thinks he doesn't even have to wipe his ass because he has some dumb Polack to clean up after him." And holding one of Maria's brushes, combing the strands of hair out and saying, "Filthy, filthy," loud enough for Maria to hear. He knew she wanted Maria to hear. How can he forget this? It is even kinder of him than it might be for one of us to forgive Maria for snapping her fingers and pointing at the thing she wanted fetched. We must ask ourselves: Burdened by the memories, the scenes, the images that Joseph carries, would we be capable of such kindess, such understanding? I fear that we would not.

Sitting in this ugly room, it's as if a field of force has bloomed around Maria. A line, transparent, sizzling blue, seems to trace the outline of her body.

But she's getting nowhere. From what he can hear, the bureaucratic buck is being passed. Maria can't speak like this professionally; she can't get people to do things by shrieking and cursing at them as she's doing now.

He's never seen Maria at work, but I can tell you what she's like: incisive, jokey, coaxing, able to listen; able to make decisions, even hard ones, and stick to them; able to walk into a room of children and see the problem, think of a solution. People who work with her love her. They are less critical of her than people in other areas of her life. Maria is an excellent boss. As a boss, no one can accuse her of being bossy. She would never talk to a colleague or an employee as she is talking to Caroline Wolf. She is terrified, uncomprehending, frustrated. How would any of us behave in a situation like this? Her daughter may be dying. Her daughter is in the hands of a doctor she doesn't know, doesn't like, doesn't trust. Her daughter refuses to see her.

"What kind of fantastic bullshit is this?" Maria is saying to Caroline Wolf. "What kind of power does the medical establishment have in this country? What is this, Russia under Brezhnev? I'm an American citizen. This is a clear human rights violation. I insist that you give me the names of some lawyers who can help me."

He sees words clanging against one another, dark blue iron rings in the dove-colored air: *citizen, rights, violation.* She can do this because she has a tie of blood to Pearl, a legal tie. None of these words would be available to him.

Caroline Wolf, he can tell, intends to resist her. She must be saying, I'll get back to you with those names.

"What do you mean, get back?" Maria shouts. "Get back from where, Timbuktu?"

He wants to laugh at the use of the name so archaically suggesting the impossible place at the impossible distance. Timbuktu. No one uses that word anymore, no one even thinks of it. What happened to Timbuktu, he wonders? Was it only a place in the mind?

He can tell Maria is frustrated by the shortness of the telephone cord. She has to sit. She cannot pace as she usually does when she talks on the phone. She has no scope, no way to express her physical force except by grabbing at her hair, her remarkable hair, long and curly, gray now. Once it rippled, blue-black; she and Devorah would walk down the street together, and everyone loved them for their hair.

"What do you mean, it's a holiday? Does this seem like a holiday situation? Are we into chestnuts roasting on an open fire?"

Caroline Wolf must be telling her she has other cases.

"I don't think any of your other cases can possibly have this urgency."

Caroline Wolf has ended the conversation. Maria puts down the phone. Caroline Wolf didn't use the words, but Maria heard them in her voice: *There is nothing you can do.*

Joseph looks out the window at a courtyard filled with hunks of plaster, rusting lengths of gutter, broken pipe. Maria looks at her watch.

It is only three o'clock. Only ten a.m. in New York. He wonders what she thinks her lawyer friends can do for her, go over the doctor's head? Insist on the primacy of her rights over Pearl's?

And it is quite hard to understand, really, that ten o'clock in one place means three in another, that someone (Who is it? Will we ever know?) has sliced the map up like a birthday cake, sectioned the globe like an orange, so that three o'clock and ten o'clock mean the same thing.

It isn't difficult to see how words spin through her brain like the close-up of a 78 record in a fifties movie about teenagers at a dance. Maria is very frightened; she is very tired. What she is experiencing most intensely, though, is rage at the idea that ten o'clock in one place means three in the place she is now.

• 25 •

Pearl hears a sound like horses tramping. Are they bringing horses into her room? They are sewing things to her nose; now they are bringing in horses to look at her. This is the doctor's voice. She is talking to the trooping horses.

"This case, Pearl Meyers, twenty, is a complex one and brings together a lot of elements in your training. Clinically, it could be described as anorexia. As physicians specializing in psychiatry, I would ask you to understand that the psychological issues are more complex. We won't go into them here; I'm assuming you've read the literature and we'll discuss this case later in detail in that context. But we must remember that in anorexia the connections between the mind and the body are inextricable. I would draw your attention to the acute physical symptoms, mostly a result of severe dehydration. Although the patient won't cooperate by giving us a full history, she writes that she hasn't eaten in six weeks and hasn't drunk in several days.

It's no wonder that she had trouble producing urine. Also tears. I've not seen this extreme a case before except in an infant. What would be some of the side effects of such severe dehydration?"

One of the horses speaks. "Kidney failure," he says.

"Right," says the doctor. "Anything else?"

"Drop in blood pressure."

"Yes. You'll note that the blood pressure dropped drastically when she moved from a standing to a sitting position. What risks would go along with hydration?"

"Risk of severe arrhythmia followed by cardiac arrest."

"Very good," the doctor says.

The horses take their fences quickly; they fly over and do not knock down any of the bars.

"We've had to take extreme measures with Ms. Meyers. She pulled the feeding tube from her throat; you can imagine the determination that took. We originally had her in restraints, but I'm very opposed to restraints; I've seen too much long-term trauma from them. But we did sew a narrow feeding tube to the side of the right nostril so she can't pull it out, an extreme measure to be sure. It's too easy for us to forget that anorexia can be a fatal disease. Starvation is starvation, whether it's in the developed world or in an African country."

"Yes, but starvation in a poor country is never voluntary. This kind of anorexia is always a disease of the affluent."

The doctor puts her hand on Pearl's arm. "Perhaps you'd be happier in another specialty, Mr. Lenehan. Orthopedics. Dermatology."

The horses make a snickering sound. One of them, Mr. Lenehan, has knocked the bar. The doctor's hand is cool on her arm. Her nails are square and short. She wears a wedding ring. The horses troop away.

"I know you're no stranger to stupidity," the doctor says. "I'll try to keep you from that sort of thing ever again."

What is she saying, that she will keep the horses away? She thinks of the horse she saw with Stevie in Mayo; its legs in the air, its dead eyes open, its teeth exposed. So that is death too. Her death is moving farther from her. No longer the companion at the clear end of the white road. Harder to get a glimpse of. Vaguer now.

• 26 •

They lie on the twin beds, side by side, reading. Joseph is reading his biography of Ruskin, Maria her weeks-old copies of *The Economist*. She would like to ask him to lend her his book, but she restrains herself. She has always found any book he was reading more appetizing than anything she might be reading at the same time, and the old *Economist*s provide no savor at all. She congratulates herself for not even hinting that he give her the book.

Joseph knows, too, that she would like to read his Ruskin book; he retreats into a pocket of what he knows is selfishness, but he will not give it to her, not this book he is so enjoying, this life he has entered into, so absorbing, so puzzling, so admirable and tragic — no, he won't give it up for her, even though it is possibly the thing he could do right now that would be of most help.

"I feel so trapped here," Maria says. "I don't dare leave the phone, but I can't get anyone in New York. Jill Kiernan's in the fucking Caribbean. She's my lawyer friend with the Irish connections. Jesus Christ, the Caribbean. Everyone's a goddam yuppie now. We slept in youth hostels with knapsacks, for Christ's sake."

"I have an idea," Joseph says. "I swear I won't tell anyone in New York. It's five o'clock, you're jet-lagged; let's go have dinner downstairs. They can get you if anyone calls. Our first early bird specials."

Joseph, as you see, has not much gift for lightness. When he tries to make a joke, it often falls flat. People who aren't taken with Joseph and Pearl often think they have no sense of humor. Maria, who is good at jokes, has never said that, never even allowed herself to think it. On the other hand, she doesn't even notice that he's tried to be funny. "All right," she says, "we might as well."

They go down to the room where Maria had breakfast, the room that at all hours smells of beer. They order grilled salmon, baked potatoes, and a bottle of Pinot Grigio in which neither of them has faith.

"I thought my love would keep her safe," Maria says. "I thought if I just loved her enough, she'd be all right. God knows I love her enough. But she's not all right, Joseph, because she thinks life is terrible and she wants to die."

"She won't die," he says. "I think the doctor knows what she's doing."

"The doctor!" Maria snorts. "Dr. Congeniality."

"She seems competent," he said. "Anyway, Pearl's safe for now."

"For now?"

"That's all we can hope for. For now she's OK. Have another glass of wine. You need to sleep tonight."

★ ★ ★

When Maria gets into bed, she's surprised at how much she wants to give in to her fatigue. How much she wants sleep. But only the right kind. Clean sleep. Not too much, not so that, waking, she's groggier than before she slept. She needs to be rested to fight for Pearl. And for her own rights, her right to be with her daughter. Her daughter who needs her. Fatigue will weaken her; fatigue will dilute her force. Fatigue kills hope. And she must act from hope. She must breathe hope back into her child. Hope breathed in through love. Absurd, the professional hygienics of the doctor, believing that with her skill, her training, she can provide an alternative to love. It is love and life that are at issue. Not specialty, subspecialty, eating disorders, invasive procedures, feeding tubes. Yet these are what is keeping Pearl alive.

Maria knows that if she falls into one of

her poisoned sleeps, one of the ones that is a vision of what is behind the scrim of our words, our civilized habits, she will be paralyzed. She will be in the place she needs to rescue Pearl from, and she cannot allow that to happen. She will not sleep.

★ ★ ★

Upstairs in room 436, Joseph has no impulse to sleep at all. He wonders whether Pearl is able to sleep. He reads about John Ruskin. Ruskin traveled through Europe with his parents, carrying with him a portable England: tools for geological expeditions, equipment for drawing, an instrument for measuring the blue of the sky, called the cyanometer. He wonders in what terms the blue of the sky is measured. What is the measure for intensity?

What is the intensity of Pearl's suffering? What does she need him to do? What can he offer her that will be of help, that will be strong enough to pull her back into the orbit of life? How can he protect her? He couldn't protect Devorah from her own failure of spirit, from the heel that caught in the hem of her skirt. He thinks that in all his life he has prevented nothing, he has made nothing happen. He would do anything for Pearl, anything that would keep her safe. But he can't think of a thing.

"The potassium levels are much better," a doctor says to a nurse. "You might want to take a look at this," he says to Tom. Tom comes toward the bed. The doctor moves the sheets; they are looking at the bag attached to the tube coming from Pearl's vagina. She is embarrassed that Tom is seeing this. "We've got a nice urine output here; it's brilliant."

Pearl would like to laugh. Brilliant to be producing urine.

"Morrisey's cut the Midazolam down. She'll be more with the program now. We're not out of the woods yet, but we're getting there."

Out of the woods. Out of what woods? What woods has she been in? There are no trees; there have never been trees. She has been here in this room that is not white but that feels white, windowless, dim, the lights making a bluish haze over everything, so that she has no idea of season or of time. Christmas. It's Christmastime.

But what does time mean to her, since

the medication — Midazolam — has turned her into a being without memory? What is time without memory? Who is the *I* without a past? Is it possible to have an *I* for whom the present is continuous, eternal, like the dead, or God, or Joseph's mother, rocking and gibbering in the Regina Caeli Home for the Aged and Infirm? Pearl is not the same person that she was several hours ago. Her memory has been robbed. Who, then, is she now?

There are tubes in her arm, her nose, her vagina. She is seeing things more clearly: the horses are doctors. And something new is happening: something she hasn't felt for many weeks. She is hungry. She is thinking of the rice pudding her mother makes, creamy and sweet, with raisins and cinnamon. How can she be thinking of raisins and cinnamon when she is so close to death? Her companion at the end of the white road has disappeared. There is only a blankness that she fears, a windless, treeless plain. They say they are giving her back her life. What they call her life she knows by another name: hunger, it is called.

I must tell you something strange, strange yet a scientific fact. The paradox:

as a starving person is given nutrition, she becomes aware of hunger, an awareness that was blocked when the starvation progressed to a critical state. Like other starving people, Pearl had not felt hunger; now, fed, she has begun to crave.

How can we understand this? Don't we believe, hasn't everything we've experienced taught us to believe, that nourishment diminishes hunger rather than increasing it? Is appetite fed on food? Must we make the one-to-one equation between appetite and life?

I find it fortunate that Pearl isn't thinking of these things. She is thinking only of the arrival of hunger. And its companions: fear and shame.

• 28 •

Maria waits till seven the next morning, which is when she knows breakfast is served, to phone Joseph. Ridiculous how meals have become the major events of her day. Like a prisoner, she thinks, or a mental patient, or a person in an old-age home.

After breakfast, Joseph asks Maria if she'd like to go for a walk; he'll man the phones. She refuses. He asks if she minds if he goes. No, of course, she says, go on.

He comes back with a book by Ngaio Marsh and two decks of playing cards. She cannot seem to read, but she can play gin rummy.

He thinks of playing cards with his mother.

Every hour, Maria phones Dr. Morrisey. And every hour she is told the same thing: The doctor is unavailable. There is nothing to report. The doctor will return your call when she is free.

"I'm going to go out and get us some sandwiches for lunch," Joseph says. "That hotel bar is just too grim. Even this room is better."

"I'll be here," Maria says.

Joseph walks out of the hotel, his book heavy in his pocket. Odd, he thinks, to be reading about John Ruskin in Dublin. The Irish humor, the Irish generosity, the Irish sense of chance and miracle would have exasperated him. And why would anyone, he imagines Ruskin thinking — he for whom the eye was all — go to a country he believed populated by dirty, superstitious beggars, a country whose great buildings could be counted on one hand, a country whose mountains lacked sublimity, a country with only minor ruins?

Joseph has only three hours for a glimpse of Dublin, a situation Ruskin would have thought barbarous. Most likely it is, he thinks, but then I am a barbarian. Unrefined. "That's very fine," he hears Dr. Meyers's voice saying, a phrase that had the power to abash or to exalt him. He wonders what Seymour Meyers would think of what his granddaughter has done. He would applaud the impulse — martyrdom — but not the terms in which it was expressed — human despair. He would have thought despair a sin. So much, of course, is in the terms. The terms determine what we see. For the first time, he makes the connection between *term* and *determine*.

What is knowing? What can be known, really known? What does it mean to know well? Ruskin knew some things well, and yet his blind spots made much of his knowing unreliable. And is knowing living? What is living? How do you understand a life? What does Pearl understand by this thing she seems so willing to give up?

He is tormented by the idea that he doesn't know what to do for her. Maria has been told she can do nothing, but she knows what she'll do when she's allowed. Maria wants him here to help keep Pearl alive. What does Pearl want? He is here to do whatever it is she wants, and whatever Maria wants. Suppose the two are different?

The air is wet and tastes of iron, or of coins. There is a smell to it that he knows he has never smelled before, yet it seems deeply familiar: sweetish, smoky, something like wood or coal yet with more soil to it. A smell with a deep brown color: is this peat? As he walks, the smell seems curative, quieteningly modest. He feels it slowing his pace.

He will ask the way to Trinity College. No, he will not. He will look at the jade-colored river, the scarlet and sapphire doors.

But as he walks, his heart drops with the sense of his own failure. He doesn't know how to look without guidance. Without an idea anterior to sight, without a context provided, not from his own imagination or experience but from the imagination and experience of someone else, he doesn't know how to look. He doesn't know what to look *for*. This makes him seem pathetic to himself. How can he become a person with a greatness of response, like Ruskin? When something pleases his eye here, he has no words for the terms by which he is pleased. The gold lettering on a store window, the shiny-green blue or red paint on a door: how should he compare these to other things that have pleased him? The things that please him here seem merely *pleasant,* and his inability to see more in them makes him feel that he has failed.

But what is he doing, thinking about Ruskin, when he is in Dublin because Pearl is trying to die? Perhaps this is his punishment; he cannot look because it is wrong for him to be looking at all. But what is right? Waiting; waiting and praying. Only he is a person who has long ago given up the possibility of prayer.

The air is raw and damp; it is the end of December. The cold of the pavement seeps through his new Italian shoes. He would like a hot drink. He imagines tea will be good in Ireland.

He walks into a café that beckons him because of its suggestion of Victorian — no, Edwardian — gentility. Cakes and scones sit solidly, reassuringly, on plates with pedestals. They offer a solid comfort without the risk of alarm or surprise. He chooses tea and cheese sandwiches and takes them to the cash register, fumbling with the unfamiliar coins. No one is impatient. The young woman at the register fishes the right amount from his open palm; he is not unpleased by the touch of her warmish fingers, at the slight grazing of her light-pink polished nails.

A waitress in a black uniform and a white maid's cap wipes the marble surface of his table with a damp blue-and-white checkered rag.

"Desperate, isn't it?" she says. "Perishing."

For a minute he wonders if she knows something about Pearl. But then he understands she's only talking about the weather. He can't get over her easy, colloquial use of the words or their cognates: *desperate, perish.*

Desperate: to be without hope. Perish from *perdere:* to lose, to be lost. To be lost and without hope: such large, truthful ideas about the nature of life. He very much likes what it suggests about a culture, that such concepts can be so domesticated, so simplified, as to apply to weather.

"It's not so bad," he says, smiling.

"You're a brave man," she says, with a smile and an intake of breath that could be a sigh, a sign of agreement, or disagreement.

He looks around him. He listens to the buzz of talk for what he thinks of as a distinguishing tone. People here are not nearly so good-looking as they are in Italy, maybe because it's rainy and cold. But no, it's more than that. No haircut here is a work of art. Teeth do not flash in triumph; eyebrows don't suggest a later assignation or an upcoming fistfight or a quick, mutually profitable deal. There is laughter, but it isn't dangerous. No knives gleam in this laughter; no outraged honor bubbles at its surface. Voices aren't raised. Yet there's not the fuzzy mutedness of London tearooms; he knows he must imagine bloodlettings here, but such imagination would require work.

Men sit alone at tables and read newspapers; women too. And some of them read books. They regularly light up cigarettes. One woman takes a flake of tobacco off her tongue.

A waitress stands beside him with a brown teapot and offers to fill his cup. The steamy air of the room has made the wisps escaping her chignon go softly curly. Her upper lip, which has a light dusting of down — traces only, bee pollen — is dampened a bit by sweat. He imagines that if he embraced her, the smell of her armpits would be pleasantly rank: an overworked young animal's. He likes the whiteness of her fingers, and the dark blue stone of her ring, and the greenish vein that travels up the inside of her arm.

So that is what I have become, he thinks, a man of a certain age, a widower, thinking of the details of the body of the young girl who brings me tea.

"You're American?"

"Yes, I am."

"I'd say Americans have the right end of the stick about most things. I'd love to go over there."

Does she imagine him as her sugar daddy? A pathetic older man who will usher her into prosperity, a life without a maid's cap, a damp rag? What is he thinking? What has become of him?

"Many people are disappointed when they actually get to America," he says.

"I wouldn't be, I know. I've got two sisters there, in Boston. You're not from Boston yourself?"

"New York."

"I'd be that terrified of New York."

"It's not unsafe, really."

He thinks of how dull he must be for her to talk to, how disappointing.

"If I went, I'd like to go someplace warm. LA, maybe, or New Orleans. But I won't go anytime soon. My mother'd be completely destroyed to send another kid there. There's only me and my brother left. He's much younger than me. Ten years old, and a right gurrier."

Joseph has, simultaneously, no notion of what a gurrier might be and at the same time a clear image of a light-haired stocky boy running down a sidewalk, fists clenched, cheeks red, legs pumping, making a roaring noise.

"I have no siblings myself," he says, and then feels ridiculous at the suggestion that he and she are in a position so that anything about them could be compared.

"Large families are grand, or they can be if you've the means. Have you children yourself?"

"No, I'm a widower."

"Well, then, you're on your own," she says, her damp cheeks turning pink. He's embarrassed her with excessive information, the implied plea for sympathy.

"I travel a great deal."

"That's grand for you then," she says. He can tell she's eager to get away.

He finishes his tea, his cheese sandwiches. He tips the waitress lavishly. She blushes once again.

"Give my regards to Broadway," she says, raising her hand as if she were waving him off as he sailed away.

• 29 •

Every time Pearl opens her eyes, he is there: Tom, her suicide watcher. He is about her age, maybe a little older. He's already beginning to lose his hair. He keeps trying to read his medical textbook, but he often falls asleep. If she really wanted to pull the tube out again, she could try when he was napping. But it doesn't matter what she wants; the tube is sewn to her, and the drug — Midazolam — even in the reduced dosage, makes any action difficult. He opens his eyes and sees her looking at him.

"How's it going?" he says.

She smiles.

"That's a stupid thing to say, I know," he says. He blushes and comes over to straighten her sheet.

"I hope I didn't get you into trouble."

"Nothing I won't recover from. Dr. Morrisey reamed me out good and proper. She's a tough one. Brilliant doctor, everyone wants to train with her, but she scares the bejeezus out of most of us. And she's got a real stake in your case. How is it with the lower dosage of Midazolam?"

She doesn't want to tell him that she has become more fearful of death now that she is moving farther away from it, as if it is punishing her by replacing love with fear. Love casts out fear. Fear casts out love. She says instead, "I think I'm hungry."

"Well, you would be, you see. The ketones start kicking in. I'm sorry, that's technical, but the odd thing is, the more you're nourished, the hungrier you feel. And you're probably more depressed, because you're losing the anorectic euphoria."

Losing anorectic euphoria. That's how they think of it then. She would like to tell him that she was happy and now she is not, that she knew what was right and now she doesn't, that she was in love with death and now she fears it. And that she is hungry for her mother's rice pudding and wants to see her mother. But this last she feels she can resist. In case it's not too late and she can still become the one thing, the one sentence, as she had planned when she was not a hungry person or a person of fear.

"Just try and rest," he says to her. "Dr. Morrisey will be in pretty soon. She'll want to hear what you're going through."

Through to where? she wants to say.

There is a knock on the door and it opens. Seeing it's Dr. Morrisey, Tom begins to blush again. He backs out of the room, as if he feels he has no right to be there.

"You seem more alert," Dr. Morrisey says. "How does that feel?"

She doesn't want to tell the doctor that she's hungry.

"Tom O'Kelley's a fine young man, very sensitive. He'll make a good doctor."

"My father was a doctor," Pearl says. Once the words are out, she wishes she could take them back. She doesn't want to give the doctor anything.

"What kind of doctor is he?"

"I don't know, I never met him. And it's *was,* not *is.* He's dead."

That, Pearl thinks, will shut her up. It is a new impulse in her, the impulse to be rude. She wants to make the doctor know that she is nothing to her and she can make nothing happen.

"You were studying the Irish language here. I understand you're a student of linguistics."

Pearl turns her head away.

"What I find interesting about the decision you made is that, for a person devoted to language, you seemed to have so little faith in it."

Pearl turns her head toward the doctor, interested despite herself.

"What do you mean?"

"You seemed to think that action, your taking your life, was the only way to communicate what you believed. As if your body were stronger than words."

Pearl would like to snort, make some sign of derision, but the tube makes that impossible. She will have to use words, words only, for that. "I did write a statement. It was on the ground next to me; I think you read it. Suppose I'd just written that and passed it out on Grafton Street. Would anyone pay attention? There are too many words spoken by too many people."

"But what you've done: not many have done that. You really have got people to pay attention."

She would like to accept this as a compliment, assert her pride.

"But for how long? If you die, there's no chance you'll be able to change anything in the world. There'll be nothing you can do."

"There's nothing I can do anyway."

"Nothing?"

"Not enough. Not enough to make it worth it."

"Life, you mean."

"Yes. I mean *my* life."

Hazel Morrisey is silent for a moment, heartened that at least there is some conversation, worried that the next thing she'll say will be wrong.

"You must be in a great deal of pain to believe that. I understand that nothing might seem worthwhile. But you didn't want to die just to be free of pain; you wanted to be saying something by your death — and that, I feel, is a sign of hope."

"Hope for what?"

"Your hope that communication is possible, that perhaps something can be changed. That you have some interest in the work of the world: what you can do in it."

"There's nothing I can do."

"We do what we can," Dr. Morrisey says.

"You sound like my mother," Pearl says.

"I'm going to assume you didn't mean that as a compliment," Dr. Morrisey says.

Pearl smiles. "I'm feeling hungry," she says. She doesn't know why she's decided to tell the doctor this. It seems less personal than telling her something about what she would call her *self*. Yes, I do think the body is stronger than words, she wants to say to the doctor, but I don't want to talk about that. If I tell you I'm hungry, that's saying something about my body. That will shut you up.

"The paradox is, nutrition makes you hungrier. Ketones," the doctor says.

"I know all about it," Pearl says, in a childish voice, a bratty voice, a voice I had never heard her use to anyone.

"I wouldn't be surprised if you're very angry at me for thwarting your plan. You felt you were in charge of your own life by deciding to take it. Then I come in and make you live, as if I had no respect for your wishes. As if I believed I knew better than you did. I want you to know that's not the case. I do want to keep you alive, because I have faith and hope that in time you'll find you want to live. I believe your death would be the waste of a valuable life. I believe you have many things to live for."

"I already told you. Not enough."

"We'll talk more later," Hazel Morrisey says.

What the doctor says has interested her despite herself. It has been a long time since anything has made her mind feel lively rather than paralyzed. She wishes the doctor would never come back.

She wonders what it can mean about words if the body is stronger than words.

Which she believes it is. She would like to tell the doctor, Don't you see what I was doing? Turning my body into a sentence, a sentence everyone would have to understand.

But the doctor wouldn't understand. All she wants is for Pearl to live. She doesn't ask: for what. She is one of those people who believes the answer is obvious. She doesn't understand.

· 30 ·

Joseph unwraps sandwiches for the both of them.

"You're good, Joseph."

He frowns. She knows he doesn't like to be reminded of his goodness.

"I can't just sit here doing nothing. Let's go to the hospital. Maybe there's a chink in Dr. Morrisey's armor."

"Do you think that's a good idea?"

"I don't think anything's a good idea. But I want to be there."

"Let's walk, then. You need some exercise, or you won't have any chance of a normal night's sleep."

"Normal," she says. "What would be normal in this situation?"

He understands that she wants him to take charge of things.

He asks the woman at the hotel desk for her advice on getting taxis; she recommends that they walk to a taxi rank half a mile down the quay. She has so thoroughly understood his wishes — a little exercise, but not too much, and then conveyance —

443

that for a moment he would like to take her in his arms.

They give the cabdriver the hospital's name and he starts off, as all cabdrivers do, gunning his engine as if he were digging his spurs into the sides of a reluctant horse.

"No one too sick, I hope," he says. "Although I suppose you wouldn't be in hospital unless you were that sick. What I mean to say is, I hope it's not critical. Terrible time of the year for sickness."

"What's a good time?" Maria says, determined, Joseph can see, to cut short his professional garrulity. But she fails.

"Now, in the good weather, like — I mean to say, spring or summer — the old don't go popping off the way they do in winter. Particularly around the New Year. It must be some kind of stress for them. Where're you from in the States?"

"New York," Joseph says. Maria looks out the window.

"Never been there. Went once to Orlando, Florida. Disney World was a great gas, I'll say that for it. Nothing like that over here."

"Why is Viagra like Disney World?" Maria says.

"Beg pardon?" says the driver.

"Because you have to wait an hour for a ten-minute ride."

This silences the cabby. Joseph isn't sure whether he didn't get the joke or was shocked that a woman told it. Whatever the reason, Maria's tactic worked. There's no more chattering. They drive through the Dublin streets in silence.

The woman behind the desk in the psychiatric section of the hospital has tight blond curls that sit on her scalp like snails on a rock; when she smiles, her eyes narrow and there is no welcome in them when she says "Welcome." Perhaps that's why they hired her, to discourage visitors. Her dentures look as if they might be made of bone; the gums are the pink of new pencil erasers.

"I'd like to see my daughter." Maria says Pearl's name.

"You'd need a special pass for that, I'm afraid. I'll see if there's one for you."

Maria knows that Hazel Morrisey has not issued her a pass. She knows there'll be no indication of permission beside her name, and she knows that when the woman sees it she'll be glad.

"I'm afraid the patient is restricted as to visitors," says the woman, flashing her eraser-colored gums. There are drops of spittle at the corners of her mouth; when she smiles they shine like bits of broken glass. Maria imagines that her power to prevent has made her literally salivate.

Maria recognizes the woman's style; it's similar to the nuns in grade school who refused you recess or permission to go out to the school yard after lunch. Joy in refusal has dried this woman's skin; it has cut ridges into her square fingernails.

"I'd like to speak to your supervisor," Maria says.

"The supervisor's gone home for the day. You may consult her on the morrow."

Her use of *on the morrow* infuriates Maria. "Let me put it another way," she says. "Either you let me talk to someone who can help me see my daughter, or I'm going to stand here and scream at the top of my lungs until someone takes me to the psychiatric ward."

Joseph is wondering if she'll do it. He doesn't know if he wants her to. He too dislikes the woman behind the desk and he has always found Maria's transgressions compelling, even when he hasn't approved.

The woman behind the desk doesn't know how to predict what will come next. Maria steps back. She plants her feet apart firmly so that the ground will give her as much support as possible; she leans her head back, closes her eyes, and puts her hands on her hips. Screams come from her mouth — one, two, three jets of water from a hose — a shock of color in the neutral-colored, anonymously furnished lobby, as shocking as if a fox or a leopard had run through. Joseph wouldn't be surprised to see claw marks on the leather of the chairs and the couches. Will someone come now? Surely someone must come, someone in uniform, a policeman or a guard, to silence her, to lay on hands. But no one in uniform appears. Maria goes on screaming. He doesn't know where she gets the strength, the voice.

"Stop that. Stop that at once!"

The woman behind the desk has risen to her feet. Her face is drained of color, except for two circular red spots on her whey-colored cheeks, like the circles on the cheeks of a cloth doll.

Maria goes on screaming.

"I'm going to call someone in authority!"

Maria doesn't stop screaming until she hears the woman on the phone reporting what she's doing to someone she's referring to as *doctor*.

"You can give over now. Dr. Morrisey's coming down."

"That's all I asked for," Maria says, wiping the corners of her lips with a tissue as if she's just finished a petit four.

"I suppose you're proud of yourself," the woman behind the desk says.

"I am, rather," Maria says, smiling pleasantly.

"This isn't the States, you know. You can't get away with that kind of behavior here."

"Yes, I know. In the States we have things like the Bill of Rights. Concepts like individual freedom."

"There's freedom and there's license, and then there's your kind of carry-on, which there isn't even words for."

Joseph thinks the two of them will go on this way until someone makes them stop, and their sniping is much more unbearable for him than the simple assault of Maria's screaming.

"Insufferable," the woman says, but Joseph sees she's running out of steam and is giving up the fight, whereas Maria's just getting started.

We have to admire Maria, or at least I do, for sheer persistence in getting something done. For a disregard for propriety in the face of what she believes is a larger good. This is why Pearl wants her kept away; her definition of the good is what *she* believes to be the good. It almost never includes refraining from doing something, and it rarely includes restraining her conviction that she knows what is best.

A woman comes out of the elevator. Young, blond, short-haired, slightly unfeminine, an athlete, a runner perhaps, some kind of track and field event: high jump or javelin, Joseph thinks. We have already encountered Hazel Morrisey, but Joseph and Maria have not. Her youth surprises them; they are uneasy having someone so much younger than they in charge of the most important thing in their lives.

She walks up to the two of them.

"I'm Dr. Morrisey. We spoke earlier."

"Actually, I wouldn't call what we did speaking," Maria says. "You offered pronouncements, and I was meant to submit."

"As I tried to suggest, Mrs. Meyers —"

"It's Ms. I'm not married."

The doctor doesn't skip a beat.

"Your daughter's welfare is my concern, not your narcissistic needs. I wonder what you think your performance here has accomplished?"

"It brought you here. I've been trying to contact you all day."

"I can see where Pearl gets her will. I only hope we can use it to keep her alive."

"You said she wasn't going to die."

"I'm doing everything possible. I've had to take some drastic measures, measures that might seem barbaric. She pulled the feeding tube out of her throat so we sewed another to her nose, beside her nostril. It's one reason I don't want you to see her."

"I'm her mother. There's nothing I shouldn't see."

"Perhaps if the world were a fairy tale, a mother could see everything, but it's not. Besides, you don't know what you shouldn't see unless you know what it looks like. Your daughter with a feeding tube sewn to her nostril is not a pretty sight, but she can't afford to be without nourishment anymore. Her friend confirms that she hasn't eaten any food in six weeks."

"Her friend?"

"The bloke she lives with."

Maria hopes it doesn't register that this is news to her.

But if she doesn't admit to not knowing who he is, she has no hope of reaching him or even finding out his name. She knows her daughter's address — or at least the place where mail was sent. But maybe that isn't where she really lived. How odd, Maria thinks, I'm a person who has been lied to. I am a parent from whom my daughter's living arrangements were kept. Which means, of course, the details of her sexual life.

For a person of Maria's age and background, the idea that someone is lying to them about sex is often a surprise. People like Maria and her friends thought *they* were the deceivers; they couldn't imagine that *they* could be deceived, not about sex. Not them.

She's never felt she needed to know the details of Pearl's sex life. A sexual person was an adult by the simple of fact of being sexual. She had no more right to know about Pearl's sex life than Pearl had to know about hers. Pearl had never offered information; Maria had never asked.

She looks into the intelligent uninflected eyes of Dr. Hazel Morrisey. She needs something from this woman; she must calculate how to get it. The gifts that make her good at her job, able to get things she needs from the people she works with, come into play. Dr. Morrisey's face suggests an amenability that her voice did not. Maria must meet her adversary at the place she is and acknowledge the rightness of her position. Establish a common ground. She has done it so often in the past, it isn't difficult to do now.

"I know you think I need to be kept away from my daughter," Maria says, as if a concession has been absolutely and unequivocally made.

"For a time," says Hazel Morrisey, blinking like a gunman momentarily relaxing his stare at the opposing gunman.

"And I understand you may be unwilling to put me directly in touch with this young man. But I was wondering if you could possibly give him my number and offer him the option of getting in touch with me."

"I could certainly do that without compromising anything. Pearl's unwilling to see the boy as well."

Joseph can see Maria's shoulders soften with the relief of a competitor who, if she hasn't yet won, cannot be said to have entirely lost. If Pearl is cutting herself off from everyone, it is far more tolerable than abandoning her mother in favor of a young man. He sees that Maria has begun to win Hazel Morrisey over. Is it just her physical presence? Or is it that, despite herself, Hazel Morrisey was impressed with Maria's civil disobedience, framed as it has become by a display of reasonableness, an ability to compromise? Whatever it is, he can see that Dr. Morrisey — like everyone else — has lost at least some of her initial will to resist Pearl's mother.

"I'll give the fella your number. It will be up to him if he wants to act on it."

"Of course."

"You see, Ms. Meyers, if Pearl is going to trust me, she has to trust me to respect her wishes. I'm already going against her by taking the measures I feel it's vital to take. I'm trying to let her know I'm really with her."

"I understand."

"She's never been on any kind of psychotropic medication? Prozac, or anything like that?"

"She's never been particularly depressed. Ordinary adolescent ups and downs but nothing like this."

"No anorexia or bulimia? Her relationship to food was normal?"

"She loved to eat and is naturally slender. She didn't think about food much, other than liking certain things."

"And politics?"

"I never thought she was very political. When I was involved with things like school board elections and city council races, she took no interest. She wouldn't go to demonstrations with me after she was quite young, and I didn't force her. She said she didn't care about voting because the whole system was corrupt. This made me very angry, so we didn't talk about it. I guess I was disappointed that she wasn't interested in politics, that we couldn't share that."

"I was wondering if maybe she thought she was pleasing you by doing something political. That this was a way she could please you and please herself."

"By giving up her life?"

"I've observed that some young women seem to have a special impulse toward martyrdom. I think of it as the Antigone complex." The doctor blushes; for the first time she is girlish. "Although you mustn't go looking for it in the medical journals. It's only the way I name it for myself."

Martyrdom. Antigone. Joseph is surprised to hear the doctor using those words to describe Pearl's situation. He wonders if there isn't another name, more clinical, more professional, used in countries less steeped in the history and language of the church by doctors who haven't had the accident of a classical education.

He watches the two women, Maria and the doctor. They are leaning toward each other. They understand each other, and they both believe they understand Pearl. The basis of their connection, he realizes, is this: they have both rejected, quickly and automatically, the concept of martyrdom as a useful idea. Thrown it out of the sphere of the acceptable, as you would throw out dirty water or sour milk.

He is not so ready to throw it out. Again he wonders if we must necessarily believe, before we can begin to speak with the assumption of a common language, that nothing is worth dying for. Is it one of the things we must all agree on as civilized human beings, like the idea that slavery is always evil?

He watches the two women talking, nodding in agreement, their heads bobbing up and down. Their nodding discomfits him. What is it to be human if you are unwilling to give up your life?

Unless a grain of wheat falls into the earth and dies, it remains just a single grain; but if it dies, it bears much fruit. . . . Those who want to save their life will lose it.

Is that it, then? Is his belief in the value of giving up your life the product of his early training in a religion in which he no longer believes? Can you lose your faith and hold on to what that faith insists on? Isn't that, in fact, the purest faith, faith without faith? Faith without hope? Faith without the possibility of faith's consolation?

But Pearl was not brought up as a person of faith. What, then, is the source of her conviction that it's worth giving your life for something? And for what? He tries to understand what she was doing before she was stopped. He senses the taste of what she's done, but the details are vague: figures in the mist, shadows of the dead in the Greek underworld.

Are they right, these two women, that it is Pearl who doesn't understand life and they who do? In their conviction that life must be by its nature desirable, good? That life must be preferable to death?

Joseph can't bear the idea that Pearl might die. The thought of her death paralyzes him, terrifies him. But he doesn't want her to have to live in a world in which the possibility of dying for something is automatically considered sick or ridiculous.

He wants to protect her against their closed pleased faces, the faces of the mother and the doctor, refusing to allow the question "Is it always desirable to live?"

Perhaps you too think this question should never be allowed. Or that the answer is so obvious that the question is simply a waste of time. Or that there is something wrong with Joseph for even considering it. He is asking these things of himself. And yet he does not choose to disallow the question, because he believes that to do that dishonors what Pearl has gone through and what she has seen.

Only now does the doctor acknowledge his presence.

"You must be Joseph Kasperman," she says. "I read the letter Pearl wrote you. It was forwarded to me by the embassy; I hope you don't mind."

"No, of course not."

"Something interesting: when I first sedated her, she said your name. 'Joseph won't make me,' she said."

What does it mean? How can it make him feel about himself that he's important to her by his potential failure to make something happen? Of course she's right.

He has never, he believes, made anyone do anything. Yet she wants something of him. Help in giving up her life. He won't do it; no matter how much she wants it of him, no matter how much she believes he's the only one who could.

He's afraid to look at Maria, to see her disappointed face, that in this area of life that is most important to her, he has won something. That Pearl wanted her mother kept away and suggested there was something desirable about him. But why think of it in those terms, winning or losing, the terms of a game? Yet he feels he *has* won something, some place or placement in the regard of the one who is most important to both of them. Once, he would have said Devorah was the most important, but she disappointed him and she is dead. There is no one who even comes close to Pearl in importance. It is possible to say there is no one else whom he can say, with certainty, he loves. Does he love Maria? Certainly he did, at one time; when he was younger, when he didn't mind her winning. What has happened is that he has lost so much he now resents her winning what he thinks is more than her share of the prizes. So perhaps we are not as surprised as he that he takes pleasure in this victory over Maria when he has spent a lifetime not competing with her, in no small part because he always knew he could never want to win as badly. Certainly, he tells himself, he doesn't want to displace her in Pearl's affections. And when he thinks of his prize, he sees how questionable its value is. His only distinction is that his pressure is light enough so he won't be in the way. It is simply this: he isn't forceful enough to keep someone alive.

When finally he looks at Maria's face, it isn't disappointment or resentment he sees there but something new, something unfamiliar. Is it humility?

"Could Joseph go and see her then?" Maria asks the doctor.

"Not just now. She's awfully weak. We want to strengthen her up with some nourishment."

They mean force-feeding, he thinks; the tube sewn into her flesh. Why don't they say what they mean? But perhaps it's better not to. There must be a reason for using language in a way that muffles the truth, that filters it rather than exposing it, a kind of language that is born not of the impulse to tyranny but the impulse to kindness. Is it possible to call it kindness rather than disregard for truth?

Joseph can feel that the atmosphere has changed. But it didn't break with the violence of a storm. It was a gradual lifting; the sky's turning from gray to silver, then a hint of blue. Hope has entered. How?

Maria has done something outrageous, unacceptable, something that should have been dealt with by punishment. And she has not been punished. The opposite has happened. She has got what she wanted.

The prodigal son. Always when he heard the story he identified with the older brother, the stay-at-home. How hurt he must have been at his father's welcome for the delinquent who had done nothing to earn love and had been loved greatly anyway, maybe more greatly.

Maria, though, has never come back for her inheritance. She believes she has given up her share of the fatted calf. Is it a trick or an equivocation that she allows him to spend her father's money on Pearl? To have used her father's money to take time off to get her degree in social work when Pearl was small. To have made certain (there was no need for this, but she felt she needed legal certainties) that, even before Devorah died, Pearl was provided for in Joseph's will. Was this another case of Maria's having her cake and eating it too?

He wonders about Pearl's physical state, wonders why Maria hasn't asked more questions, wonders whether it's his place to ask. Perhaps Maria doesn't want to know details; she often prefers not to have too much information; it might get in her way. He thinks, though, that it might be all right to ask one question of the doctor. Only one.

"Is she in any pain?"

It says something about Joseph, I think, that he asks a question rooted in the present. A modest question, an answerable question, one that doesn't ask for a dangerous prediction that could be proved humiliatingly wrong. I wonder what he would think if he knew that the doctors believed that because Pearl had no memory of pain, her pain was not real. But Dr. Morrisey wouldn't think of discussing that with him. I think we can understand why she is relieved to have been asked a question she can answer.

"No, she's rather heavily sedated at the moment. She's taking a lot of medication: sedatives, nutriments, antidepressants. They'll get her out of this crisis. But it's going to be a long haul before anyone can be sure she's out of danger as a suicide. Because whatever else she's doing, whatever else we call it, whatever she calls it, moral witness or political statement, we have to understand it's at least in part a suicide attempt."

So the doctor is frightened too, Joseph thinks. This makes him feel safer.

"Come upstairs to my office," she says. "It's ridiculous to have this conversation standing in the middle of the corridor."

The receptionist sniffs. "They'll be needing passes."

Dr. Morrrisey signs something. None of the three of them looks at the receptionist.

The doctor's office is a windowless cubicle. There are a few medical books on the shelves, a picture of her in a rowboat with a dark man and two dark children. None of them fair like her. So we share something, Maria thinks, in having children who do not resemble us. She'd like to mention that but decides against it.

"Pearl has never shown any signs of being suicidal," Maria says, "so do you really think this is a suicide attempt? The terms of her statement are moral and political rather than emotional."

"Of course, it's very complicated, and a political death by self-starvation is not unheard of here in Ireland. You can't go far around Dublin without seeing some image of Bobby Sands. Some people think he was a martyr, some people think he was a murderer; after all this time there's still no consensus. But his death is still very much on people's minds."

"What sort of sense would it make to call Bobby Sands's death a suicide?" Maria says. "I mean, to classify it with other suicides, which are a result of some sort of depression or personal despair. It wouldn't make any sense to call Bobby Sands a neurotic."

Joseph is glad she's said that. He remembers thinking of the Buhddist monks during the Vietnam years, setting themselves on fire to witness to the injustice of the war. Had their death had any effect? Was any effect worth Pearl's death? No, not to him. Yet he would not call what she did a suicide attempt; that would dishonor her.

"Well, what your daughter's done has a lot of different aspects to it of course, we can't discount that, but unlike Bobby Sands and other political martyrs she acted entirely alone; she had no community. So that makes it more like a suicide, in my opinion. And then the first reason she gives for her death is to mark the death of the young man for whom she feels responsible. That's a response of private guilt, private remorse, private atonement — even though the boy had relatives who had political connections, Pearl's connection to him wasn't political.

"And like anyone who wants to commit suicide, she believed her life wasn't meaningful. At least not as meaningful as her death. A suicide is essentially overwhelmed by feelings of hopeless passivity. Suicides can't imagine that anything they do matters at all. So when a suicide looks at something horrible, or a series of horrible things, she's not the only one to see it, but to her it has a force that blots out anything else in life. All of us have our days when life doesn't seem worth it, but we usually get over them. A suicide has no other kind of day. It's as if she's always looking directly at the sun or at some sort of unfiltered light. Not that the light isn't there, the rest of us retain our vision by a series of filters that block things out and protect us. A suicide can't protect herself from the things that most of us protect ourselves from. It's not that what she says about the world is wrong, it's not that she's seeing things that aren't there or that the rest of us have never seen, but we push them out of our field of vision because we have to."

He sees Pearl on a desert landscape,

parched, burned by a relentless sun. There are caves she could seek shade in, rocks she could shelter behind, if only for a moment. But she won't. She won't get out of the light. Is there no one who will say that there is reason for this, even courage in it? He dare not say it here, not in front of these women.

"She's going to need extended treatment. I assume you'll be taking her home to New York; I hope you'll be in support of that."

"Of course," Maria says.

Who will treat her? Joseph wonders. How will she be treated? He worries about a rough touch on this skin that has been seared by the too-bright sun, from which she has refused shelter. Her burnt skin needs soothing, protection. What if the hand is clumsy? He looks at Hazel Morrisey's square hands. They have shoved tubes in Pearl against her will; they have sewn things into her flesh. If the touch that thinks of itself as *treatment*, even cure, is too harsh, what will happen to the wounded, abraded skin?

"You see, the drugs and the nutrition we're giving her will help temporarily. But what we need to do, or what she'll need to do for herself, is to have some sense of her own strength to choose to live her life, some ability to forgive herself for the death she thinks she's caused so she doesn't believe she deserves to die. It's a lot easier to prescribe medication than to track the course of her guilt. She'll need a great deal of support."

Hazel Morrisey knows this is a clumsy attempt to put into words the questions that take up her mind: What is the relationship between psychotropic drugs and real inner change? Yet she has to make things clear to Pearl's mother; she has to say what she believes: that both are needed, both medication and the slow cure of the soul. A soul she cannot, as a scientist, prove the existence of and therefore cannot publicly call by name.

"It goes without saying that we'll give her all the support she needs."

"It will need to be on her own terms and at her own pace."

"Of course," Maria says.

Joseph wants to say to Maria, I'm afraid to leave her in your hands. But he doesn't know what his own hands — lacking, as he does, authority or any kind of leverage — could keep Pearl from.

"There's nothing much to do, now, but wait."

"If you asked me to do anything else," Maria says, "run a hundred miles, move a mountain, it would be easier."

"I understand," the doctor says. "I wish I could say something different."

They understand each other, Joseph thinks. What, he wonders, does Pearl understand?

• 31 •

"Your mother's a real piece of work," Tom says. It's the first time Pearl's seen him laugh.

"What do you mean?"

"They wouldn't let her in to see Morrisey, so she just stood in the lobby and screamed until they sent Morrisey down to talk to her. I see where you get your determination."

"I'm nothing like my mother."

"Well, I don't know her, and I don't even know you. I was just thinking of *my* mother. My mother wouldn't stand up to anyone, she's terrified if anyone says boo to her, and she's always letting people get ahead of her on the bus queue or at the supermarket. I guess I'm like that too. We're a pretty quiet family."

"How many are you?"

"Six brothers and sisters, my father, and my mother. We all live on a farm down in County Clare."

"It's just my mother and me."

"Well, we're pretty ordinary."

"You're lucky," she says.

"Yeah, well, you're lucky to have a mother who sticks up for you fearlessly. You're less alone in the world that way. My parents — they never went to college — they'd be terrified to say the first word to Dr. Morrisey. I'd die a thousand deaths if they ever met her."

"Do you miss living in the country?"

"I do, yeah. I hope to go back after the training. But who knows? . . . How are you feeling, then. Is there anything I can do for you?"

"Just tell me some things about your life."

"I'm not much of a talker. I don't think you'd find anything I had to say that interesting."

"Tell me something about your animals."

He feels on the spot. He was never good at talking to girls. And now he knows, somehow, it's terribly important to say the right thing. She's asked for a story about animals. That's a good sign; an interest in animals is always a hopeful thing. He's read about experiments where some depressives were given dogs to care for and others put on Prozac, and the ones who had the dogs to care for did as well as the ones on medication. He feels himself begin to sweat, but he always feels like this when he talks to a girl. Of course, she isn't a girl, she's a patient, Morrisey's patient, and he's already screwed up once. Frantically, he tries to remember everything about every animal he's ever known. A story comes to him. Perhaps she'll like it. People have liked it in the past.

"I'll tell you this one story, about a dog, his name was Nick, and a cat, his name was Scooter.

"Nick was part collie: long fur, mostly white with gold and brown marks, a beautiful plume of a tail, and ears that stood up halfway and then flopped. He hardly ever walked: he pranced, he bounced; he was always curious, like a puppy.

"One day we saw Nick carrying something that looked like a black rag. One of the barn cats had recently had a litter; it was one of the kittens. Nick had its entire head in his mouth and was trotting proudly about, once in a while setting the kitten down and pawing it gently and cocking his head to watch it. Every day Nick would walk around with the kitten for a while and return it to the litter when he was done playing. Then he would come again when the mood hit, take out the black kitten, and play with it for a while.

The kitten flourished. When he was a little bigger, we would see Nick carrying him around by the nape of the neck, the way many animals carry their young. Nick invented a new game — bowling, we named it. He would put Scooter down, trot off a few yards, turn around and charge, knocking the kitten to the ground. Why Scooter put up with it, we couldn't imagine, but he seemed to think it was his destiny to play bowling pin to bowling-ball Nick. He grew to a size where Nick could no longer carry him, but that didn't stop the game. Whenever he saw Scooter, Nick would charge; the cat would gather himself into a bowling-pin shape and wait to be hit.

"One day the following spring, Scooter disappeared. He was a good-sized tomcat at that point, so when he didn't come back all summer we sort of gave up on him. But then one day there was Scooter in the path. I have never seen a cat express joy the way this one did. He purred like a motorboat, rolled around on the ground, took leaps into the air. He jumped into my arms; he felt like a different animal; he was muscular and tough, like a wild animal, not like a pet. Then around the corner of the barn came Nick. He took one look and charged. Scooter just gathered himself up and waited to be knocked down."

Pearl tries to laugh, but it is difficult with her tube. Tom is worried about that, and when the nurse comes in he asks her to check Pearl out.

"She's fine," the nurse says. "You can take a bit of a break. I'm taking your place."

Pearl wants to say she's very sorry someone's taking his place, but she's afraid of embarrassing him.

"I'll be back in a while. You're all right, are you? You're in good hands."

Not as good as yours, she wants to say, but says only, "Thanks. That was a great story."

"See you soon, then." His story has been a success after all, and that isn't the kind of success he is used to.

· 32 ·

The restaurant the young woman in the hotel recommended is traditional: paneled wood, carved chairs, mahogany tables. For a moment Joseph thinks he should refuse food, out of solidarity with Pearl. But he tells himself his weakness won't help her. He needs his strength. He still does not know what for.

They order a bottle of claret, the best on the menu, twenty pounds. The dollar is good against the pound, Maria says, and besides, we need it. She has always had a talent for indulging herself in small pleasures. Of course she could always do that because her father's money was always there, whether she acknowledged it or not, to break her fall, and Joseph was always there too, the fireman holding the net. It was true that she wasn't extravagant, but it was also true that she did not hesitate when she needed something only money could buy; when public school seemed inadequate for Pearl by sixth grade, she could move her to Watson rather than send her to Hunter or Stuyvesant, because languages were better at Watson and the smaller classes meant more personal attention. The bills were sent to him.

The waitress is wearing a straight black skirt that doesn't cover her distressingly bony knees. She must be in her sixties and should know better, Joseph thinks. Or she should be told by someone to wear a longer skirt. Is it because she's being paid to serve me, paid to make my life pleasant, that I feel the right to indulge in such anger toward her? He feels her knees are a visual aggression a paying customer shouldn't be made to endure. Her knuckles pop out of the flesh of her ringless hands. Her teeth are too big for her skull, and when she smiles it can only look false, coming from a countenance of such impoverishment. He believes that if she took off her rubber-soled black shoes he would find bunions on the sides of her fish-flat feet. Her shoulders are bent like crushed coat hangers; she never quite straightens up, and when she takes their order she says yes sir, yes ma'am, thank you sir, thank you ma'am after each item so it comes out many more times than is required. Her servility creates in him an impulse to insult her.

It is a strange impulse, isn't it, the impulse to insult. As if it would relieve some unbearable pressure, re-create right balance in the world: the unbearable weight shifted once more to its proper object.

But Joseph does not, tonight, indulge this impulse. He wishes, though, that the waitress understood that in a falsely democratic world she must work particularly hard not to appear servile. Her failure, her refusal, calls up in him the old terms: master, servant. His mother was a servant. He is the son of a servant. The waitress calls up these terms because they are her terms. She might allow herself to be insulted and then dream of cutting his throat as he lay in his bed.

The waitress brings the wine, a silver — perhaps tin — basket of rolls, a dish of four butter pats like rosettes sitting on a cube of ice. Maria drinks her wine very fast and he disapproves: it's a good wine and should not be gulped. She slathers butter on her roll. He knows how much she loves butter; as a child she would eat it plain. In Italy, butter is not brought with bread, and he prefers it so. The pale fat of the northern palate: he has never liked it.

Maria looks at the menu, which the waitress, having taken their order, has failed to remove. "December twenty-eighth," she says. "Feast of the Holy Innocents. I can't help it; those feast names pop up when I hear certain dates. Like August fifteenth, Assumption; March twenty-fifth, Annunciation. It happened with Pearl's father; it's how we both knew we'd had a Catholic education."

The skin on the back of Joseph's neck prickles. Pearl's father: has Maria ever said anything about him before? He doesn't even know the man's name; she never used it.

"Holy Innocents," she says. "I always hated that day; it was one of the things that made me lose my faith. I didn't want any part of worshiping a God who could have saved thousands of babies but allowed them to be slaughtered. And then to celebrate that and call it a feast? It's disgusting."

An old picture, readily brought to mind: mountains of babies, mothers tearing at their own breasts, tearing at the muscular arms of soldiers who ignore them and throw their babies onto a pile. A pile mixed in his mind with piles of bones and shoes in Auschwitz. And how many others for which he has no pictures and no words. Holy Innocents. If there is holiness he believes that their innocence, their very helplessness, has made them holy.

"I never felt that way about it," Joseph says. "I always thought it was right to commemorate that kind of horror, rather than pretend it didn't exist."

But Maria isn't listening. "All you had to do to be called holy was to be slaughtered. Without protest. Why are there no feasts celebrating heroic resistance? Or attempts to change the injustice of power?"

Because that is not hopeless, not helpless, and this feast honors helplessness; that is its greatness, he wants to say. But he knows that whatever he says she's not listening.

She butters another roll, puts down the knife, puts a piece of roll into her mouth, chews, swallows. "The canonization of victimization. *Une spécialité de la maison catholique.* It's not hard to sympathize with victims. Victims don't change anything. It's what disturbs me most about what Pearl's doing. It's such a weak act; it denies the possibility of change. Of standing with others and putting up a fight. That's what changes things, not somebody wasting away. Solitary acts like that are always hopeless."

All the time Maria is talking, she is chewing. She has ordered steak, bloody-rare, and she is dipping pieces of it into a little pyramid of salt she's made at the edge of her plate. She's put butter on her potatoes and her roll. The blood from her steak makes a pinkish pool on the white plate. The tablecloths are pink; there are pink shades on the small lamps that sit on every table. He is revolted by the pinkness all around him, by the heavy, too-rich food, the overheated air, the noisy conversation all around him, no words distinguishable. Gesturing, Maria has spilled some of her wine. It makes a dark rose blot on the pink cloth; she spills salt onto it: a housewife's instinct. She plays with the salt, pushing it around with her fingers until it looks like pink snow. Diamonds of grease swim in the blood that oozes from her steak. She dips a forkful of potato into it.

"We can change things, people can, by thinking clearly and cooperating with one another. But no one can do anything alone. People must stand together, or the darkness wins."

He has kneaded his roll into crumbs. His fingertips are dry, abraded by the sharp crusts. He feels the blood pool at the top of his skull, collect in a dark clot, a caul between his brain stem and his neck. The thick blood boils up, creates a pressure that makes him feel the shape of the bones that make up his head.

Maria picks up the empty butter dish, looks over her shoulder, puts the dish back down.

"Where the hell is that waitress?" she says, and looks around again. "I need more butter. Joseph, can you get me more butter?"

He sees his mother's face in the dining room of the Regina Caeli nursing home. She is wearing a hat made of a paper towel, the hat she makes for herself every day at lunch and wears all afternoon until it's taken off her head at bedtime. He sees the spittle at the edge of her lips when she says "Filthy, filthy!" to Maria. And Maria's hands, wringing themselves, pressing her nails into her palms, her hands red with hatred as if she'd dipped them in cold water or in blood. He sees Dr. Meyers's fine white hands, counting out bills and coins into the hands of his mother: large, red, and pawlike. His mother the servant.

He has been a servant to Maria, to her father, to his mother, to Devorah. He has been a servant all his life. And Maria knows, she must always have known, although she has pretended to forget it. But she has never forgotten it, not for a minute, and now it strikes him as unbearable; he will not put up with it anymore.

479

He takes the butter dish from her hand and bangs it, hard, onto the table.

"You've had enough butter," he says. "You've had more than enough."

She blinks at him; she doesn't understand. He is refusing her something. It may be the first thing he has refused her. The waitress scurries over. "Is everything all right with your dinner here? Can I get you something else?" Wearing a wholly wrong, false, ingratiating smile. Maria wonders what she's heard, what she makes of it.

"Nothing for me," Joseph says to the waitress. "I'm afraid I've been taken ill." He gets up and leaves, saying nothing to Maria, as if the waitress were his hostess at a dinner party and she's a guest he's been seated with, whose name he hasn't caught.

She watches him put on his coat and his scarf, one she had bought him as a Christmas gift, as he walks out between the tables. He's accused her of greed. He's said she's eaten too much. And Pearl is starving. The irregular oblongs of meat, the ovals of potatoes, less than half consumed, stare up at her reproachfully. She knows she mustn't follow him, so what should she do? She looks down at her food. The salty smell of the excellent meat rises up to her. Her mouth fills with water. It's terrible, she knows, how much she wants to finish her dinner. The waitress is waiting to see whether she'll follow the man out of the restaurant or go on with her meal. She must decide right now. Should the food be taken away or left? Joseph has fled, hungry, into the gloomy night. On an empty stomach, she thinks. Ridiculous, he isn't crawling on his stomach. She feels helpless, and the churning juices of her own stomach make her feel worse. Something enormous has just happened, and all that is open to her is the decision of whether or not to eat.

Eat to live. Live to eat. What does this have to do with the question of whether or not she should finish her steak? Why does it seem wrong to eat when something enormous has just happened? What is *not eating*, fasting? Her daughter is fasting. Days of fast and abstinence: requirements loosened by the Second Vatican Council but never given up by her father: always, he refrained from meat on Fridays, refused to eat between meals during Lent, ate nothing from Good Friday to Easter morning. So what did that mean about him? She tries to make the connection between fast and virtue. My father, she thinks, was a man who could give up meat but not the use of the word *mine*.

You should not be surprised that at this moment, by any definition a moment of crisis in her life, the terms of her childhood come up to her: *fast, abstinence, sin, virtue.* If you had lived in exile, even if you had exiled yourself and had learned or taught yourself a new language, would it be surprising if, in a dire time, the words you grew up speaking were the ones that came to your lips? Maria shakes herself, like a wet dog. She must decide what to do, right now, and not be calling up the old wrong terms of the past.

And yet they will not go away. The sin of greed, she says to herself. Am I greedy like my father? Joseph has accused her of being greedy. His mother accused her of being greedy: "You are a greedy girl." She thinks of Marie Kasperman's face, red, sweating, always reminding her of raw meat. And she is suddenly afraid of the food in front of her. At the same time, her mouth waters from the smell.

He is his mother's son. And she is her father's daughter. Nothing can change that. If she could have, she would have destroyed me, Maria thinks. But I held my tongue. For him.

She is right to be proud of that because

it was a struggle, holding her tongue, her silence a hard-won victory. She will not say this of herself, but I can say it for her: she did it out of love. Because she loved Joseph's goodness, his restraint, his doing quietly whatever needed to be done. She loved these things, yes, but it is also possible to say she needed them. They were her buckler and her shield. So she kept silence, difficult for her, and he kept silence, a habit that came to him more easily.

But what was their silence? Was it perhaps only a glass floor laid over a pit? Had they been tiptoeing all their lives on a floor of glass, thinly covered by a silken carpet? And now, it seems, he has stepped hard and broken through.

What should I do? Maria asks herself, because this is the question she always asks.

She tells herself she must grab on to something. She must stop her fall. She must concentrate on what needs to be done. Is it possible that everything is centered on the decision whether or not to eat? The food is here; it is still hot; it is less than a minute since Joseph left the restaurant. She must think of what can make a difference. To think of that would be to break the fall.

For now, strength is required, strength to wait. To endure her own helplessness. To wait for the boyfriend to get in touch. To wait for the doctor's word. To wait for her daughter's word. To wait and see what Joseph will do next.

It's simple, she says to herself. I should eat. Food brings strength. I require strength. Therefore food.

She cuts into the meat and salts it, dipping into the pyramid of salt she's already made. She puts the salty meat into her mouth. Chews, swallows, sips wine. Another taste: bitter. Bites into the potatoes. Soft: pleasantly dull.

She can do nothing but eat. There is no one to talk to and she has no book to read. She tries to be curious about her fellow diners but cannot attach the slightest importance to any of them. She opens her mouth. Chews. Swallows. Alternates flavors.

She is full now; she is strengthened. She made the right decision. It was better that she ate.

She asks the maître d' if he can call her a cab. "I can so," he says, and she is charmed by his diction. She's reminded how much easier it is to be charmed by other human beings if you've been well fed.

Are you appalled by Maria's finishing

her supper? Would you like her better if she couldn't eat? I understand that possibly you would. Perhaps, though, you should ask yourself: What is the relation between love and appetite?

The cab drives her across the quay. The water under the electric lights is reptile colored. The whole city, with its flat house fronts, its dark squares of only dimly apprehended windows with the occasional silvered rectangle, suggests nothing of a holiday; she imagines people weary in their beds.

She lets herself into her room and takes off her coat, which threatens to overbalance the plastic chair she throws it on. She dials Joseph's number. There is no reply.

· 33 ·

Someone Pearl has never seen, a woman in her sixties perhaps, is sitting in Tom's chair. Then he comes back into the room. "I'm here to relieve you," he says to the woman. And Pearl thinks, I am relieved that he is here.

"I think the patient's asleep," the woman says.

She was asleep but she is glad not to be sleeping now. In her sleep, memories swim up; she is frightened, people are holding her down, they are putting things in her nose. She does not know if this really happened or if it is a dream. She touches her nose. A tube is attached to it. So it was not a dream. Yet she does not remember.

She is very hungry.

· 34 ·

In the dark, lying on her back, her head entirely flattening the unsatisfactory pillow — made, Maria guesses, of some synthetic material that didn't exist when she was a child — she tries to understand what happened. What did she do to cause Joseph's outburst? An outburst in someone who has, as long as she has known him, her whole life, never burst out? Or almost never. Only twice does she remember him losing his temper. There was the time in 1995 when they were speculating about the nature of the response to the millennium. He said it would be hard to celebrate the end of the century because he believed it was the bloodiest in the history of the world. She and Devorah had disagreed with him. They said the numbers might be greater, but that was an accident of technology. The impulse to destroy had always been the same. And the same technology, they had said, the two of them tumbling over each other like good-natured puppies to agree with each other and disagree with him, had saved millions of lives. And what about antibiotics?

The blood had risen to his face. He stood up and grabbed the chair he'd been sitting on, lifting it slightly off the floor. "You do not, do not, do not know what you are talking about!" He banged the chair on the floor with every repetition of *do not*. And he had done the same thing, repeated a phrase three times, when she and Devorah suggested that Maria might become an egg donor for them. "You will not, will not, will not speak of this ever again!" Both times he had walked out of the room. But both times, at least in her memory, it was summer, and his walking out into the leafy daylight did not have the desolating effect of his walking into the bitter Dublin night. And both times Devorah had been with her. She is alone now.

She remembers the time she and Devorah came up with the idea, a foolish one; they were both forty-three and Maria was too old to be an egg donor; any medical student could have told her that. But they didn't talk to any doctors; they came up with the plan themselves over brunch and burst into the house — no, it wasn't the house, it was the apartment on 89th Street — one Sunday morning. Joseph and Pearl had just come home from the museum, and Pearl had gone home. I think it's a good thing Pearl didn't see what happened: Devorah and Maria bursting in, telling Joseph they'd come up with a wonderful plan; there was no reason why Devorah's early menopause meant she couldn't have a child. And then Joseph banged the chair down and said, three times, as if it were a spell, that they weren't to speak of it again. *Devorah,* she thinks now, *you were my beloved friend, and you are dead. I don't understand anything: what Pearl's done, what Joseph did just now. Do you, among the dead, understand things I cannot?*

If you understand, you must help me. Help me understand.

Pearl cannot be allowed to become one of the dead. Like Devorah. Like her father.

The thought of her father's death is, as always, a sheet of slate pressed down on her, hardening her heart. Making it a heart of stone. She will not regret what she did, what she had to do, in the name of justice. She won't think about her father now. It is Devorah among the dead whom she misses, not her father, tapping the white tips of his fingers together, light bouncing off the glass of his rimless spectacles. Her father and the pope had had the same glasses: Seymour Meyers and Pius XII.

She was glad when it had come out that Pius XII had done nothing to save the Jews. Had collaborated with the Nazis and could not be admired in good faith. As she no longer admired her father, had given up admiring him when he allowed her friends to go to jail. She will not think about her father now.

She gets out of bed. A bath is what she needs. She lowers herself into steaming water, almost too hot for her to bear.

In the hot water, she lets her eyes fall on her breasts, which have lost, she knows, their prized youthful allure. She thinks of when her breasts were, for Pearl, a source of perfect nourishment. And this daughter is dying from starvation now. Loss and loss and loss. She weeps for the consolation, lost, of nursing a child, those moments when it was impossible for either of them to fail, to disappoint. She doesn't care what her face looks like. If she could catch a glimpse of herself in the mirror it would mean nothing to her. She would not be herself.

In the water, which is cooling in a way that makes her feel her skin belongs to someone else, her tears no longer seem authentic; it is as if someone else has entered the room; it is as if she is being watched.

She quickly gets out of the tub.

She dries herself on thin cotton towels, more like diapers, she thinks. She rings Joseph's room. And once again there is no answer.

· 35 ·

"Such a shame, such a beautiful girl," Pearl hears a nurse say to Tom. What does she mean by that? That if she hadn't thought Pearl beautiful she wouldn't consider what happened to her such a shame? What, then, would she have considered it?

Words, ideas, are coming into greater focus in her mind. She can think of things following each other. Things leading from each other. Things she understands. She is very hungry.

Beautiful girl. It is important to be a beautiful girl; she has known for a long time that it was important, that those words made things possible. But did she want those things? *Beautiful girl.* Was it being something or having something? Something she had and her mother had but not every woman had. And something people wanted. Wanted from you if you had it. They wanted it from her mother too. She had got whatever it was from her mother: a way of being looked at, favors granted, allowances made. And some other things, not nice, connected to it. Something people wanted that she might not want to give, that had nothing to do with her, something because of which people would give her things she didn't want and want things from her that she didn't want to give.

Such a beautiful girl.

How can this be? There is a tube sewn into her nose, a tube stuck in her vagina. This is not a body anyone could want anything of. It is no longer even hers. It is the doctor's body now. The doctor makes things happen that she does not want. But she no longer knows entirely what she wants. Starved, she knew exactly her desire. Now she is hungry and afraid.

My mother, she thinks, is in this city now. The city where I am.

The doctor is speaking to Tom. "We're cutting the Midazolam way down. She'll be much more lucid now. She might want to communicate more. But be careful. Her will is very strong."

• 36 •

In the late night air, supersaturated with raw dampness, Joseph walks and walks. His gloves are good and keep his hands warm, but his shoes are wrong for this climate, bought in a different world with a different set of considerations. Yes, it is sometimes cold and damp in Rome — in all of Italy, particularly in the north — but they don't seem to think of that; it isn't in the forefront of their minds when they're designing their shoes or their houses.

He is walking because he can't think of anything else to do. He doesn't even know where he's walking. The city is a closed box to him because he's refused what he has come to think of as the easy out of maps and guidebooks. He was going, like Ruskin, to depend on the strenuous exercise of his eye. And when he dressed he hadn't thought he would be walking tonight; he was going to the hospital, the restaurant.

His shoulders ache; his throat constricts from the strain of unnatural effort. Perhaps from all the years of never having said,

"But that isn't what I want, you see, that isn't what I want at all."

Never wanting to go along with Maria's plans, to the synagogue at Yom Kippur, to the Village to buy marijuana, to demonstrations against the war. "Let's talk about the worst martyrdoms we can imagine," she would say when they were children. No, he wanted to say. Let's pray that we'll be spared, that we'll never have to think of it. And never saying to his mother, Please be quiet, please don't talk to me about your skin rashes, your insect bites, your constipation, Maria's hair in the bathtub, the traces of Dr. Meyers's shit on his underpants. Please, please, is there nothing you will not say?

And the money. He'd believed it was his responsibility to keep the business going. Of all imaginary accusations, the one he'd most feared was lack of gratitude. He was his mother's son. He was unable to attach a face to his father's name. As his mother's son, his fate ought to have been that of the son of a domestic servant. A laborer. With luck, a minor clerk. Insurance man. Accountant. But he'd been given magnificent opportunities. Access to the highest culture. A splendid education. How could he complain about being placed at the head of a successful business?

It had never occurred to him to say, But this isn't what I want. It had never occurred to him to take seriously the question that preoccupied his generation: What makes me happy? He'd thought a better question, a fuller, finer one, was: What is the right thing to do? Perhaps that was why he didn't know what to say when Maria had asked him, desperation in her voice, "But Pearl's always been happy, hasn't she?" He hadn't thought of happiness for her, any more than he'd thought of it for himself. It didn't seem the appropriate category for her, as it hadn't for him.

He knew he couldn't be happy if he thought he wasn't doing the right thing. It hadn't occurred to him that there were different kinds of rightness. The rightness, for example, of his absorption in the works of art he loved.

Try and imagine, if you will, the nineteen-year-old Joseph, student of art history. Absorbed, taken up, electrified by his mind's devotion to this new subject: medieval reliquaries. A subject he could think of as *his*, truly his own, perhaps the first possession he could think of in that way, even believing that it might be deserved because it had been earned. He wrote his senior thesis on a reliquary in the Cloisters, a triptych, with lapis and gold angels forming the outer wings and, in the middle, glass revealing the relic lined with pearls. It was meant to have been given to a convent in the city of Buda by St. Elizabeth of Hungary. Do you know about Elizabeth, queen of Hungary in the thirteenth century? I will tell you the story.

Elizabeth was the virtuous wife of a tyrant husband. During a famine, he forbade her to feed his starving subjects. Against his will, she walked into the streets, bread hidden in her skirt. Her husband discovered this and threatened to have her killed by his soldiers as a punishment for having defied his orders. He accosted her at the castle gate. He demanded that she loosen her skirt. She did and behold! There was not bread but roses. He fell to his knees, begged her forgiveness, and became a virtuous benevolent ruler.

Joseph had loved that story from the first time he read it, in one of Maria's books, *Fifteen Saints for Girls.* He'd read the whole book; he found it fascinating. He remembers a description of a Blessed Margaret Clitherew, an Englishwoman martyred by Henry VIII, or maybe it was Elizabeth. The priest she is hiding in her house says of her, "She is not an English rose but rather a firm white hollyhock."

When he was a boy, that story generated a kind of proto-arousal, an excitement that was not yet sexual, when he thought of the connection between women and flowers. Roses in a skirt, the firmness of a hollyhock. When he had first seen a woman's body, Devorah's, the only one he's ever seen, he had not been disappointed, just delighted that the metaphors were so apt.

Now he believes he must think of himself as a man who has fallen to imagining sniffing the armpits of waitresses. He is not a specialist in medieval reliquaries but the head of a corporation whose business is the spread of ugliness.

But he believed he had lived his life above reproach. He could not have borne reproach: from Dr. Meyers or from his mother. But Dr. Meyers is dead and his mother is rocking and gibbering and Devorah made a mockery of his idea of the great gift and Pearl has made a mockery of all their ideas of safety. Now he can reproach himself for being a fool and, worse, a betrayer. Just now, over a plate of meat in a restaurant where everything was pink or pinkish, because he thought Maria was eating too much butter, because she asked for more, asked him to get her more, he allowed his anger to break through, the anger he had always hidden, swallowed, killed.

But what if she hasn't really understood? Or if she's been able to convince herself, as she often can with uncomfortable truths, that it really wasn't what it seemed? He thinks of Pearl saying, "My mother is distractible." He knows she believes that the center of the world is not impenetrable but porous and susceptible to change. That things are not done once and for all. So maybe he can say, "Sorry, I don't know what got into me. I guess we're both under a lot of stress." Strange, isn't it, the history of the word *stress,* once used primarily by engineers, now called on to explain almost everything.

And perhaps she'll say, "Forget it. Let's concentrate on what needs to be done."

Perhaps, in a little while, he'll do it. He'll say, "Sorry . . . stress." But not now. Now he wants to walk.

· 37 ·

Maria wakes at seven in the morning and forces herself to the discipline of brushing her teeth and washing her face before she telephones to see if Joseph is in his room. An old habit: small penances, minor sacrifices, wages offered up to the unseen. So she will brush her teeth before she calls but allow herself to telephone before she takes a shower.

He isn't there. This means something terrible, something else she can do nothing about. Whatever he does when they see each other, she thinks she'll be able to respond well. If he's apologetic, she'll say, "It's nothing. We're all under stress." If he pretends nothing has happened but leaves her a message naming a time for lunch, for dinner, she'll say nothing.

But what if he wants to talk about it? That would be quite unlike Joseph. Yet what he did last night was quite unlike him also. If he wants to talk about why he was angry with her, she'll do that. She can do anything he asks of her. What is unbearable is what is being asked of her now: that she wait. Her only possible act a mental one, to understand the implications of there being nothing for her to do.

She showers. The thin transparent cap is insufficient to protect her hair. Her hair will be wet, and this will be unpleasant in what she imagines is the day's damp cold. Her window looks out only on the empty — no, rubbish-strewn — courtyard; she has no idea what the weather is really like. She goes down to the breakfast room, still smelling of beer, praying that she won't run into the women from breakfast two days ago.

She eats oatmeal with milk, butter, and sugar. She butters her toast and adds a thick film of marmalade. What would Joseph say to that? She feels shame at the memory of last night. She knows she is eating like a child, but it's what she wants.

She doesn't know what to do with the rest of the day. Dr. Morrisey will speak to her at four. It's now nine-fifteen. She doesn't know where Joseph is. She can't think of anyplace she'd like to go.

When she gets to the lobby, the woman at the desk says, "There's a young man to see you."

For a moment, Maria thinks she means

Joseph. Then she remembers: Joseph can no longer be described as young.

"I'm Finbar McDonagh."
You have, I hope you will remember, the advantage over Maria. You know a certain amount about Finbar; she knows nothing. She has been given nothing but a name. The young man says his name as if it were enough. His hair is lank, red, shoulder-length; he's wearing an army greatcoat — it could be from any army — and black lace-up boots that overbalance his slight body. The fingernails of his childish freckled hands are bitten; he's tried to grow a mustache but it's a mistake, a sign not of bravado or virility but of an inner despondency so habitual it's impaired the growth of his facial hair. When Maria looks into his eyes, she sees blue-green stones, impatient eyes that don't like to rest too long on any one thing, eyes that reveal that this boy has read many books and wishes it weren't so, but he will always read many books; there's nothing he can do about it. His eyes are red-rimmed as if he hasn't slept or has been crying.
"I'm Maria Meyers."
"I know. I'm Pearl's friend."
Friend. This means lover. They shared a

domain. She's disappointed for her daughter. Another rescue mission, she thinks, comparing this boy's weedy body, his failed masculinity, with Pearl's realized beauty, her long legs, straight spine, hair that falls down her back like a shower of dull gold. She wishes that Pearl had picked someone more attractive, so that people would have smiled when they saw them on the street. So that Pearl could have had the fun of that. But Maria has never grasped the idea that perhaps that kind of fun would be to Pearl beside the point. Or not fun at all.

It's always been difficult for Maria to understand that Pearl hasn't taken pleasure in being looked at. And you may find it hard to understand: a child whose mother's eye always fell on her with joy, a beautiful girl, looked on favorably by the eye of the world. I don't know quite why myself, but from early childhood Pearl felt that being looked at was being stolen from. The actor's joy in performance — so much a part of her mother's life — was never part of hers. How do we explain, then, what she's doing now, insisting that she be looked upon, studied, taken in? I must admit I don't quite understand how she came to it. Except perhaps that the pain of this visibility was something she thought of as the price she paid for witness. The price of atonement.

Maria and Finbar look at each other in silence. It's impossible for them to behave normally with each other. There is too much or too little to say.

From somewhere, a voice tells her that at moments like these, when it's impossible to imagine the right thing to do, it's best not to rely on the imagination but to fall back on convention. The habitual or formal gesture is the one that best serves. He is coming here because she is his girlfriend's mother. What would a girlfriend's mother do if the circumstances were ordinary? That the circumstances are not ordinary is the part that must be pushed aside.

"Have you had your breakfast?" she asks.

The boy begins to cry. He's appalled at himself. I think that if he could have done anything else in the world — hit Maria, set fire to the hotel, vomited on the carpet — he would have found it preferable.

From the basketful of gestures in her repertoire she pulls up one and hands him a Kleenex from the packet in her handbag. She doesn't look at him. She pretends to be fumbling for something at the bottom of her purse.

"You need protein," she says. "Come upstairs with me to the horrible breakfast room: my treat. You can have eggs and sausages. I'm sure you don't have to worry about cholesterol, not at your age. Unless you're a vegetarian. Pearl was a vegetarian for a while. But she gave it up. I must say it made life easier."

She realizes that this chatter is the wrong thing; she's losing him. Her first instinct was right. She should be a mother: Pearl's mother, anybody's mother. The most typical of her kind.

She is sorry for this boy, as if what he's gone through had nothing to do with her daughter. She can see he's gone through a great deal. She remembers something she read once about a knight going through an ordeal. This boy has gone through an ordeal, she keeps saying to herself. The word *ordeal* presses itself on her shoulders; she feels its heaviness and its extent.

In the tale she'd read, the knight who needed to gain access to magic asked another suffering knight, "What are you going through?" And this was the right question, the one that unlocked magic.

What are you going through? she would like to ask this young man, whom she sees not as himself (she knows nothing about him) and not as anyone connected to her daughter, but simply as a young man standing for all young men who have gone through ordeals. No, not gone through. He isn't out of the woods yet.

She wonders why she isn't angry at him. Then she understands it's because she could never imagine his making Pearl do anything she didn't want to do. She knows her daughter's force, and she sees that sitting across from her is a person of no force.

The waitress shows them to a table in the farthest corner of the room. Even from there, Maria can't help hearing American conversation.

"You from the South?" a man asks the two young women at the next table.

"Charleston, South Carolina."

"I was in South Carolina once. Not once. I mean, once for a long time. When I was in the Marines. Parris Island. We used to call it 'the land that time forgot.' "

The waitress brings them tea in a brown pot. "Please fill up," Maria says. "It's the same cost no matter how many times you go back."

"I'm not a vegetarian," Finbar says. "Pearl loved our sausages. She said she couldn't stand American ones, they were too fatty."

"She always hated fat on meat," Maria says, alarmed that they are both speaking about Pearl in the past tense.

"She said we wouldn't like each other," Finbar says, stirring a third spoonful of sugar into his tea. "She never wanted us to meet."

"I tended to give her a hard time about her boyfriends. I never thought they were right for her."

"What made you think you knew what was right for her?" he says, and his mouth suddenly looks nasty. She's tempted to answer him in the tone that his remark and the line of his mouth deserve, but she needs this connection; she needs to learn things from him.

"It's an occupational hazard with mothers," she says, hoping she hasn't lost her power to charm. "Maternal narcissism is a widespread disease."

"That most don't want the cure of."

She likes his syntax but can see that, nevertheless, he's one of Pearl's lame ducks. Of the foreign variety, therefore exotic, therefore with more obvious appeal.

She looks into his eyes, smiling, and he blushes.

"Actually, what I'd like is porridge," he says.

'That's what I had," she says, as if this bond between them were profound.

When he walks over to get himself porridge, she sees how young he looks from the back. She wonders how old he is. Hard to tell with the young, she thinks, feeling her own lack of youth.

He piles the overfull bowl of porridge with butter, sugar, and cream. A version of her own bowl, but the boy's version. A fearful child's habit, a child who fears that his delight will be interrupted, stolen, or forbidden, arbitrarily kept back.

"Are you a student?" she asks.

"I guess, yeah. I'm doing Irish. That's how we met — I mean Pearl and I."

He doesn't say Pearl and me. He is a middle-class child, despite the excessive helpings of butter and sugar.

"She's good at it. She's bloody fantastic for someone who never did it before. I mean, in a few weeks, she was caught up with people who'd done it for years. I'm in the advanced class."

He is struggling, an age-old struggle not to brag about his intellectual achievements because he knows, he has always known, it won't win him friends. And friends are what he desperately wants. So he's trying to pretend it doesn't matter to him, being in the advanced class.

"It wasn't meant to turn out like this," he says, his cheeks flushing in a way that reminds her of Devorah, the one redhead she'd known well.

"How could it possibly have been meant to turn out like this?"

She doesn't know what her tone conveys; she understands that he wants understanding from her, forgiveness maybe, absolution best of all. She isn't tempted to withhold it, perhaps because he is so obviously weak.

"What I mean is, she got me confused. I misread her. I thought she was with us in a way she turned out not to be."

"Us?"

"Our movement. What we call the Real IRA. Those of us — and we're not a few, and we're not thugs or madmen as the media would like you to believe — those of us who think the peace treaty is a great betrayal. A betrayal of hundreds of years of sacrifice. Just for the sake of Eurodollars."

"Go on. I'm a bit lost."

"Pearl and I were in accord about people all over the world being motivated solely by greed these days. The almighty dollar. We talked a lot about how the collapse of the Berlin Wall meant there was no idea in the world now except the idea of profit. I know she was with me on that. I thought she understood how the whole treaty thing is a part of it. Then she started talking about tales and stories and how we needed stories and not tales. I'd no idea what that had to do with the treaty. I thought it was just literary theory; she was more literary than I was. It's hard sometimes to know what she's really thinking."

"I know."

"You see, she can do these silences and if you talk a great deal, like me, you can assume those silences are filled up with whatever you've just said."

"I know what you mean," she says. She understands that this boy loves her daughter, that he feels he failed her and, at the same time, that she failed him. His thin shoulders are bowed down by the weight of all that failure; his babyish chest is narrowed by it.

"So it was only at the very end, after everything went so wrong, after all the business with Stevie, that I realized she wasn't with us, she was *for* the treaty, she could only see wanting the violence to stop, not that violence was the only weapon that we had and would lead to less violence in the future. She couldn't see that. She had no idea that the violence was a tragic but necessary price, she was just listening to me, pretending to agree with me and waiting till she knew just what she wanted to say. But she only made that clear after the whole Stevie business."

"I don't know what the Stevie business is."

"Yeah, well, you wouldn't, would you," he says, nasty again. "I don't think Pearl was exactly confiding in you toward the end."

"We were three thousand miles apart."

"Whatever."

Maria is irritated, as she always is, by the use of that word, a tic among the young. *Whatever.* Without an adverbial objective. Strange to hear it in an Irish accent, a noxious American import, like Muzak or McDonald's.

"You were going to tell me about someone called Stevie."

"He was the son of a very good friend of mine. A sad case, really. My friend did everything he could. He's American. You probably don't know him."

She nods, as if it were surprising that there is an American she doesn't know.

"The thing about Mick is, he never lost the faith."

For a minute, she thinks that Finbar might mean that the man is still a practicing Catholic. But he can't possibly mean that, although it's the only context in which she's ever heard the term. Lost the faith. Among her father's friends, it was a common locution. But this boy must mean something different.

"Stevie came from a noble line. A noble line," he says, slipping into the language of saga, assuming the bardic tone. "His uncle's been in prison since 1982. You've probably heard of the Leeds Eight. Reg Donegan. Stevie's mother is his sister."

Maria doesn't dare confess that she hasn't heard of the Leeds Eight or of Reg Donegan. She assumes it's something to do with an IRA bomb. She notices that Finbar doesn't give a name to the female he's mentioned. Someone's mother. Someone's sister.

"Stevie was Mick's child, but of course he couldn't marry the mother."

"Why was that?"

"He has a family in the States. She knew it all along. But he never abandoned Stevie, he always acknowledged him and sent her money and came over here to be with them one month of every year. There's not many men would do that."

He takes a few spoonfuls of oatmeal, a few sips of tea.

"There was something slightly wrong with Stevie, not quite the full shilling. A bit slow. Pearl said she thought he was dyslexic. She was trying to help him. They got on great, the two of them. She was devoted to him, and he to her."

Maria remembers Pearl asking her for advice, materials, for dealing with a dyslexic kid. "How old is he?" she asks.

"Fifteen at the time of his death."

Always, this is a shocking sentence. The conjunction of the word *death* and a number so near the beginning of life.

"You see, Stevie's mother, Breeda, couldn't take it in the north anymore. The Gardai were always ripping up her place in Belfast whenever there was any trouble, on account of her brother, even though she's never been involved, not the least little bit. She's not so much on the brain power herself. So she came down here, works as a char in an office building. They seemed to be doing all right. Stevie loved it. Mick would come over and take him everywhere. Stevie loved sitting around with all of us. We didn't think he got the political stuff, but he seemed to like being one of the blokes, you know, sitting about, having a few jars. It made him feel a part of things. I think it was hard for him at school. I'm not sure he could actually read before Pearl came along and started working with him. When we'd all be together in the sitting room — the blokes, I mean — the two of them would be in the kitchen working at the reading. I thought it was great at the time, but it probably wasn't a good thing for Stevie. As Mick said, it raised unrealistic expectations. Unrealistic hopes. And he wanted to be a big man in front of Pearl. Stevie, I mean. And then we all got carried away that one time and the whole thing became unfortunate."

She pours more tea into his cup, nudges the sugar bowl toward him.

"Mick was very big in the antiwar movement in the Vietnam days. Pearl says you were involved, but I'm sure not to the extent that Mick was."

Maria wants to say, You have no idea of my past, no idea about what price I've paid. But it is not the time for this kind of talk, and she doesn't want to think about her father now.

"Mick was close to Abbie Hoffman. He was with him in the Yippies. At the beginning part, particularly."

I'll bet, Maria wants to say, thinking of

all the people who claimed to be close to Abbie Hoffman, or on the Pentagon March, or at Woodstock, or to have seen *Hair* while it was still off-Broadway.

"Mick's story is really remarkable. He comes from a wealthy New England family. I believe they came over on the *Mayflower*. He left his family over Vietnam. It wasn't till much later that they were reconciled. He really lives poor; he gives vast sums to our fellows over here. He'd give more, only he has to provide for his own family — well, the two families, the biological families, he calls them, which we all understand, of course. We cod him about being part of the Protestant Ascendancy. I don't know if you know what that means over here. It's the English-born Protestants who have all the land and the money."

She almost says, You are simply going to have to stop condescending to me. But she needs to keep his favor. She still hasn't heard Stevie's story, which seems to be connected, somehow, to Pearl's. Without this information, she's paralyzed.

"So this one day, Mick's telling us about one time with the Yippies. About how they brought down the war machine with laughter. He started talking about the spirit of carnival, how the only real challenge to the bourgeois was guerrilla humor. He showed us this picture of a demonstration he was in, during the Gulf War. Him and his mates had made these huge lips out of red satin, and hundreds of them appeared in front of the White House with these six-foot satin lips tied to their heads. All of them, men and women, were wearing pink slips over their clothes. They were carrying signs: GEORGE BUSH, READ OUR LIPS. OUT OF THE GULF OR GET A PINK SLIP. And of course, you know, after that, Bush was defeated. We were all passing the picture around, laughing; I guess we were all a bit jarred by then. Pearl wasn't around. I don't know if things would have got so out of hand if she'd been around. She tended to keep a lid on things. I think Mick sort of resented that. He used to tell her she didn't know how to enjoy herself, she should let herself go more."

I used to tell her that, Maria thinks, with shame.

"This day, then, we came up with the idea. It seemed a great bit of gas at the time. I think we were all downhearted about how the other side seemed to be winning so big, almost everyone being behind the treaty. And then after the Omagh thing, we seemed to be losing all support.

No one wanted to hear about our side. We thought we needed to change the tone. That would be really radical, we thought. Introduce comic irony, you know. You know how you can do wild things when you get downhearted."

Yes, she thinks, oh, young man, you don't know how well I know!

"So Mick comes up with this idea. He says it'll be great street theater. We go down to one of the new sex shops, we buy a whole bunch of these dildoes. . . ."

She sees he's blushing and looking over to see if she'll censure him. She wonders what his mother's like.

"Well, we tied all these dildo things up in a ribbon and wrapped them in a parcel: brown paper, string. We talked Stevie into leaving it in the hallway of the Central Gardai Station. We called in a bomb threat, saying the package was left in the name of those who wouldn't stand by for the selling-out of our history. Then we called the media, to make sure there'd be coverage. Stevie was supposed to leave it and get right out. But for some reason, he just hung about."

Finbar sounds like a miffed first-grade monitor whose slower charges haven't responded properly to his directions about a fire drill.

"I'm not saying it was exactly his fault. I know he was disabled. All the same, what he did was daft. They ask him if he has anything to do with the package and he says yes, so they arrest him and his mother comes and they find out about him being the nephew of his uncle, and it got in the papers — well, not the whole thing, but parts that made Stevie look bad. One bad part about Pearl helping him with his reading was he promised her he'd read the paper every day. So he took the whole thing in. Especially the headline: THE BLOOD RUNS THIN.

"He was let go, of course, they could see he was disabled. When Pearl found out about the dildo thing, she went berserk. And Stevie was very upset. Mick gave him and his mother money to go to his house in Mayo. I don't know how it happened. He was walking down a country road, Stevie — in the rain, or the fog, maybe — and the fella that hit him said he didn't see him at first, then he beeped his horn, but Stevie didn't get out of the way and he just couldn't stop in time. Then his mother — you know, Breeda — came around, and she just lost it. I think Pearl started to go crazy after that."

"Why didn't she get in touch with me? I

didn't know anything about any of this."

"I told her to, Mrs. Meyers, I told her maybe she should go home. But she didn't answer me. She just sat by the window all day, writing in her notebook. She wasn't eating, but I didn't think much of it at the time, maybe just that she was upset over Stevie.

"Then one day when the mates were over she came in with this strange look on her face and said she'd show them guerrilla theater, but she'd do it right. She had a kind of funny smile, I can't forget it. She told us about not having eaten for six weeks and planning to chain herself to the embassy. We couldn't believe she hadn't eaten for six weeks, but she said she'd planned it very carefully and we should do just as she said. She wanted us to call the media just as she was doing it. I'm not accusing her of anything, but she deliberately misled us. We thought it was about our movement, in memory of Stevie, like she said, but because of who he was. His family, you know, his uncle's history, his roots. When I said that to her she said, That's right, memory and blood and roots."

He looks at Maria with those eyes that are like stones, wanting forgiveness and wanting to hurt. He's waiting for her to say something. But what can she possibly say?

"I wish she'd called me. I wish I'd been able to do something."

"There was nothing you could have done. It had nothing to do with you."

"I'm her mother. Everything she does has to do with me."

Both of them are shocked at what she's said, the utter lack of modesty and restraint. And yet Maria can't take it back, pretend she didn't mean it. They sit and look at each other; appalled at the chasm that has opened up. Now he will need to punish her; she waits to see its shape and extent.

But it doesn't come, the punishment. He looks at her with pity, as if she were a child who'd heedlessly run into a wall. She thinks he might be a good father someday. But not for Pearl's child, no.

"Well, it's a terrible thing," he says, and she is touched by the largeness, the indefiniteness of the reference.

"She doesn't want to see me," Maria says.

"Me either."

"Maybe when she's stronger."

"I don't think she'll ever see me again," he says simply, scientifically, as if he were talking about the extinction of a species of wildflower. "I mean, like, she has to see you, you're her mother. She can perfectly well get by without seeing me. I guess that might be better. Too much has gone on. Some things that can't be fixed. Not if the boat was a little rocky to start with."

"Wait and see," she says.

"I've put her things together, books and clothes. If you want to collect them. You could come over to the place. Only not today. One of the blokes is there with some company."

"Tomorrow, then," she says.

"Tomorrow, teatime."

He writes the address on a paper napkin. The edges of the letters blur into the softness of the paper, become a pattern rather than a message, hard to read, abstract.

"What time, exactly?"

"Four o'clock."

"Could it be morning? I see the doctor every afternoon at four."

"We tend not to be early risers."

"How about eleven?"

He nods. She hopes she's sounded accommodating.

"The doctor thinks she'll probably be all right."

He nods again and turns. His brown

greatcoat disappears into the brownish air.

Maria tries to understand what has just happened. Do you find it hard to understand? This impatient woman, who is where she is because her daughter is close to death, has treated this boy with compassion instead of turning on him in fury. You now know this about Maria: she is capable of surprising and sometimes erratic kindnesses, ignoring the most likely, most deserving candidates for mercy in favor of the insulting rogue, the ungrateful *mutilé de guerre*.

She asks herself: What did he come for? What did he want from her? Was it only because the doctor told him she wanted to see him? Did he think he was doing something for her? What did he think he was doing? What does he think he's done?

What has he done, and how can she understand it? New names swirl in her mind: Mick, Stevie, Finbar. One woman's name: Breeda, a name she'd never in her life heard. People she didn't know existed an hour ago, so for her these people did not exist at all. It is as if a sorcerer arrived in the breakfast room of the Tara Arms Hotel and conjured three new people whom she now was forced to know. One a dead boy, dead in mysterious circumstances, all of them involved in a political act so puerile, so anachronistically ridiculous she doesn't know how to think of it. She can only imagine the rich Yankee with the memory of the glory days he probably never had anything to do with. A trust-fund baby with a dream of revolution, transplanted here so he can't be understood to be the loser that he is. And a mother with a dead child. "She went crazy." What does that mean, what does any of it mean, and how can she connect it to her child, who may be on the brink of death? How did these people, these names without faces, bring Pearl to the place she now is? A place she will not allow her mother to be, a place Maria doesn't understand — nor does she understand her role. What is my place in this place? she says to herself.

The boy, Finbar, believes that what happened is connected to the dead boy, Stevie. A living boy talking about a dead one. What does it have to do with politics? He did say that things started to change after the Omagh bombing. But how?

Pearl had phoned to talk about the Omagh bombing. Had she paid enough attention? Had she failed to take in its full significance? Had she passed over it as one more atrocity in a world blood-glutted with them? And this event that she nearly passed over, is it at the center of her daughter's will to die? And who is Stevie? The dead nephew of an imprisoned revolutionary? The love child of a feebleminded mother and a father whose parents came over on the *Mayflower*? The *Mayflower*, she thinks, I'll bet.

Perhaps Dr. Morrisey knows more. Perhaps she will tell her. But she still has four hours to wait. She tries Joseph's room again. No answer. She has to get out of the hotel. She will walk. She'll buy a map and walk all the way to the hospital. This is a task that will absorb her; finding her way will drown out the tormenting voices that she can't now afford to hear. She will walk. Find the next street. Concentrate on whether to turn right or left and how far to go before the next turn. Do not think of what it is unbearable to think of. Do not see anything before your eyes except the names of streets, the blue lines on the map, the green oblong of the river.

• 38 •

In another part of Dublin, Joseph is walking too. He has been walking all night and half the day, stopping only for cups of tea, a bun, a sandwich. He feels worn out, empty. The surface of his mind is like a battered basin, shiny, holding nothing. His mind is a muscle whose existence makes itself felt only on account of, or in rebellion against, overuse.

He has done a terrible thing. That it was only a thing of words makes it no less bad. He doesn't know what should be done next. He hopes, somehow, that it will come to him, seep into his skin like the cold moisture from this gray sky, weakly underlit from time to time by a sun that is a flat disk of beaten silver.

There is no stopping for him, no sitting down, not on the wet grass, and certainly there is no entering cafés for a warming breakfast. He isn't ready for that; that would be premature, it might suggest a false answer, a snare. He must keep walking. If he takes tea or something to eat, it must be standing up. He mustn't stop until he is entirely worn out or has found the answer.

• 39 •

Maria is only fifteen minutes early at Dr. Morrisey's office, not so early as to be embarrassing, she tells herself. She sees that Dr. Morrisey is harried, distant. She is the professional again, and in her case that means, if not cold, then cool.

"There's nothing much to report. I think she's gaining strength; she's less agitated; she's more alert, as we've cut down on the sedative; it's a crucial moment, and I don't want to put it at risk by having her see you before she's ready."

"I can't see her yet?" Maria says. She wants to say, This is what I've been waiting all day to hear? But she's weaker than she was yesterday; she has lost some of her fight. The encounters with Joseph and Finbar have exhausted her.

"Not just yet. Another twenty-four hours of medication, of nutrition, could make an enormous change. Let's give it twenty-four hours. The prospects could be entirely different."

Maria wants understanding from the doctor, compassion: she needs to be listened to. Particularly after what happened with Joseph. I'm sure you can see why this would be the case.

"I keep trying to go over my part in it," Maria says. "What I did wrong. I just thought if I loved her enough, everything else would take care of itself. Maybe I wasn't attentive enough, maybe I was too much the animal mother, maybe I loved her too much as a cub. Oh, I loved her body so much as a baby. I loved being the mother of a baby, I never understood people who didn't. I never got impatient. She seemed so good to me. She always seemed so good. So surprising in her goodness, a kind of goodness I could never have had any hope of. She's very different from me, you know. She's very reticent and I'm, as I'm sure you've noticed, talkative. She could do things I could never do. Sew. And be quiet. But even as a little child, she couldn't defend herself very well. I came to understand she didn't want to. Once someone in school said to her, 'People like you, Chinese people, have no eyelids.' And she just crumbled in the corner. I told her she should fight back, I told her that so many times. And the last time, the time when that child insulted her about her Asian eyes, she said to me, 'Fighting back is not what I do.' As she might have said, 'Cornflakes are not what I like for breakfast.' "

"All this will take time to sort out," Dr. Morrisey says. Maria feels she is distracted, not really interested. Not really interested in *her*, not even as Pearl's mother. That she has been chattering, wasting her time. What she doesn't know: Hazel Morrisey's daughter, six years old, is about to celebrate her birthday. Hazel Morrisey must be home before the party starts. Her husband, also a doctor, has done the preliminary work, but she mustn't fail her daughter, not today, not as she has already done too many times in favor of a patient whose needs seemed more pressing to her than her own child. She likes Maria Meyers; she is even sympathetic to her, but she cannot give her any more time.

"We just have to give Pearl time," the doctor says. "Which I don't have much more of today, I'm afraid."

There is nothing to say. Hope for better prospects. Wait and hope. Wait and see. Give it time.

What is time? What can it do of itself, that giving it to something would make a difference? Maria feels time stretching out in front of her, dark and empty, growing larger instead of smaller as it is eaten up. She goes to her hotel room and orders a sandwich and a drink. Tries to watch television. Tells herself her daughter is out of danger. She orders a brandy to be brought up. She wonders if she seems disreputable to Orla at the desk, a pathetic older woman with nowhere to go. Every ten minutes she phones Joseph's room. There is never an answer. It is more than twenty-four hours since he left the restaurant. Where can he be? Is he in danger too? It's another thing she mustn't think about. She has, she thinks, become one of those women grateful to her brandy for dulling the edges of her mind.

★ ★ ★

In the morning, she finds Finbar's street on the map. She walks up two back streets flanked by recently done-up shops. She is passed by many young people; this is an area where students live. The businesses cater to them: chip shops, music shops, and one called Condom-inium which advertises "Something for everyone." So the church has lost its grip, she thinks with satisfaction. Even here. But the young people she passes seem sullen, worried, ill at ease, like young people everywhere these days. Not like the young Irish in the tourist posters, their red cheeks a sign of their high spirits.

The address Finbar gave her is in a building that looks so new the cement seems barely dry. It could be anywhere in the world, and the young people coming out of it, with their jeans and heavy boots and serviceable coats, could be from anywhere.

She rings the bell and is buzzed in. Finbar doesn't come to the door. It's answered by a man about her own age, wearing jeans and a fawn-colored corduroy shirt. His thinning gray hair is cropped close: a good concealing device, she thinks. He's barefoot; her eyes are drawn to his bare feet, which are, as she imagines he very well knows, beautiful, slightly golden, a sign of grace in this climate where she has not yet seen real sun.

"I'm Mick," he says. "You're Maria. Finbar's showering. This is the crack of dawn for him."

He takes her coat; he actually helps her off with it. She smells his soap and shaving cream. Her eye falls on the dark hairs on his squarish hands. She wants to keep looking at his feet.

"He doesn't need to trouble himself. I'm just here for my daughter's things."

"Sit down. I've made some good coffee. You can actually get it here if you know where to shop. Don't tell me you're not dying for a good cup of coffee. Sit down for a minute, for God's sake. You're going through hell. Is there anything I can do for you? It's horrible to be alone in a strange city and have to go through this kind of thing."

"I'm not alone."

"Is Joseph with you?"

"How do you know about Joseph?"

"Pearl talked of him so fondly. And of the relationship you and he had. Children together, all those years. It always sounded so very very unique. And now the two of you here together, in this crisis."

"Don't make a Kodak moment of it," she says, congratulating herself for her restraint at not telling him that nothing can be *very unique*. And particularly not *very very unique*. I can tell you that for Maria this was no easy thing.

"I have no one left from my early life. Too many changes, too many roads not taken, I guess. Theirs or mine. But our generation made a lot of big journeys, when you think about it."

The smell of the coffee is difficult to resist. And the sound of American speech, even if its content is foolish, seems somehow benevolent, comforting. Is this compromising her mission, to sit and talk and drink coffee? Pearl and this man had some sort of conflict. Perhaps she shouldn't be talking to him. But she can't think about it now.

"I'm so terribly sorry about what happened to Pearl. It's a crazy outcome. I must say we were all surprised."

"All?"

"Me and some of the lads I work with politically. Finbar and his friends."

"What politics are we talking about?"

"Well, the group we identify with is known as the Real IRA. The group opposed to the treaty. I'm sure you know better than to believe what the media says, we all learned that during Vietnam, and it's particularly true of this group. Not that we're really involved that closely. We're really more anarchist revolutionary ourselves. But we don't want to see the commitment of centuries, the poetry of history, generations of sacrifice and honor, a long tradition of resistance to colonialism thrown down the drain for consumer greed. There's got to be more to life than money."

"Nobody believes there's nothing to life but money. They call it other things.

Security. Quality of life."

"Yeah, well I'm against it. Down with quality of life," he says, raising the espresso pot over his head. "At least in the sixties, we knew there was more to happiness than consumer goods. A lot of us put a lot on the line for that."

She follows the line of his arm as it travels, admires the corduroy of his well-cut shirt. She can't imagine his putting anything on the line for anything. He is prosperous, healthy, well fed. A hero to a bunch of wannabes, one of whom was her daughter's lover.

She thinks of Ya-Katey, her daughter's father. Her lover once. She thinks of Billy Ogilvie, jailed because of her father. She thinks of her father. She will not allow this buffoon to include her in any category he might consider himself part of.

"The sixties weren't the same for everyone. They involved a lot of irreparable loss. It wasn't one big love-in."

"I couldn't agree with you more. I've come to believe that history as it's given to us is a tragedy, and it's up to us to turn it into a comedy. That's what I try to do with my politics and with my work in theater."

"What happened to your son wasn't comic."

"What happened to my son was very sad. But it was just an accident. I think it knocked Pearl off her center. Of course with the Omagh bombing, she started to get a bit unbalanced, I think, really fell for the whole media deal hook, line, and sinker, stopped thinking for herself, in my opinion. She bought the media's interpretation that it was a terrorist act. Not understanding that one man's terrorist is another man's freedom fighter, one man's violence is another man's liberation. Or woman, for that matter. And that in revolution there are always tragic errors."

"In this case the tragic errors resulted in dead children. A dead child is not an error. She refuses to deal with life and death as an abstraction. That's why she's done what she's done."

"I know, the personal is political — particularly for young women, I've found. I have two of my own, and God knows I find them hard enough to understand. They're in their mid-twenties, but sometimes I think their understanding of things is very adolescent. I've read they're changing the definition of adolescence to include twenty-five-year-olds now. Stevie, my son Stevie — well, his death got all mixed up for your daughter with politics and her eating issues, which is a big thing for young women these days. My Caitlin went through a little bulimia phase in high school."

"My daughter does not have an eating issue. She was experiencing despair about the nature of the world, she wanted to mark a tragic death, she wanted to bear witness to a larger tragedy, a public one. She wasn't worried that she was fat. It had nothing to do with how she looks."

"But let's face it. The stage she played everything out on is the stage of her own body. It's what I do: theater. I have my own company in Roxbury. A lot of the women are involved with pieces acted out on the stage of their own bodies. I mean, as theater what she did was very potent. Everyone looked, which was obviously the point."

"She didn't want people looking at her. She wanted people to listen to what she said. There was nothing theatrical about it. It isn't a performance. It's life and death to her: what she believes in seems worth her life. She wants to bear witness." Maria knows she is using Pearl's words, not her own, that she is expressing what Pearl believes, not what she herself thinks. But she will not allow this man to misinterpret her daughter so carelessly, so foolishly.

"I can't support that kind of martyr trip," Mick says. "Maybe it's your Catholic background, it makes you more sympathetic."

Maria feels a band of heat spread across the back of her neck. I think you've seen that Maria's relationship to Catholicism is, to say the least, quite vexed. No one is more critical of the Catholic Church than she; she has left it — unequivocally, she believes — in protest against aspects she considers repressive, heinous even. Yet she hates it when someone feels free to make an assumption about Catholics — especially when she is one of the ones being assumed about — that she considers coarse, clichéd, or overlarge. Is this just a version of defensive tribalism, is the band of heat on the back of the neck just that? Yes and no. Maria would say no, absolutely. I would not be able to entirely agree.

"I'm sure your ignorance of Catholicism and my relationship to it is near absolute," she says, "but I have no impulse to go into that now."

"Look, I don't want to argue with you either. I can imagine you're feeling incredibly overwrought."

Like many women, Maria reacts to the

word *overwrought* as if a gauntlet has been thrown down and she must pick it up and perhaps choke the thrower with it. She doesn't want to spend any more time with this man. But she can't resist saying something to his accusation that she is *overwrought,* a word she knows he would never think of using for a man.

"I am not overwrought. Nothing I have said or done justifies that adjective. I am not overwrought simply because I don't go along with some male version of the world."

"Don't gender it, OK?" he says. "I'll get Finbar. You just sit here and enjoy your coffee."

She refuses to sit down, refuses to touch her coffee mug. She stands behind her chair, black plastic, easily overturned. She would like to turn it over; she would like to break something, simply to make a point: that she could.

Finbar comes into the living room wearing a terry-cloth robe the color of peanut butter and yellowish suede slippers with fleece cuffs. She's sure his mother bought those slippers for him, as she is sure his parents are paying for the apartment, which is entirely featureless. Books and papers spill everywhere; full ashtrays and beer cans cover the black plastic coffee table. There are cigarette burns on the tan corduroy couch and chairs. The lettering on the posters is in Irish, so she doesn't know what anything means, but she imagines they're proclaiming solidarity with the Republican cause. Pride of place belongs to a poster of a young man in pageboy hair, a dazzling smile. Finally something is legible: the name Bobby Sands.

Finbar must know she and Mick have had words. He's no abashed, ingratiating, wounded boy now; she's the enemy, the woman here to ruin male peace.

He hands over a box that's taped on the top. It's remarkably heavy; she doesn't know how she'll get it down the stairs.

"Here, give me that," Mick says. "There's no elevator. I'll take it outside and we'll get you a cab."

"I can manage, thank you," she says.

"Look, it's easier for me. Don't make a battle of it. Save your strength for the real enemy."

He takes the box out of her arms and is already out the door. She can't possibly run after him and struggle for the possession of the box. Finbar watches her follow Mick down the stairs; he closes the door before they're at the bottom.

Mick has gone out without a coat, but he doesn't seem to notice the raw cold. He carries the box two streets down to a taxi rank and helps the driver put it in the trunk.

"Thank you," she says, refusing to meet his eye.

"Hey, if you need anything, you know where we are. Day or night. Absolutely," he says, and cocks his thumb and forefinger at her as if they were a gun.

When she gets back to the hotel, the bellboy carries the box into the elevator and then into her room. She unpacks it as if it would provide clues. The clothes in the box are remarkable only in their neutrality: grays, blacks, whites. No nightgowns or pajamas. Pearl and this boy slept naked. A warm red velvet robe, familiar to her: a present from Joseph and Devorah five Christmases ago, worn — overworn — on weekends when Pearl's not getting dressed till three in the afternoon drove Maria to distraction. Toilet articles; several products — Nivea lotion, under-eye cream — for dry skin. She hadn't known Pearl suffered from dry skin. Maybe it was only in Ireland. But wasn't the climate of Ireland wet? A package of condoms. Our generation did not use condoms, she thinks. The new etiquette — my condom or yours — was foreign to us. It was supposed to give women more control, although she couldn't see how. Her daughter's condoms. Her daughter's life with men. Men? Finbar is a boy. What was her daughter doing there? She shudders, thinking of Mick — what was his name, Cabot, Lodge — one of those names. Winthrop. She wishes she'd been with Pearl to help her interpret him. She could have said, at least, It is impossible to act well in a room with a man like that. Impossible to be natural. "Don't gender it," he had said — ridiculous use of language; surely Pearl would have seen through that. But seeing through that kind of man didn't seem to help. You saw through him as if he were transparent, but the transparency didn't matter; his weight was what mattered. They were heavy, these men; you felt the weight of their bodies on you, pressing you down, making it hard for you to breathe. As if they were fucking you; in a room with them you always felt fucked, fucked by a man who was too heavy on top of you, whom you had to wriggle around to be free of, knowing that if they wanted to they could, with their strong arms, pin you down. You acted trapped, like a wild animal. You did wild things, trapped things. You said, "I can carry that box," when you really couldn't, when it was clearly the case that he had more physical strength, could carry it more easily than you, and you ended up following him down the stairs, a fool, a failure, a weakling, a girl. And then your rage flared up, and you wanted to do something wild to show him — to show him what? That kind of man was transparent but impermeable. A wall of glass bricks that could crush you but would never fracture, never even have its surface scratched.

What should she have done in that room with Mick Winthrop? What did Pearl make of him? How did he treat her daughter? Who did he think her daughter was? And how did she act with him? If only she had been there. But Pearl had never mentioned Mick or Finbar, or living with a boy whom she bought condoms for, kept in her toilet kit along with her under-eye cream, moisturizer, nail clippers, deodorant, cake of eyeliner, and thin black-handled brush.

She's almost afraid to look at the books, as if they might give too much information. Most have to do with language. Irish grammars, books by De Saussure and

Chomsky. A collection of Irish fairy tales. And one she recognizes as her own: *Butler's Lives of the Saints.* Not her own, her father's; his signature is on the bookplate. Her father's study comes to her. Days when she would sit reading on the rug, the delicious smell of paper making her wonder if the books she was reading might themselves be edible.

Pearl must have taken the book from her shelf without asking. Or, no, it wasn't on her shelf. She must have gotten it from Joseph; Joseph had kept her father's books.

She won't think about her father now. Only to wonder what Pearl knows of him. Has Pearl asked Joseph questions about her grandfather? If so, it's been kept from her. But Maria has never asked to be the custodian of her daughter's thoughts.

She puts everything back into the box. None of it has made anything clearer. If Pearl were in front of her right now, the first thing she would say to her is, I don't understand.

· 40 ·

Pearl opens her eyes, closes them, opens them again. The doctor is gone, but she is not alone. Tom is always with her, or a nurse. There is very little she can do. This interests her, as if it were a situation she was observing in the life of someone else. There are bars at the side of her bed that she can't lift. She hasn't the strength, and besides she is attached to poles with tubes; there is a tube in her nose and throat; in her vagina. She has only a vague memory of how they got there, a distant sensation, like a wind rushing, violent, tearing, dark, but without a single image clear enough to explain anything.

The doctor is gone. The doctor has kept her alive. The doctor said her death would be a waste. Didn't she understand how insulting that was? Like saying someone's lover was a fool.

Did the idea of death make the doctor angry? Was it anger that gave the doctor the strength to hold her down when she'd put the tube, hard as a pencil, in her throat, the tube she'd pulled out? Had the doctor been impressed by that? Or did it make her angrier; was it anger that made her stitch the tube beside Pearl's nostril? For the first time in her life, force has been used against her. Odd, she thinks, that force should be used against me, a person of no force. "You have a lot to live for," the doctor said. The doctor who spoke kindly was the same one who pressed her shoulders down, shoved a tube into her throat, then sewed another to her nose. Pearl feels she must thrash against her. She sees the doctor as a bush with branches that keep growing in front of her, scratching her eyes out, choking her, like in a fairy tale. The bush keeping her from something she has worked to get to, that the doctor thinks she must be kept from, because it is a waste.

She is losing her weakness, a thing she cannot will herself not to lose. It is very odd, she thinks: as she loses weakness, she becomes more afraid; as she is fed, she becomes hungrier. In losing her weakness she has lost something of great value to her. She is giving up her place outside the ring of force. When she was not afraid of death, she was saying that there were things more important than her own life. That seemed an entirely good thing. Now, in fearing death, in no longer desiring it, she is helping to keep the iron ring closed. She no longer breaks the circle. She had cast her lot against all safety measures and all prudence. Her hand became so thin it was translucent if she held it to the light. She raised her thin translucent hand and in this gesture was her exaltation. And in her exaltation she was exultant.

Starved, she was exalted and exultant. But with nourishment, she has grown hungry and she has begun to fear. Starved, she needed nothing. Now she knows her own aloneness. Before, she saw or sensed her companion, waiting for her at the end of the road. Now she can see no companion, only a long darkness, and feels the sense of being unaccompanied.

Fear has entered, now, and taken root. It has taken its time; its time is now. When she tries to tell herself death is desirable, she must work to conjure the face at the end of the white road, and often she is distracted: by a tearing hunger, and by the doctor's words.

She is frightened; she is hungry; she is confused; she is interested; she must work to see the face at the end of the road.

Her mother is in Dublin now. If she calls for her mother, her mother will come. The doctor has said she will bring her mother to her, if she wants, or keep her away, if that is what she wants. Only a little while ago — but how long? Time has been lost to her — she knew she didn't want her mother. Now the image of her mother, coming in from the winter with cold on her hair, stirs up in her a hunger, a hunger that is similar to her desire for her mother's food. Her mother's mashed potatoes. Her mother's rice pudding. Her mother's body, the cold clinging to her hair.

She turns her head to where Tom sits, reading under the bad light. "Tom," she says, "I'd like to see the doctor."

"She's just outside. I'll get her right away."

· 41 ·

Joseph has walked for a second night through streets that seemed desolate rather than dangerous, walked down prosperous streets of houses set far back from the road, houses behind walls or hedges or gates. He has taken buses, got off anywhere, read signs that said Howth, Dun Laoghaire, Chapelizod. He feels the pavement through the thin soles of his shoes; this is an appropriate sensation, he thinks, ungiving, punishing, without variation or surprise. Once he stopped for a glass of wine. This he regretted, because it blurred the edges of his fatigue, making him feel he should succumb to it.

And why not? He has a room that has been paid for. He could bathe so that he won't dread the glimpse of himself in a shop window: grizzled, derelict.

He is waiting for something, an understanding or the lifting of a burden. But his mind won't focus; all it will do is press again and again on the dull wound of his mistake.

The sun comes up, a joke effect, a whitening, not an illumination: colorless. He tries to remember: if you stare into the sun do you go blind? Not this sun, he thinks, it hasn't enough power. He rests his gaze on the circle of a more silvery white, concentrates on the whiteness pressed into the whiteness, loses himself in the question: What is the difference between white and white?

White, absence of color, pure color. He thinks of white stone, arches of white stone, a white stone fountain. He thinks of the hateful pinkness in the restaurant two nights before: the pink lamp shades, the pink tablecloth, salt poured to absorb the spilled wine on a pink hill on the flat pink plane of the cloth. He thinks of Maria eating meat and butter. Animal fat. Pure animal. Even an animal has its purity, because no animal is capable of excess. That's it, he thinks, excess rather than mixture is the opposite of the pure. Maria has always been excessive. His mother was right. What she said was dreadful but it was the truth; Maria is greedy. Greedy for everything: for weather, talk, expression. Most of all sensation. The word *sufficient* has never crossed her mind.

A pure gesture, he thinks, has no excess.

Purity. Impurity. He has suffered because of the ideal of purity; he remembers the shame of being sent away to Portsmouth Priory; the guilty anguish at the strange, perhaps criminal desires of a thirteen-, fourteen-, fifteen-year-old boy; his torment in the days when he desired Devorah's body and knew that any touch would be a violation. He has suffered from the ideal of purity, but he would not have it given up. Without the ideal of purity, too much would never have come to be: Matisse's empty oval, the face of St. Dominic, holding only air; the arias in the St. Matthew Passion; the credo in the Magnificat that changed Devorah's life. She was right to change her life for it, wrong only later when she said it wasn't worth it. What was the *it* that it wasn't worth? he wanted to ask her.

He has always thought of Pearl as pure. A white flower hidden in a cool green sheath of leaves. Did she think she was emptying herself of all excess? Did this emptying mean she would become one of the dead? She has approached the territory of the dead, intending to give herself to it. He looks at the white sky with the whiter sun pressed into its surface and thinks of the desire to be part of it. That whiteness.

That quietness. Withdrawn, set apart from the world. Of course Maria can't understand that. She is sated, clotted. Pearl is a white flower without fragrance, or the fragrance only of leaves, nearly toneless, a pale green sheath. Maria wants to force the sheath. To force the flower with her sharp nails, her thick fingers. People did that with flowers. Devorah did it — in the name of what? Paperwhite narcissus, the bulbs were called; she had forced them, as if that were a good thing. And the flowers overfilled the air of the winter room with their insistent smell — was it supplication? protest? He didn't know what it smelled of, only that it had made him sick. Forced. They forced things because they wanted them for themselves, in their own time. They wanted what they wanted *now*. That was all they saw, all that was real to them. Paperwhite narcissus. Butter.

He remembers a story Professor Stivic told him: Professor Stivic, whom he had had to disappoint; Professor Stivic, in his crowded, chaotic office, with his caterpillar eyebrows that became completely vertical when he was excited or alarmed. Or distressed. This day he was distressed, because Joseph was apologizing for the mediocrity of his work. They both knew what he had written was mediocre. "You are forcing it," the teacher said. "You mustn't force things. Forcing is always a mistake. I must tell you about forcing. A story about forcing, the story of the worst thing I ever did. I was very young, but not so young as to justify it."

Joseph was frightened. Was he going to hear a story of a murder covered up, of a rape, of pointing the Nazis to a hideout of hidden Jews?

"I was with my best friend, we were walking in the woods, and we saw a butterfly about to hatch from a cocoon. For a while we watched it, but I got impatient and took it in my hands, the cocoon, and I breathed on it, to provide warmth to hasten the course of things. It worked, the butterfly hatched, but because the time was wrong, because it had been forced, its wings withered and it died in the palm of my hand. It died because of my impatience, because I forced something that should not have been forced. Go home to your beautiful new wife, let her sing to you, walk with her in the sunlight. What will come will come in its own time. Never force."

Professor Stivic. Each year a Christmas card; from Champaign-Urbana, lately

Krakow. Joseph did go home; he and Devorah walked by the river; they made love. He did no more work that day. But eventually he did write a thesis, his thesis on medieval reliquaries, that he knew was very good.

Pearl must not be forced. How can he protect her — from her mother, from this doctor, from other doctors who most certainly are to come? What is the difference between force and protection? The doctor has said she needs protection in order to be kept alive.

Pearl could die. Her body could consume itself, because she would rather be a skeleton than be part of this life, a life she feels is unbearable. Because of what she did to that boy. The will to harm, she calls it; he calls it the unreasonable appetite. The hot breath, gasping *Mine, now.* Whatever they call it, he and Pearl mean the same thing. Both of them have felt themselves torn at, eaten up, by the hand that grabbed and grabbed, the mouth that chewed and chewed. What they have both understood is the real nature of the world. But he hadn't understood before that he was feeding the maw with the substance of his own life.

Only now does he understand that he

has given too much. He has given too much because others had felt free to take too much. He has given too much to the wrong ones, the ones who wanted the wrong things: Maria and Devorah and his mother and Dr. Meyers; they wanted sensation and position, safety and placement, attention, the demands and the desires of the flesh. What about his desires? He desired beauty and fineness; he gave over his substance to others, who wanted what would perish, what the moth would eat, what rust would turn to nothing, what would go in their mouths and end up in the drain. Wasn't that what Jesus was saying, that this sort of desire was wrong? Where your treasure lies, there will your heart lie; hadn't Jesus said that too? He and Pearl were alike. They did not desire what the moth could eat or what rust could consume. What they desired was not consumable. He remembers her telling him, and begging him not to tell Maria (and he did not), that she decided not to apply to Harvard because she didn't want it enough and her friend Luisa wanted it so much, and she knew the difference between really wanting something like that and not, knew she could never want something like Harvard the way Luisa did, and she was afraid that because her mother was an alumna and because Pearl had two 800s on her college boards, she would get in before Luisa when it wasn't something she wanted nearly as much. Luisa is hungry for it, she had said. I'm not.

The hunger of the world. He has fed the hungry. That's how he's lived his life, feeding Maria, feeding Devorah, feeding his mother, feeding the hunger of the world for ugly objects thought of as a type of god. Idolaters. Appetite and ugliness and force. He and Pearl are talking about the same thing. They are talking about the real nature of the world. It might have killed her. And then what in life would be pure, would be lovely, would be worth his life?

Feeding others, he has allowed Pearl to starve. The prospect of losing her is unbearable. He sees now what the shape of his life must be: to protect her. The doctor has said people like her need protection. He has not protected her; he has not kept her safe. Now he must live his life to keep her someplace where she will be safe from the assault of the world's force. A life where she need not suffer, where she won't be afraid to live. So she won't die.

But now he can't do anything for her,

because he has no legal standing. Her mother is the only one with legal standing. Only her mother can invoke the law. In Pearl's name, for her protection, he must be able to invoke the law. So that she will live. He must be able to do it, not her mother. Her mother doesn't understand her. Her mother and the doctors can save her body; only he understands what will save her soul. If her soul isn't saved, she'll find another way of destroying her body.

Joseph is thinking in ways that he has never thought before; in his mind he is using words that have not, until now, been his. Never before has he said *must* in relation to something he wanted to do. Never before has he thought *only he* could do something. But no, that isn't true. He had thought only he could give Devorah the life she wanted; only he could help her honor her gift. Only he could protect her. In losing that conviction, he lost the habit of thinking himself singular in any way.

He had not been able to protect Devorah, but he must protect Pearl. He knows this is most important; he must not fail, as he did with Devorah. Pearl must be protected. Something must be invoked that will protect her. He tries to think of a suitable law. But what law can help him guard her? Guard, he thinks, and then the word comes to him: *guardian*. To become her legal guardian, he would have to have her mother declared unfit, and no one would think that of Maria. But if he were her guardian, he could protect her. Her mother and the doctors don't understand what she needs. Life, they keep saying, more and more life. But what of the flowers that wither in the sharp wind, the burning sun? What of the butterfly, forced outside? Some need enclosure. A garden enclosed is my sister, my love. The Song of Songs: what greater love poem has there ever been than this? He sees lilies of the valley, unprotected, turning brown exposed to air. She is in danger. How can he keep her from danger? Her doctor said it: she needs protection. How can he provide protection?

It comes to him: he will protect her. By marriage. He will invoke the law that is invoked by marriage. A man and a woman, kept by marriage from the encroachments of the world. He sees it now, he sees it: they must marry. She must take his name; they must have it as the visible sign of his protection of her. What is marriage but a story of the law? It goes without saying that he will never touch her, but if they tell the story of a marriage, she will be protected. He is the one who will be called; he is the one who will have to give consent; the doctors will have to abide by his decisions should she ever need a doctor.

When he was married to Devorah, she was connected to him by law. When she died, the decision of what to do with her body was his. Her parents had had to call him for her body; it was up to him.

He looks up at the white sun in the white sky. The whiteness is illumined now; it spreads itself, a sheet of silver whiteness. He can look at this sun without danger; nothing in it seeks his harm. Pearl must not be forced. She must be protected. This, he knows, is the right thing. He will find a place for them, a quiet place, a sanctuary. Old stones to take the sun's heat, the splashing of a small fountain. Days drenched in peace, shaped by silence. Their meals as plain as she likes. Everything will be simplified. She can study her languages. He imagines a plain white table piled high with dictionaries and grammars. No poetry or novels, no history or science, no politics or philosophy. It will mean he will give up some things important to him, a kind of reading by which he has understood himself and his place in the world, but of course, he tells himself, he can make this sacrifice in the interests of simplicity. He will cook for her. He doesn't know how to cook, but he will learn. He is sure she will eat properly if he presents her with this plan to keep her from the force of her mother, the force of the doctor, the force of the world.

He will devote his life to her. To her protection. Her claustration. From the Latin *claudere, clausus:* enclosed. The enclosure of the sacred: tabernacle, temple, shrine, sanctuary. The sanctuary of marriage, the safe place, the inviolable place, the locked door that keeps out danger.

★ ★ ★

I want to tell Joseph that he's made a mistake, it's not the sanctuary of marriage, it's the sanctity. But you might want to cry out: Why of all the wrong things that he's done would I choose to remark on a mistake of language? Perhaps it is because I am aware of how little I can do, how little I can change. Don't you imagine that if I could have stopped Joseph from thinking in this way I would have?

What Joseph understands is this: Pearl will be kept safe by their marriage, which will be a good story, a strong story, a story that explains the shape of things, even if the explanation isn't true. Finally, a story that doesn't sicken him, that does its proper work.

He will go to her with this plan, this plan to keep her from force and ugliness and fear and sorrow. To live a life of quiet, of the contemplation of beauty, under the sign of the law. She has looked too long and too hard at the unfiltered sun. That's what the doctor said. He will keep her from all that. He will provide sanctuary for the contemplation of the beautiful. He will see to it that these things, these things alone, will make up her life. He will live his life for that. She will no longer be subject to her mother, to her doctor. He and she will be alone together.

Joseph is lost to himself, but he doesn't know it. "He's gone round the bend," we might say, and those words would indicate what has happened: we have lost sight of the man we knew, as he has lost sight of himself. He, of course, doesn't know this, so he is exhilarated by the new man he has become. He feels he has been born again. A new life will be his: of freedom and of beauty. This is what he calls it, these are the words he uses: freedom and beauty. What words would we use? Would we say, instead: This is a kind of madness? He would tell us that we cannot see, as he sees, the vision that came to him while he was looking into the white circle of the early sun.

But he believes Pearl will see as he sees, what he sees. She will share his vision. He will tell her everything, and then he will leave for Rome, where he will search out the place where they will live. Perhaps an abandoned convent: he has heard there are many such now in Italy. He sees a cloister. He sees them walking around the cloister in the afternoons, digesting their light lunch. He hears the plashing of the fountains, sees the slim silver-barked trees.

He knows now what must be done. All at once, the burden of his dirtiness, his soiled shirts and shorts, becomes intolerable. He longs for a shower and a shave. He can imagine the hot coursing water, reassuring him that everything he's thought of is possible and right. He looks up at the white sun. Light without heat. Light without color. Light without force. Pure light.

• 42 •

"I want to see my mother now," Pearl says to Dr. Morrisey.

"You're sure you're ready?" Dr. Morrisey says.

"I want to see her."

"She may have a strong response. There may be tears, reproaches. You need to be ready for a variety of things."

"My mother's not like that."

The doctor touches the tube sewed to Pearl's nose. "You're ready for me to take this out of you? You're ready to say you are committed to leaving the other tubes in?"

Pearl makes the OK sign.

Dr. Morrisey cuts the stitch under her nose. The sound of snipping is a shock but there is no pain attached. "I hope this will be the last bad thing I'll be doing to you," she says, and pulls the tube out of Pearl's throat. Pearl feels a bit bereft at first, and her throat feels raw, robbed of its newly comfortable false vein.

"I didn't want your mother to see you that way. I'd say she's a powerful person to have in your corner."

Pearl nods her head.

"I'll stay around. If it seems too much, or you want to be alone again, ring the buzzer and we'll do whatever you want. You're in charge: remember that."

Pearl says, "You don't know my mother."

"I've met her," Dr. Morrisey says, "and you're still in charge. You probably don't want to hear this, but your mother loves you very much. She very much wants you to get well. None of that means she'll know how to behave. So you must call the shots."

The shots, she thinks. What shots? Bang bang, you're dead.

But who dies? she wonders. She or her mother?

Neither, she thinks. We are both alive.

Maria answers the phone that sits on the table beside her bed. It is Dr. Morrisey, whose voice is, for the first time, warm.

"She's ready to see you now."

"She wants me?" Maria says humbly, a rejected lover, a cast-off wife invited back.

"She's asked for you."

★ ★ ★

Maria leaves a message for Joseph but doesn't wait for Orla to call her a cab. She runs down the road to the taxi rank and tells the cabby to take her to the hospital. Pronto. Where did that word come from? What movie? Whatever it is, the taxi driver has seen the same movie. "Pronto it is," he says, meeting her eyes in the mirror.

★ ★ ★

Maria hears her heels and the doctor's heels on the linoleum of the corridor; she feels they aren't walking fast enough, but she can't think of a way of making the doctor walk faster. Maria knows she must follow the doctor: her low-heeled tan shoes, her blond head, the thin white cloth of her jacket. They don't speak.

The doctor goes into the room first. Maria stands a bit apart from her. The light in the room is dim and Maria thinks of the words *twilight sleep,* a drug she seems to remember that was intended to anesthetize women in childbirth. The light is bluish, the lamp beside the bed the only illuminating source; the far wall can only be sensed, not seen. She is entering a split cone of darkness, in the center of which only one spot of the visible emerges: the bed, its white sheets only a plane blocked by the doctor's back.

"Your mother's here."

There is no sound and then, Maria sees, Pearl is weeping. Tears are coming down her cheeks, but there is no sound coming from her.

"It's all right now, love," Maria says. Her eyes fill with tears too. She sits beside the bed in a turquoise plastic chair and slips her hands through the bars, in between the tubes, and takes Pearl's hand, gingerly, because a needle is attached to the skin with a Band-Aid.

Maria's tears are as simple as sweat. Her body doesn't struggle against them; her throat isn't choked by sobs; the tears are silent. Her breath comes easily, naturally.

The two of them are experiencing the same thing: they are weeping with no sense that anyone will tell them to stop. Grief without struggle, without contradiction.

"I'm hungry," Pearl says at last. "I want to eat something."

"Not so fast," Dr. Morrisey says. "Not immediately."

She pronounces it *immijitly*, and Maria feels the warning in her voice.

"What would you like to eat when the time comes?" Maria asks.

"Rice pudding," Pearl whispers.

"A shark-infested rice pudding," Maria says to her, thinking of a children's book they both liked. She can't remember a thing about it but the title. Most children's books bored her; she couldn't wait for Pearl to get past them, a secret she hopes she successfully kept. She hated the coyness, the archness, the creation of a falsely pristine or falsely jokey world. She couldn't wait till it was time for *Jane Eyre*. But Joseph liked children's books; Joseph read to Pearl a lot when she was little. When Joseph comes, Maria thinks, swallowing her fears for him, she'll remind him of a shark-infested rice pudding.

"We'll think about rice pudding in a few days," the doctor says, and leaves the room.

In the half-light, Maria closes her eyes, lightly holding her daughter's hand, cool, damp, the nails bluish, or perhaps it is only the light. I am, she thinks, strangely happy. She remembers being happy when she nursed Pearl as a child with a low-grade fever. The same feeling of purposely useful action perfectly completed, and the peace it brought, comes back to her now. A stillness that seemed immaculate because there was nothing else that could possibly be done. An island, a cutting off.

There is no noise but the buzz of the fluorescent light in the hall, which ought to be disturbing but is not. It's soothing, like the heavy buzz of bees over a field on an August afternoon. She thinks of the words *August afternoon,* and as she thinks of them her eyes close and she feels herself smiling.

Tears are still coursing down Pearl's face. My body is working now; I can make tears again, she thinks. She is not so unhappy now and, with her mother near her, she is not quite so afraid. She can make tears and she is not alone. But the fear is still there, the fear of what she knows is inside her, the thing that made her want death, the thing that is flesh of her flesh. She thinks of her face, what her face must have been like when she said to Stevie,

"How can you be so stupid!" She still has that face. As long as she is alive, she will have it. She is frightened of her own face. She cannot see Stevie. Her mother is with her. Her mother can hold her hand. But she cannot take away her face.

• 44 •

When Joseph finally goes back to the hotel, Orla gives him the message: He can come to the hospital and see Pearl. He takes this as a sign. His intuition, earned by two days and nights walking, the tentative noons, the damp cutout moons against the twilight sky, the pastel sunsets, the false-lit darkness, the silvering whiteness of the rising sun: it was all right. It is a great moment now; a great change will come, a liberation. All their lives will be different, and everything will be better than it was. Maria will have to suffer for a while, but that's not important. Maria is distractible; Maria will get over it; Maria has, for too long, taken too much. What's important now is what's best for Pearl.

He enters the hospital room and sees Maria there, her eyes closed. She may be sleeping. She is holding Pearl's hand, but awkwardly, through the bars. It's beautiful, of course: mother and child. But that is a misleading beauty. The ancient forms must no longer be obeyed. The new law must come into effect.

Maria gets up and kisses him. She doesn't ask him where he's been or say anything about what happened when they last saw each other. She says only, Do you want to be with Pearl?

Are you surprised that she would leave him alone with her daughter without asking him to explain what's happened between them and where he's been? For Maria, letting Joseph speak to Pearl was the next thing to be done. And that is how she has always proceeded with her life: do the thing to be done, then the next thing to be done. The only way to get through things is to get on with them.

He says yes, he'd like to be alone with her. His face is sore from a shave with insufficiently hot water and the sting of his sandalwood cologne. He wore it because he knows Pearl likes it. Sometimes she wears it as her own scent. He wonders if people will notice that they wear the same scent or if they'll assume it's a natural product of their life together. But they will not be seeing many people: perhaps no one at all.

Her hair is spread out behind her like a fan: gold on white cloth. He leans over to kiss her forehead, which has always been very beautiful to him. Wide, a wide brow leading to her remarkable arched eyebrows, darker than her hair, and thick. She opens her eyes. Her eyes are not dull; her skin is not unhealthy; her head is not a skull but a clean oval, something by Matisse. She smiles at him. Her eyes are calm, not the eyes of torment; her fingers, reaching out to him, are not sticks but the rather blunt fingers he's seen holding a needle, a pen, a dog's leash, a hairbrush, a spoon. She is still beautiful. My young queen, he thinks to himself, unembarrassed to be using the word *my*.

He knows everything that needs to be said must be said quickly.

"You're feeling better."

"That's hard to say."

"You've been through a lot."

She takes his hand with the hand that has a tube taped to it.

"Joseph," she says. "I'm afraid of things."

"I know you are," he says. "I understand."

"I knew you would. I knew that, whatever I did, you'd understand."

"I do understand. And I understand what needs to happen next."

"I can't even think what will happen next. I don't know where I'll go. I guess I have to go back to New York for a while. I suppose I could go back to school eventually, but right now I don't want to go back to New York, and I don't want to go back to Wesleyan. I don't want to stay here, though. I know that's not possible."

He hears everything she is saying as a sign that she has been waiting all along, without knowing it, for him to say what he is going to say. Isn't she asking him to take her away, somewhere far from her old life, her old connections?

"You could go anywhere; you don't need to think either of going home or going back to school. There are many more places we can think of."

"I just don't know how to think right now."

"You don't need to. I'll think for both of us."

She smiles. "I know I shouldn't think that's a good idea, to let someone else think for me, but right now I'm so tired."

He takes her hand, her ringless hand, the one not taped to a tube.

"I know how unhappy you've been, and for so long."

"It seems like a long time, but it hasn't been that long really."

"Probably much longer than you think. As it has been for me."

It occurs to her that he is going to talk about himself, which might be the first time in her life this has happened. Does he need something from her? That seems strange; she can't imagine being of any help to anybody now, she feels so weak.

"I didn't know you'd been unhappy for a long time," she says.

"It doesn't matter. We were both unhappy, but we won't be anymore."

She's confused. Why is he saying *we?*

"You must listen to me, Pearl. I know you'll understand because we always, always understand each other, we always have, and we always will."

He kneels beside the bed; he puts his mouth close to her head. He cups his hand around her ear; the side of his hand feels hard against her skull. He begins talking, but it isn't talking, it's a breathless whisper. Why is he doing this, why is he talking this way, as if there's something he's trying to catch, something he's afraid of not catching? He has never ever spoken this way; his speech has always been deliberate, considered, words chosen as if they were precious, turned over, laid down slowly, and then used. She doesn't understand the breathlessness behind his voice. And what is he saying? Phrases detach themselves, each one incredible, each one comprehensible. He cannot be saying this. That it came to him while he was walking, that he was walking all night, that he didn't sleep, and it came to him, looking up at the sky, looking into the sun. He tells her about the white sky, the white stones, the plashing fountains, the trees around the cloister where they will live. He tells her about the protection of the law: that she needs protection and only he can give it. He tells her that marriage is only a story of the law. He assures her he will never touch her. He will marry her only to keep her safe.

★ ★ ★

I told you long ago, at the beginning, that I wished I could protect them, these three people, but I could not. Never would I like to protect them more than now. But I cannot. Joseph has said the things he had to say. There is nothing to be done about it.

Pearl shakes her head back and forth on the pillow. "No no no," she says. She would like to put her hands in front of her face, her fingers in her ears, but he is holding one of her hands and the other is connected to a tube. What is he saying, what can he possibly mean, what is happening in and to the world? Who is saying those words? Can it be Joseph? Saying, *must* and *must* and *must*. You must do this, we must do this together.

In all her life, he has never said she must do anything. You must listen to me. I must protect you. We must get married. Married to Joseph? What could that possibly mean? That they must live together just the two of them, away from the world. Must? Must not? That she must stay away from her mother. That there are things she must not look at. As if she were a child or an invalid. That he must live for her. Meaning that she must live for him?

Something has happened to Joseph, so he is no longer Joseph. Joseph who stood beside her, so she always knew that if she fell, she'd be caught. She was not alone. It was what having a father meant. Now he says he doesn't want to be a father but a husband. Her husband, but he will not touch her. She must look only at what he arranges for her to look at. They must be closed in together. Claustrated, he says, kneeling beside her, his mouth to her ear, conjugating Latin verbs: *Claudo, claudere, clausus.* Who is this beside her? What can these words mean?

She tries to understand: Joseph has lost his mind. She must be rid of him; he is a danger to her, and she isn't strong.

Everything she is saying to herself is

right: He has lost his mind. Where has it gone, and will he get it back? He is not himself, he is a stranger and a danger to her, and she is right that she isn't strong. She is right in pushing him away, she couldn't do anything else. Not in her condition. Not in the condition of having taken the first steps away from her death.

Pearl is right to do what she does, but when I see the effect it has on Joseph I could almost ask her not to. Not to do it. But what could I suggest instead? Nothing. In this situation, there is no right action. Her action is, of all possible actions, the most right.

She pulls her hand from his grip. She holds it up to indicate that he should move far away from her. She wants him far away. He must be kept away. He is not anyone she knows.

"Don't come near me," she says.

He doesn't understand what she's doing, moving around like this, thrashing like this; she'll pull the tube out of her hand, the tube connected to the pole with the clear plastic bag with whatever is keeping her alive. She must be kept alive, so he can live for her. Why won't she be still? When he came in she was still and beautiful. Now she is thrashing.

Her thrashing sets off a buzzer. A young man comes running in. He must have been just by the doorway the whole time. What did he hear? Who is he? She is moving wildly, although the tube attached to the pole limits her range of motion. "Calm down, Pearl," he says, "it'll be all right."

Joseph is startled by the presence of the young man in the room. Shocked. It is one of those moments when a cliché seems to come alive: *I jumped out of my skin.* We say that, don't we, for the slightest thing: running into someone we haven't seen since grade school, being cut off by a truck on the highway, catching ourselves in the mirror unawares. But the sight of the young man, who calls Pearl by name, jolts Joseph with a force that makes him feel he has left his body; he sees a skin, kneeling by Pearl's bed, and it is loathsome, empty: it cannot be anything that he would once have called himself. But of course it is himself. He rises from his knees. A nurse comes into the room.

"I'm afraid you'll have to leave," she says to Joseph. "She seems to be upset. Perhaps two visitors in one day were too much. She seemed fine with her mother. But we've overdone it a bit, perhaps."

The wildness of Pearl's thrashing makes the phrase *overdone it a bit* seem ridiculous, and he and the nurse both know it. She presses a button and another nurse comes in from the hall. "Best get the doctor," the first nurse says. The other disappears into the hall. A doctor — a young man, not Hazel Morrisey — comes into the room with a syringe. He injects Pearl. Then he and one of the nurses leave the room.

Maria pushes her way in.

"You must tell me what's happening," she says to the other nurse.

"Something's upset her. We're just giving her a sedative. We can't have her pulling the IV out."

Maria tugs on Joseph's sleeve, a supplicant, with a starved supplicant's desperate pull. "What did she say? Did she say anything? Something must have happened. What did she say to you?"

"She didn't say anything," he says. He knows himself to be a liar.

The nurse tells them Dr. Morrisey has said they must go home. She will phone them in the morning. Pearl is sleeping; she's sedated. Everything is all right for now.

But everything, he knows, is not all right

and will never be again. He moves like a man who has just been electrocuted, shocked; his body is flooded with pulses that thrum and burn. He thinks of the words *shock treatment* — a switch is thrown and the madman's sanity is restored to him. He has been shocked. He would like to fall onto the floor and roll around, bash his head against the wall: anything to stop this terrible sensation.

He lost his mind. The ideas he had, the words he said to Pearl, were the ideas and words of a madman. Now that he is in his right mind, he can see it, and the seeing is unbearable. He wishes he could do something to block the vision.

Maria is trying to understand. "I thought everything was all right. I was so happy; I felt so at peace. Was I wrong, Joseph? Was I completely wrong? I couldn't have been. But then what happened? What went wrong?"

He sees her trying to find fault in herself, in her behavior. But she can't find anything wrong, and it wouldn't occur to her to blame him.

"I thought I understood."

You did, he wants to say. There was nothing you didn't understand, and nothing you can understand now.

· 45 ·

They have injected her with something new. It is making her sleepy; it is making her forget whatever it is they want her to forget: something Joseph said that took away her understanding of her life. That made her feel her heart in her mouth. Her small, nearly invisible heart. *My heart was in my mouth,* people say, describing fear. If your heart is in your mouth, what do you do with it, swallow it? Spit it out? And then what are you left with? Then you are no longer alive.

He was kneeling beside her whispering in her ear, frantically whispering words that made no sense. He wants to carry her away. How can that be? To a hidden place where she would be his wife. Where her mother would not be allowed. Where the doctor would not be allowed. He wants to take her from the world and keep her to himself? His wife? How could she be his wife? He is Joseph; he has been with her all her life, the one who made her feel all right when she was frightened, when she lost faith and hope, the one to catch her if she fell. And now he wants to carry her away. All this is what they want her to forget, but she cannot forget it. A stone is on her head, trying to press her down to sleep, but she cannot be pressed down; she is floating. She will not be pressed down, but she would like a place of rest.

· 46 ·

Joseph and Maria are both silent on the cab ride home.

"I just don't understand," Maria says yet again, when they get to the hotel.

His own understanding horrifies him. An understanding that is at the same time a failure to understand. How could he have done what he did? What came over him? A drunkenness, a madness, a fever. It is broken now, the fever and his heart and all their lives; he has broken everything. He had wanted to protect Pearl; now she must be protected from him. He wants to turn to Maria and say, *Do you understand what I've done?* But the error had happened when he said what he wanted, the thing that could be the ruin of them all. He must not say what he wants to say; he must say what Maria needs.

He thinks of the young man running into the room, calling Pearl by name. Rescuing her from him. From *him:* the man who has always thought of himself as her protector, the man who planned on devoting his whole life to keeping her safe. Does the young man know who he is? Will she tell him everything that happened? Who is he? He's not a doctor. What can he be doing there? How quick he was to rush into the room, rush to the rescue. A knight in shining armor. Where did he come from? On what white horse?

He can't think about that now. He must answer Maria.

"Pearl's very fragile now. We must remember that."

Neither of them has any inclination to speak. They say goodbye when the elevator reaches Maria's floor.

For the first time, Maria has lost hope. She had believed something in her daughter had broken but that it could be fixed. Her love would fix it — that was what she'd thought at first; later she began to have faith in the skill of the doctor. But suppose what was wrong with Pearl was beyond either love or science? What if Pearl was damaged beyond repair?

Repair. What do you repair? A pair of shoes. A washing machine. A bridge. A watch. A road. How was the soul repaired? Reparation. What was it that was needed to be paid back?

She lies in the dark, her eyes over-wide,

excruciating, in their hyperalertness. What needs to be paid back? What is her debt? She knows she has never been in literal debt, because of her father. She thinks of her father now. What was broken between them was beyond repair. She had taken her broken heart and turned it to a heart of stone. *My father who art in heaven.* If he is in heaven, what sort of place is that, and who else is there, and does she want to be there herself? Does she want her daughter there? Not now. Her father may be in heaven but Pearl will not be. Not anytime soon. She will see to it. She can't get it out of her mind: *My father who art in heaven.* And then, my father who bought us cream puffs in Rumpelmayer's, who told us we must learn to eat a cream puff comme il faut. She will not think of her father in Rumpelmayer's; she will not think of Pearl in heaven. She will turn her heart to stone.

Perhaps you have found this stony heart unsympathetic, incomprehensible. To harden your heart to the father who gave you life, your one living parent, to refuse to mourn his death, to invoke the name of justice whenever the temptation to grieve arises?

What happened, you may wonder, when other images of her father, kindly images, loving images, arose? Is the image of her father in Rumpelmayer's followed immediately by the policeman telling her, "Go home to your father. You have friends in high places"? She convinced herself that the face of her father was the face of surveillance, of a judgment she felt had taken a way of life, everything from her that was colorful and lively, and crushed it, that felt entirely free to say *my treasure* and cut out the rest of the world. When it appeared to be kindly, it was only a face tried on, perfected in front of a mirror, a mask used to achieve ends it always had in mind: surveillance and control. So the tender glance, the loving smile: they were not to be trusted. They were in service of a force to which she would not yield. The force that allowed her father to say, "My treasure. My own."

She understands the need to say it now: *My treasure. Protect my treasure. My own.*

She sees her father's face, his light-blue eyes behind his rimless glasses sparkling with judgment. Then she sees his face, white, against the pillow, the last time she saw him, the time he pretended to be close to death. What was his face like when he was really close to death? She will never know. And until now she has refused to think about it.

She no longer refuses. She understands herself a thief. Because of her, her father lost a daughter. She understands for the first time what the weight of that loss might be. She turned her heart into a stone and did not count the cost.

What if the stone could be rolled back? The stone was rolled back at the Resurrection. She thinks of Easter — the risen body, vulnerable to light, comes, fragile, back into the world. *Noli me tangere.* Don't touch me. Don't.

If you roll back the stone, what is there in the darkness?

I do not believe in the resurrection of the dead. My father died, once and for all, bereft of my forgiveness. And I of his. The dead are dead. Silent. Out of our reach. This is the way the story ended. Ends.

But suppose, she wonders, it is not? Suppose the dead can forgive and be forgiven? How would the story end in that case? And what would that mean about what the story always was? If she is to think about it, she will have to stand — or sit, perhaps — in an unbearable place, the place of unbearable grief and loss. She will have to be in this place for a time if the story isn't over. To take the next step, she will have to sit, not in the place of stone but in the bog of loss and grieving. Always she was afraid of drowning, of being entirely swallowed up. But is there some ground now, not a place of stone but simply a sliver of dry land, on which she can, for a moment, get her footing? A place where she can stand and say *my father* without feeling she has bent the knee before the tyrant, towering above her with his raised arm?

She asks herself, supposing it was possible to stand on a sliver of dry ground and say "My father," what will happen if she is wrong? What would constitute wrongness? She is not under surveillance. If she is wrong, no one will blame her, for the very reason that no one will know.

So why not act as if the story weren't over? As if, somewhere, in a place she has no need either to locate or to name, her father is reachable, on the other side of words. She feels the sliver of dry ground beneath her feet: the place from which she can begin to speak.

Father, forgive me.

Father, I forgive you.

Father, forgive me, but I knew exactly what I did.

I wanted to harm you. And I did.

And there was no repairing it. You died. You did not rise.

Repair us, now, Father; forgive me, keep her safe.

Roll back the stone.

In the dark, she weeps for the lost face of her father, the face of her child, in danger of being lost to her forever. What if there is no end of weeping? Then, she wonders, how will I live my life?

Father, forgive me. Keep her safe. There is nothing I understand; there is nothing I can do.

She lies weeping, helpless, the child she always refused to allow herself to be. Was the refusal based on pride or fear? Who knows? We can know this. She has relinquished what she once held dear: an old refusal.

Joseph runs a bath so hot it will scald his skin. This is what he must live with now; he has betrayed the innocent. He hears the words: "I have sinned in betraying innocent blood." Judas the betrayer said that. Like him, Judas was in charge of the money; he was also the safeguarder of the wealth.

Going over the story of Judas, he tries to understand what might have happened to his fidelity, his devotion, his trustworthiness. Judas had been given the purse; he must have been trusted. When did it come to him that it would be a good idea to betray Jesus? Most likely, he didn't use the word *betray* at first; perhaps in his mind he called it *handing over*. How did that come about? he wonders. What could it have been like? Did it happen after he'd made a fool of himself over the perfume and Mary Magdalene? When he reproached her for spending money on perfume to wash the feet of Jesus, money that could have been spent on the poor? "You always have the poor with you," Jesus had said. Did Judas feel then that everything he'd done was useless, that he'd followed this man because he was devoted to the poor and then he said the poor didn't matter, it was more important that a whore pour perfume on his feet and wash them with her hair? Was that what tipped him over the edge, feeling his whole life had been wrong, a waste? Did he tell himself he was turning Jesus over because Jesus had betrayed his own ideals? Did he convince himself that he was betraying Jesus in the name of the poor?

He imagines Judas, walking as he walked, hour after hour, looking as he had looked into the white sun pressed like a coin into the white sky; convincing himself that he'd come up with a good idea, acting on the idea, and then almost immediately seeing what he's done. Appalled, he tries to undo it, to give back the money; he throws it at the high priests. The high priests say, "What is that to us? See to it yourself." The gospel does not record what Judas does between hearing that and going out to hang himself. He can imagine no good idea now but death by his own hand.

Now he, Joseph, can imagine no good idea, either, only to stay away from Pearl. To wait for her accusation. Perhaps to wait for nothing. It is possible she will refuse to see him. He would, of course, deserve that too.

"See to it yourself." Joseph cannot imagine what it is that he must see to. He takes the thin towel and wraps it around himself to cover his nakedness. Also called his shame, his manhood. "I am a worm, and no man." The words of the psalmist come to him; was it David or is David's authorship of the psalms another story too weak to withstand the test of time? The words of scripture, the characters of scripture, dregs at the bottom of his unbelief: "I am a worm, and no man. Can these bones live?"

· 48 ·

Something has pressed her down to sleep. But she is bobbing up now. And Tom is walking with something that bobs, something so light he is having trouble holding it. They are a strange thing for a tall man to be carrying, too light, too little weight for him to easily transport. How can it be that something's lightness should make difficulties? Her body is losing its lightness.

Tom unwraps the parcel. Puts it down on the radiator. Has she fallen asleep again? When she wakes, they are no longer flowers on the radiator, they are silver disks, bobbing like insubstantial lollipops on stems of ribbon. Somehow they move but she doesn't understand how. What are these silver circles bobbing in the air? The stone of sleep is pressing on her head, but she forces herself to bob up. She must focus on those silver disks, somehow attached, moored in their box on the radiator, and the heat from the radiator is making them bob in its generated breeze. But why are they here?

Her throat is very sore. If she whispers, will Tom the watcher hear her? Joseph knelt by her bed and whispered. The words made no sense. She will try to make Tom the watcher hear.

"Why are they here, those silver things?"

"It's a bouquet of balloons. A present for you."

A bouquet of balloons. That is a very strange thing. Bouquets are flowers. She asks if she can see them.

Tom carries them over.

There is writing on the silver disks, but the writing is flowers. Sometimes she begins to make letters of the flowers and sometimes she sees only patterns. She must focus. If she can read words, she can begin to understand. Gradually, capitals form, *G . . . W . . . S. W . . . S . . . G. S . . . G . . . W.* And then the small letters become comprehensible: *Get Well Soon.*

But I wasn't sick, she wants to say.

"There's a card with it," Tom says. "Shall I read the card?"

"Yes, please."

"*Dear Pearl. I hope you're fine. I'm fine. I miss you. Wishing you all the best. Let's get together soon. Love, Breeda.*"

She doesn't understand. This must be a trick, a mistake. The last time she saw

Breeda, Breeda said what she'd done was unforgivable. That she was the worst of all of them because she'd made Stevie think she understood him. That it was the thing she said — How could you be so stupid? — that sent him over the edge. His blood was on her hands.

How can it be that Breeda said Stevie's blood was on Pearl's hands and now she is sending her balloons and saying *Let's get together soon?* It is beyond her understanding; she feels as helpless now as when Joseph said the things he did.

There is nothing she understands. If she could understand one thing, she could take one step and then another. Does this mean Breeda has forgiven her? That what she has done is not unforgivable? Is there forgiveness without a forgiver and if Breeda has forgiven her is she no longer unforgivable? And what about what Breeda said before? Her mind is bobbing. Suddenly she remembers the name of the material the balloons are made of — Mylar — and the room is full of bobbing silver disks, too light, flying up, more and more of them: Mylar, yourlar, everybody's lar. Forgive. Give for what? Writing that is flowers. Get well soon. I hope you're fine. The disks bob up. Sleep, like a stone, presses down.

She is tied to her bed but she is riding a horse, a silver horse whose name is Princess. He is riding a chestnut horse named Lucy. He says their names, Princess, Lucy. He says, These are the horses in my story. Do you remember my story, the story we wrote together? Yes, she says, I do. They are riding together, and the manes of the horses are light in the wind. The horses' hooves don't touch the ground. He rides a little ahead of her; she calls to him; she's afraid he can't hear. Forgive me, Stevie, she calls. He slows down his horse so they are right next to each other. Forgive? he says. Forgive? With so much to be forgiven, it would be strange not to forgive. And he smiles and the horses are close together; their heads nearly touch. She hears more horses behind her, and when she turns she sees the others: Miss Alice and Janet Morehouse and John Lennon and Bobby Sands, and Jolene and Sean and Avril, the Omagh dead. Riding together in the air that turns silver as they ride into it and are taken up.

She is on a horse but she is tied to a bed. Silver disks are bobbing; are they heads or faces? No, there is writing on them. Or is the writing flowers? Her mother will keep her safe, and Joseph wants to take her away so he can marry her because only he can keep her safe. Balloons, that kind of silver balloon. Mylar. Why are these in her room and what is the writing that keeps turning into flowers? She wants to weep with the effort to understand.

"Forgive," he said. What does that mean, forgive? She had said, "How could you be so stupid?" to a boy whose shame was that he felt stupid already because people said he was. And at the moment when he was covered with the greatest shame of his life, she had joined the camp of his accusers: she, who had said to him, "They're wrong. You're *not* stupid." Breeda was right, she was the worst because he believed she understood him. She had thought she did.

And Joseph had said, "I am the one who understands you. I am the only one." Which meant he wanted to carry her off, keep her for himself, keep her from the world — safe, he said, but what he meant was hidden. Marry her. The man she thought was like her father. So what was his understanding? And if you understood at one time or maybe most of the time, why didn't that keep you from the error that could undo all the understanding you believed you had, that you might actually have had?

Forgive. Give for what?

Was Breeda saying she forgave her? Did that mean she was forgiven? If you were forgiven, could you still be unforgivable?

How could Breeda have forgiven her? This is what she needs to know. But she is tied to her bed. They will not let people in to see her. Tomorrow, they said. But she can't wait till tomorrow. She has to know now.

She tells the nurse she must see Dr. Morrisey.

"Dr. Morrisey is off, she's not at your twenty-four-hour beck and call. She has a family of her own, you know."

The nurse doesn't like her. The nurse resents Dr. Morrisey's attention. Forgive me, she wants to say to the nurse. But for what?

"Please, she said I could call her at home at any time. I'm sorry. Please."

Tom stands beside the bed. He is tall, very tall, taller than the nurse. He will be a doctor one day. "I was here when Dr. Morrisey said it. She made quite a point of it. She repeated it several times so Ms. Meyers would know she meant it. I hate to think what she'd do if her wishes weren't respected."

Tom is on her side. Tom is with her. She

would like to say, I am very grateful. Grate-ful. Gratitude. The gratitude has made me full. But I am not full, I am empty. There is no greatness in me.

The nurse disappears down the hall, comes back with another doctor. He concurs: Dr. Morrisey has said Pearl could call her at home. Her throat is very sore; she's frightened that when they hand her the phone she'll be inaudible.

They hold the phone for her; her hands aren't free. "Hazel Morrisey here," the voice says, and Pearl tries to marshal all her strength to appear reasonable. If she appears reasonable, they are more likely to grant her request. But nothing feels reasonable to her. Joseph is incomprehensible to her, and Breeda, and the silver disks bobbing in the air. But she must appear to be a person who has understood the way of things.

"It's terribly important that I see someone," she says to Dr. Morrisey. Her voice sounds like a croak in her own ears. "If I can clear something up, it will make all the difference to me."

"In my judgment, you're not ready to be seeing people. I think it was seeing too many people that drove you to this point. I can't allow it."

She can't tell anyone what drove her to

this point. She can't let anyone know what Joseph whispered, kneeling at her bedside, his hand cupping her ear, the side of it pressing into her skull.

Appear reasonable.

"I'd have to know who it is you want to see."

"The boy who died, Stevie. His mother. We parted on bad terms."

"And what if you're still on bad terms after you've spoken? The risk is far too great."

"I understand your concern," Pearl says, "but she sent me a bouquet of balloons and a note that said she hoped we'd see each other soon."

"I'm afraid I can't go along," Dr. Morrisey says.

She has said she understands, but she understands nothing. If she can see Breeda, if she can understand what Breeda meant by sending her a bouquet of balloons that are supposed to be flowers, that has writing that is flowers, if Breeda says that the unforgivable thing that she did to Stevie wasn't unforgivable, that she has in fact been forgiven . . . then there will be something she can understand. But it can only happen if Dr. Morrisey believes her to be reasonable.

"I know what happened won't happen again."

"And suppose this visitor of yours doesn't give you the response you want? You can't guarantee it, and I can't take the risk. I'll allow your mother to come in tomorrow. You've been heavily sedated; you're not up to much in any case. Just try and rest."

The phone is hung up, taken away from her. She gives over to the wave of confused sleep. She can't fight anymore; she can no longer pretend to be reasonable.

• 49 •

Maria is lying in the dark, her eyes focused on the ceiling. She is trying to understand, but it is beyond her grasp. She keeps trying to pluck an idea from the dark air, an explanation. No one was with Pearl but Joseph.

The phone's ringing shocks her.

"Hazel Morrisey here. You may go and see your daughter in the morning. She says there's someone she's eager to see, but I'm not going to allow that right now. I'm only permitting you to visit for the moment, and only for a little while. Try to keep things on an even keel."

"Do you have any idea what precipitated her agitation today?"

"None at all, but I haven't seen her in person."

She phones Joseph's room; he isn't there. She leaves a message: She'll be going to see Pearl first thing in the morning, and for the moment she's the only one allowed.

She rushes to the hospital without breakfast, runs to get a taxi. When she arrives, she has to pass her enemy in charge of hospital passes. She hands Maria hers, holding it at arm's length with the tips of her fingers as if any contact would be contaminating. Maria thanks her, insisting on a sincere-looking smile. She nods at the hall nurse and makes her way into Pearl's room.

"Mom," Pearl says, "I need you to do something." Maria is shocked by Pearl's hoarse voice.

"Does your throat hurt? Do you need something for it?"

"Never mind my throat. I need you to do something. Do you know about Stevie?"

"I know what Finbar told me."

She nods, unsurprised that her mother and Finbar have met. She points to the balloons on the radiator. "Stevie's mother, Breeda, sent me these. We were friends — I mean we used to be. Then she told me Stevie's blood was on my hands. That what I'd done was unforgivable. And I knew she was right. What I did *was* unforgivable: I told Stevie he was stupid. Breeda was right. She said she didn't ever want the sight of me again. Then she sent me those balloons, with that card."

Maria picks up the card and reads it. "She seems to feel differently now. I'm sure she spoke in a moment of terrible grief. It sounds like she really wants to see you."

"But she was right. What I did *was* unforgivable."

"I don't know what that means, unforgivable. Everything is potentially forgivable. Or unforgivable. If you've been forgiven, that means what you've done is forgivable. Forgiveness implies a forgiver, after all. It doesn't come from the sky."

Forgiveness, Maria is thinking, is a choice. She remembers the words of the gospel, when Jesus gives the apostles the power to forgive sins — or not. "Whose sins you shall forgive they are forgiven. Whose sins you shall retain, they are retained." Has the woman forgiven Pearl? Maria doesn't know if she would be able to forgive in the same circumstances.

"Mom, you have to go and see her. You have to ask her if Stevie's blood is on my hands, like she said."

And how exactly would you like me to go about doing that? she wants to say to Pearl. Am I supposed to ring her bell, introduce myself, and say, Excuse me, you don't know me, but do you think your son's blood is on my daughter's hands?

She looks at Pearl's hands, the nails

bluish. Thin, useless, tied down to blocks of wood attached to the railings of the bed. Blood on her hands? Her hands are tied.

"OK," she says. "Give me the address."

When she gives the cabby the address, he whistles. "You wouldn't mind me saying I'd advise you not to go there?"

"I have no choice. I'll just be a minute."

"Would I wait for you then? You'd never get a taxi in that part of town."

"That would be very kind. It's quite important."

"An errand of mercy, then. So is it an angel of mercy I'm supposed to call you?"

"I'm much too substantial to be an angel," she says, and he laughs.

"The Lone Ranger, then. Heigh-ho, Silver," he says, and steps on the gas.

The housing project is called Fatima Mansions. Fatima has an association for Maria, as it did not for Pearl; it is the town in Portugal where the Virgin Mary was said to have appeared to three peasant children in 1917, warning against the evils of communism. The Virgin dictated a letter to the children — Maria remembers two of their names, the girls, Lucy and Jacinta; the boy she can't remember. The letter was meant to be opened in 1960. A rumor went around the Universal Church that the pope opened the letter and fainted. The report given to the world, which no one in the world believed, was that the letter said, *Pray for Peace*. This, you see, is the universal aspect of the Universal Church. All over the world, people of Maria's age (but no younger) heard Fatima and saw a silvery Virgin on a puffy cloud. Now they think of it in Goa, in the Philippines, in Peru, in Latvia. Their children, however, do not think of it at all. And what, I wonder, are we to think of that? The shortened shelf life of truths once sold as eternal, now relegated to the back of the store, the remainder bin, recycled to the third world, the unsavvy consumer.

The housing project's atmosphere, made up of children's cries and adult acrimony and shouted greetings and snatches of music, is familiar to her from the projects in New York she's entered hundreds of times on home visits to children's families. Empty whiskey bottles and beer cans border the entry. She has no hope that the buzzer will work, but she presses the button next to the name B DONEGAN anyway. It doesn't work. She walks up three flights of dark dangerous-looking steps.

She's out of breath when she gets to Breeda's door. She knocks and hears a woman answer. What can she possibly say to this woman? She can't think about it now. She'll just ask Pearl's question and take whatever answer the woman gives. Whatever the woman thinks of her, if she gives her the information Pearl needs, Maria will have done her job.

The door is opened by a small woman with over-permed blond hair, large blue eyes with sandy lashes, teeth destroyed by smoking and bad food. Her slight body is muffled in a turquoise quilted robe; she wears fuzzy turquoise slippers. In the background, Maria can hear the television: an American show called *Friends* that some of the younger people she works with habitually watch. They've urged it on her, and she's tried, but she can't pick up the thread. Perhaps she could say to the woman, Oh, I see you're watching *Friends*. Well, your son and my daughter were friends. She understands, as she did with Finbar, that it's best in an impossible situation to rely on formula. Cliché.

"I'm Maria Meyers. I'm Pearl's mother. I've come from the United States."

"Come in."

The room is dark, although it's only ten

in the morning. It is a room entirely without natural light. And Breeda has not put most of the lights on; she has been watching television at ten in the morning in the semidark. Something is hanging on a string from the ceiling — many things. In the dim air they seem more colorful than they would be in full light. Maria can't comprehend them at first, but gradually it comes to her: they are paper birds, origami. Pearl had said she taught Stevie origami. The room is a jungle of paper birds; his mother had allowed him to hang them everywhere. Red, orange, yellow, blue. Light, so light, the slightest breeze moves them.

Or they move of their own lightness at the end of their nearly invisible strings. Maria understands that Breeda was right to let him hang them; they make the room come alive, even though it's difficult to walk there; you have to keep parting them in front of you, like Moses at the Red Sea. The waves of colorful birds part, rustle, fly lightly on their strings, return. Without them the room would be merely dispiriting, with its ceramic figures of cats with wagging heads and aqua eyes, a painting of a baby seal, and several of uprearing horses. Maria knows she must move carefully. She is aware that the waves of birds on strings may be all that is left to Breeda of her son.

"Will you have a cup of tea?"

Maria is anxious to get the information that Pearl needs, but she will not be inhumane. Tea, of course; probably there will be cookies, called here, as in England, *biscuits*. In the corner of the room, where the television blares, there is a table with a wooden base and Formica top, blond-colored. Breeda takes a cloth and wipes the table quickly. She fills the electric kettle; in seconds steam appears. Neither woman has said a word.

"She's all right, Pearl, is she?"

"I don't know. She's in the hospital. They've been feeding her with tubes."

"Force-feeding? They did that to some of the hunger strikers."

A thrill of fear goes through Maria. The Irish hunger strikers died.

"I think she's willing to eat now."

"Thank God," Breeda says.

Maria thinks that she probably means it literally, and this is both a comfort to her and a source of estrangement. Breeda believes in a prayable, thankable being. This makes her, at the moment, more fortunate than Maria herself. Yet Maria has a living child; Breeda does not. She cannot, there-fore, be counted among the fortunate.

"I'm terribly sorry about your son."

Breeda nods. Her eyes overflow with tears that come effortlessly from her body, like sweat, as if weeping were her habitual and ordinary state.

"Life was hard for Stevie, always hard. The thing with Pearl was, I felt she got the good of him. She got his goodness, she was able to enjoy him, to understand that he had gifts, you know, even if most people couldn't see them. She could see them. We'd have good times here, you know, just watching the TV or chatting or having a take-away meal."

"She loved him. His death was shat-tering to her. I think she feels in some way responsible."

"That's probably my fault. I need for-giveness of her too. She wasn't to blame, not the least little bit. But you see, I was out of my head when Stevie died, out of my head. He's all I have. All I had. And they made a fool of him with the parcel at the Gardai station. A laughingstock was what he was. And then what Pearl said to him — well, I understand she was just fu-rious at the stupidity of it, only she turned on him, and she shouldn't have done that.

It took the last heart out of him. But the other thing is, he was a boy the sun never shone on. What happened to him was an accident. It was an accident that he was killed before he and Pearl had a chance to make it up. It was an accident of time."

For the second time, Maria feels a thrill in her spine. If what Breeda has said about Pearl and Stevie is true, that it was an accident of time, is it possible that this could be true of her father and her? If they'd had more time, if he hadn't died when she was away, if Pearl had been born . . . is it possible that things could have been different? Was it only an accident that death and circumstances butted up against each other in a way that was unfortunate? If Breeda can say it about her own dead son, can't Maria say it about her dead father? She would like to tell Breeda the story of her and her father and ask her if what she just thought of could possibly be the case. But she isn't here for herself. She is here for Pearl, who has given her a great gift: she has asked Maria to do something, something she thinks her mother can do, rather than just wait.

"He was deaf in one ear, Stevie," Breeda says. "He covered up a lot, he wouldn't wear his hearing aid, no one knew about his bad hearing, really, and the night was foggy — he just didn't hear the car beeping its horn. It was an accident, in one way, But I can't help thinking in another way he's another victim of the Troubles. And I wanted to scratch the eyes out of them. Out of his father. Because when I went over there, and he was just so calm, that American kind of calm, you know, and I was raving, and all he said was, 'Get hold of yourself. It was a terrible thing, but it happened.' Like I didn't know it happened. Like he had to tell me that. And Pearl was there, saying nothing. I guess I wanted her to stand up to him, and when she didn't I turned on her. Because it *had* upset me, what she'd said to Stevie. But later, I was able to understand. She couldn't stand up to Mick because she was shattered herself. She'd lost heart too. There wasn't much left to her, but I couldn't see that. All I could see was that she was one of them, and she wasn't standing up to Mick for saying 'It happened.' So I said the thing I did.

"But then when I read about what she did in the paper, when I read that she talked about Stevie and said Stevie was great, then I understood. She was mourning Stevie just as I was. We were the only ones. Like she said, she was marking his death. I didn't want his death marked with another death. I didn't *want* another death, and yet the fact that she wanted to mark my boy's death meant something to me. Now, if she died, it would just be another dead child, and there's been too much of that.

"I needed her. I need her now. She's the only one I can talk to who really got the good of Stevie. She's the only one I can remember things with. My family never got the good of him: he wasn't political; he wasn't strong, you know, or quick. I think that's one reason he wanted to do the thing they put him up to, being the son of his father, coming from my family. And when I thought of Pearl so near to dying, I thought, No more dead. No more dead children. Because she's only a child herself, isn't she?"

Maria leans her head back in the dimness. She watches the birds fly in the quiet air — the air that would be quiet but for the blaring of the television. She lets her eye follow the gentle movement of the birds. Real birds, living birds, would not move so gently. They'd be getting somewhere. She thinks of the words used to describe the flight of birds. *Soar, swoop, hover.*

But that implies a wingspan. Stevie's birds have folded wings. Moveless movers.

"She wanted me to find out from you: Do you forgive her?"

"Of course. We were both out of our heads with grief. We weren't neither of us ourselves. You must ask her to forgive me too. You must tell her she's got a special place in my heart. And in my prayers."

"I want to get back to her now. What you've said will mean the world to her. It means the difference between life and death. We'll see each other when she's well."

"Perhaps you could both come over for a meal. I could show you some of Stevie's things. It would help if I could talk to the two of you about him."

"We'll do that," Maria says, putting her coat on.

"God bless you," Breeda says.

As she runs down the filthy stairs, Maria feels blessed indeed. And she wonders if it's possible to believe in blessing, in having been blessed, if you don't believe in blessing's source. Maybe it doesn't matter. She can't think about it now.

★ ★ ★

When she gets to the hospital, she encounters her nemesis behind the desk again.

"There was only one pass for you and you've used that up."

"I understand, but I was only gone for a little while. I had to get some breakfast."

"I don't know about that. I only know that going out and coming in you'd be needing two passes, and I've only the one for you and you've used it."

"There's another one for my brother, isn't there?" she says sweetly, concealing her murderous true heart. "Perhaps you could look in the folder and get that one for me."

The woman knows she's been outfoxed. Maria won't take her eyes off her, but she keeps her smile pasted on. The woman goes to the folder. She doesn't quite have the nerve to refuse the other pass. In two minutes, Maria's lied to the woman twice: that she went out to get breakfast and that Joseph is her brother. Well, it's almost true; she has been nourished and Joseph is like a brother to her. In the old days in the Church that was called a Mental Reservation. If you made a mental reservation — if you said to the Jehovah's Witness, "My father isn't home" and you meant in your mind, My father isn't home *to you* — you hadn't really committed a sin.

She runs into Pearl's room.

"What did she say?"

"She said there was nothing to forgive. She said you weren't yourself. She said you spoke out of the heat of anger as she spoke out of the heat of grief. She feels you need to forgive her because none of it was your fault and she made you feel it was; she sees it all as a combination of accident. Stevie wasn't wearing his hearing aid that night, you know. And something much older, much larger, part of the tragedy of this country. She called it an accident of time: if you'd had time, and had been able to work through time, you'd have worked it out. And she needs you to mourn with her, to be with her in the work of mourning, of remembering. I think she blames Stevie's father for not mourning. For wanting to forget their son. *That* she finds unforgivable."

"Then some things *are* unforgivable. How do we know what they are?"

"We know if we're forgiven."

"And then what?"

"And then we live our lives."

★ ★ ★

Pearl had been desperate for her mother to find out what she's found out. And now she doesn't know if it makes any difference. Because now she has the information, she doesn't know how to interpret it.

Breeda says she's forgiven her and says that she, Breeda, is also in need of forgiveness. Or is she saying that neither of them needs forgiveness because they were in the grip of anger and grief? What does it mean, then — that anything is forgivable if you're enraged enough, suffering enough? Breeda doesn't want to blame her, although she deserves blame. But what happens if blame isn't cast? Does it disappear? Vaporize like the fog the night Stevie died? Where, then, is justice? Isn't it lost if nothing is unforgivable?

Consider, if you will, the questions Pearl faces now. If she accepts Breeda's forgiveness and forgives herself, what will she have lost? What if, rather than saying, *This is itself and nothing else,* the truth says, *That is what you thought to be itself, but it is also other things you may never have thought of?* Is this the more frightening possibility, that we must live with mercy and forgiveness, which may be a series of mistakes, of overpayments, rather than the blame we seize, the blame we believe is shining, singular, the burning brand we use to mark with our own name? These are the things Pearl must consider in her weakness and exhaustion, tied down as she is and drugged.

Her mother sits down on the turquoise plastic chair. She takes her coat off; she is trying to catch her breath. She pats her upper lip with a Kleenex; she is sweating with exertion; there are two deep curves like parentheses cut into her face. Her mother is no longer young.

Suppose Breeda forgives her. What does that mean if she does not forgive herself? Her mother has said, If someone forgives you, you are forgivable. But what if what you did resulted in a death? The dead cannot forgive.

Stevie can't forgive, but Breeda has forgiven in his name. Can you forgive in the name of the dead? And must the living always forgive? Breeda said Pearl did what she did because she wasn't herself, so she must be forgiven. But who is the self who did the thing and who is being forgiven? Perhaps Joseph wasn't himself when he said what he said. What he said made her feel that nothing on earth was safe, nothing was dependable. Can that be forgiven? Is it possible to say he wasn't himself because he had suffered too much, maybe from Devorah's death, maybe for a reason she will never know? If she can be forgiven in the name of the dead, must he not be forgiven by her, in her own name?

And then what? We live our lives, her mother said. What did that mean? And why do it?

Her mother is no longer young. This fills her with a terrible tenderness. Her mother, her strong invincible mother, will one day be weak and old. Her mother will one day be among the dead. Will her mother be lonely, among the dead, without her? Before this moment, she never believed her mother would die. She had always believed that, moving decisively, as she always had, her mother would somehow move quickly out of death's way. She had never pictured her mother as not alive. She had never imagined life without her mother in it.

It had been easier to imagine life without herself in it. She had imagined her mother mourning her, weeping for her in a dark room. She had not imagined herself weeping for her mother. She had not imagined facing life without her mother. What did it mean, to face life? What was the face?

Stevie's face flattened; it became featureless, like the moon, like the desert, when she had said, "How could you be so stupid?" He became a creature without a face. How can Breeda believe her to be forgivable, believe she doesn't even require forgiveness? Because she was not herself? If you are not yourself, who are you?

The silver disks bob in the overheated air. Her mother will one day be among the dead. Some things are unforgivable or everything can be forgiven as long as there is a forgiver. Some things cry out for punishment, or punishment is quite beside the point. There are accidents. It was an accident of time; if they'd had more time, they would have worked things out. He could have forgiven in his own name. Would he have forgiven her? She would know she had been forgiven because she would have had the words of forgiveness from a living mouth. It would have been a great gift. But supposing he didn't want to give it? Supposing Stevie didn't think she was forgivable? In the dream he had said, "With so much to be forgiven, it would be strange not to forgive." But dreams are not life. You have to live your life; a dream is something you wake from. Some things you do not wake from. *How could you be so stupid? We must marry.*

And one day, her mother no longer in this life.

Does her mother understand? Her mother doesn't long for death, doesn't believe there is a scrim — thin, easily traversable, infinitely desirable in its lightness — between life and death. Wanting life so, she must understand why people resist taking their place among the dead when one day they will have no choice. Her mother, so alive Pearl could not until this moment imagine her dead. Her mother who gave her life. Her mother who said that after forgiveness you must live your life.

She must ask her mother, "Why is it that it's life we want?"

What do you make of this question? Do you think it's unanswerable? Do you even go so far as to say it's a question no one has the right to ask? Do you assume there's nothing else wantable except for life, and so it is absurd even to ask the question? What would you do if someone asked it of you, would you try to answer on the spot or would you say, "I'll get back to you" and consult libraries, wise friends, authorities across the disciplines? Maria doesn't have that luxury. Her daughter has asked her a question. She must answer it.

And she knows Pearl wants a real answer, not a rhetorical one. She is encouraged that Pearl used the word *we*.

She tries to think of the things people live for: Love. Beauty. Pleasure. Virtue. Fame. Friendship. None of these things seems real enough, strong enough, to be a proper answer to Pearl's question. She knows what the answer is for herself, but this answer she cannot give: "I live for you." She thinks of Breeda, who must live having lost her only child.

Pearl has asked her a question, Why do we want life? There must be a good answer. She does, she believes, want life. But if Pearl died she would want to die. Yet Breeda goes on living. So perhaps she is the one who should be asked. But Breeda is not here. Breeda has not been asked; she, Maria, is the one who must answer.

She tries to remember once again why people have said that life is good. Love. Friendship. Beauty. Pleasure. Virtue. Fame. Fame is irrelevant. Virtue may be its own reward, but is it real enough for Pearl, who has always been virtuous, to prize? Even the virtue that relieves suffering comes up against the reality that the number of the suffering is overwhelming; there are always more, no matter how many are relieved. She has never wanted to die, but she can't imagine that the good she has done for children would be enough to make her want to live. And what about beauty? Can you say, "You must live for Beethoven, for Vermeer, for the Alps?" Friendship? "You must live for your friend Luisa." Love? Certainly the boy in the breakfast room in the Tara Arms Hotel, the boy in his peanut-butter-colored bathrobe, wouldn't make the difference between life and death. Pleasure, then. What has Pearl enjoyed? Food, weather, physical movement. She sees Pearl running with her dog, Lucky; Pearl sitting with her head on Lucky's head; Pearl next to Lucky, eating ice cream. It is a ridiculous thing to say, Life is worth living because of ice cream and your dog. But it seems preferable to saying, Life is worth living because you must live for me.

Maria sees two scales: one with the horrors of life, one with its goodness. The first is much, much heavier. Only some trick could make them seem equal, some thumb placed on the tray of goodness to give false weight. She sees a butcher's bloody thumb; her eye falls on a butcher's bloody apron. She hears the words *false weight*. She sees a thumb. An apron. But she does not see a face.

And then she does: the face of Aldo Osani, the Italian butcher whom her father liked because he seemed old-fashioned. He had one of those old-fashioned scales: two trays hanging from a chain, two trays that needed to be balanced. There was meat on one tray, lead weights on the other. He would give Joseph and Maria a piece of bologna while Joseph's mother waited for the order. His fingers were beautifully shaped, and yet his nails were rimmed in blood. Aldo Osani, she is sure, did not give false weight. But now this is what she needs: a belief in the possibility of false weight on the side of goodness. She needs a bloody thumb to tip the scale.

But even if the scale is tipped, she doesn't know who does the tipping, or why the tipping happens, or if at any moment it might stop. And she must say only what she knows. Pearl has asked her, "Why is it that it's life we want?"

She can only answer, "It seems we're meant to."

Pearl is frightened when she hears her mother say this. Her mother doesn't know any more than she does. "It seems we're meant to." But why and by whom? Who is the one who means and what is the meaning? This is what her mother doesn't know. Is the answer only "We want life because we're afraid of dying"? When she wanted to die, she was not afraid of death. When she became afraid of death, she wanted life.

She thinks of Breeda, Breeda who has lost everything, who has refused to blame her, who has sent her balloons that bob in the overheated air, who is sitting, Pearl is sure, in her aqua robe drinking tea and smoking cigarettes in front of the television, Stevie's birds hanging from their strings, a paper jungle. Why does Breeda want to live? How can Pearl understand it? She can't understand it; she thinks of Breeda and she is stupefied.

There is no reason for Breeda to forgive her. Pearl has hurt her son, perhaps done something to lead to his death, and now her son is dead. Because of this Pearl has wanted to die. But Breeda goes on living; Breeda has said there is nothing to forgive. There isn't any way of understanding it. It isn't sensible, it isn't reasonable: therefore incomprehensible. What Bobby Sands's sister Bernadette did was comprehensible. Her brother died; she planted a bomb in revenge. Revenge is comprehensible, she thinks, forgiveness is not. Comprehensible. *Comprehend* means to include. *Claudo, claudere, clausus,* Joseph had said. Include means to enclose. I cannot include this, I cannot enclose it with the power of my mind. I cannot comprehend.

Comprehension. Incomprehension. She feels the pressure of her incomprehension, a weakness that is at the same time a force. Whatever Breeda is or does, it is greater than Pearl's comprehension. Or her incomprehension. I cannot comprehend. Meaning, I cannot take it in. Does *it* take her in then: does *it* surround her, include her, enclose her, the way she thought death would enclose her, the enclosure Joseph wanted, that would save them from the world? Is that what saves us, then, the incomprehensible?

After everything, Breeda has forgiven her. Breeda wants life.

This is incomprehensible. It cannot be taken in. Yet to refuse to take it in, to refuse to look at it, to refuse to acknowledge its force, to choose death because you are unforgivable when she says you are forgiven, to choose death when she refuses it — this cannot be done. It dishonors Breeda. It cannot be done.

She sees Breeda, sitting in the dark apartment under the origami birds, the television blasting, the pictures of uprearing horses, of white seals. She looks down the dark road: windless, treeless: there is nothing. Is this the choice then, or is there no choice: the incomprehensible or nothing? Is there no choice, or is there only one, the one Breeda has made, the one Breeda has offered her? It would seem impossible to refuse her. It would seem dishonorable to say no.

She thinks of Breeda's face, her thin eyelashes, her ruined teeth, her eyes almost too large, too undefined. Breeda says she needs her, for the work of memory. Breeda has said she is forgiven. If she has been forgiven, she must do the needed work. Work that is needed to be done by her. *By her.* By her and no other. Done by her or left undone. The work of memory. Work.

She remembers the definition of work from physics class: "Work is the product of force acting upon a body and the distance through which the point of application of force moves." She got an *A* in physics; she liked physics very much, but she never thought it would come back to her in this way. Force and movement. Work uses force for change. Forgiveness opens the door to believing that work can be done, that you can do it, that it matters if you do it. That you, a body that possesses a force, can move through space to touch something, move something else.

Breeda has said she is forgiven. Needed. To do the work of memory, which only she can do. None of this is comprehensible. But to deny its force, its power: that would be dishonorable. That would be a lie.

She has always wanted to tell the truth.

Breeda's face. Her face. Incomprehensible. Pearl sees Breeda's face. She understands that you cannot see a whole face at once, even in memory; she focuses on one feature at a time. Mouth, nose, eyes, eyebrows, forehead. And, for the first time since the news of his death, she sees Stevie's face. No longer flat, white, dish-shaped but a set of features: the light-blue eyes, the full lips, the mole the size of a dime on his left cheekbone, the light wheat-colored hair. Feature by feature, Stevie's face is hers again; he has come back to her. He has come back to her when she was looking for his mother. His mother who has sent her a bouquet of Mylar balloons: "I hope you're fine. I'm fine. I miss you." His mother who has said that she needs Pearl to do the work of memory with her. His mother who, despite everything, has said that they are friends.

"Breeda is great," Pearl says.

"Great," Maria says. "Absolutely great. God, the place she lives in is a nightmare. You know, Pearl, I was thinking maybe she'd like to get away from Ireland, too many sad memories for her here. Maybe she'd like to come to America. We could find her a job in New York; there's a big Irish colony up by the Cloisters. I know people up there; we could get her a green card eventually, I'm sure we could. I mean, I know a million people, there must be a way. Then we could see her a lot and she could have a whole new life. I'm going to start calling some people I know."

Pearl laughs. It's the first time she's laughed hard for a very long time, and it hurts her throat. Her mother is absurd. She met Breeda for — what was it? — ten minutes, and she has a plan for Breeda's whole life. And if she tells Breeda, Breeda will be taken up with an idea she'd never have thought of before her mother walked into the room with the force that makes you think the only good thing is to go along, or you'll be missing something wonderful. Ridiculous, her mother's sense of possibility, her endless belief in the goodness of change. An old instinct tells her that her mother must be wrong. But what if she isn't? What if change is, as she always says, "much more possible than people are willing to think"? Her mother is a person of faith and hope. Her mother believes in change.

Her mother believes in change; her mother will never change. This is the sort of thing, this inconsistency, that in the past had made Pearl angry with Maria. But now her mother's combination of constancy and inconsistency amuses her, delights her. The spectacle of her mother's life, this lively life, these habits of hers, this head-long rushing ahead, tickles Pearl's palate like the imagination of a tart dessert. She had said to her mother: Go and do this thing for me, and her mother had done it. She hadn't hesitated; Pearl had known she would not hesitate. Her mother is her mother. My mother is my mother and I am I. This seems quite amusing; she could repeat it to herself just for the pleasure of the words.

My mother is my mother and I am I.

Of course, her mother is wrong about Breeda. Breeda can't be taken up, seized in her mother's beak on one of her swooping flights. How can she trim her mother's beak and not curtail her flight? Her mother is a swooping bird, a galloping horse, a ship in full sail, an airplane soaring, barely visible, a black dot in a wide blue sky. Her mother is not death, but sometimes she moves too fast.

Pearl looks at Maria. The eagerness in Maria's eyes makes her seem to Pearl terribly young. How can this be when just moments ago she saw her mother as not young at all? How can it be that she now feels herself much older than her mother? Her mother is running headlong, running too fast; she may crash into something, she may hurt herself, hurt someone else. Pearl can see that. Her mother cannot.

"Mama," she says. "Slow down."

Maria looks at her daughter and blinks, as if she's just heard the most intriguing sentence of her life. And then they both begin to laugh. They laugh as if what Pearl just said was the best joke in the world. They feel they may never stop laughing and it doesn't matter, because it's the best thing to do.

★ ★ ★

Dr. Morrisey comes in while they are laughing. Of all the responses she would have predicted, laughter was not among them. Words of anger, gestures of recrimination, anxious sobbing, clinging, followed by a push to separate: all these and many others had occurred to her. But laughter?

No, she had not thought of that. She wonders what this means about her, what it means about the body of her knowledge, that this common act, one of the most common in the world, the act that some philosophers said make humans human — man is a laughing animal — is one she hadn't thought of. She is humbled by the sight of them, mother and daughter, holding hands, laughing.

But when we think about it, how can we blame her for being surprised? In the iconography of mothers and daughters, laughter has not taken much of a place. Desperate loyalties; struggles to the death, struggles against death; bosoms of comfort, choking hands; get out of the house, stay in the house; find yourself a man, no man will ever love you; this is the way to bake bread, to clean, to keep your body beautiful: in all this lore, who has mentioned a mother and a daughter laughing? Why not? I don't know.

Dr. Morrisey can't stop to think about it. She checks Pearl's vital signs and is satisfied. Later, she will try to discover the cause of Pearl's agitation of the day before: the thrashing and the panic, the call asking for Stevie's mother, then her own mother, who has done something, changed something, so that they sit here laughing. Later, she will speak to Pearl. But for the moment she will let it be. Tomorrow, she will act once more as a doctor, as a scientist. She knows how troubled Pearl must be to have acted so radically, to have planned her own death. As a scientist, she knows better than to believe in the miraculous once-and-for-all turnaround, the bend in the road irrevocably taken, that leaves the path of sickness far behind for good. But for now, looking at Pearl and her mother, she can hope: that things will be all right. That there is enough health here to have faith in. What, she wonders, scientifically speaking, is the place of faith and hope?

"Sorry to break this up, ladies, but my patient needs her rest."

"Dr. Morrisey," Pearl says, "can I see Joseph later?"

Hazel Morrisey makes a calculation: Is she pushing it again, is she taking a risk? Wasn't it Joseph who precipitated the last crisis? She has no scientific basis for her judgment, but she believes her instinct: Pearl has turned a corner. She is better than she was. The road is long, she knows that, but a corner has been turned.

"You can see him for a little while."

"Mama, will you send Joseph over? So I

can talk to him alone."

"Of course," Maria says. At last, an easy request: no plunging into the lives of strangers with impossible questions, impossible requests. All Pearl wants is for her mother to deliver a simple message: *Pearl would like to see you now, alone.* But really, Pearl could ask her anything. She can do anything now; the reign of terror is lifted, life is possible once again, knives cut, clocks can be believed, the earth can be stepped upon with confidence.

She walks home, enjoying the damp air. Joseph can see that she is happy.

"She seems much better. I think she's going to be all right, Joe, I really think it. She wants to see you alone. And I've done something celebratory, maybe a little rash. I can't stand this place anymore. It's just too depressing: the spread, the curtains, the fake stained glass. I've booked us into the Shelbourne. It's madly expensive, but I'm in love with the naked ladies on the art nouveau lamps. And it's just across from St. Stephen's Green, so we can walk somewhere nice and not be run down by trucks. Don't say we can't afford it."

So Pearl has told her nothing; Maria knows nothing of what came between them. He is grateful for that, of course, but

Pearl's good behavior makes his bad behavior stand out even more. Just a few hours ago, the sight of her was the most desirable thing on earth to him. Now he dreads it as he has dreaded nothing in his life. But he must take his punishment. What will she say to him? Whatever she wants to say, he must listen.

He looks at Maria, her eyes lively with the prospect of her new luxurious hotel, and realizes she has no idea of how much money she has. Of what shape the business is in. Of what the nature of their investments is. And this knowledge makes him feel, for the first time in three days, undefiled. This is what he can do: he can make sure that Maria and Pearl will never have to worry about money. Will be free of its press and its entrapment and corruption all their lives. Yes, he will do that. From Rome, occasionally from New York, he will guard their fortune, the fortune provided by her father. He will be the good steward: a Judas who kept the purse. What if he had gone on keeping the purse instead of hanging himself?

They will live as they always have, without thinking about money. He won't see them often, but he will guard their prosperity.

"I'm going back to Rome tonight," he says. "Everything's fine here."

"Oh, Joseph, please don't," she says, then looks repentant. "Oh, I know. I'm being selfish. I have to get used to your not being around all the time. You're going to move to Rome, aren't you?"

"Yes, I think I am."

"Are you seeing someone there?"

"Yes," he says. He *is* seeing someone: himself, a well-dressed middle-aged man in a wide Roman piazza. The sun falling straight and indiscriminate. Young people laugh and smoke and ride their Vespas. Tourists enter churches; old couples walk arm in arm; Asian and African nuns walk in pairs; Japanese teenagers in groups of twenty pose for photographs before a fountain. He isn't part of it, but he watches, and no one wonders, Who is that man? because he isn't someone who is looked at, he is one who looks.

"Pearl will be fine," he says. He believes it because he must.

"I hope," she says, and he knows she believes it because she is a person of hope, and so she hopes.

• 50 •

The doctor says, "I'm lowering the dosage of your medication. I'm going to trust you."

Pearl nods. She is trusted. Forgiven. Once again.

· 51 ·

Pearl's eyes are closed when Joseph walks into the room. The room is dark; her white bed is brilliant in the darkness. There is discoloration under her nose. There is a tube attached to her hand. Her hands are ringless and her nails, unvarnished, are nevertheless luminous in the darkness, like moons.

He sits in the turquoise plastic chair and waits for her to open her eyes. She is very beautiful, silvery in her cone of darkness, transected by the rectangle of her bed.

"Oh, Joseph, things have been so strange. I've had all kinds of things happen, and then these strange dreams. Some of them were beautiful, some were quite disturbing, and I have no idea, because of the drugs and what's going on with my body, what things have really happened and which were dreams. I've given up trying to figure out what really occurred. It doesn't seem terribly important."

What is she saying, that she doesn't believe he said what he said? That it was a nightmare she can relegate to the world of useless nightmare images: the winged creatures with talons and teeth, the bottomless well, the door that will not open? Is that what she's saying? Does she believe it, or is she trying to let him off the hook?

She mustn't let him off the hook; hanging from the hook of her blame is where he belongs. He has harmed her. He has betrayed her. He wanted her for himself. He suggested marriage, when that would be a terrible betrayal; he didn't see it as the betrayal it would be. He only saw what he wanted. He looked harmfully. He wanted to make sure she would never suffer, so he committed the sin of idolatry. He wanted her to be a creature he could worship, a treasure, hidden in a tabernacle, hidden from the world. He committed the sin of greed. He committed the sin of theft. He stole from her the belief that there are in the world safe corners where nothing jumps out, where there is no possibility of ambush or destruction in the form of unexpected visitations.

How can this be forgiven? He doesn't want any forgiveness from her, and certainly not forgiveness that is only a mistake. She must know what he has done, so that she isn't haunted by it, so that in future it won't rise up, another ambush, and in a vulnerable moment cut her down.

"It wasn't a dream, Pearl. I said what you think I said. I can't explain it. I can only offer you — I don't even know what the word is; apology is far too light. I am terribly sorry. I can only ask your forgiveness. I wanted so to protect you."

Never has she seen a face so taken up by its distress. This distress, the absolute giving over to it, makes him seem innocent and, as her mother seemed to her a short time earlier, very young. Young in his suffering, defenseless. How can she defend him? It is himself that he must be defended from, and she has no idea how to do that. She knows what it is like: to feel that you must be defended from yourself. She would like to help him. She knows how much he needs her help.

"It's not important, what you said. You've been good to me all my life."

"I don't understand," he says. "I hurt you."

"It's not important. I'm all right."

He is abashed by her generosity, by her kindness, but also angered by it. He would rather have her blame. Does she really believe what she's saying, that what he said wasn't important? Or is she just being kind? He feels shaken, clumsy, like a fumbling, dangerous animal, dangerous in his largeness, in his maladroit lunges toward the human world. He thinks of a poem by a Polish poet, about a bear who is afraid neither of men nor fire. He steals meat off the porches of houses. The friend of the poet shoots the bear under the shoulder — only understanding the bear's odd behavior when he tracks him down and sees his jaw half eaten away by abscess. The poem acknowledges that the problem of the bear was insoluble. The bear had to be shot. He was a danger. The fact that his behavior was explicable did not mean he didn't need to be destroyed.

But she has said his dangerous lunge was not important. That she's all right. How can that be? He has lunged dangerously, like the wounded bear, and failed to do harm. What, then, protected her? Certainly not himself, with his pathetic passion for protection. What was it that has kept her safe?

He would like to say, Look out for me. In both senses of the term. He would like to ask her for her protection. He has already asked her forgiveness and been given it. How will he live with that? Forgiveness for betrayal. Judas the betrayer. He remembers a brother in Portsmouth Priory, Brother Luke. "Poor Judas," he always said. "He didn't know how easily he could have been forgiven. He was overcome by despair. By shame." As if he were telling a slightly obscene story, he nearly whispered into Joseph's ear, "I believe he is forgiven. I believe he is beside Jesus in Paradise. Along with the Good Thief. Because despair can turn you deaf, and he couldn't hear the word that would have been his consolation. He was deafened by despair; all he had to do was ask. But I think he was forgiven anyway, even without asking."

He has asked her forgiveness and has been given it. He doesn't yet know what this might mean. He knows he must go away. He will stay away.

"Joseph," she says, "I've had all these ideas, my brain's a little wild, I know that, but one idea keeps coming back to me, and I need your help. I was thinking that after a while, after I'm better, what I'd like to do is go to Cambodia. Look for something connected to my father. Try and find records, something. I don't know what there is but I'd like to try; in any case I'd like to see the place. I know that would cost a lot of money. Do you think we have enough money for that?"

In all the years he has been in charge of the Meyerses' money, in all the years he has seen to it that Maria and Pearl — and Devorah, of course — had everything they wanted, none of them ever asked what Pearl has just asked. The question allows him to give an answer that lightens the burden of what he has done to her. He has been clever with her money; there is more than enough. And he can tell her that: with pride, with pleasure. Yes, he can say, there is enough money to do what you want. He has protected her wealth; he will continue to protect her wealth. The Judas who kept the purse.

"You've had a windfall with one of your mutual funds," he says.

Windfall. Mutual funds. She sees dollar bills twirling like leaves; she sees figures dressed as dollar bills, dancing, holding hands. She smiles. He doesn't know what she's smiling at. He hopes it doesn't mean she's lost her understanding.

"I've had a lot of ideas, things I'd like to do before I go back to school. After I go to Cambodia, maybe I'll travel around Asia. And then I think I'd like to work on a farm. I'd like to learn about animals. Maybe I'll come back here, I have a friend whose family has a farm."

He's never heard her talk this way: chattery, girlish. She seems younger to him than she has for years.

"Slow down, kiddo," he says.

"That's what I said to my mother," she says. "Slow down."

"I'm going to leave you now. I'm going back to Rome."

They both know what he means. That he is distancing himself from her, that he is keeping himself away from her, exiling himself in reparation for what he has done. Is the price too high? He made a misstep, a grievous misstep. Maria has made many; Pearl at least one. And yet they will go home. He will live a stranger in a strange land. Isn't there any other way, some slow process of return? He doesn't think so. He believes, unlike Pearl, unlike Maria, that, although forgiven, he will not be given a second chance.

"Rome," Pearl says. "You love Rome. That will be good for you."

Does she mean that? Or does she mean, It will be better for me? Whatever she means, neither of them will question her words. And so, I suppose, we will not either.

Maria knocks lightly, shyly, at the door, then enters, although no one has told her to come in. She stands beside Joseph, puts her hand on his arm, leans awkwardly over the bed so she can touch Pearl's hand.

"I've got to get my plane now," Joseph says. Maria kisses him goodbye.

He bends over the bed to put his lips on Pearl's cheek. She pats his head. Like a mother, he thinks, and feels the cool light touch his own mother never gave him. She moves her hand so that her fingers come to rest on his forehead. Her fingers are far cooler than his forehead, as if he were feverish, the kind of fever he hasn't had since he was a child, the kind of fever that makes the touch of a cool hand feel like a poultice. What does a poultice do? It draws poison into itself. Ringless, these fingers, resting on his forehead, not moving at all, but still and cool on his thin skin, and he thinks: the skull beneath the skin, the brain beneath the skull. *Brain fever. The fever broke.* Those were the words used; that was what people said. And something in him does break, or break up, at the touch of her cool fingers, wonderfully still, drawing — what can it be? — the poison of his harm into themselves. She might have been harmed by him, but she does not seem harmed; he feels the strength in her cool fingers, the competence. Not delicate, those fingers, perhaps a bit too short for the wide palm. Her fingers on his forehead make it difficult, terribly difficult, to leave her, but he must go. He walks to the door. Maria blows him a kiss, and Pearl waves her one free hand.

"Bon voyage," Maria says. She would like to say, Go with God, but she won't allow herself.

He closes the door. They are together. They are safe. He hears his heels on the mole-colored linoleum and thinks of them holding hands lightly in the damp and overheated air.

• 52 •

We will leave Joseph walking down the corridor. We will not follow him; he would not wish to be followed.

And we will leave Pearl and Maria to themselves.

We will hope for the best.

ABOUT THE AUTHOR

Mary Gordon is the author of the novels *The Company of Women*, *The Rest of Life*, and *The Other Side*, as well as a critically acclaimed memoir, *The Shadow Man*, among other books. Winner of the Lila Wallace–Reader's Digest Writer's Award, a Guggenheim Fellowship, and the 1996 O. Henry Award for best short story, she teaches at Barnard College and lives in New York City.